THE ULTIMATE CONSPIRACY CONTINUES . . .

W. A. Harbinson first exposed the nightmarish truth – a truth so terrifying that it could only be presented as fiction – about UFOs in his international bestseller *Genesis*. Now he has taken the themes and many of the characters from that groundbreaking work and developed them into further dimensions of cosmic horror with other astounding novels in the PROJEKT SAUCER series. *Phoenix*, the second self-contained *Projekt Saucer* epic, takes the story on from the end of the Second World War and through the postwar years of humankind's first tentative explorations of space. During this historic period, the sinister earthly forces behind the UFO conspiracy begin to show their hand more openly – and start to exert a deadly stranglehold on the destiny of the whole Earth . . .

PHOENIX: THE SECOND BOOK OF THE EPIC *PROJEKT SAUCER* TERROR SERIES

Also by W. A. Harbinson in New English Library paperback

Inception

About the author

W. A. Harbinson has been a journalist, magazine editor and TV scriptwriter. Born in Belfast, Northern Ireland in 1941, he left school at fourteen, studied mechanical engineering, then joined the Royal Australian Air Force. While serving in the RAAF, he drafted his first novel, *Instruments of Death*. In 1980 he completed the classic *Genesis*, the epic novel of the world's most fearsome secret that became the inspiration for the *Projekt Saucer* tetralogy. (*Phoenix* is chronologically the second novel in this sequence.) Harbinson lives in north London.

Phoenix

W. A. Harbinson

PROJEKT SAUCER: BOOK TWO

NEW ENGLISH LIBRARY
Hodder and Stoughton

Copyright © 1995 W. A. Harbinson

First published in Great Britain in 1995
by Hodder and Stoughton
A division of Hodder Headline PLC

A New English Library paperback

The right of W. A. Harbinson to be identified as the Author of
the Work has been asserted by him in accordance with the
Copyright, Designs and Patents Act 1988.

10 9 8 7 6 5 4 3 2 1

A CIP catalogue record for this title is available from the British
Library.

ISBN 0 450 61751 3

Typeset by Avon Dataset Ltd, Bidford-on-Avon, B50 4JH

Printed and bound in Great Britain by
Cox & Wyman, Reading, Berks.

Hodder and Stoughton Ltd
A division of Hodder Headline PLC
338 Euston Road
London NW1 3BH

For
Perrott & Irena Phillips
&
For Anna

Part One

CHAPTER ONE

SOCORRO, NEW MEXICO

JULY 2, 1947

When that thing flew overhead Marlon Clarke could hardly believe what he was seeing. As he had been doing too often lately, he was sitting out on his porch, in his old rocking chair, slugging beer from the bottle, muttering under his breath and gazing out over the parched lands of his failed farm, flat and eerily desolate in moonlight. He was just a small farmer who'd had a bad few years and he liked to sit out there in the evenings, feeling bitter and murmuring angry words to himself, getting drunk enough to sleep without too much anxiety. Tired and thinking of bed, he had just glanced at his watch and noticed that it was ten-thirty when the whole porch shook a little, his last bottle of beer fell over, and he heard an exploding noise right overhead.

Shocked back to the real world, his heart racing too fast, he looked up to see a glowing, saucer-shaped object screeching, wobbling, spinning and pouring steam or smoke as it flew at tremendous speed across the night sky on a descending trajectory.

Before Marlon had a chance to get a grip on himself, the glowing object fell towards the Plain of San Augustin,

3

between Magdalena and Socorro, about five miles from his farm, then turned into a growing fan of white and red flames in what looked like a billowing cloud of dust. The explosion came a second later, as the fan of flames grew bigger, illuminating the rising cloud of dust and obliterating the stars.

The blast rocked Marlon's house.

Startled this time into a state of near sobriety, he got out of his rocking chair as the fan of flame shrank back to a tiny flickering that soon disappeared, letting the star-studded night sky return.

'Kee-rist!' Marlon exclaimed softly. Instantly, on an impulse, both fearful and curious, he grabbed a bottle of whisky from the floor of the porch, hurried down the steps, clambered unsteadily into his battered old truck, and tore off towards the scene of the crash.

As he drove across the flat plain, through pale moonlight and the shadows of cacti and sagebrush, he controlled the steering wheel with one hand, held the bottle in the other, drank too quickly and felt his heart racing. It was the whisky, he guessed, but it was also what he had seen: that glowing, saucer-shaped flying object of the kind he'd heard so much about lately.

'Jesus!' he whispered to himself as the old, battered truck growled and rattled across the windblown plain. 'Jesus H . . . I don't believe . . .'

He kept glancing outside the truck, growing more apprehensive, half expecting to see another of those objects gliding under the moonlight. He even thought of turning back, but his curiosity kept him going, and he convinced himself, even as his fear was growing, that it had just been an airplane.

He was wrong.

On the broad, flat plain near the town of Magdalena, about halfway between the road and the distant Black Mountain, he saw a dark pile of still-smouldering debris. Driving off the road, he bounced over the rough, sage-strewn plain until he came to the location of the crash. Stopping the truck, he had another drink of whisky, wiped his lips with the back of his hand, then looked out at the smouldering debris.

It was the wreckage of a large, saucer-shaped craft, about half of it smashed to hell, the remainder glinting a dull grey in the moonlight.

What looked like three scorched corpses were still strapped into the central cockpit of the crashed object.

'Lord Almighty!' Marlon exclaimed softly.

He was too scared to get out, but he had a good look, making sure that his eyes were not deceiving him. The object was round alright, shaped like two plates, one inverted and placed on top of the other. It was about twenty-five to thirty feet in diameter, obviously made of a metallic substance, and had smooth sides that rose gracefully, seamlessly to a smashed-up, transparent, domed cockpit. The charred bodies were still strapped to their seats.

That's when Marlon grew really scared. Blinking, rubbing his eyes, he looked out again.

The three corpses were burned beyond recognition. They were wearing grey-coloured one-piece suits, or coveralls, which were charred black, in tatters and still smouldering like the pieces of metal scattered widely around the broken, circular craft.

Nauseated by the smell of roasted flesh, Marlon looked beyond the crashed object to the distant mountain range. It was black in the night, but its sides were streaked with moonlight that also fell across the Plain of San Augustin. Marlon looked around him, expecting to see something else, but there was nothing out there but empty land and the wind's constant whispering.

Taking a final look at the charred bodies in the crashed flying saucer, he shivered with revulsion and fear, then turned the truck around and burned back to his ranch.

When the men from the Roswell Army Air Base came to

see him, Marlon was surprised by how many there were. They arrived in a jeep and troop truck as the sun was rising over the horizon to flood the flat plain with light. Marlon was still sitting in his rocking chair, more drunk than ever, when the armed troops jumped out of the truck to form a semi-circle around the yard, some with their backs turned to the house, others facing the empty plain, all holding their weapons at the ready.

More frightened than he had been by the sight of the crashed saucer, Marlon was wiping his dry lips with the back of his hand when a man in a plain grey suit, accompanied by a uniformed Air Force officer and two others in plain clothes, descended from the jeep and approached him. Stepping up onto the porch, the two in plain clothes hurried past Marlon and entered his house without his permission, slamming the mesh-wire door behind them. As Marlon was about to get out of his rocking chair and protest, the Air Force officer removed his peaked cap, revealing stark black hair and warm brown eyes in a slightly plump, friendly face. He offered a natural, easy smile.

'Mr Clarke?'

'Darn right,' Marlon said. 'And when I called, I didn't expect—' He nodded back over his shoulder, indicating the two men who could now be heard noisily searching his home.

'I'm sorry, Mr Clarke, but it's necessary. I'm First Lieutenant William B. Harris of the Eighth Air Force, stationed at Roswell Army Air Base. The two men in your house are members of the intelligence team of the 509th Bomb Group, also at Roswell. And this—' he indicated the unsmiling man in the plain grey suit – 'is CIA agent, Jack Fuller, who's flown here straight from Langley, Virginia.'

'You called about a crashed saucer, I believe,' Fuller said in an oddly threatening tone of voice.

'Right. It crashed last night, about ten. I was expecting you people a lot sooner. I've bin sittin' here all night.'

'I'm sorry about that,' First Lieutenant Harris said, 'but I had to wait for Mr Fuller to arrive.'

'All the way from Langley, Virginia,' Marlon said, glancing at the unsmiling Fuller who was, he noted, still under thirty, but had eyes as grey and wintry as Antarctica. 'You musta taken me serious.'

'It's strictly routine,' Fuller informed him, sounding as cold as he looked. 'It's just one of the rules. All the flying saucer scares we've had since last month—'

'The Kenneth Arnold sightings.'

'Right. They're mostly false alarms, but they have to be checked out. That's why I'm here.'

'This is no false alarm.'

'You actually saw the saucer?'

'Sure did. It's out there on the Plain of Magdalena with three dead bodies in it.'

Fuller glanced at Harris, then down at Marlon's whisky bottle. 'Have you been drinking, Mr Clarke?'

'What do you think?'

'I think you were drinking last night – you have a reputation for it – and just imagined you saw those dead bodies. I think you saw a crashed weather balloon, related it to all the flying saucer stories that have been in the papers since the Kenneth Arnold sightings, and let your imagination get the better of you.'

'The hell with that,' Marlon said, outraged. 'I know what I saw there last night – and it wasn't any goddamned weather balloon. It was big and made of metal and had three dead bodies in it. They were burnt all to hell.'

'Come with us, Mr Clarke.'

Before Marlon could protest, Fuller took him by the shoulder and tugged him to his feet. Marlon jerked his head around, indicating the noisy search still going on in his shack, but Harris told him not to worry and walked at his other side as Fuller led him between the armed troops to the jeep and coaxed him up into the rear seat. Fuller sat beside him, Harris sat up front, then the driver took off

along the road that ran as straight as an arrow across the
flatlands, towards Magdalena.

Marlon's stomach was churning. The sight of the armed
troops had scared him, the people searching his house
more so, and now he was confused as well as frightened,
not too sure if he had done the right thing in making that
phone call. Jack Fuller, the CIA agent seated beside him,
was only half Marlon's age, but had a cold-eyed, obscurely
threatening manner, never smiling, just watching. He was
making Marlon feel as guilty as hell, though he didn't know
what for. He had simply tried to behave like a responsible
citizen – reporting the crash and what he had seen – and
now this Fuller was making him feel like a criminal, or
even a madman. Thinking of all the stories he'd read about
UFOs in the past few weeks (ever since the June sightings
by Kenneth Arnold, the papers were full of them), he started
wondering if he *had* imagined the whole thing.

Marlon desperately wanted another stiff shot of whisky,
but the bottle was back on the porch where it could do him
no good.

They covered the five miles in about ten minutes and
soon were bumping over the flatlands, towards the crash
site, which now, Marlon noted, was surrounded by armed
troops just like his house. The sun was up and the heat
made Marlon sweat; he was also sweating with nervous
tension when the jeep braked to a halt, its wheels churning
up a cloud of dust that spiralled around him and the others
to be carried away on the moaning wind.

Marlon didn't have to get out of the jeep to express his
surprise.

Fuller turned unyielding eyes upon him. 'Is this what
you saw, Mr Clarke?'

It was not. Now, in the centre of that large circle of armed
troops, where the flying saucer with the three dead bodies
had been, Marlon saw only some white-smocked
technicians picking up a thin scattering of silver-foil and
narrow balsa-wood beams. There was no sign of the large

flying saucer. No dead bodies. No ambulance.

'This isn't what I saw,' Marlon said. 'What I saw was—'

'This is what we found,' Fuller told him. 'The remains of a crashed Rawin weather balloon. Easily mistaken for flying saucers, Mr Clarke. We sometimes see what we want to see.'

'What do you mean by that?'

Fuller glanced at First Lieutenant Harris. 'One of the worst lightning storms we've had in a long time,' Harris explained with a gentle smile, 'took place about seventy-five miles southwest of here last night, about the same time as this weather balloon crashed. Since then, we've had lots of reports of unidentified flying objects in the vicinity. Most turned out to be natural phenomena caused by the storm. In other words, false alarms.'

Marlon felt more confused, but he knew what he had witnessed. No way were those pieces of silver-foil and balsa part of what he had seen here last night.

'That thing I saw last night was big – very big – and it had dead bodies in it.'

'It was night,' Fuller told him. 'You were drinking. You saw what you expected to see. Did you get out of your truck?'

'No, but—'

'So you'd been sitting out on your porch, drinking half the evening, then you saw this saucer-shaped object falling from the night sky about five miles away. Remembering all the stories you'd read in the papers this past few weeks, about so-called flying saucers, you assumed that's what you'd seen, drove out there to find it, and maybe got scared when you *did* find it and imagined the rest.'

'With all due respect, sir, that's bullshit. I know what I saw.'

'You were drunk and frightened.'

'I'm more drunk now than I was last night, but that don't mean I'm imagining all this.' Marlon waved his hand to indicate the ring of armed troops and the white-smocked men picking up pieces of silver-foil and balsa beams to load them into the army truck nearby. 'And I'm telling you that what I saw last night was no weather balloon. It was at least twenty-five feet wide and had—'

'Dead bodies in it.' Fuller sighed. 'So where are the dead bodies, Mr Clarke? Where's the large, presumably metallic, flying saucer?'

'That's right. It was metallic.'

Fuller smiled in a mocking way and pointed to the men carrying the debris of the weather balloon. 'Silver-foil,' he said. 'It would look metallic in the dark. The moonlight, the drifting dust, your state of mind, the drink, combined could have made you see all the rest. Enough said, I think.'

'Well, maybe . . .' Marlon felt confused and nervous, no longer sure of his senses, and wished he could have a stiff drink to put his thoughts in some order. Okay, so he was drunk, but he wasn't that dumb . . . and when he noticed a lot of tyre tracks leading away from just beyond this much smaller area of wreckage, heading towards Roswell, he was convinced that another team of men from the Roswell Army Air Base had cleared away the real wreckage and taken it back to the base.

Frightened, he decided to keep his nose clean and get involved no further. After wiping his dry lips with the back of his hand, he deliberately shook his head from side to side, as if chastising himself. 'Dammit, I guess you must be right. I sure as hell hung one on last night. I guess that *could* explain it.' He glanced again at the tyre tracks that started beyond the perimeter of armed troops, then at the truck into which the white-smocked men were putting the last of the debris from the weather balloon. 'A weather balloon?' Harris nodded and smiled at him. 'Well, I'll be damned,' Marlon said like a real country yokel. 'It's amazin' what a man sees when he's drunk. I feel a right goddamned fool now.'

'No need,' Harris said, raising the peak of his Air Force cap to offer a genuine, friendly smile. 'You'd be surprised at what people think they see at nights – and these weather balloons, they fool a lot of people.'

'Sure fooled me. Say, you haven't got a drink in that there jeep?'

Harris smiled more broadly. 'Nope, I'm afraid not. But you've still got that bottle on the porch and we're going back now.'

'Yeah, let's do that.' Pretending to be more drunk and tired than he was, Marlon glanced at the CIA agent, Jack Fuller, whose grey gaze was coolly searching, then at the white-smocked men who were still placing pieces of debris into the truck. Comparing the size of the craft he had seen last night and the much wider area of scattered debris with what he was seeing now, he was more convinced than ever that his senses had not deceived him as Fuller had suggested.

No, those tyre tracks clearly visible beyond the ring of armed troops belonged to the trucks that had taken the debris of the flying saucer, as well as its dead occupants, back to the Roswell Army Air Base. This coldly handsome young CIA agent, Fuller, and the friendlier Air Force First Lieutenant Harris were undoubtedly covering up the real crash. Convinced of this, Marlon became even more determined to keep his mouth shut. He was therefore relieved when the driver turned the jeep around and headed back to the ranch.

See no evil, hear no evil, Marlon thought, keeping his gaze fixed resolutely on the road ahead.

It was best to be silent.

Marlon awoke in the early hours of the morning, haunted by the remnants of bad dreams and frightening realities. At first confused about where he was, hardly remembering going to bed, he saw his bedroom in darkness, stars framed by the window, then recalled that crashed flying saucer and the three strange, scorched bodies. He groaned aloud, hearing something – *feeling* something – and remembered

waving goodbye to Fuller and Harris as they drove away
from his house, having grimly warned him to forget flying
saucers and accept that what he had seen was a crashed
weather balloon.

'Shit,' Marlon said, hearing something – *feeling*
something – then realised that he'd been awakened by a
strange bass humming sound that seemed physical and
made his head hurt. 'Shit!' he said. 'What the hell . . .?'

The sound was growing louder, as if descending on his
roof. As it did so, the whole house shook to the pulsations
of a dazzling light that had suddenly obliterated the stars
as it poured in through his window.

The house shook more violently as the pulsations
became more rapid and the light blinded Marlon. The bass
humming sound grew louder and more . . . *physical*,
threatening to crush his skull.

He jerked upright on the bed and covered his ears with
his hands, letting out a scream of anguish and terror.

The noise cut out abruptly and the pulsating light
disappeared, leaving normal darkness – and unnatural
silence.

Marlon lowered his hands, staring fearfully at the
window. Hearing and seeing nothing other than starlit
darkness, he jerked the sheet from his sweating body and
slid off the bed. He put his pants on, picked up his shotgun,
then went to the window and looked out. Seeing nothing
unusual, he padded back to the front door and stepped out
onto the porch.

A large, silvery, saucer-shaped craft was resting on the
ground at the end of Marlon's moonlit yard. It appeared to
be seamless and had no protuberances other than four
retractable legs.

It looked just like the crashed flying saucer that Marlon
had seen on the Plain of San Augustin.

Even as a wave of fearful disbelief swept over him,
making him drop the shotgun, which made a godalmighty
clattering, the landed saucer suddenly gave off a bass

humming sound that shook him to his bones, vibrated slightly, and became surrounded by an aura of pulsating white light. A transparent dome rose up from the saucer's raised centre to reveal three human-shaped silhouettes inside. Then a beam of dazzling light shot from the saucer, almost blinding Marlon.

Crying out and covering his eyes with his hands, he fell back against the wall of the house. The light shone through his fingers, showing the blood beneath the skin, and the bass humming sound pressed in on his skull. Marlon slid down the wall, whimpering in pain and terror, until he was resting on the porch with his chin on his raised knees. Then the light faded away, the bass humming sound cut out, and Marlon looked up as a trap-door opened silently in the bottom of the saucer, tilting down to the ground.

Three men, all dressed in black to match the night, dropped out, one after the other.

They spread out across the yard to advance upon Marlon.

Something about those three men in black told him that they had come to take him away and that he could not escape.

Marlon just sat there, paralysed by terror, until the men stepped up on the porch and closed in around him. Then something exploded in his head and he sank down through spinning stars.

Chapter Two

Captain Dwight Randall, of the Air Technical Intelligence Centre, or ATIC, was not feeling too happy when introducing himself to First Lieutenant William B. Harris, Flight Intelligence Officer of the Roswell Army Air Base. Back in Wright-Patterson AFB, in Dayton, Ohio, Dwight's wife, Beth, nursing their first child, Nichola, was also nursing her resentment because he was on a trip away from home again. She knew that he had no choice, being compelled to obey orders, but that hadn't helped him when he waved her goodbye for the third time in the four weeks since Nichola had been born. Dwight had optimistically promised her that he would be at home a lot more, at least during the first few months of their new baby's life, but unfortunately the recent, unexpected spate of UFO sightings had taken precedence over domestic matters. Now, as Dwight returned the salute of First Lieutenant Harris, then shook his hand, he felt guilty that he was here instead of in Dayton, looking after his family.

'Please, Captain,' Harris said, indicating the chair at the other side of his desk, 'take a seat. Can I get you a coffee?'

Dwight glanced out the window at the distant aircraft hangars, then shook his head and sat in the chair. 'No, thanks. I've drunk gallons since leaving Wright-Patterson, so I'll beg off this time. Do you mind if I smoke?' Harris just spread his hands in the air and offered a natural, charming smile, so Dwight lit up, inhaled, blew a smoke ring, and watched it drifting away ... like a flying saucer.

'So,' he said, 'I've been sent by ATIC to investigate the so-called Socorro Sighting of last week. Do you resent my intrusion?'

'No, sir,' Harris said. 'My intelligence training didn't include flying saucers, so any help I get will be appreciated. It's also good to know that the Air Force, which has so strenuously denied the existence of the phenomenon, now has some tangible evidence.'

'One of the functions of the Air Technical Intelligence Centre is to gather data on Unidentified Flying Objects. The fact that most of them turn out to be natural atmospheric phenomena may explain our former reluctance to accept the reality of the UFOs.'

It was a disingenuous statement. What Dwight could not tell Harris was that, contrary to the Air Force's own publicity, it was in a state of near panic over a whole series of recent UFO sightings, particularly those over Muroc Air Base – the top secret Air Force test centre in the Mojave Desert – on July 8, just two days ago and six days after the Socorro sightings.

The first UFO flap had actually occurred in 1946 when, throughout the summer and fall, thousands of 'ghost rockets' appeared in the skies over Scandinavia and western Europe. Mostly seen at night, they were reported as being 'cigar-shaped' and with flames issuing from the tail. Estimates of their speed ranged from that of a 'slow airplane' to five hundred miles per hour. In the month of July alone, the Swedish military received more than six hundred reports, which encouraged the Swedish general staff to declare the situation 'extremely serious'. Then, when sightings of the unidentifieds spread out from Sweden to Finland and close to the Soviet border, the Americans also took the phenomenon seriously – certainly enough to express their fear that the rockets might be secret weapons developed by the Russians with the help of captured German technical specialists and material.

Their fears were in no way eased by the knowledge that

whereas the mysterious 'Foo Fighters' of the recent war had not shown up on radar, the ghost rockets certainly did, and therefore could not be classified as hoaxes, misidentifications or the products of mass hallucination.

The Soviets denied any knowledge of the rockets, but US suspicions remained unabated while sightings of the rockets continued to be reported from as far afield as Greece, Turkey, French Morocco and Spain, before gradually fading away the following year.

However, on June 21, 1947, only a couple of weeks ago, a harbour patrolman, Harold Dahl, accompanied by his fifteen-year-old son and two crewmen, was on patrol near Maury Island in Puget Sound, off Tacoma, Washington, when he observed six objects shaped like 'inflated inner tubes' hovering about two thousand feet above his boat. Five of the objects were circling about the sixth as it descended to about five hundred feet above the boat, where, appearing to hover magically, it was seen more clearly. The object appeared to be about a hundred feet in diameter, metallic, with no jets, rockets, wings, or propellers, but with a 'hole' in the centre, or base, symmetrically placed portholes around the perimeter, and observatory windows on its underside. After discharging what appeared to be a cloud of aluminium-coloured debris, which littered the sea, where they gave off clouds of steam, which suggested that they were hot, the circular craft ascended to rejoin the others, then they all flew at high speed toward the open sea and soon disappeared.

Three days later, on June 24, an American businessman, Kenneth Arnold, reported that when flying his private Piper Cub airplane near Mount Rainier in the Cascades, Washington, searching for the debris of the Marine Corps C-46 transport that had crashed against the south shoulder of Mount Rainier the night before, he observed nine disc-shaped, apparently metallic objects flying in 'a diagonal chain-like line' and making an undulating motion 'like a saucer skipping over water'. According to Arnold's report, the objects performed impossible manoeuvres in the sky, before flying off at supersonic speed to disappear in the direction of the Canadian border.

As Arnold had been a deputy sheriff and was a reputable businessman, as well as an experienced mountain air-rescue pilot, his story was taken seriously and the term 'flying saucer' came into being. It was therefore used widely over the next few weeks when the media spread Arnold's story nationwide and encouraged a spate of similar sightings, many of which were hoaxes, some of which were by trained observers and seemed highly credible.

By this time the US military, while publicly ridiculing the reported sightings, were secretly in a state of panic over their own plague of UFO sightings: the first, on June 28, over Maxwell Air Force Base in Montgomery, Alabama; the next, on June 29, near Alamogordo, New Mexico, right over the top-secret White Sands Proving Ground; then, on July 8, a whole spate of sightings of spherically shaped, white aluminium-coloured objects flying over Muroc Air Base, the supersecret Air Force test centre in the Mojave Desert.

Because these particular sightings were made by trained technicians and pilots, and because the reported objects were appearing increasingly over top-and-supersecret military research bases, a growing suspicion in intelligence circles was that the men and material transported from Nazi Germany to Russia had led to a dangerous Soviet lead in space technology. And now one of the damned things had crashed and all hell had broken loose.

'Anyway,' Dwight continued, 'the so-called Socorro Sighting has caused quite a stir in the media and placed us in an uncomfortable position. I believe you're the one who compiled the first official report on it.'

'Yes, sir. I take it you've read it.'

'About a dozen times,' Dwight told him. 'I kept re-reading it because I couldn't believe my own eyes.' He withdrew Harris's report from the briefcase on his lap, leafed through it, then looked up again. 'You say the UFO appeared to have suffered damage in a lightning storm near Roswell, but managed to fly on to Magdalena, where it crashed on the Plain of San Augustin. It was a real flying saucer – or at least a disc-shaped aircraft – and the wreckage contained three dead bodies. Naturally the report came as a shock. Are you sure— ?'

'I stand by that report,' Harris said, brushing a lock of dark hair back from his brown, candid gaze and offering a slight, nervous smile. He looked like an honest, reliable officer, but clearly he was uncomfortable over this matter. 'What that farmer told me, I was able to confirm with my own eyes: a crashed flying saucer with three dead bodies in it.'

'Marlon Clarke was the farmer.'

'Yes, sir.'

'A known drunkard who was drinking at the time.'

'Not that drunk – and I confirmed with my own eyes what he'd told me when he phoned us shortly after finding the wreckage.'

'You say the bodies seemed human.'

'They were burnt beyond recognition and I couldn't examine them thoroughly, but they certainly *seemed* like human beings.'

'This is quite a story, Lieutenant, but not one I'd want public. How the hell did it get out to the press?'

'Not guilty. The story was picked up by Johnny McBoyle, reporter and part-owner of Radio KSWS in Roswell. McBoyle personally investigated the case and found that a lot of people had reported seeing the UFO fly overhead. Others reported hearing a loud banging sound as the object flew through that lightning storm over Corona – presumably when it was first damaged. Others in Magdalena reported hearing an explosion from the Plain of San Augustin – when the object crashed. As soon as I heard that McBoyle was going to put the story out on the teletype, I blocked the message with one of my own – sent anonymously, of course

18

– telling him not to transmit. That scared him enough to make him cancel his transmission. Unfortunately, the following day, our enthusiastic young public information officer, Lieutenant Walter Haut, acting on odd bits of information coming into Roswell, issued a press release without the authorisation of myself or the base commander. His vague story of a crashed saucer – no mention of the dead bodies – was subsequently published in the Roswell *Daily Record* of July 8 – the day after the crash. Hunt has been reprimanded and will probably be posted out of here.'

'Alas, too late to kill the story.'

'I'm afraid so.'

Dwight turned over another page in the report, then looked up again. 'The saucer wreckage and dead crew members have been removed from the scene of the crash?'

'Yes, sir. We did that immediately. At the insistence of no less than the Deputy Chief of the Air Force, General Hoyt Vandenburg, the three charred bodies and the debris from the crash were picked up by an intelligence team from the 509th Bomb Group and transported in strict secrecy to Carswell AFB, Fort Worth, Texas. There's no trace of it left at the crash site.'

'Subsequently you paid Clarke a visit.'

'Yes, sir. On the instructions of CIA agent Jack Fuller, we scattered the pieces of a Rawin weather balloon around the crash site and went through a charade of picking them up for examination when Fuller and I took Clarke back out there. We insisted it was the balloon that had crashed and that Clarke had simply imagined the dead bodies. Clarke finally pretended to believe us, but I don't think he did.'

'I better have another talk with this Clarke.'

'You can't. He vanished the day after the crash and hasn't been seen since.'

'*Vanished*?'

'Completely. We've searched high and low, but we can't track him down. Neither could the Roswell *Daily Record*. He's vanished into thin air.'

Dwight leaned forward in his chair, suddenly feeling cold and frightened. 'Christ, you must have *some* idea of what happened to him. This is a small, intimate community, Lieutenant. Someone must know *something*.'

Harris simply shrugged and raised his hands in a gesture of defeat. 'No-one knows anything. When we checked Clarke's shack, we found his bed unmade – suggesting he'd slept in it the night before. His old truck was still parked out the back. The only clue to his disappearance was what might have been a group of footprints in the earth, leading from the steps of the porch to just outside the front yard, where they stopped abruptly. There were no signs of tyre tracks, but a circular patch of brush, about twenty-five feet wide, was flattened and slightly singed in an odd way – I mean, not from the sun. A real mystery there.'

'A circular patch of brush, about twenty-five feet wide – approximately the same size and shape as the crashed saucer.'

'Right. It bears thinking about.'

'What's the story on Bradley? It says here that as soon as you received word of the crash, you invited former intelligence officer, now UFO authority, Mike Bradley to go with you to view the crash. Bradley, normally obsessed with flying saucers, surprised you by not turning up and by later refusing to discuss his reasons. Has he talked to you since?'

'I haven't been in touch with him since.'

'Can we drive out and see him right now?'

'Yes. He lives out in Eden Valley, near Robert Goddard's old rocket-launching ground. It's not a long drive.'

'Okay, let's go.'

Dwight slipped the report back into his briefcase and got to his feet while Harris phoned through for a jeep to come around and pick them up. The jeep was waiting for them by the time they got outside. Dwight glanced up as three F-86 jet interceptors roared over the great semicircular hangars along the edge of the runway, under a cloudless blue sky. He did it automatically, perhaps looking for a flying saucer, and felt instantly foolish when he realised what he had done.

Sitting beside First Lieutenant Harris in the rear of the jeep being driven by a US Air Force corporal, Dwight put his head back, closed his eyes, and let the beating wind cool his face as they left the base and headed for Eden Valley, just outside Roswell. Opening his eyes again, he saw the El Capitán Mountain rising from the foothills near the southwestern horizon and, to the east, the sunlit slopes of the Caprock where, not so long ago, the Comanche Indians, Spanish explorers, and even Billy the Kid had roamed. It therefore seemed incredible that this same area was already filled with highly advanced defence installations, including atomic research, aircraft, missile and rocket development, and a lot of highly advanced radar-electronics and stratospheric flight experimentation. Not far away, in Los Alamos, was the top-secret 'Manhattan' atom bomb project. The White Sands Missile Range and Proving Ground, at Alamogordo, was the most important of its kind in the United States. Also, the only combat-trained atom bomb group in the world was the 509th Bomb Group of the US Army Air Force Base, located right here in Roswell and given high prominence in Harris's report. This area was also, incidentally, the one producing the most UFO reports in the whole country, most of them by professional pilots and military observers.

Dwight sighed, thinking of the recent spate of saucer sightings that had overturned his life in the past month: first the Harold Dahl and Kenneth Arnold sightings in Washington State, then the spate of sightings over various top-secret military establishments right here in New Mexico. Recalling those sightings, he realised that he was getting into truly unknown, perhaps even dangerous, territory.

He was also working too much for his own good, which was upsetting Beth. Imagining her back in their small house in Wright-Patterson AFB, Dayton, Ohio, breast-feeding baby Nichola, his heart swelled with love and concern for her. Then, to distract himself from his feeling of loss, he went back to reading First Lieutenant Harris's report.

Harris had included a brief resumé of Bradley's career, so Dwight knew he was about to meet an impressive man. Bradley had been a biplane pilot during World War I, spent a good many years as a successful Wall Street lawyer, became a member of OSS during World War II, and was known to have been involved in a major intelligence operation in occupied Europe. The exact nature of that operation was still top secret, though it certainly concerned German secret weapons. Badly wounded in an explosion at Keil Harbour during the last days of the war, Bradley had recovered, been discharged from OSS, married a former Roswell *Daily Record* reporter, Gladys Kinder, and moved back to Roswell with her. Now, when not making a living by the drafting of contracts between the many US Air Force and civilian aeronautical establishments in the area, he was conducting his own investigations into UFO sightings.

Bradley's interest in UFOs, Dwight was convinced, related directly to what he had discovered during his intelligence gathering in Germany during the war. Why he had rejected First Lieutenant Harris's invitation to check out the Socorro UFO crash site was therefore a matter for some concern.

'Apart from the formal resumé contained in your report,' Dwight said as the jeep crossed the sun-scorched flatlands between Roswell and Eden Valley, 'what do you know about Mike Bradley?'

'He's been to the base a few times to discuss UFO sightings with me. He's intelligent, good humoured and, given his background, unpretentious. A lot of experience in his face, a kind of air of quiet authority, but also something guarded, even secretive. He never talks about the war. Says his work is still classified. I wouldn't call him the obsessive type, but he's certainly obsessed with UFOs. That's what keeps us in touch.'

'And his wife?'

'A terrific lady. Bit of a local character. Used to be a reporter on the Roswell *Daily Record* and was known to be as tough as any man. Still is, in fact. Likes to wear stetsons and high-heeled boots. Pretty sharp with her tongue, too.'

'How did she meet Bradley?'

'He was out here in 1931, trying to run down a physicist – called Wilson, as I recall – who'd worked for Robert H. Goddard on his rocket experiments in Eden Valley. Reportedly, Gladys was briefly involved with Wilson and Bradley went to see her about him. I don't know if anything occurred between them here in Roswell, but certainly they met up in London, England, during the war, after Bradley's wife had been killed at Pearl Harbour. Bradley and Gladys seem unusually close and are popular locally.'

'When did Bradley's obsession with UFOs begin?'

'For him, it's more specific than unidentified flying objects – it's flying saucers. He's been interested in them as long as I've known him. We first met a few weeks after he arrived here with Gladys, which was about four months after the war, about November or December, 1945. I met him at a welcome-home party given for Gladys by her old buddies on the Roswell *Daily Record*. As soon as Bradley learnt I was the Flight Intelligence Officer at Roswell, he pinned me to the wall to enquire if I ever received reports of saucer- or disc-shaped aircraft. This, mind you, was about twenty months *before* the first sightings by Harold Dahl and Kenneth Arnold. Of course I'd never had reports of any such thing – at least not until last month – and when I asked him why he wanted to know about them, he just murmured vaguely about his interest in unusual airplane configurations. After that, he regularly asked me if I'd received any unusual reports, but until last month, I'd nothing to give him.'

'Then, remarkably, when you got that report on a

crashed saucer, he failed to show.'

'Right,' Harris said. 'Damned amazing – and he won't tell me why.'

'Maybe this time we'll be lucky,' Dwight said as the ranch-style house on the edge of Eden Valley came into view.

'Yeah,' Harris said. 'Maybe.'

The driver braked to a halt by the gate of the front yard, causing a cloud of dust to boil up around the jeep. Dwight slipped out his side of the vehicle, waving the dust from his face, then was dazzled by sunlight as he walked up the yard path, beside First Lieutenant Harris. When Harris rang the bell, a woman came to the door. She was tall and lean, wearing a long belted dress with high-heeled boots, and had a head of short-cropped, greying brown hair, which made her seem slightly mannish. Her grey eyes were disconcertingly steady over a full-lipped, sardonic smile.

'Bill Harris!' she exclaimed as her gaze flicked inquiringly to Dwight. 'What brings you here?'

'We've come to see Mike.'

'Who's your friend?'

'This is Captain Dwight Randall, of the Air Technical Intelligence Centre, or ATIC, based at Wright-Patterson AFB, in Dayton, Ohio. He's here to investigate the Socorro sighting.'

'Mike doesn't know anything about that.'

'Dammit, Gladys,' First Lieutenant William Harris said, smiling with considerable charm, 'stop giving us a hard time and at least invite us in for a coffee.'

'It isn't coffee you want, Bill.'

'Okay, it isn't coffee we want. But can we at least step inside and talk to Mike?'

'What about? He knows nothing about the Socorro sighting. As you know, he didn't go to the crash site with you.'

'Yeah, I know,' Harris said. 'And what I now want to know is – why? He's been hounding me about saucer-shaped aircraft since he came to live here – and then, when one actually crashes, he doesn't turn up when he's invited. Why?'

'Who is it, Gladys?' The man asking the question appeared in the doorway behind Gladys. In his early fifties, he was short but muscular in an open-necked sky-blue shirt and denims. Though silvery-haired, he was handsome, but the skin on the right side of his face was livid from severe burning caused by the explosion at Kiel Harbour in 1945. 'Bill!' he said, sounding pleasantly surprised. 'Hi! Come on in.'

Gladys rolled her eyes, but opened the door and stepped aside. 'This,' she said, indicating Dwight, 'is—'

'Captain Randall, of the Air Technical Intelligence Centre,' Dwight said, holding out his hand. 'Call me Dwight.'

'Dayton, Ohio?' Bradley asked, shaking his hand.

'Correct.'

'Welcome to Roswell.' He started leading them into the living-room, but when Gladys mentioned that they were here about the Socorro sighting, he stopped in his tracks, blocking their way. 'The Socorro sighting? Why come to see me? I know nothing about it.'

'That's the point,' Dwight said. 'First Lieutenant Harris here tells me you're fascinated by disc-shaped aircraft, or flying saucers, and yet you didn't turn up at the crash scene when you were invited. Why was that, Mr Bradley?'

'I just didn't feel inclined.'

'You hound First Lieutenant Harris for a year-and-a-half about disc, or saucer-shaped, aircraft and then, when he tells you one has crashed, you don't feel inclined? Do you expect us to believe that, Mr Bradley?'

'Why not? I've just lost interest in the subject.'

'But when I rang you,' First Lieutenant Harris said, 'you didn't sound like you'd lost interest. In fact, you sounded real excited and said you were going to meet me at the main gate of the air base to join me on the trip to the crash site. So what stopped you, Mike?'

Bradley glanced at his wife, then turned a closed gaze back to Harris. 'I'm sorry, Bill, but I just changed my mind. The reasons are personal.'

'You must have changed your mind shortly after First Lieutenant Harris rang you,' Dwight said. 'What kind of personal reason could make you change your mind so quickly?'

Now Bradley wasn't smiling. 'That's my business, Captain.'

'And you still insist that you're no longer interested in UFOs?'

'You're not deaf,' Gladys said aggressively. 'You heard what he said.'

'I heard, Mrs Bradley, but I find it hard to believe.'

'That's your problem.'

Dwight turned back to Mike Bradley as First Lieutenant Harris became embarrassed. 'Would you mind at least telling me what stirred your interest in UFOs in the first place?'

'Like a lot of folks, I was intrigued by the Kenneth Arnold sightings.'

'Which took place a month ago. First Lieutenant Harris tells me you've been interested in disc- or saucer-shaped aircraft from the moment you first came to Roswell, at the tail end of 1945 – about twenty months before the recent sightings.'

'Okay, I'll admit that.'

'Long before there was any talk of so-called flying saucers.'

'Right,' Bradley said, looking uncomfortable.

'Which means you picked up the interest during, or just after, the war. Is that also correct?'

'I can't answer that question.'

'Because the job you did for OSS was classified?'

'Correct,' Bradley said. 'Now, I think—'

'You better leave,' Gladys said. 'My husband doesn't want to discuss this any further.'

Dwight ignored her. 'What happened on the night of July second, Bradley, after First Lieutenant Harris called you about that crashed saucer? What stopped you from turning up to see what you'd been so desperate to find?'

'I've nothing more to say,' Bradley responded, his face more flushed than the livid flesh on his right cheek.

'Whatever it was that stopped you, it also made you give up your UFO investigations. Isn't that the truth, Mr Bradley?'

'Goodnight, gentlemen. Goodbye.' Bradley turned away and disappeared back into the house as Gladys, with a grim, no-nonsense expression, pushed them out through the front door. 'You heard the man,' she said harshly. 'Now get the hell out of here.'

'Does the name "Wilson" ring a bell, Mrs Bradley?' Dwight boldly asked her.

She looked startled, then blushed.

'Back in 1931, when you first met your husband, he was investigating a scientist called Wilson, who'd worked right here, in Eden Valley, with Robert H. Goddard. I believe you knew Wilson, Mrs Bradley.'

'I don't know what you're talking about,' Gladys said, then slammed the door in their faces.

Dwight stared at the closed door in amazement, then at the uneasy Harris.

'Well, I'll be damned,' Harris said. 'I knew Bradley wouldn't be keen to talk, but I've never known him or Gladys to be *that* unfriendly.'

'They're both frightened,' Dwight said. 'They're just trying to cover it up. Come on, Lieutenant, let's go.'

They stepped down off the porch, climbed into the jeep, and let the corporal drive them away, back across the parched flatlands on the edge of Eden Valley. Dwight thought of the rockets that Robert H. Goddard had launched from this desolate area, then tried making the connection between Goddard, whom Bradley had visited once or twice with regard to the mysterious Wilson, and Bradley's later obsession with disc- or saucer-shaped flying objects. He came to a blank wall.

'Bradley was obsessed with UFOs,' First Lieutenant Harris said like a man in a trance of bewilderment. 'I just can't figure what's scared him.'

'*You're* scared,' Dwight informed him. 'First a flying saucer crashes, then it's spirited away to Carswell, then the only civilian witness to its existence disappears, and now Bradley and his wife have clammed up and won't discuss UFOs. So you're scared . . . with good reason.'

'Yes, sir, that's right, I'm scared. What about you?'

'Yeah,' Dwight confessed, glancing up to be dazzled by the brilliant, vast, empty sky. 'I'm scared too, I guess.'

Chapter Three

Wilson, Ernst Stoll, Hans Kammler and Artur Nebe were together in the underground viewing bay as the *Kugelblitz II*, a twenty-five-foot diameter, piloted flying saucer, descended at hovering speed through the deep well formed by a circle of soaring, ice-capped mountain peaks. Its lights were flashing kaleidoscopically around its sharp outer edge, but its bass humming noise, the infrasounds of its power source, which could tighten a human skull at a certain intensity, was blocked off by the thick plate-glass window of the viewing bay. Eventually, the saucer started settling gently on the steel-plated landing pad constructed at ground level in the cavernous space hacked out of the snow-covered Antarctic rock.

The base seemed to be underground, but was actually at ground level and hidden from the view of the pilots flying overhead by a ring of soaring, snow-capped mountain peaks. However, working from this valley floor, beginning during World War II, Wilson's *Slavenarbeiter*, or slave labour, under the ruthless supervision of the former SS officers, Stoll, Kammler and Nebe, had worked night and day at hacking their way into the base of the mountain to create aircraft hangars, workshops, laboratories, the first two of what would be many landing pads for the flying saucers, offices, staff accommodations, and underground quarters for the slave labour.

The slaves had originally been shipped out from the occupied territories of Nazi Germany and, more recently, abducted from various countries and flown here in Wilson's flying saucers. Only two saucers were operating right now, but more were being constructed. Within five years there would be a whole fleet of them, each one better than the last, with no end to their technological evolution in sight. While not feeling pride (a redundant emotion) Wilson certainly felt satisfied as he watched the saucer rocking lightly on its base before finally settling down.

Its bass humming sound receded into silence, then its flashing lights winked off one by one. The arc lights powered by self-charging generators and fixed high up on the walls of solid rock to illuminate the gloomy, cavernous landing area, gave the saucer's metallic grey surface a silvery sheen. It looked alien and beautiful.

The other saucer was at rest beside it, but covered in a tarpaulin, and both were surrounded by white-coated technicians and slaves, men and women alike, dressed in identical dark grey coveralls that just about kept out the biting cold. It was not unmitigated Antarctic cold, since that had been reduced by the installation of phase-change solar-heat pumps that could store enough energy to also get the colony through the long Antarctic night; but it remained cold enough to be uncomfortable for the unfortunate labour force.

Now, as the *Kugelblitz II* settled down on the landing pad on its four retractable hydraulic legs, the technicians, armed guards and *Slavenarbeiter* moved in to surround it. As the latter placed specially-made stepladders along the sloping sides of the saucer, to begin checking and polishing its seamless sides, a trap-door opened in the base, sloping downwards, and a slim man dressed in a pinstripe suit lowered himself to the landing pad and looked around in a dazed, disbelieving manner, before the armed guards closed in upon him. A second man emerged from the saucer almost immediately, this one big and bulky and wearing dirty bib-and-brace overalls. He, too, looked around him as if dazed, until he was surrounded by the armed guards and led away with the first man.

'Good,' Kammler said. 'They got both of them.' Blond and blue-eyed, he glanced at the dark-eyed Nebe, who merely nodded solemnly and stroked the pistol strapped around his waist. Both men, like Wilson and Ernst Stoll, were wearing heavy roll-neck pullovers under thick coats and trousers. All of their clothing was coloured black.

Wilson merely nodded and smiled. He was feeling good today. He needed advanced prosthetic replacements for his artificial elbow joints and the man they had captured could do the job – that and many others. Sometimes it all seemed so simple. Faith could move mountains.

The two men surrounded by guards moved out of view far below, approaching the lifts that would carry them up to the upper level of the colony, occupied by Wilson and his most senior staff, including those now grouped around him. He glanced at Ernst Stoll, once an enthusiastic rocket engineer, then an SS policeman, now an embittered, therefore malleable, administrator responsible for the collection and welfare of the slave labour. Stoll was looking down at the parked flying saucer, showing little emotion. He had left his heart and soul in conquered Germany; now he lived for this colony. Wilson was satisfied.

'Let's go and greet them,' he said, turning away from the window and leaving the viewing bay through doors that led into a gloomy corridor hacked out of the inside of the mountain. The corridor led into a larger, brighter room, which also overlooked the landing area for the saucers, but contained comfortable armchairs and settees on an Italian tiled floor partially covered by large Moroccan carpets. The wall overlooking the landing area was mostly thick plate-glass framed in ugly reinforced concrete. The back wall had been hacked out of the mountain and was simply the original rock covered in concrete and damp-proofing black paint. The two side walls were also of reinforced concrete, but contained steel-plated doors, one of which was for the lift, with a row of indicating lights above it. As Wilson entered the room with his entourage behind him, the lights came on one by one, indicating that the lift was ascending. The light stayed on at the marking for the fifth level.

The lift doors opened and the two captives emerged, being prodded by the automatic weapons of two guards wearing old SS uniforms. The slim, grey-haired man in the pinstripe suit and tie was, Wilson knew, Dr Paul King, of the Powered Limbs Unit of West Hendon Hospital, London, England. The bigger man in the dirty brace-and-bib overalls was the farmer, Marlon Clarke, who had witnessed the crashed flying saucer near Magdalena, New Mexico. The sophisticated Dr King, while clearly bewildered and frightened, was in control of himself; the other one, Clarke, was terrified, practically dribbling with fright.

'Dr King?' Wilson said, as if this meeting and the circumstances were routine.

'Yes,' King replied, his voice admirably calm, though his eyes betrayed confusion and fear. 'Who are you? Where am I?'

'My name is Wilson. You will address me as that. You are in a colony hacked out of a mountain in Neu Schwabenland, or Queen Maud Land, in Antarctica. You are here as my prisoner.'

Clarke started sobbing, uncontrollably, like a child, wiping the tears from his cheeks with a grubby hand as he stared down at his own feet.

'Oh, Christ,' he said. 'Oh Jesus, I don't believe . . . Oh, God help me, I'm dreaming.'

'No, Mr Clarke, you're not dreaming. Nor are you imagining things. This is real. We are real. What's puzzling you, Dr King?'

'Something about your face.'

'I'm seventy-seven years old, doctor, but look fifteen years younger. My face lacks a certain mobility due to crude plastic surgery. I also need improving in other ways, which is why I need you.'

'Oh, Jesus,' Clarke sobbed. 'Why me? What the hell am I doing here?'

'You have been brought here,' Wilson informed him, 'because you were unfortunate enough to witness the debris of a crashed flying saucer and its three dead crew members. We cannot permit you to talk about that, so you are here to be silenced.' Clarke burst into tears again as Wilson turned to the other man. 'As for you, Dr King, you're fortunate enough to be one of the world's leading specialists in research into the myoelectric control of external prosthetics, or artificial limbs. You will therefore be invaluable to this community and need have no fear if you co-operate.'

'Co-operate?' King asked as Marlon Clarke sobbed hysterically beside him. 'What do you mean?'

'This is a secret community devoted to science,' Wilson explained, 'with no moral impediments to progress. We'll do anything necessary, no matter how ruthless, for the advancement of the technology we're creating. We're a society of masters and slaves, scientists and their servants, and we live beyond the reach of so-called civilisation and its antiquated moral constraints. You are either for us or against us, Dr King – willing worker or slave. The choice is all yours.'

'I think I'm hallucinating,' King said. 'I just can't accept this.'

'Don't be as foolish as him,' Wilson warned, indicating the still sobbing Clarke, 'by putting this down to imagination. This is real, Dr King, and it cannot be stopped. Outlawed by the world we may be, but we're well out of reach. The saucers are my creation and just the tip of the iceberg, so to speak. My ultimate purpose is a new kind of man, both physically and mentally: the mythical superman made real in a world based on logic, not emotion. We're a unique community, Dr King, and you will be part of it.'

'What if I refuse?'

'You don't have the choice. Either you do it willingly or

we compel you to do it. We have our ways, Dr King, and
you can't escape from here. Outside this mountain is the
Antarctic wilderness. Where would you go?'

As the full implication of what Wilson was saying struck
home to Clarke, he sobbed again and started shaking. When
Wilson nodded, one of the guards took hold of Clarke's
elbow and managed to steady him. Dr King, though clearly
frightened, remained in control of himself and stared about
him in wonder.

'I take it you're human beings,' he said, turning back to
Wilson, 'and not creatures from outer space.'

Wilson smiled coldly. 'Alas, yes, we're all too human.'

King glanced at Stoll, Kammler and Nebe, then nodded,
indicating the armed guards. 'You look like a bunch of Nazis
to me.'

'I'm an American,' Wilson said, 'but one without political
allegiance. These men, it is true, were in the SS, but all
that is behind them now. There are no nationalities here;
we've all disowned that. Here, our only religion is science.
We don't worship false gods.'

'I know that I'm not hallucinating,' King said, 'but I still
can't believe this. I don't know who you are or how long you've
been here, but you won't be able to stay. Sooner or later, the
West will learn about you and put a stop to your madness.'

'Some of them know we're here,' Wilson said, 'but they
can't get us out. No-one can get us out of here. No-one has
the technology.'

'I don't believe that,' King said.

'It's true,' Wilson insisted. 'The US Government knows
we are here, but they can't get us out.'

'You mean they've already tried?'

'Yes. Last January they launched the biggest Antarctic
expedition in history, Operation Highjump, led by the
explorer and naval officer, Rear-Admiral Richard E. Byrd.
The resources of the assault force, which was disguised as
an exploratory expedition, included thirteen ships, two sea-
plane tenders, an aircraft carrier, six two-engine R4D

transports, six Martin PBM flying boats, six helicopters, and a total of four thousand men. When this supposedly invincible assault force reached the Antarctic coast, it docked, on January 12, near Queen Maud Land, or Neu Schwabenland, then divided up into three separate task forces. When the expedition ended, in February, much earlier than anticipated, there were numerous stories in the press about Rear-Admiral Byrd's references to enemy fighters that came from the Polar regions and could fly from one Pole to the other with incredible speed. The machines to which he was referring are the kind that brought you here and were created by me in Nazi Germany. As for Admiral Byrd's mission, it was deemed a disaster and the United States has since declared that it's withdrawing from the Antarctic for at least a decade. They know they can't get us out of here. Like I said, they don't have the technology.'

Dr King did not reply, but he licked his lips and glanced about him, still in a state of disbelief, trying to accept the reality of this nightmare as the farmer, Marlon Clarke, sniffed back his tears and looked frantically around him, his eyes stunned by dread.

Ever curious about human emotions, since he had so few himself, Wilson decided to take the confused, disbelieving Dr King and terrified Marlon Clarke on a tour of the colony.

'Come,' he said. 'Follow me.'

Confident that neither King nor Clarke would try to escape, since there was nowhere to go, Wilson nodded at the armed guards, who put up their weapons and left the room through the door leading to the corridor. Wilson then entered the lift, followed by Dr King and the trembling Clarke, then Stoll, Kammler and Nebe. Stoll pressed the button for the third level. When the lift had descended and the doors opened again, Wilson led the group out into a clamour of hammering, pneumatic drilling, and echoing voices.

Another tunnel was being hacked out of the mountain and walled and roofed with reinforced concrete and steel wiring. As Wilson led Dr King and Clarke through churning dust in the arc-lit gloom, it was clear that the work was being done by the filthy men and women who slaved under gunpoint and to the cracking of the whips of other guards.

'All this started in Nazi Germany,' Wilson explained. 'Contrary to popular belief, the Antarctic continent has many unexplored arid areas, many of which are well hidden from view by vast ice sheets and mountains. In other words, Dr King, we are not quite underground, but rather hidden by high mountain peaks. We're carving the rest of the space we need from the interior of the mountain.'

He saw that King was gradually accepting that all of this was real, now glancing about him with as much awe as fear at the many unfortunates slaving in this dust-filled, arc-lit rocky hell.

'Nazi Germany,' Wilson continued, 'had a genius for the construction of immense underground production plants and factories, most completed with the ruthless use of captured slave labour. Indeed, most of the underground research centres of Nazi Germany were gigantic feats of construction, containing air-shafts, wind-tunnels, machine-shops, assembly plants, launching pads, supply dumps, accommodation for all who worked there, and adjoining camps for the slave workers – yet few German civilians knew that they existed.'

A whip cracked and someone screamed. Dr King twitched beside Wilson, but walked on, though Clarke, growing ever more terrified, let out an audible groan.

'Take Peenemünde, for instance. The full enormity of that research complex can only be gauged from the fact that apart from its wind tunnel – the most advanced in the world, containing its own research department, instrumentation laboratory, workshops and design office – it also had its own power station, docks, oxygen plant, airfield, POW camp for specially selected prisoners who provided

cheap labour, and social and medical facilities associated
with a town of twenty thousand inhabitants. It was therefore
the prototype for the even larger underground factories to
be built secretly in Germany and Austria, notably at
Nordhausen in the southern Harz mountain range of
Thuringia, which is where I created my first piloted flying
saucer, the *Kugelblitz*. Do you know about Nordhausen,
Dr King?'

'No, I'm afraid not.'

'It was an immense rocket research and construction
facility, consisting of a series of linked tunnels carved out
of the Kohnstein Mountain near the town of Nordhausen.
The parallel tunnels were eighteen hundred metres long,
and leading off them were fifty side-chambers, a main work
area of one hundred and twenty-five thousand square
metres, and twelve ventilation shafts which had been bored
down from the peak of the mountain. Work at converting
the tunnels into a mass-production facility for rockets began
in September 1943 with the use of two thousand engineers
and fifteen thousand inmates from the nearby concentration
camps. The slaves were kept in a separate camp located in
a hidden mountain valley, less than a kilometre from the
entrance to the tunnel. A new underground complex, to be
linked to Nordhausen by another network of tunnels, was
in the process of being built deep under the ground around
the town of Bleicherode, twenty kilometres away. Between
them, Nordhausen and Bleicherode constituted the first of
the SS underground factories – virtually living towns – and
what the Nazis were doing there, under the earth, we are
now doing here, in the Antarctic.'

'I can't imagine how you managed to get so much
equipment and so many of these unfortunate wretches
here,' Dr King said, glancing around him at the sobbing,
sweating captives now slaving in abominable conditions.

'The labour force and equipment were shipped in many
submarines, in the course of many voyages, over a period
of years, throughout the war, when other Nazi boats and

submarines were protecting the South Atlantic coastline of Antarctica. Bear in mind that the normal U-boat of that time could cover seven thousand miles on each operational cruise. Also, the Germans had submarine tankers spread across the South Atlantic Ocean at least as far as south of South Africa, and any one of those tankers, which had a displacement of two thousand tons, could supply ten U-boats with fuel and stores, thus trebling the time that those submarines could stay at sea. It took a long time, but we managed to get enough men and equipment here before the war ended. We should have enough to last a couple more years, by which time we will have more and bigger saucers to fly in what we need.'

The tunnel led into another large viewing bay in which the plate-glass windows had yet to be inserted. Far below was a workshop of massive dimensions, with jibs and cranes, whining machines, and sheets of a metallic substance, dull grey and in various shapes, being swung to and fro. There were many workers down there, also, as well as long work benches, steaming vats, blast furnaces, screeching electric drills, and the ribbed bodywork for other, larger saucers. The walls of the workshop were solid rock, hacked out of the mountain's interior, but the vast ceiling was reinforced concrete, as was the floor.

'The workshop's three hundred feet long and a hundred and thirty-eight feet wide,' Wilson explained. 'Its roof is eighty feet high and made from twenty-three-feet thick reinforced concrete. To pierce it, you'd need a bomb weighing about twelve tons and striking the ceiling at a speed of Mach 1, the speed of sound. In order to construct it, we needed forty-nine thousand tons of steel and concrete for the roof alone. Hundreds of jacks were used to raise the roof slowly, inches at a time, with the walls being built up beneath it, as it was raised. The enormous amounts of steel, cement, sand and gravel needed were brought in by U-boat and plane over a period of years, like the rest of the material and the labour force. The site used about five thousand workers, who were shipped here from the occupied territories, mostly from concentration camps. At any one time there were always at least a thousand men at work. This went on around the clock in twelve-hour shifts, and my guards had no hesitation in executing anyone too ill or exhausted to do it. For this reason, we managed to complete the construction of the workshop in a year. With logic, Dr King, and not emotions, men can do the impossible.'

Dr King gazed down on the skeletal saucer prototypes and the great steel plates being swung to and fro. 'So it was one of your flying saucers that crashed at Socorro, New Mexico.'

'No,' Wilson said bluntly, almost angrily. 'Not one of ours.'

King started to respond, obviously wanting to know about the other saucer, but before he could do so Wilson waved him into silence and led them all across a catwalk, then through another, shorter tunnel, eventually entering a steel-plated room which had rows of frosted glass cabinets on the shelves and naked, dead bodies inside them.

Clarke stopped walking when he saw the bodies, letting out another groan, but the dark-eyed Artur Nebe, who still had his hand on his pistol, roughly pushed him on. Dr King merely gave a slight shudder, but continued walking behind Wilson. They soon emerged from the tunnel to another room, a laboratory, its steel-plated walls climbing to a ceiling of chiselled rock that was part of the interior of the mountain.

The members of staff looked perfectly normal, men and women in white smocks, reading and writing, peering down through microscopes, checking printouts and gauges and thermometers, working quietly, intently. What was different were the specimens in the cages and glass jars: human heads, artificially pumping hearts, floating brains and intestines. There were also cabinets containing artificial joints and various prosthetics.

'Oh Jesus!' Clarke groaned. He covered his face with his hands, started shaking even more, and became so weak he had to be propped up by Ernst Stoll. Clarke started sobbing again.

'Take him away,' Wilson said. 'Might as well prepare him immediately. Stoll, come and see me in five minutes. I'll be in my office.'

'Yes, sir,' Stoll said. He and Kammler then slipped their arms around Clarke and practically carried him out of the laboratory, leaving only the dark-eyed, expressionless Artur Nebe with Wilson and Dr King. The latter was gazing around him in amazement, but not shock, as prosthetics were what he had been working on in the hospital in England.

'A familiar sight?' Wilson asked, pleased to see that Dr King was in control of himself.

'The prosthetics, yes. The rest of it, no. We work under certain moral restraints, as you've already noted.'

Wilson smiled thinly. 'The work that goes on here,' he explained, 'is not only for the production of advanced prosthetics and organs. Its ultimate goal is life extension, first through the transfer and replacement of bodily parts, eventually by discovering the secrets of longevity. Right now, we need primitive life extension through prosthetic replacement, which is where you come in. Your work will involve human prosthetics and the creation of cyborgs: half men, half machine. I'm sure you'll find it highly satisfying.'

'You realise I think you're insane.'

'I'm not. I'm just logical.'

Dr King was not swayed by Wilson's brand of logic. 'I'm fifty years of age. I have a family and friends. Even were I to accept that I can't escape from here, I'd still find it psychologically impossible to adjust to the loss of everything I've known, loved and need. In short, even if I tried to co-operate, I don't think I'd succeed.'

'You worry unnecessarily. We have ways of indoctrination. Drug therapy, combined with psychological persuasion, will aid your adjustment while letting you retain all your faculties. That process of indoctrination begins today.' Dr King just stared at him, blinking too much, turning pale. 'Are you frightened?' Wilson asked.

'Yes, I'm very, very frightened.'

'You won't be for long.'

Wilson nodded at Artur Nebe, who removed his pistol from its holster and indicated the nearest doorway with it. Dr King licked his lips, then walked out, followed closely by Nebe. Wilson sighed, then stepped into another lift and ascended to the level directly above – the highest level so far, though others were planned.

Emerging from the lift, he entered a sunlit, dome-shaped room, its white-metal walls gleaming, enormous windows running right around the walls, framing the dazzling sky and snow-capped mountain peaks of the Antarctic wilderness. Between the windows were doors, steel-plated, all closed, computer consoles jutting out just above them, their lights flashing on and off. The room was fifty feet wide. There was a desk in the middle. On the desk was an intercom, a microfilm viewer, a pile of books, notepaper, pens and pencils, a panel of switches. There were chairs in front of the desk, all leather, deep and comfortable; there was no other furniture in the room and the floor was laid with plain tiles which, in combination with the steel-plated walls, made the room cold and sterile.

Wilson walked across the floor, his footsteps reverberating, passing the desk and stopping at the window, to look out over his kingdom of snow and ice, the impossibly blue sky. He only turned away from that view when the door opened and Ernst Stoll entered the room. Stoll stopped by the chairs at the desk, but he didn't sit down.

'You wanted to see me?'

'Yes.' Wilson remained at the window, gazing steadily at Stoll, aware that the man would not like what he was about to hear. Stoll was in his middle thirties, but looked older, no longer handsome, ravaged by the loss of his family and idealism during the war. Now loathing the outer world, having nothing to return to, he was devoted to Wilson and his work with this Antarctic colony. He would not want to leave.

'The colony is expanding rapidly and requires more workers,' Wilson said, 'and the original labour force is dying off. We therefore need more workers. We also need human specimens for our laboratory experiments. Finally, we need smaller people for use in the saucers, either in human form or, given time, as cyborgs. We can find a plentiful, constant supply of the small Ache Indians in Paraguay. That country remains sympathetic to the Nazis and will welcome your overtures.'

'I'm to go to Paraguay?'

'More than that, Ernst. Not for a mere trip. You must give up direct participation in the running of this colony and instead take up residence in Paraguay. There you will cultivate a close relationship with General Stroessner, organise the purchase, collection and shipment of the Ache Indians, and keep constantly vigilant for signs of betrayal by Stroessner or his government. In other words, you will leave here for good and settle in Paraguay.'

'I don't want to leave here, Wilson, and I certainly don't want to settle in Paraguay. While it's true that the country has become a haven for Nazi refugees, most of them live in protected enclosures in the jungle and go mad with boredom.'

'You will not be bored, Ernst. I promise you that. You'll be busy rounding up the Ache Indians and liaising between the Paraguayans and me. You'll be in frequent contact with us here, and will receive regular visits from myself and others. You'll also be our main contact with the rest of the world, which will involve a lot of travelling and meetings. I am certain that you'll find it far from dull and might even enjoy it. This work is important, Ernst.'

'I'd rather stay here, but if you insist . . .'

'I insist. I don't trust anyone else, Ernst. Kammler and

Nebe are men who like intrigues and live by betrayal. I want them here, where I can keep my eyes on them. You're the only one I'd trust outside the colony, so it has to be you.'

'I'm honoured,' Ernst said, as stupidly as he had to Himmler during the war. 'When do I leave?'

'Not immediately. Right now, Paraguay is in the middle of a minor revolt, which I believe will be defeated by President Morínigo. While this is going on, and causing great confusion, we're having long and frustrating negotiations with the corrupt general, Alfredo Stroessner. We don't expect to have matters resolved too soon. I'd think in six or seven months from now. Say early next year. Is that satisfactory?'

'Yes, of course.'

Wilson smiled thinly and shook his hand. 'Good, Ernst. I'm pleased.'

Ernst nodded solemnly and left the office, having foolishly believed everything Wilson had told him.

What Wilson had told him was essentially correct – at least regarding the work required. Where he had misled Ernst was in telling him that life in the jungles of Paraguay would not be dull. In fact, it would be hell, which is why Wilson had chosen Ernst. Kammler and Nebe would both have refused to go. Ernst, then, with his perverted idealism, was the natural choice.

Pleased with himself, Wilson took the lift from his office back down to the third level. Once there, he made his way to the steel-plated laboratory with the ceiling of chiselled rock and gruesome collection of human heads, artificially pumping hearts, floating brains, intestines, and all kinds of prosthetics. Passing the men and women in white smocks, he entered the operating theatre, where the unfortunate Marlon Clarke, now almost mindless with terror even though slightly sedated, was strapped by his legs, arms and forehead to a surgical bed and surrounded by silent, white-smocked surgeons.

'Oh, please,' Clarke whimpered tearfully. *'Please!'*

Wilson leaned over him, to smile coldly at him. 'We wish to remove your head while you're still fully aware, in order to check if we can preserve it in its conscious state. Your neck has been anaesthetised, so you shouldn't feel a thing, though you'll be aware until the very last moment of exactly what's happening. Treat it as an experience.'

He then stepped back to observe as the leading surgeon switched on the electric guillotine and moved it on its pulley into place on the throat of the pop-eyed, sweating, violently shaking Marlon Clarke. As the surgeon proceeded to surgically remove Clarke's head, Wilson calmly looked on, curious to see how the unfortunate man would react before death blotted out his mind.

Chapter Four

This place is the pits, Fuller decided as he parked his jalopy in front of the hospital annexe in Fort Bliss, New Mexico, which was now being used to house the German rocket scientists under contract to the US Air Force. Fuller was an urban man who hated the country, and having driven from the White Sands Proving Ground, located between Alamogordo and the site of the first atomic explosion, across eighty miles of desert distinguished only by endless sagebrush, he was convinced that he had passed through a world inhabited solely by mountain lions, coyotes, wildcats, and rattlesnakes. He was therefore relieved to be in Fort Bliss, within sight of the Organ Mountains (which, he had been informed, reminded the German scientists of the Bavarian Alps), though was *not* thrilled to step out of his car into yet more dust and scorching heat.

How he longed to be back in Langley, Virginia, with his CIA pals.

As he walked up to the door of Count Wernher von Braun's rooms in the wood-frame building, an Army Stinson L-5, a small liaison plane, flew overhead, reminding him that this was a military base and that the Kraut scientists housed here, including von Braun, were reportedly conducting, in collaboration with Americans, a highly secret research project for the government.

Things sure change quickly, he thought with unsullied cynicism.

Ringing the doorbell located beside the mesh-wire

screen, he reminded himself that the man he was about to meet was not an American, but a former Nazi scientist who had created the V-2 rocket that had devastated London and Antwerp during the war. Now classed as a civilian with civilian staff, von Braun remained in charge of a hundred and seventeen of his own German scientists, engineers and technicians, albeit under the supervision of US Army Major James P. Hammill, a physicist and German-speaking Fordham graduate. The Germans had come into America in 1945 as so-called Wards of the Army, thus requiring no entry permits, all signing one-year contracts with the Army. These were soon changed to five-year contracts, and now the Krauts, while still quartered in this hospital annexe, were acquiring automobiles, wearing sombreros and cowboy boots, going to movies and nightclubs, and sending their kids to schools in El Paso.

A better life than we're having, Fuller thought as the front door opened and a paunchily handsome face appeared behind the mesh-wire screen. Defeat has its rewards.

'Yes?' Count Wernher von Braun asked.

'Jack Fuller, from Langley, Virginia.'

'Ah, yes, the CIA. You're expected. Come in.'

He opened the mesh-wire door to let Fuller enter. Inside, the house, or conversion, was neat, if rather spartan and obviously not meant to last. Soon, as Fuller knew, von Braun would be moving to Redstone Arsenal, Huntsville, Alabama, as director of research-and-development projects of the Army Ordnance Guided Missile Centre.

Another reward, Fuller thought as he and the imposing German shook hands.

'Please,' von Braun said, indicating a soft chair in the living-room. 'Be seated.' Fuller sat. 'I'm afraid my wife isn't here at present. A drink. Some tea? Lemonade?'

'Beer?'

'This I have,' von Braun said, his great bulk looming large over Fuller, casting its shadow upon him. 'One moment, please.' When he disappeared into the kitchen,

Fuller had a good look around. No TV set yet, but the radio was on: Benny Goodman's orchestra and a lady singing the swinging 'Bei mir bist du Schön', which made Fuller want to snap his fingers and dance. A copy of *Forever Amber* was on the table, in the shadow of a vase of fresh flowers. Clearly someone was perfecting their English with popular music and fiction. Von Braun soon returned with a tall glass filled with beer, which he gave to Fuller, and a bottle of Pepsi Cola for himself. 'I am sorry it's not German,' he said. 'American beer is not good, no?'

'No,' Fuller said. He sipped his lousy American beer. Von Braun sat in the sofa directly facing him, his thick legs outspread. He had the build of a wrestler and the ease that came with huge egos. He would not be pushed easily.

'Nice place,' Fuller said.

'You know that's not true. It is merely adequate, but better than we deserve – and, of course, temporary. I look forward to moving on.'

'You like it in America? Apart from the beer, I mean?'

'At first I was lonely. A lot of us, we were lonely. But recently we were joined by our parents, wives and children. Three hundred in all. Included in these were my parents, the Baron and Baroness Magnus von Braun – whose ancestral estate in Silesia has been confiscated by the Russians – and I have also been joined by my bride. I was given leave to marry her in Landshut and bring her back here. The Americans are generous.'

Damn right, Fuller thought. And an eighteen-year-old bride, a second cousin, at that. 'We're not so generous with our own citizens,' he said without the trace of a smile.

Von Braun smiled for him, though his gaze remained cool. 'No, I suppose not.'

'Where's your wife now?' Fuller asked.

'I thought our conversation would bore her,' von Braun said, 'so I sent her out for a walk.'

Which means she can't say the wrong thing, Fuller thought. Some fat pumpkin we have here.

He sipped some more beer. His throat felt dry in this dusty hole. 'What do you most like about America, Count von Braun?'

'American sport. Joe DeMaggio and Rocky Graziano.' Von Braun shrugged. 'Apart from that, I like my work. Now what do you want to know, Mr Fuller?'

Fuller smiled, admiring von Braun's bluntness. A twenty-eight-year-old hard case from Brooklyn, New York, Fuller was the child of moderately wealthy, uncaring parents, a clear-eyed product of Havard, and a veteran of many relationships and one failed, childless marriage. Not a man for finer feelings, he admired those who were nimble on their feet and ruthless in pursuit of what they wanted. This von Braun, though built like a wrestler, clearly had those attributes.

'I've come to enquire about your rocket construction programme. The V-1s and V-2s.'

Von Braun sighed. 'I've been over this so many times. There is nothing secret about it anymore. It is all in the files.'

'It's easier for me to talk to you than try to get at the classified files. I have clearance for this, but not for your records. That's why I'm here.'

Von Braun sighed again, sipped some Pepsi Cola, then rested the dripping bottle on his lap. 'So what do you want to know?'

'You were, I believe, one of the founder members of the German amateur rocket society, also known as the Spaceship Travel Club.'

'Yes. The *Verein für Raumschiffart*, or VfR. It came into being in 1927 when a group of space-travel enthusiasts took over an abandoned three hundred-acre arsenal, which they called their *Raketenflugplatz*, or Rocket Flight Place, in the Berlin suburb of Reindickerdorf. From there they actually shot some crude, liquid-fuelled rockets skywards.'

'When did you join it?'

'About 1930, I think. By then the VfR included most of

the rocket experts of the day, including Rudolf Nebel, Hermann Oberth, Willy Ley, Max Valier, and Klaus Riedel. I was very proud to gain admittance to that august company.'

'How did you end up in the German Army?'

'I know what you are implying, but it's not true,' von Braun said with no sign of anger. 'I was never a Nazi. In April 1930, the Ordnance Branch of the German Army's Ballistics and Weapon Office, headed by General Becker, appointed Captain Walter Dornberger to work on rocket development at the Army's Kummersdorf firing range, approximately fifteen miles south of Berlin. Two years later, after many experiments to find the most promising method of propulsion and the most stable means of flight, the VfR demonstrated one of their liquid-fuelled rockets to Dornberger and other officers at Kummersdorf. In 1933, when Hitler came to power, the VfR was taken over by the Nazis and became part of the Kummersdorf programme. Many of the German engineers, including myself, were therefore conscripted in a very real sense. We were, and remain, scientists – not soldiers.'

'You ended up in Peenemünde, working on the V-1 rocket programme.'

'Yes, but the prototype was known as the A-2.'

'Is it true that much of the German rocket research was based on the work of the American rocket scientist, Robert H. Goddard?'

'A genius shamefully ignored by his own country. Yes, it is true. We all revered Goddard and based our work on his brilliant theories. While in the United States those theories were being received with indifference and even contempt, we in Hitler's Germany were spending fortunes on rocket research that was, by and large, based on Goddard's work. As early as December, 1934, two highly advanced A-2 rockets, constructed at Kummersdorf, gyroscopically controlled, and powered by oxygen-and-alcohol fuelled motors, were launched from the island of

Borkum in the North Sea and reached an altitude of one-and-a-half miles. Those stabilised, liquid-fuelled rockets were, at the time, the only known, serious challengers to the rockets of Robert H. Goddard.'

'But the work didn't end there.'

'No. On March 7, 1936, we demonstrated some more motors at Kummersdorf, including one with an unprecedented three thousand, five hundred pounds of thrust. Those demonstrations so impressed the German Commander-in-Chief, General Fritsch, that permission was given for us to build an independent rocket establishment in a suitably remote part of Germany, where research and test firings could be carried out in the strictest secrecy. The chosen site was near the village of Peenemünde, on the island of Usedom, off the Baltic coast. The rest is now history.'

'According to an Operation Paperclip report, when the V-2 rockets were inspected by Allied scientists in the captured Nordhausen Central Works at the close of the war, they were found to be remarkably similar to the rockets of Robert H. Goddard.'

'Of course. The most notable features of the propulsion unit were the shutter-type valves in the fixed grill, the fuel injection orifices incorporated in the same grill, the combustion chamber, spark plugs and nozzle. We stole those from a Robert H. Goddard patent that was reproduced in the German aviation magazine, *Flugsport* – about January 1939, as I recall.'

'In 1944 many Allied pilots were being harassed by what appeared to be balls of fire which were under some kind of remote-control. The pilots called them "Foo Fighters". Were they connected in any way with your work or Goddard's early experiments?'

'No, I don't believe so. I had heard that they were some new kind of German secret weapon, radio-controlled from the ground, and designed either to foul the ignition systems of the bombers or to act as pyschological weapons, to confuse and unnerve Allied pilots. Certainly they were not designed or constructed at Peenemünde. However, given that they might have utilised some of our technical innovations, it is possible that they were created by rocket engineers other than my own.'

'Such as?'

Von Braun shrugged. 'We were scattered far and wide.'

'What about Kummersdorf or Peenemünde?'

'Not at the latter; possibly at the former. There were actually two rocket research centres at Kummersdorf, separated by an old firing range. We were transferred from the original site to the new site at the other side of the firing range, then another development team took over our old site.'

'Anything unusual about it?'

Von Braun smiled knowingly. 'You mean the reports about a traitorous American physicist?'

'Wilson. You know about him.'

'Not much,' von Braun said, shaking his head. 'I never met him or saw him. I only heard reports about his extraordinary presence as part of a research team involved in a top-secret project. I never found out what the project was, but certainly ideas and innovations were swopped across the firing range. The other establishment was even more heavily guarded than ours.'

'Do you think Wilson had anything to do with the so-called Foo Fighters?'

'There were rumours about disc-shaped aircraft. Frightened whispers. No more than that. Certainly nothing of that nature was tested while I was at Kummersdorf.'

'Do you think disc-shaped aircraft were on the German agenda?'

'Yes. I myself did not believe that such a craft could be made workable – I believe in rockets, not flying discs – but certainly Germany had a long history of research into vertical-rising, spherical or disc-shaped aircraft. In fact, the idea itself was first conceived by a German: the nineteenth-century mathematician and aeronautical theorist Wilhelm Zachariae.'

'A theorist,' Fuller said impatiently, now listening, also, to the Glen Miller orchestra on the radio and wondering what had caused the famous band leader's unexplained disappearance over the Atlantic. 'Were his ideas ever put into practice?'

'Yes. As early as 1939 Dr Alexander Lippisch, at Messerschmitt, Augsburg, was developing his Delta-Rocket Jet ME163 and testing its circular wing in the wind tunnel of the AVA company at Göttingen. Meanwhile, Arthur Sack, of Machern, near Leipzig, had for years been obsessed with the idea of disc-shaped aircraft. He tested various models at the model-airplane competition at Leipzig-Mockau on July 27 and 28, 1939, with disastrous results. A larger, piloted model, the AS 6, was constructed at the Mitteldeutsche Motorenwerke factory in Leipzig and failed to fly during its test flight at the beginning of February, 1944, on the airfield at Brandis, near Leipzig. He tried again at Brandis on April 16, 1944, but the airplane barely lifted off the ground. Shortly after, the Allied advance brought Sack's experimentation to a halt for all time.'

'Any more?'

Von Braun sighed, obviously finding the subject tiresome. 'Not much. Viktor Schauberger claimed to have designed and constructed a small, remote-controlled flying saucer in 1940 in the Kertl aircraft company in Vienna. Reportedly, during a test conducted in 1943, the saucer went through the ceiling, but by and large it was otherwise unworkable – like most of the other prototypes. Then there were the so-called flying wings, or all-wing airframes, of the Horten brothers, which excited the interest of your intelligence, but which in fact were of value purely for research into wind velocity and drag. Finally, as you doubtless know, by the closing months of the war there were many rumours in German aeronautical circles about the imminent appearance of radically different airplanes, without wings, tails, rudders or other surface protrubences, and powered by special turbines or jet engines. I think it unlikely that such projects were completed – if indeed they ever existed in the first place.'

'Which gets us back to the rockets.'

'I'm afraid so,' Von Braun said.

'What about Nordhausen, towards the end of the war? Were there other rocket engineers in that area?'

'You mean Wilson again.' Von Braun was sourly amused by Fuller's interest. 'More rumours,' he said. 'We heard that another group, heavily guarded by Artur Nebe's most ruthless SS troops, had been shipped in from Kummersdorf to Kahla, which was not very far from Nordhausen. There were also rumours that a jet-propelled aircraft of unusual configuration, but possibly spherical or disc-shaped, had been test-flown over Kahla in February 1945. The results of that test, if indeed it took place, were not known, but in early April the Kahla complex was evacuated, as was Nordhausen, and that was the last I heard of Wilson.'

Fuller knew the rest. At the end of the war, Germany's scientific papers were hidden, and eventually found, in tunnels, caves, dry wells, ploughed fields, river beds and even cess pits. Also found across the length and breadth of Nazi Germany and its occupied territories were the well-known V-1 flying bombs and V-2 rockets, as well as lesser known, but equally formidable, heat-seeking ground-to-air missiles, sonic-guidance torpedoes, the highly advanced U-XX1 and U-XXIII electrical submarines, ME-262 jet-fighters, rocket planes that flew even faster than the Messerschmitts, the beginnings of an atom bomb project, and the prototypes for other, vertical-rising jet aircraft.

Because of this, there was a race between the Allies and the Russians to capture as many of the rocket scientists and engineers as possible, as well as the invaluable technical documentation. Deals were thus struck between the conquerors and their former enemies, particularly with regard to those involved in rocketry and other advanced weaponry.

Along with a hundred and fifty of their best men, General Dorberger, Walther Riedel, and Wernher von Braun came to the United States to work on secret government projects. The Russians, however, also gained a wealth of documentation and material, including the plans for V-2 rockets, buzz bombs, ocean-spanning surface-to-surface and surface-to-air missiles found in Peenemünde, and about seventy per cent of the twelve thousand tons of technical equipment stranded on the docks at Lübeck, Magdeburg, and the Gotha plant. They also captured six thousand German technical specialists, including Dr Bock, Director of the German Institute of Airways Research; Dr Helmut Gröttrup, the electronics and guided-missile expert; and a particular aeronautical engineer, known only as 'Habermohl' and reported to have worked under the American, Wilson.

'Why are you so interested in this Wilson?' von Braun asked while glancing impatiently at his wristwatch. 'Has he vanished completely?'

'Yes.'

'He was probably killed by the Nazis.'

'That's what was reported, but we don't think it's true. We have reason to believe that Wilson, when in Nazi Germany, was indeed working on highly advanced, supersonic aircraft of unusual configuration, possibly spherical or disc-shaped, and that he might still be doing so in a location I'm not allowed to disclose.'

'You mean the Soviet Union? The V-2 they launched recently?'

'No. Somewhere else. I can't say where. I *can* tell you, however, that my government is seriously concerned with what Wilson might be constructing at the present time. This is why we were so keen to place you and your rocket scientists under contract, irrespective of negative public opinion.'

'I'm not sure I get your drift.' Von Braun's command of English was admirable, as was his gift for casually easing people out of his house. He simply sighed, glanced again at his wristwatch, then stood up and stretched himself, which made him look even more enormous. 'But I'm sure you know what you're about,' he added. 'Your intelligence is thorough.'

Fuller stood up as well, then walked to the front door. Von Braun, acting as if he had been shaken out of a trance, said, 'Oh, I see you're leaving! Please, let me.' He held the door open until Fuller had walked out and turned back to face him. 'So why did you risk negative public opinion to put me and my men under government contracts?'

'It is imperative,' Fuller said, 'that we get into space before Wilson does. Do you think you can do that?'

'Chuck Yeager has already broken the sound barrier,' von Braun said. 'So the answer to your question is "Yes".'

'Good,' Fuller said, then he nodded goodbye, walked down to the car, climbed in and drove out of Fort Bliss.

Chapter Five

Nichola Randall, already blonde and beautiful, was covered in mushy food and hammering the rim of her high chair with a rattle as if beating on a tin drum. At least that's what it sounded like to her dad, Captain Dwight Randall, who winced as he ate his cornflakes, even though he could not be angry with her, not even this early in a bleak morning in January, 1948.

'Honey,' he said, 'I know you're just seven months old, but couldn't you quieten it down just a little bit? Between you and those damned airplanes taking off, I can hardly think straight.'

'Don't blame my daughter,' Beth said. 'Blame the US Air Force and their planes. Always making a racket.'

'*Your* daughter, I note,' Dwight said with a smile. 'I don't get a look-in. You'd think I'd nothing to do with her.'

'Stop fishing for compliments.'

'As for the US Air Force, don't forget it's our bread and butter. Here we are in a tract house in Dayton, Ohio, secure as little bunnies in their burrows. What more could we ask for?'

'A house outside Wright-Patterson Air Force Base. A little home of our own.'

'Time will bring us everything.' Dwight finished his cornflakes and pushed his plate aside as another F-51 jet interceptor roared overhead. Nichola gurgled happily in her high-chair, banging away with the rattle and smearing food over her face, but Beth rolled her eyes as if she couldn't

56

bear it another minute. Still as slim as an adolescent in loose sweater and slacks, she had short-cropped auburn hair and the face of a lovely urchin, full-lipped and round-cheeked. They had been married for just over two years and were still in love, Dwight hoped, but Beth was increasingly frustrated by life on the base and by Dwight's constant working for ATIC, the Air Technical Intelligence Centre, located here in Wright-Patterson. If anything, his workload had become even heavier since the start of the UFO flap last year. In the seven months since then, Dwight had virtually worked around the clock and it was giving them problems. Now Beth, ironing the clothes by the window, was looking disgruntled.

'When are you going to get a few days off?' she asked.

'Soon,' he replied.

'You've been saying that for months.'

'Our new boss is arriving this morning, so I can't ask immediately, but as soon as he's settled in, I'll put in my request for some leave.'

'Promise?'

'I promise.'

The telephone rang. Carrying his cup of coffee, Dwight leaned across the table, kissed Nichola on her messy cheek, then picked up the phone.

'Captain Randall,' he said.

'Hi, Dwight, it's Bob,' said his friend and sidekick at ATIC, Captain Robert Jackson. 'Are you awake yet?'

'I'm just about to leave.'

'I'm at the office already.'

'Bully for you.'

'I'm gonna make your day, Cap'n.'

'Oh, how?'

'We've just received a classified Memorandum for the Record from our Commanding General. It states that last September General Nathan Twining, Chief of Staff of the United States Army, wrote to Brigadier General George Schulgen, Commanding General of the Army Air Force, expressing his belief that the UFO phenomenon is something real, that it is not, quote, visionary or fictitious, unquote, and that the objects are disc-shaped, as large as aircraft and . . . wait for it . . . *controlled*.'

Dwight whooped with delight, making Beth stare at him, surprised. He couldn't contain himself because for too long he had been working on a project that many thought was a waste of time, if not downright idiotic. Twining's letter would give the project validation, as well as priority, and Dwight felt good about that. He therefore grinned like a schoolboy and gave a puzzled Beth the thumbs-up.

'According to the memo,' Bob continued, 'the letter wasn't intended to support the extraterrestrial hypothesis, but came about because US military fears that the UFOs might be Russian have been exacerbated by the knowledge that the Soviets tested their first A-bomb last November.'

'Right,' Dwight said. 'I *thought* that might get them jumping.'

Bob chuckled. 'Anyway, because of Twining's letter, the Army Air Force is going to establish an official UFO investigation unit with a 2A classification. Called Project Sign, it'll be located right here, in Wright-Patterson, with you in charge and me remaining as your side-kick. We're to start it as soon as we can, but no later than next month, so you better get your ass over here, Cap'n.'

'I'm on my way,' Dwight said. Exultant, he hung up the phone, gulped the rest of the coffee, put the mug back on the table and tightened his tie. As he slipped on his jacket and reached for his peaked cap, he saw Beth's sulky face.

'Whoops!' he murmured.

'What's up?' Beth asked. When he told her, she said, 'There goes our vacation. A 2A classification is second only to top priority. You'll be working night and day with this new project. I'll hardly see you at all.'

'I won't, I promise.' He placed his peaked cap on his head.

'Send me a postcard,' Beth replied. 'Let me know how you're keeping.'

Dwight smiled uneasily, then gave her a hug and kissed her. 'Don't worry, I'll be back in time for dinner. Have a good day.'

'Yeah,' Beth said flatly.

She was already returning to her ironing when he left the small house and walked quickly, too eagerly, to the ATIC offices located at Wright Field. Saluting junior and senior officers en route, he looked fondly at the aircraft flying overhead, under grey clouds pierced by weak sunlight. Recalling Beth's sulky face, he was ashamed of his own eagerness, but knew that it could not be helped. The truth of the matter was that he was too easily bored and, though still loving Beth, was having problems adjusting to the domesticity of marriage and fatherhood.

During the Second World War he had been a B-29 bombardier and radar operator, flying to India, China and the Pacific with the original B-29 wing. Though returning to college after the war, he had kept his reserved status, flying as a navigator in an Air Force Reserve Troop Carrier Wing. This had only increased his low-boredom threshold for normal life, so immediately upon receiving his degree in aeronautical engineering, he married Beth, whom he had met at college, then went back on active duty. He was posted straight to ATIC, which was responsible for keeping track of all foreign aircraft and guided missiles, and he and Beth moved into married quarters here at Wright-Patterson.

Beth was the beloved only daughter of Joe McGinnis, an amiable car salesman and his good-humoured wife, Glenda, both Dayton residents. Their benevolent parenthood had turned Beth into a fine woman, a loving, loveable wife, but one not familiar with life on an air base. They had been here for a year now, during which time Nichola had been born, but Beth was increasingly desperate to kick off the shackles of Air Force protocol and be nearer her parents in Dayton.

Like Mr and Mrs McGinnis, Beth was both good-humoured and quick-tempered, which had made for some tempestuous moments when the first small, inevitable disillusionments of marriage took place. Unfortunately, Dwight's growing fascination with the UFO phenomenon, which he found more intriguing than the tracking of foreign aircraft and guided missiles, had revitalised his flagging interest in the peacetime Air Force even as it increased Beth's frustrations by keeping him away from home more often. Trouble was brewing, he realised, and he didn't know how to deal with it.

His sidekick, Air Force Captain Bob Jackson, was in the operations room of ATIC with their only assistant, a pretty blonde WAC corporal, Thelma Wheeler, from Huntsville, Alabama. Bob, in his late twenties like Dwight, was a recruiting officer's dream in his Air Force uniform, with short-cropped dark hair, a sleekly handsome face, and a ready smile that always made Thelma squirm with pleasure. When Dwight entered, Bob was sitting on the edge of the WAC's desk, obviously flirting with her while leafing through the morning's mail, but he looked up and grinned when he saw Dwight.

'Lo!' he said. 'Our supervisor has arrived! I *thought* that phone call would get you out of bed.'

'I *was* already out of bed.'

'Tell it to the marines.'

Thelma touched her piled-up hair with exploratory fingers and asked, 'Would you two like a cup of coffee?'

'Yes, thanks,' they replied in unison.

Thelma pushed her chair back, stood up, and went into the small kitchen, looking very attractive at this hour of the morning in her standard WAC skirt and blouse. Dwight thought there was something going on between her and Jackson, but he couldn't be sure of it. Right now, Bob was removing his admiring eyes from the door through which Thelma had disappeared and instead casting a more thoughtful gaze around the one room that constituted the operational centre of ATIC.

It was a spartan office, with a few desks, lots of filing

cabinets, typewriters, phones and a mountain of paperwork, most of it technical information sheets for official UFO reports. The walls were covered with incident maps, charts and graphs showing most of the reported UFO sightings, including the Foo fighters of World War II, the Scandinavian sightings of 1946, and the wave of American sightings that had started with the two famous incidents in Washington State in July the previous year.

So far, the coloured pins on the maps revealed no definite linking pattern to the flight paths of the reported UFOs, apart from a general southerly drift in direction. It wasn't much to go on.

Grinning, Bob lifted a couple of sheets off the desk and waved them at Dwight, who immediately snatched them from him and started reading. The papers included a copy of General Twining's original official letter, dated September 23, 1947, to the Commanding General of the Army Air Force; another letter from Major-General L.C. Craigie, Deputy Chief of Staff of the Air Matériel Command, dated December 30, 1947, instructing the Commanding General of Wright-Patterson AFB to form a project, to be codenamed Sign and classified 2A, for the serious evaluation of UFO reports; and finally, a Memorandum for the Record from the Commanding General of Wright-Patterson to Dwight, ordering him to set up the project forthwith from his present office in Wright Field.

Reading the letters with increasing exhilaration, Dwight saw all the words he had longed to hear from his superiors: 'the phenomenon reported is something real . . . not visionary or fictitious . . . appear to be disc-shaped . . . as large as aircraft . . . controlled either manually, automatically or remotely . . . might be of foreign origin . . . possibly nuclear . . . collect, collate, evaluate and distribute all information . . . of concern to national security . . .' These words had finally come from the very top to cast the UFOs out of mythology and bring them into reality. Dwight was overwhelmed.

'Here's your coffee, sir.'

Dwight looked up with a start. Thelma was smiling at him and holding out a cup of coffee. When he took it, she gave the other cup to Bob, who was grinning wickedly at him.

'Feels pretty good, right?'

'Right,' Dwight said.

'Christ, where do we start?'

'Let's go through all the reports—'

'*All* of them?' Thelma asked in dismay.

'Yes, Thelma,' Dwight confirmed, glancing sideways at her as she sat on the edge of her desk – hitching up her skirt to reveal her flawless knees – and looked despairingly at the thick files piled up on it. '*All* of them.' He turned back to Bob. 'Now, at last, the top brass will be taking an interest, so we better make sure we're prepared.'

'By isolating the major sightings from all the others and trying to find some pattern in them.'

'Exactly.'

'You're the boss,' Bob said.

The day passed so quickly, they hardly knew it was fading. While Thelma fed them on a constant diet of black coffee and, at lunchtime, sandwiches from the PX, Dwight and Bob went through most of the files of UFO reports, or technical information sheets, whittling out the weakest cases, selecting the strongest, and then exchanging those selected and going through them again.

By 5.30 p.m. Thelma was suggesting that it was time to finish work. By 6.30 p.m. she was complaining that she didn't get paid overtime. An hour later she was pouring them more coffee and insisting that she was going to miss dinner. At 8.00 p.m. she was finally allowed to leave, waving at Dwight as she did so, but smiling more meaningfully at Bob. By 9.00 p.m. Dwight and Bob were facing each other over a mountain of reports and through a haze of cigarette smoke, summarising what it was they had to go with.

'Okay,' Bob said, puffing smoke from yet another

cigarette, but now sipping whisky instead of coffee, 'the basic scenario is this . . . The UFO scare didn't really start last July. It appears to have started before it, during World War II . . .'

On December 13, 1944, Marshall Yarrow, then the Reuters special correspondent to Supreme Headquarters in liberated Paris, syndicated an article stating that the Germans had produced a 'secret' device, thought to be an air defence weapon, which resembled the glass balls used on Christmas trees. According to Yarrow, they were coloured silver, seemed slightly transparent, and had been seen hanging in the air over German territory, sometimes singly, sometimes in clusters. A second article by another reporter, published in the New York *Herald Tribune* of January 2, 1945, described the devices as 'weird, mysterious "Foo Fighter" balls' which raced alongside the wings of Beaufighters flying intruder missions over Germany. According to the reports of Allied pilots, the 'balls of fire' would appear suddenly and accompany the planes for miles. They seemed to be radio-controlled from the ground.

'Either because of the famous line from the popular Smokey Stover comic strip, "Where there's foo, there's fire",' Bob explained, reading from his notes, 'or simply because the French word for "fire" is *feu*, those "eerie" weapons soon became widely known as "Foo fighters".

'Official "Foo Fighter" reports were submitted by pilots Henry Giblin and Walter Cleary, who stated that on the night of September 27, 1944, they had been harassed in the vicinity of Speyer by "an enormous burning light" that was flying above their aircraft at about two hundred and fifty miles per hour; then by Lieutenant Edward Schluter, a fighter-pilot of the US 415th Night-Fighter Squadron based at Dijon, France, who, on the night of November 23, 1944, was harassed over the Rhine by "ten small reddish balls of fire" flying in formation at immense speed. Further sightings were made by members of the same squadron on November 27, December 22 and December 24.

'In a report published in the New York *Times* of January 2, 1945, US Air Force Lieutenant Donald Meiers claimed that there were three kinds of Foo Fighter: red balls of fire that appeared off the aircraft's wingtips, other balls of fire that flew in front of them, and "lights which appear off in the distance – like a Christmas tree in the air – and flicker on and off." Meiers also confirmed that the Foo Fighters climbed, descended or turned when the aircraft did so.

'The Foo Fighters were witnessed both at night and by day, yet even when pacing the Allied aircraft they did not show up on radar screens.

'Allied intelligence was concerned enough about the reports to establish a classified project in England, under the direction of Lieutenant General Massey, to examine them. Massey was able to confirm that the Foo Fighters were balls of fire which flew in parallel formation with the Allied aircraft, often pacing them for great distances, at speeds exceeding three hundred miles per hour, frequently causing their engines to malfunction and cut in and out. While a few reports of crashing Allied aircraft suggest that Foo Fighters caused the crashes by making the aircrafts' engines cut out completely, most reports indicate that this was unlikely, and that the Foo Fighters merely tailed the planes and caused psychological harm, rather than physical damage. They also flew away when fired upon.'

'But in the end, no official designation of the Foo Fighters was given,' Dwight said.

'No,' Bob confirmed. 'Unable to solve the mystery, both the RAF and the US Eighth Army Air Force concluded that they were the products of mass hallucination. Subsequently, they did no more about them. In any event, sightings of the Foo Fighters tailed off and ceased completely a few weeks before the end of the war.'

'But the first post-war UFO flap came in 1946 with the appearance of so-called ghost rockets over Scandinavia and western Europe – cigar-shaped, with flames issuing from the tail, and mostly seen at night, often by airline pilots and radar operatives.'

'Which led to speculation that both the Soviets and the Americans, utilising the men and material captured in the secret research plants of Nazi Germany, including those at Peenemünde and Nordhausen, were developing advanced saucer-shaped aircraft.'

'That could have been possible,' Dwight said. 'Certainly when World War Two ended, the Germans had several radical types of new aircraft and guided missiles under development. The majority of such projects were in their infancy, but they were the only known craft that could even approach the performance of the objects reported by UFO observers.'

'Right,' Bob said. 'And it's worth noting that whereas the mysterious Foo Fighters didn't show up on radar, the ghost rockets certainly did – so they couldn't be classified as hoaxes, misidentifications or the products of mass hallucination.'

'The Soviets denied any knowledge of the rockets.'

'Sure, they did. But US suspicions remained unabated while those things continued to fly. They only faded away the following year.'

'Then came the first known American sightings: pilot Richard Rankin's sighting of ten discs, about thirty to thirty-five feet in diameter, over Bakersfield, California, on June 14, 1947; the Maury Island sighting of six, much larger discs by Harold Dahl on June 21, 1947 over Puget Sound, off Tacoma, Washington; and three days later, Kenneth Arnold's famous sighting of nine disc-shaped, apparently metallic, objects flying in formation and making an undulating motion, near Mount Rainier in the Cascades, also in Washington. In the latter two cases the UFOs flew off and disappeared in the direction of the Canadian border.'

'Thus strengthening the belief that they could be American secret weapons, also based on captured German designs.'

'In other words, both the Soviets and the Americans could be producing secret weapons, or aircraft, from designs and material captured during the war.'

'Which would lend credence to the reality of the original Foo Fighter.'

'Right. Then came last year's plague of UFO sightings over top-secret military bases: the first, on June 28, over Maxwell Air Force Base in Montgomery, Alabama; the next, on June 29, near Alamogordo, New Mexico, right over the White Sands Proving Ground; then, on July 8, a whole spate of sightings of spherically shaped, white aluminium-coloured objects flying over Muroc Air Base, the supersecret Air Force test centre in the Mojave Desert.'

Bob nodded assent. 'And because those particular sightings were made by trained technicians and pilots, and as the reported objects were appearing increasingly over top-and-supersecret military research bases, a growing suspicion in intelligence circles was that the men and material deported from Nazi Germany to Russia had led to a dangerous Soviet lead in space technology.'

'Either them or extraterrestrials.'

'Yeah, right,' Bob said. 'Little green men.'

'Either way,' Dwight summarised, 'what we're dealing with is a combination of small, fiery, probably remote-controlled discs and large, aircraft-sized, obviously piloted, so-called flying saucers.'

'I guess so,' Bob said.

Dwight sighed, put his feet up on the desk, then lit yet another cigarette. 'It's now probably too late to investigate the Maury Island and Kenneth Arnold sightings, but I certainly think we should re-examine the ones that took place over our own military establishments, particularly those at Muroc Air Base.'

'That may be easier said than done,' Bob pointed out. 'I think we'll have to be careful. I mean, even though we've now been given official sanction to go ahead with Project Sign, I don't think we should forget that many of the personnel involved in UFO sightings, either reporting them or investigating them, have gotten into hot water with their superiors, often for no apparent good reason.'

'Yeah,' Dwight said thoughtfully. 'That's always baffled me. Given that UFOs have been classified as a threat to national security, it's strange how much resistance there's been to investigating them – particularly from our own intelligence services. I mean, even that famous Socorro sighting of last year . . . Remember that?' Bob nodded that he did. 'Well, first the Roswell Army Air Base public information officer, Lieutenant Walter Haut, was reprimanded and posted to some shit-hole for releasing the story to the press; then First Lieutenant William Harris, the flight intelligence officer who helped me with my investigations, went the same route. To that you can add the disturbing fact that the major civilian witness to the actuality of the crashed saucer, local farmer Marlon Clarke, has disappeared completely. Last but not least, the former, highly decorated, OSS member and local UFO authority, Mike Bradley, refuses to even discuss the matter, which suggests that he's pretty frightened of something – or someone. So . . . yes, I think we've good reason to be concerned.'

'I don't wanna sound paranoid,' Bob said, pushing his chair back, placing his hands on his hips and stretching his spine, 'but we've already had two officers killed under suspicious circumstances while involved in UFO investigations. Only four months ago. August 1, 1947. Captain William Davidson and Lieutenant Frank Brown, both members of A-2 Military Intelligence of the Fourth Air Force. Engaged in an investigation of Harold Dahl and the Maury Island mystery. They were flying back to the Fourth Air Force, Hamilton Field, California, with a box containing the debris that had fallen from the damaged UFO into Puget Sound, when their B-25 malfunctioned and crashed, killing both of them. Even more surprising is that the only other two passengers on board, Technician Fourth

Grade Woodrow D. Mathews and Master Sergeant Elmer L. Taff neither experienced flyers, both of whom had, reportedly, cadged a lift at the last moment, managed to parachute to safety while our two highly trained intelligence officers failed to do so. That anomaly still hasn't been explained.'

'You think it was rigged?'

Bob simply shrugged. 'All I know is that two experienced intelligence officers died – and the only physical evidence for flying saucers we've had so far was lost in that crash.'

Dwight shivered, feeling cold. He glanced out the window, saw that it was dark, looked at his watch and lowered his feet to the floor as if they'd been scorched. 'Shit!' he exclaimed. 'I should have been home for dinner three hours ago. Beth's gonna kill me!'

'The joys of marriage,' Bob said, putting on his peaked cap and buttoning up his jacket. 'I think I'll go and have a drink with a friend.'

'I hope it's not the delectable Thelma,' Dwight said, pushing his chair back, getting to his feet, and likewise preparing to leave. 'A good officer doesn't get involved with his staff, no matter how much he's tempted.'

'I think I get the message, Dwight.' Bob grinned and patted Dwight on the shoulder, then they turned out the lights and left the office, locking the door behind them. Once outside, Dwight looked across at the huge hangars, parked planes and silent airstrip of Wright Field, thinking of the other kinds of aircraft now haunting the skies. Now, when he saw a shooting star, his heart gave a leap. It was almost instinctive.

'Project Sign,' he said. 'It sounds good. I think I'll enjoy it.'

'You will,' Bob replied, 'but Beth won't. Good night and good luck, my friend.'

'Tread carefully,' Dwight said.

They walked off in opposite directions, Bob to have a drink, probably with Thelma Wheeler, no matter what

Dwight said, and Dwight to return and face the music for being late for dinner again. As he walked away from Wright Field, the silence was broken by the deep rumble of an RB-29 coming in to land, reminding him that the air base never slept. Glancing up at the sky, which was a mosaic of cloudy patches and stars, he contemplated the possibility of equipping some RB-29s with the latest aerial cameras and using them to photograph unusual phenomena by day and by night. The Air Matériel Command laboratories at Wright Field, he was convinced, would be ideal for the processing of such photos. Determined to put his idea into immediate practice, he turned into the silent streets of the married officers' quarters, then entered his own temporary home.

As anticipated, Beth was not amused. Dwight's cooked meal, now cold, was sitting untouched on the table and Beth was reading a book, smoking a cigarette, and listening to Arthur Godfrey on the radio at the same time. She did not look up when Dwight entered.

'Sorry,' he said. When she didn't reply, he crossed the room and kissed the top of her head. 'Really, I'm sorry.'

'Your dinner's cold.'

'I noticed.'

'Nichola's in bed.'

'I guessed.'

'I didn't get my postcard,' Beth said, 'and you seemed to be gone that long.'

'Okay, Beth, that's enough.'

'Your work.'

'Yes, my work. We have to set up this new project and we don't have much time.'

'No time for us, obviously.'

'That's not an issue, Beth. I was only ten minutes' walk from here. It shouldn't be a big deal.'

Beth stubbed her cigarette out, closed her book, turned off the radio. Standing up, she said, 'Maybe not to you, but I know what it means.'

'What?'

'More UFO investigations. Even more than before. Since those first sightings, last July, you've been travelling all over the place. Now that you're in charge of the whole thing, it's bound to get worse.' She headed for the bedroom, then turned back to face him. 'And you like it,' she accused. 'That's what maddens me the most. It's not that you have to do it, it's that you enjoy it so much. You'd rather be travelling and investigating UFOs than be at home with me and your daughter. I could hate you for that.'

'That isn't true, Beth.'

'It is. And damned well you know it. Goodnight, Dwight.'

'Goodnight.'

When she disappeared into the bedroom, Dwight poured himself a drink, a stiff bourbon, and drank it sitting by the window, looking up at the night sky. He felt guilty because he knew that Beth was right, so the drink went down well. He was just finishing and contemplating bed when the telephone rang. It was Bob, sounding shocked.

'When I left you,' he said, 'I went back to the office—'

'What for?' Dwight asked, realising immediately that the office was the only place on the base where Bob and Thelma Wheeler could get together.

'I forgot something . . . Anyway, what's the difference? What I'm saying is that I was back in the office when I received a call from a buddy at Fort Knox, Kentucky, informing me that Air Force Captain Thomas F. Mantell, an experienced pilot and air hero during the Normandy invasion, was killed in a crash today – reportedly when trying to pursue a UFO over Godman Field.'

'Oh, my God!' Dwight blurted out, hardly able to believe his ears. 'What made them think it was a UFO?'

'I haven't got the full facts yet. Godman have promised a detailed report, but in the meantime all I've got is what I was told over the phone.'

'Yes?' Dwight demanded, feeling breathless.

'There were a series of sightings this morning all over the area, beginning in Maysville, Kentucky, less than a hundred miles east of Louisville, where Godman Air Force Base is located. The object was also sighted over Owensboro and Irvington, located in northwest Kentucky. The cumulative sightings, called in to the local police, indicated a circular, metallic object about two hundred and fifty to three hundred feet in diameter, heading in a westerly direction, towards Godman Field. Early that afternoon, the state police contacted Godman, but the control tower operators could confirm no similar sighting at that time. However, half an hour later, the assistant tower operator picked up the object, which was subsequently observed by the operations officer, the intelligence officer, the base commander, his executive officer, and a band of other ranking personnel.'

'Christ!' Dwight exclaimed.

'A flight of four F-51 fighter planes, headed by Captain Mantell, was sent in pursuit and was observed disappearing in the southward wake of the UFO. According to the control-tower operators, by the time the four planes reached ten thousand feet, Mantell was well ahead and far above them. He reported to the control tower: "I see something above and ahead of me. It looks metallic and it's tremendous in size. Now it's starting to climb." He then said that the UFO was above him, that he was gaining on it, and that he intended going as high as twenty thousand feet. Those were his last words before he crashed. Losing contact with him, the other pilots returned to base, where they were informed that Mantell was dead. The UFO wasn't seen again.'

Bob went silent, though Dwight imagined he could hear him breathing. He then realised that he, too, was breathing heavily and that his heart was racing. Taking a deep breath, he glanced up at the clouds and stars, then he let his breath out again.

'Make sure you get the full report,' he said.

'Sure,' Bob said. 'Goodnight.'

The line went dead and Dwight put his phone down. He thought of Beth in their bed, already concerned for him, and wanted to lie quietly beside her and press himself into her. Instead, he poured himself another drink and let it last a long time. He drank while gazing up at the night sky, until it seemed to press down upon him, threatening to crush him. That sensation, he knew, was caused by fear. He would have to get used to that.

Chapter Six

'They weren't ours,' Wilson said as he gazed out from his office of steel and concrete near the summit of the mountain to the vast, white desolation of Antarctica. 'Neither the Maury Island sightings, nor those made by Kenneth Arnold over the Cascades, were of our saucers. The ones that flew back towards Canada belonged to someone else. Not to me. Not from here. We must look to America.'

He sipped his mineral water and placed his glass back on the table by the panoramic window while Hans Kammler, still blond, handsome, and cold-eyed, likewise gazed over Queen Maud Land, his beloved Neu Schwabenland, and smiled thinly, bleakly, to himself.

'Ah, yes,' he said, 'the Americans. Perhaps the Soviets as well. Our captured V-2 rockets were shipped from Germany to New Mexico in 1945. The launch of American V-2s commenced at the White Sands Proving Ground in March the following year, under the direction of that traitor, Count von Braun. We have since received a report confirming that North American Aviation are planning to go into the production of rocket motors under a USAF contract and will be basing their work on the original V-2 motor.'

'How ironic,' Wilson said, smiling, 'that the V-2 in turn was based on the rocket motors of America's own badly neglected Robert H. Goddard, with whom I also worked when he was based in Roswell, New Mexico, now the

W. A. Harbinson

location of the White Sands Proving Ground. It has all come full circle.'

'It's nothing to be pleased about,' Kammler said testily. 'The Russians have Habermohl and the Americans have Miethe, who also worked on Projekt Saucer. Miethe was formerly stationed with von Braun at Fort Bliss but is now located at Alamogordo, the centre of American rocket development. God knows what he's constructing there.'

Wilson glanced at the launching pad far below, carpeted thinly with snow and shadowed by the encircling rock face soaring high above it. The Antarctic sunlight beamed down upon the latest three hundred foot flying saucer like a torch shining into a dark well, making the machine's metallic grey surface take on a silvery sheen. The many men in black coveralls, who had been swarming all over the saucer, were removing the ladders and hurrying behind the shock-proof protective shields located in small caves hacked out of the rock. From this high, behind the thick, plate-glass window, Wilson could not hear the saucer's bass humming sound, but he could see it rocking slightly from side to side, its heat turning the thin snow into steam as it prepared for lift-off.

'Yes,' he said, 'the original Projekt Saucer team are a problem. Now that pompous fool, Schriever, who managed to escape from Prague, is living back in his home town of Bremer-Haven, West Germany, telling all and sundry that the Allies are building flying saucers based on the one he constructed during the war. Though the press are viewing him with scepticism, he is in fact correct. The Canadians and Americans are both working on a flying-saucer development programme based on designs found in Germany at the end of the war. The Canadian project is being undertaken by the A.V. Roe Company in Malton, Ontario; the American one is hidden somewhere in the White Sands Proving Range, reportedly Holman AFB.'

Far below, the *Kugelblitz* Mark III lifted off the ground, swaying gently from side to side, then ascended silently,

74

growing wider as it came up to Wilson's level. The higher it climbed, the more sunlight it caught, which turned it from dull, almost invisible grey to dazzling silver.

It looks alien and beautiful, Wilson thought. Or beautifully alien. We have done a good job this time.

'If their work is based on the Schriever designs, we have little to fear,' Kammler said.

'Not at the moment, but time could change that, and already the Americans and Canadians are more advanced than they should be. While grossly exaggerated versions of what Harold Dahl and Kenneth Arnold saw over the Cascades have enthralled the world, both men *did* in fact witness the test flights of a series of remote-controlled, pilotless discs, based on our original *Feuerball* and constructed at the A.V. Roe Company in Canada. A larger, piloted saucer is also being constructed there, as well as another by a US Naval Laboratory team in that hidden location in the White Sands Proving Range. While reportedly neither machine is very good, both have had satisfactory test flights.'

'Which have been witnessed by various pilots and other trained military personnel,' Kammler noted.

'Yes. As have ours,' Wilson said. 'Which means that the Canadian and US saucers have been mistakenly credited with the kind of capabilities that only our machines possess so far. This, at least, is to the good. The Americans think the more efficient saucers have been made by the Russians, who believe that they've been made by the Americans. Thus, we can fly our own saucers with impunity, not having to worry if we're seen. By attempting to build their own saucers, based on our old designs, the Soviets, Americans and Canadians have actually given us greater freedom of movement. They should get an award.'

His smile was not returned by Kammler, a man of limited humour, so Wilson concentrated on the three hundred foot diameter saucer as it reached the level of the window and hovered there, swaying gently from side to side, as if in salute. In fact, it was just testing itself. The steel covers on the raised dome were open, revealing the transparent pilot's cabinet with six crew members inside, but they would close when the saucer actually took off on its long flight to Paraguay, making it look like a seamless spinning top in flight. Now, as if obeying Wilson's instinctive nod of approval, the saucer dropped out of sight below the window, descending back onto its landing pad.

'Is Stoll ready to leave?' Wilson asked.

'Yes,' Kammler replied. 'Not too happy, but prepared to do his duty. I'd better go down and say *Auf Wiedersehen*.'

'Tell him I'll be down before take-off, after I've visited the laboratory and talked to Dr King.'

'He responded well to his indoctrination. Particularly after hypnotic-drug treatment, which helped change his mind – for the rest of his life, I hope.'

'He's a man of considerable will-power. He'll serve us well in the end. So, Hans, let's go.'

Pushing his chair back, Wilson glanced again over that vast, spectacular panorama of Antarctic wilderness, then stood and walked across the immense, dome-shaped room, with Kammler behind him, and took the lift down to Level 3. Leaving Kammler in the lift, to continue his descent to the ground level where the flying saucer was parked, Wilson walked through a short tunnel hacked out of the rock and entered the laboratory containing its ghoulish collection of human spare parts and artificial replacements. By now, some larger glass cabinets had been built into the walls of bare rock and contained drugged, unconscious, and frozen human beings who had been abducted by Wilson's flying saucer crews. Wired up to machines that showed their declining heartbeat and brain-waves, they would eventually freeze to death, though not before providing valuable information for the ongoing researches into longevity.

Surrounded by other white-smocked physicians and surgeons, Dr King was at a long table, examining a drained human torso which had a prosthetic replacement attached to the stump of one of its amputated arms. The interior of the prosthetic arm had been left open to reveal a complex of electric wiring that ran from the shoulder down into the artificial hand. A white-smocked assistant was applying electric charges to the prosthetic while Dr King checked the mobility of the twitching artificial fingers. He looked up and stopped what he was doing when Wilson approached him.

'Good day, Wilson,' he said, sounding calm enough, but not smiling.

'Good day. How's it going?'

King glanced down at the prosthetic arm fixed to the drained human torso. 'Not bad,' he said. 'I think we'll get there eventually. Working with human cadavers, instead of animals, short-circuits a lot of otherwise time-consuming experiments and aids progress tremendously. It's really quite exciting. I think we'll have working, myoelectric limbs before the year's out. They won't be all that brilliant, but once we've got a working model, the rest of it will come even more quickly.'

'What about head transplants?' Wilson asked. 'Or even just partial replacement of the face and head: the mouth, throat and jawbone? I mean for the development of cyborgs. For survival in outer space and on the sea bed. To man the saucers indefinitely.'

King glanced at the guillotined human head, now frozen in a small glass case on a nearby table, that was wired up to an EEG machine, which was actually recording weak, dying brain-waves. The eyes of the head were open, staring wildly, seeing only God knows what. It was the head of the unfortunate Marlon Clarke.

'A long way off yet,' Dr King said, 'but we'll get there eventually. At the moment, we're concentrating simultaneously on many different aspects of the problem and discovering the biological and physical interrelationships between them. Experiments already undertaken in the animal laboratory have convinced us that animal gut, intestines and even skin can eventually be transplanted successfully into humans. Similarly, the heart and lungs might be used, but this will take longer. Regarding artificial bones, joints and sockets, it's my belief that the main alloys required will be of the cobalt and chromium variety: tantalum, titanium, niobium and molybdenum. Limited success has already been attained in the preservation of human heart valves, bone, blood and even the cornea of the eye.'

'Very good,' Wilson said. 'Have you been able to make any advances on what you were doing in the Powered Limbs Unit of West Hendon Hospital?'

'Yes.' The doctor spoke precisely, but rather like one of the automatons he was hoping to create. 'In external prosthetics, the myoelectric control of limbs is racing ahead.' He waved a hand, to indicate the prosthetic arm joined to the limbless human torso on the table. 'As you can see.' Wilson nodded. 'Already we've perfected a hand-arm prosthesis in which all five fingers are capable of closing around objects of variable shape, though not yet with the precision of a human hand. We are also working on other advanced prosthetics, including myoelectric arms with interchangeable hands. From there, I hope to progress to a more sophisticated arm that will be able to move at any angle, speed or force simply by being *thought* into action. Such an arm will pick up muscle signals generated to the natural stump, transmit them to a small amplifier, and use that to drive a compact electric motor. The machinery for all this will be housed inside a flesh-coloured, fibre-glass casing that resembles a real arm.'

'Like the one on the table.'

'Correct.'

'But the head?' Wilson insisted, glancing at the wide-eyed severed head of Marlon Clarke, which may or may not have been aware of its own existence, though the brain inside wasn't likely to be sane any more.

Ignoring the head, Dr King pointed at the large glass cases containing unconscious, frozen human beings. 'Our biochemists and mechanical, electrical, chemical, and biomedical engineers are already exploring the possibility of collecting healthy human specimens, rendering them unconscious, and freezing them to just under the point of death for as long as possible. If we can perfect a workable form of cryonic preservation, even though the brains of these living cadavers will have ceased functioning, they'll still be potentially respiring, pulsating, evacuating, and excreting bodies that could be maintained for many years as a source of spare parts and for medical experimentation of all kinds.'

'But the head?' Wilson repeated impatiently, glancing at the staring eyes of Marlon Clarke. 'Can we ever transfer the entire *head* from one human being to another?'

Dr King nodded affirmatively. 'I think it can be done. In the other laboratory isolated animal brains are being kept in cold storage and others, less lucky' – here the doctor smiled bleakly – 'are functioning, warm brains kept alive by hook-ups to blood machines or to live individuals of the same species. Right now we can't speculate as to what's going on mentally inside those disembodied brains, but our latest two-headed dog has survived for a week now and is eating, sleeping and performing its physiological functions normally, as if nothing has happened. In other words, it appears to accept itself as perfectly normal.'

'And longevity?'

'We'll require a steady supply of live fetuses. The heads will be cut off and then injected with radioactive compounds to enable us to study brain metabolism. We also need mature adults who can be injected with various diseases, including live hepatitis virus and cancer cells, to determine if the diseases can be so induced and suitable antidotes found.'

'We conducted similar experiments in the Nazi concentration camps,' Wilson told him, but they didn't prove much.'

'You lacked both knowledge and proper facilities,' King replied. 'I'm expecting much more here.'

'I think you're beginning to enjoy this, Dr King.'

'It's more exciting than my work at Hendon,' King said without the slightest trace of humour. 'Here, the possibilities are limitless. The mysteries of longevity will eventually be solved here – and the cyborgs will come even before that. You have no cause to worry.'

'I'm not the worrying kind,' Wilson said. 'Thank you, Dr King.'

Taking a final, curious glance at the wide, staring, unreadable eyes of the guillotined head of Marlon Clarke, Wilson left the laboratory, crossed a catwalk, and glanced down a dizzying drop to the mass of men in black coveralls working on skeletal saucer structures in the immense, arc-lit workshop with walls of solid rock. He then entered a tunnel still being hacked out of the mountain's interior with the sweat of slave labour. Reminded by the gloom, bedlam, dust and cracking whips of the Nordhausen Central Works in the Harz mountains, he was glad to get through the nightmarish tunnel and emerge to the viewing bay overlooking one of the proliferating landing pads for the saucers. As this one was located directly below his immense office located near the summit of the mountain, he found himself looking down on the three hundred foot diameter saucer that had ascended to his level during his discussion with Kammler – the one that was taking Stoll to Paraguay.

Wilson took the lift down through the interior of the mountain and emerged to the cleared area that had become a landing pad. The saucer was resting on its four hydraulic legs, with its exit door tilting out from the base to form a short flight of steps down to the ground – a recent, much welcomed innovation. The raised transparent dome was uncovered and Wilson could see the crew inside. Ernst Stoll and Kammler were standing near the front edge of the saucer, talking with the artificial smiles of men who secretly despise one another. They stepped away from each other when Wilson approached them.

'Well,' Wilson said, 'the day has come at last. It's been a long wait. No regrets?'

'No regrets,' Stoll said. 'Naturally, I'd rather stay here with you, but I'll do what I have to.'

'I'm glad,' Wilson said, looking into Stoll's dead gaze and realising just how much he had changed since first they had met in Berlin in 1938. Since then, Stoll had lost his dream of becoming a rocket engineer, lost his faith in the Nazis, lost his wife and child – lost everything. Now he only had Wilson who cared little for him but was all too willing to use him. Wilson glanced at Kammler, then nodded at the flying saucer. 'Is it ready to leave?'

'Yes,' Kammler said. 'We were just waiting for you.'

Wilson shook hands with Stoll. 'Enjoy your work – and good luck.'

'Thank you,' Stoll said, releasing Wilson's hand, shaking Kammler's hand less readily, then ducking low to slip under the base of the saucer and clamber up the ladder into the machine. The ladder was pulled up electronically behind him, sealing the exit, then Wilson and Kammler moved back with the other men to take their positions behind transparent protective shields in the small caves hacked out of the rock. Artur Nebe, the deadly former SS officer now in charge of Wilson's security, was already there with some of his armed guards. He looked at Wilson with dark, inscrutable eyes, resting his hand, as always, on his holstered pistol.

'Do you think he can be trusted?' Nebe asked.

'Yes,' Wilson replied. 'At least until he goes insane. Until then, just to be sure, we will visit him on a regular basis and check what he's up to. I'm sure he'll do the job well.'

'Let's hope so,' Nebe said.

A high-pitched whistling sound came from the saucer, then it changed into an angry roaring. The glittering machine lifted up off the ground, swaying from side to side and bobbing gently up and down. The saucer remained like that for a few seconds, swaying and bobbing magically, roaring angrily, turning the swirling snow into great clouds of steam that made the light from the arc lamps bend and quiver to form a dazzling web. The machine ascended slowly, vertically, as if on invisible strings, until it had cleared the snow-capped peaks of the mountain, just above Wilson's office. There it roared even louder and seemed to quiver like a bow-string, until suddenly it went silent, became motionless for a second, then shot abruptly, vertically up into the blue sky and almost instantly vanished.

'Perfect,' Kammler said.

'And here comes the other one,' Nebe said, his dark eyes glinting watchfully.

The other saucer, also three hundred feet across, had appeared out of nowhere to hover just above the snow-capped peaks and then begin its descent. It came down as gracefully as the first one had ascended and landed as lightly as a feather on the same launching pad. When it had whined back into silence, its trap-door opened and angled down to the ground to form steps. A middle-aged man emerged, wearing a black coverall and boots. He was followed by the five crew members, all dressed in grey coveralls. When Kammler stepped forward to receive the flight records from the crew members, the man in black walked up to Wilson and gave a slight, formal bow.

'Well?' Wilson asked him. 'Did it go well?'

'Yes, sir,' the man, Flight Captain Friedrich, replied. 'We flew over quite a few air bases without much success, but finally, at Godman Field, near Louisville, Kentucky, we were pursued by four F-51 fighter planes. One of them was more foolhardy than the others and pursued us to nearly twenty thousand feet. We let him catch up with us. When he was still climbing and just below us, as close as he dared come, we used your new laser-weapon against him. It worked, sir. Beautifully. The F-51 cut out, went into a spin, and was splitting in two even before it crashed. We later heard on the radio that the pilot was killed. Air Force pilot Thomas

F. Mantell. A World War Two hero. A good choice, don't you think?'

'You didn't exactly choose him,' Nebe coldly corrected him, 'but certainly, for our propaganda purposes, you couldn't have come across a better victim. Now the US Air Force will be very frightened indeed, which is what we require.'

'It's also good to know that the laser weapon developed in Kahla now works,' Wilson said. 'We're pleased, Friedrich. You've done well.'

He squeezed Friedrich's shoulder, glanced at Kammler and Nebe, then turned away and walked back into the mountain.

CHAPTER SEVEN

Fuller made good use of his time before interviewing the former Projekt Saucer scientist, Walter Miethe. Forced by his assignment to return to New Mexico, he decided to learn as much as he could about the V-2 rockets before discussing them, and more important related matters, with the Kraut scientist now working for the Army's First Guided Missile Battalion located in White Sands.

Driving out of town at dawn, past the bright orange-and-white signs saying ALAMOGORDO: HOME OF THE ATOMIC BOMB, CENTRE OF ROCKET DEVELOPMENT!, Fuller headed for White Sands, where a V-2 launching was to take place later in the morning. The drive took him across desert filled with nothing but sagebrush, past isolated gas stations charging twenty-five cents a gallon, to the three thousand six hundred square miles of even more parched desert, sand dunes, and cattle-grazing land, which formed the White Sands Proving Ground, surrounded by the distant, closely bunched peaks of the aptly named Organ Mountains.

Not particularly fond of ranchers, rattlesnakes, mountain lions or coyotes, Fuller was glad to reach the government's first rocket centre. He knew he was getting close when he hit Highway 70 and found it clogged with motorists trying to get themselves a good vantage point for the launching. Rather than being classified, the V-2 launchings (or 'shoots' as they were commonly called), which took place every couple of weeks, were treated as gala occasions and used as military PR exercises on the local populace. Fuller was therefore not surprised, when he approached White Sands in the morning's dazzling light, to find himself in the thick of cars and buses coming in from Las Cruces, Alamogordo, and El Paso, bringing farmers, cowboys, housewives, young mothers with new-born babies, schoolchildren, Boy Scout troops, students from the international rocket school, ROTC men, National Guardsmen, and members of the Chamber of Commerce and civic clubs. Many of these would tour an assembly hangar and the White Sands Proving Ground Museum, housed in a long Army van, where a V-2 rocket was on display, see a movie about guided missiles, visit the launching site, then scramble for a good position in the camp viewing area, located approximately seven miles away.

American know-how, Fuller thought proudly.

He was even more impressed when he entered the White Sands camp and found it swarming with state and municipal officials, retired and active Mexican generals, ordinary GIs, naval ratings, Air Force engineers, and top brass from the Pentagon, West Point, and Annapolis.

'It's like the goddamned Fourth of July,' he said to Captain Edward 'Ed' Gunderson of the First Guided Missile Battalion, in his office near the Proving Ground museum. 'I thought all this would've been top-secret, but these folks are having a party.'

'It's a kind of festive day,' Ed said. 'The rocket shoots are still exciting. You can't keep a shoot secret – I mean the rockets are so damned visible – so everyone's invited to come along. The real secrets are the payloads in the rockets – and the public don't see those.'

'What kind of payloads?'

'The permanent personnel of the Proving Ground are both civilian and military, so it depends on who's financing and sharing the individual rocket. In this instance, General Electric has thermometers on board because they're interested in the problems of heat transfer; the Naval

Research laboratory is sending up a spectrograph to measure the spectral qualities of light at high altitudes; and the University of Michigan is contributing an air-sample bottle, to suck in a sample of the atmosphere and then seal itself. Even Harvard University, would you believe, is sending up a packet of seeds to learn how cosmic radiation affects them. So while the rocket shoot itself isn't secret, the results of the tests certainly will be.'

'Who's most interested in the rockets?'

'Military men and scientists are equally interested, but for very different reasons. The scientists are mostly interested in pure scientific research – an orbital satellite for the checking of weather and other atmospheric data is their long-term aim. But the military men – wouldn't you know it? – are after an atom bomb transported by guided missile. That says it all, doesn't it?'

Fuller's instinct was to say, 'Why not? We've got to protect ourselves from the Commies and other enemies.' But realising that this would antagonise his new friend, he said instead, 'Yeah, I guess it does, Ed. So, when do I get to talk to the Kraut?'

'Dr Miethe?'

'Yeah.'

'Right after the launch. He's out in the desert right now with one of the Recovery Officers, waiting to pick up the rocket's scientific instruments at the point of impact. You can see him right after that.'

'Can you take me out to the launching site?'

'Sure,' Ed said. 'No problem.'

They left the First Guided Missile Battalion HQ and drove in Ed's jeep to the launching site, burning along the camp's only paved road, which ran through seven miles of sagebrush and dunes, with the organ-pipe peaks of the mountains to the west, on the far edge of the otherwise flat terrain. The journey only took ten minutes, but the wind was hot and filled with sand, making Fuller feel dry-throated and sun-scorched by the time the V-2 appeared as a patch

of glinting white in the distance. A minute later, the jeep
was close enough to let Fuller see that the rocket, painted
white but with a pointed, silver warhead, now raised into a
vertical position, was being planted on a portable launching
platform by a specially equipped truck. Ed drove on to
where the rocket was and they got out of the jeep.

The V-2 looked lonely in the desert waste, even though
a good hundred-odd men, civilian and army, were gathered
around it.

The rocket was now straddled by a sixty-foot tall crane,
which had platforms at different levels, where the launch
crew were working like beavers while technicians climbed
up and down ladders, opening and closing the instrument
panels, and, on the ground, the surveyors checked the
vertical alignment. It looked like organised chaos.

'Come on,' Ed said to Fuller. 'Let's check out the
blockhouse.'

'What's that?'

'Headquarters for the shoot.'

The blockhouse was a long, low concrete structure about
a hundred yards west of the launching platform, reminding
Fuller of the pillboxes he had attacked as a Marine during
the war. Inside, it was blessedly cool and contained only
instrumentation relating to the V-2, with lights flickering
constantly on the consoles and other equipment making
rhythmic clicking sounds. The thick, protective walls of
the blockhouse contained three narrow viewing windows
of thick laminated glass which, when Fuller looked, showed
only the fins at the bottom of the V-2 being prepared for
launching. There were also oxygen masks and bottles
hanging on the walls.

'The rocket could keel over and fall into the blockhouse,'
Ed explained reassuringly, 'cutting off our exit. The walls
of the blockhouse are so thick they probably wouldn't cave
in, but the masks would be needed to protect us from the
toxic gases that could seep out of the rocket and fill this
place before we could escape. Come on – only twenty people

are allowed in here during a shoot and you're not invited. You can come with me as part of a field crew. They're stationed right across the Proving Range, in the desert and mountains. Their job is to keep track of the rocket's flight and phone their reports in to the blockhouse. You want to come?'

'Hell, yes,' Fuller said. He hadn't enjoyed himself so much since fighting the Japs at Iwo Jima and was glad to get out of the packed, gloomy blockhouse. Once outside, he noticed that the technicians were no longer swarming over the raised V-2, but had been replaced by a lot of civilians, all on the third platform, about fifty feet up.

'The guys in charge of instrumentation,' Ed explained. 'Let's get in the jeep.'

They drove away from the blockhouse, heading into the desert, arriving a couple of minutes later at Radar Station D, an encampment of half-a-dozen trailers, containing radar and other equipment, located a mile east of the launch area. When Fuller got out of the jeep and looked back where he had come from, he saw heatwaves rising off the plain in front of the rocket.

Wiping sweat from his face, he followed Ed into one of the trailers. It contained the telemeter, which would transmit data on temperatures, wind pressures and cosmic rays during the rocket's eight-minute flight, and three special cameras, which would make a pictorial record of the flight. Men stripped to the waist and wearing shorts, their torsos sweat-slicked, had taken up positions behind the cameras. As this meant that the shoot was imminent, Ed led Fuller back outside, where they could get a good view.

As zero hour approached, more people poured into the encampment, including a lot of full colonels. Instructions were being broadcast from a PA system which linked up all the field stations. Shortly after a pair of Stinson L-5 observation planes appeared in the sky, the count-down began and continued until it reached X-minus One. Then the seconds were counted off: 'Ten, nine, eight, seven, six, five, four, three, two, one – *Fire!*'

A distant, bass rumbling sound soon became a mighty roaring, then flames shot out around the base of the rocket and turned to boiling black smoke. From where Fuller stood, it looked as if the rocket was on fire, about to explode, yet remarkably it didn't move immediately. Instead, the thrust from one thousand nine hundred pounds of explosive fuel built up beneath it, only gradually lifting it off the launching tower. The rocket rose slowly, dramatically, as if about to fall back again, but kept climbing in that oddly leisurely manner out of geysering yellow flame and boiling smoke. When it broke free from the launching tower, spitting flame from its tail, the roaring washed over Fuller like a wave and the ground shook beneath him. He covered his ears with his hands and put his head back, looking upwards, feeling tremendous, almost sexual excitement as the roaring turned into the loudest noise he had ever heard and the rocket started putting real distance between itself and the earth. Fuller's neck could bend no further when the rocket became no more than a flickering flame, curving up and away, until it disappeared altogether, leaving Fuller to squint into nothing but the vast, empty sky.

When he straightened his neck to look about him, he saw Ed's grin and raised thumb. Fuller felt extraordinarily alive, completely physical, and at last had a very real sense of the world that was coming.

No wonder they're scared, he thought.

Fuller didn't like Commies, Japs or Germans, but he tried to be civil when he interviewed Walter Miethe later that afternoon in the headquarters of the First Guided Missile Battalion. The office was small and spartan, containing a desk and three chairs. There was nothing on the desk. Two of the chairs were at one side of it, with Miethe in one of them. Fuller, at the other side, had a good view of White Sands, its chapel framed by the window, which was open.

The bawling of GIs playing on the basketball court came in loud and clear.

'Cigarette?' Fuller asked. Miethe shook his head, indicating refusal. He had black hair and eyes as dark as pitch, though they still revealed wariness. He was a man who had been asked a lot of questions and didn't want to hear more. 'Do you mind if I do?' Fuller asked, lighting up before Miethe could answer. 'No,' Miethe said. 'Of course not.' Fuller grinned. 'You don't smoke at all.' Again Miethe replied by shaking his head in a negative gesture. 'Filthy habit. Never start,' Fuller said, puffing smoke rings and watching them drift away, pretty close to Miethe's face. 'So you know why I'm here, right?'

'I can guess,' Miethe replied.

'You worked for an American called Wilson and we're trying to find him.'

Miethe sighed wearily. 'I'm sorry, I can't help you. I can tell you what I know about Projekt Saucer, but I don't know anything more about Wilson. He's probably dead.'

'What makes you think that?'

'There were two saucer construction programmes: one run by Flugkapitän Rudolph Schriever, the other by Wilson. The two saucer teams were separated in 1944. Wilson's team was placed under the command of SS Brigadier Hans Kammler and transferred under the supervision of Captain Ernst Stoll to Kahla, near the underground rocket construction plant at Nordhausen, in the Harz Mountains. I went with Schriever and his team to Prague, so I never saw Wilson after that. My closest associate on Projekt Saucer, Habermohl, was sent by Schriever to work on part of the programme in Breslau, where he was captured by the Soviets. As for Schriever, the last I saw of him was when he was running away from murderous Czechoslovak partisans at the BMW Plant in Prague, when the Russians were advancing on that city. However, just before that happened, we received unofficial notification that Wilson's team had been evacuated from Kahla in April 1944 and that

Wilson had been shot by General Kammler, to prevent him falling into the hands of the advancing Americans.'

'Bu you had no proof of his death.'

'No.'

'And you've heard nothing about him since?'

'Absolutely nothing.'

Fuller gazed at Miethe's dark, wary eyes and wondered if he was telling the truth. Maybe, maybe not. Wilson was a shadowy figure, a teasing conundrum, but what Fuller had learnt about him so far convinced him that the man was cunning and dangerous, with a long, deadly reach. Lots of people had reason to be scared of Wilson and Miethe might be one of them.

'Your recent boss, Wernher von Braun, was in charge of the Nordhausen Central Works about the same time Wilson was in Kahla. Did he and Wilson co-operate?'

'I don't know. I wasn't there. I was with Schriever in Prague. However, I doubt that they had anything to do with one another. Indeed, I don't believe von Braun even knew that Wilson was in Kahla. Ernst Stoll, who was in charge of Nordhausen and Kahla during Kammler's many absences – Kammler was then overseeing the firing of V-1 rockets from the Hague – kept Wilson's presence in Kahla a tight secret. No-one got in or out of Kahla, other than Stoll and Kammler, so I doubt that von Braun knew they were there.'

'What about the early days? You worked directly under Wilson in Kummersdorf, when von Braun was on the other side of the firing range. Did they co-operate then?'

'No. Von Braun knew about the American, but only through gossip. Though Wilson was compelled to pass on certain innovations to von Braun, this was not reciprocated and the two men never met. Then, of course, von Braun's rocket team moved to Peenemünde, leaving Wilson with the whole of Kummersdorf.'

'So how did you end up in Fort Bliss with von Braun?'

'When the Czechoslovak partisans overran the BMW plant in Prague, I managed to make my escape. Like

Schriever, I just fled across the fields until I lost my pursuers. After that, like thousands of others, I made my way back to Germany, by foot and by begging lifts, until I was captured – luckily, by the Americans, not the Russians.'

'Lucky indeed,' Fuller said.

'By that time,' Miethe continued, ignoring the sarcasm, 'Brigadier Hans Kammler had transferred von Braun and his men to an army barracks in Oberammergau in the Bavarian Alps. There, they were held behind barbed wire and under SS guard, until joined by General Dornberger, when they were allowed to move into the village of Oberjoch. The Americans had since transported me to the town of Reutte, in the Austrian Tyrol, for lengthy interrogation. Shortly after the Führer's death, on the second of May, 1945, Dornberger and his men, including von Braun, surrendered to the American 44th Infantry Division in Reutte and I was naturally placed in custody with them. By June I was on my way to America with von Braun and many of his V-2 specialists. Now . . .' Miethe shrugged indifferently. 'Here I am.'

'You like America?' Fuller asked him.

'I like my work,' Miethe replied, 'and here I can do that.'

Don't do me any favours, Fuller thought, outraged that American generosity could be treated with such contemptuous indifference. 'What about the beer?' he asked, grinning. 'You like American beer?'

'I don't drink,' Miethe replied.

Fuller lit one cigarette with the stub of the other, then sat back in his chair and blew smoke rings, watching them drift towards Miethe's face before dissipating.

'I've seen the drawings of Schriever's saucer,' he said. 'It looks just like the real thing.'

'The real thing?'

'Yeah. The ones that have been causing such a stir over the past year or so. Do you think there's any connection?'

'Yes, I do. I agree with Schriever on that. He's been telling the West German press that the UFOs are man-made and based on our original German designs. I think he's correct.'

'How good was Schriever's saucer? The one you tested in Prague in 1945.'

Miethe smiled bleakly. 'Not very good. It barely hovered above ground level, wobbling wildly, then it crashed back down.'

'So what makes you agree with Schriever?'

'Schriever was a pretender who always tried to get credit for ideas that he stole from the American. I do not agree that the present UFO scare is caused by saucers constructed from Schriever's designs, which in truth were incomplete; what I believe is that they are saucers based on Wilson's designs for a much better saucer known as the *Kugelblitz*. While even that saucer did not have the widely reported capabilities of the UFOs, it was highly advanced and could have been the prototype for the saucers now being sighted. Whether Wilson is alive or dead, it is my belief that enough of his designs, if not the actual prototype, were captured by the Soviets or Americans – or both – to let them build more advanced models. It is my belief, then, that the UFOs are man-made saucers, constructed here or in Russia – maybe in both countries.'

Studying Miethe in silence for a moment, Fuller considered his options. One was to invite him for a drive into the desert, then slit his throat and bury him under the dunes. The other was to utilise his knowledge for the new saucer programme. Miethe knew too much already to be allowed to run loose, which meant either that he should be allowed to work for the US government or that he should be taken out totally, obliterated. Fuller had his own preference – a quick burial in the desert – but unfortunately he was prevented by his superiors and his country's long-term needs.

'What I'm going to tell you,' he said, 'will commit you for life. If you listen to what I tell you, I won't be able to pretend you didn't hear it. That means I'll have to take strong action if you try going elsewhere. If you want to spend the rest of your days working on saucer projects, then you'd better listen to what I say; but if you're frightened of making that kind of commitment, you'd better tell me right now to shut up. You understand, Miethe?'

The German stared steadily, suspiciously at him, then nervously wiped his lips with his hand.

'What if I don't listen?'

'You'll be free to return to Germany,' Fuller lied, thinking longingly of that burial in the desert, 'which may well be the only choice you'll have, as you'll find no work here. Either you work for the US government or not at all – at least not in this country. So what way do you want it?'

Miethe was silent for a considerable time, but his pitch-black gaze was steady and intense, searching Fuller's face for hidden meanings. Eventually, taking a deep breath and letting it out, he said, 'You believe Wilson's still alive, don't you?'

'Yes,' Fuller said.

'And the saucers?'

'We now have our own, but they're not that advanced. We based them on designs found in Nazi Germany and have reason to believe they were done by Wilson. We think we can advance on what we've already got, but it's gonna take a lot of time and money. In the meantime, we have the other saucers to contend with, and certainly they're too advanced to be our own.'

'The Russians?'

'We know they got Habermohl and a lot of rocket scientists, but even if they were constructing their own saucers, they'd have the same problems as us: not enough time or money. In other words, if the Russians have saucers, they're not likely to be much more advanced than ours.'

'Which leaves Wilson.'

'Right.'

Now Miethe looked frightened. 'Do you know where he is?'

'We think we know approximately where he is, but I can't tell you where that is just yet.'

'Because I haven't committed myself.'

'You committed yourself by asking about Wilson. Now you can't back out, Miethe.'

Shocked, Miethe straightened up in his wooden chair, staring beyond Fuller's head, doubtless recalling his early days in Kummersdorf with the Machiavellian American. Fuller saw that Miethe was now truly scared and would want his protection.

'If we're right,' he said, 'Wilson is far away . . . but he has a long reach.'

'With his saucers.'

'Correct.'

Miethe nodded, rubbing his sweaty hands on his pants, then bit his lower lip. 'So,' he said, sounding like he was sighing. 'I am in. I am yours. What do you want with me?'

'You have a wife and children in Germany,' Fuller said. 'A boy and girl, twelve and ten years old respectively. Hans and Irena.'

'Yes,' Miethe said, looking even more concerned. 'Why do you— ?'

'You'll want them with you,' Fuller said. 'And you'll want them out of reach. A new flying-saucer project, based on a combination of Schriever's earlier designs and the more advanced designs found in Kahla, Thuringia – presumably Wilson's work – is about to be financed jointly by the US and Canadian governments. The contract was won by the A.V. Roe Company and construction will take place at their plant in Malton, Ontario. That's in Canada, not America, and we thought you might appreciate being there. Do you agree?'

'Yes,' Miethe said.

'Good. I'll make arrangements for your wife and kids to be flown out of Germany and you'll go to Canada shortly after. Any questions, Miethe?'

'Not for now, Mr Fuller.'

Fuller nodded, stood up, and shook the German's hand. He wiped his hand on his trousers as he walked from the room.

Early that evening, Fuller phoned his wife from his temporary accommodation in the officers' quarters at White Sands. The marriage between him and Belinda Wolfe had been a battlefield from the first day to the last and they had separated eighteen months ago, two years after the honeymoon. Belinda, the ravishing brunette daughter of wealthy natives of Georgetown, Washington DC, had been unable to tolerate Fuller's blatent promiscuity, distaste for domesticity, love of danger, gratuitous cruelty with enemies and friends alike, and horror at the very thought of having children. Fuller and Belinda hadn't met since the acrimonious separation, though they had good reason to speak often by phone: the impending divorce. Now, when they spoke, Belinda told him that the divorce papers were coming through and she was thrilled to be rid of him.

'Thanks a million, Belinda.'

An hour later, Fuller was celebrating at a dance in the Rocket Room of the Officers' Club. High on a bellyful of good American beer, which he loved (those lousy, tasteless Krauts!), he enjoyed the live band, danced with a few ladies, then played the slot machines standing along the pine wall adorned with stag heads. Also playing was the wife of an Army Air Force captain who was on a two-week flying course at Nellis AFB, Las Vegas, Nevada. Fuller engaged her in conversation, bought her a few drinks, played ping-pong with her on the porch, then drove her out into the desert, where, under the dark-blue, star-filled sky, he fucked her brains out. When she recovered and was sobbing, filled with guilt and remorse, though displaying some confusion by saying she loved him, he dumped her well outside the base and told her to walk it off.

Ten minutes later, having packed to leave the next day, he fell into his bed in his room in the officer's quarters, went to sleep almost instantly, and dreamt about a V-2 rocket flying across the curved earth and being tailed by one of Wilson's flying saucers. He awoke with an erection the size of a V-2, but his hangover didn't permit him any pleasure, so he rolled out of bed. Wondering about the elusive thread that led obliquely from the V-2s to the UFOs, or flying saucers, he showered, put on his clothes, and left White Sands for good, gratefully heading back to the real world and its many mysteries.

CHAPTER EIGHT

Even in the desert of the Southwest, just north of
Albuquerque, New Mexico, it was freezing at night.
Squatting in the sand beside the other members of his UFO
tracking team, looking up at the moon and stars but seeing
no unidentifieds, Dwight was torn between his excitement
over what he was doing and depression caused by being
away from home again, leaving Beth hurt and angry. It had
been his own idea to send special sighting patrols out into
the desert around Albuquerque in a determined bid to
resolve the mystery of the recent plague of green fireball
sightings. A good idea from the point of view of ATIC, not
so good for the marriage.

The sightings had begun in November 1948, just three
months ago, when a lot of folks around Albuquerque had
reported seeing what seemed like green balls of fire flying
across the skies. At first, because thousands of conscript
GIs had recently been discharged from the army, taking
souvenirs such as Very pistols, local Air Force Intelligence
at Kirtland AFB had written the sightings off as flares.
However, they were forced to change their tune when, on
the night of December 5, Air Force pilot Captain Goede
and his co-pilot, flying a C-47 transport at eighteen thousand
feet ten miles east of Albuquerque, observed a green fireball
the size of a huge meteor flashing across the sky just ahead
of them. Later, in their official report on the sighting, Goede
and his co-pilot both insisted that it could not have been a
meteor, as it had *ascended* from low altitude, near the slopes

of the Sandia Mountains, then arched upward and levelled out, just like an airplane. A few minutes after that sighting, the captain of a Pioneer Airlines Flight also reported seeing a green ball of fire east of Las Vegas, Nevada, when he was flying en route to Albuquerque. He, also, confirmed that the ascending flight of the green fireball proved that it could not have been a meteorite.

After that, the fireballs appeared practically every night and most of the reports landed on Randall's desk at ATIC, in Wright-Patterson AFB. While analysing the reports with the help of Bob Jackson, Dwight arranged for Dr Lincoln La Paz, head of the University of Mexico's Institute of Meteoritics, to look into the sightings. Subsequently, La Paz reported that he had personally witnessed the green fireballs both from the ground and from an aircraft, in the company of some distinguished scientists from the AEC Los Alamos Laboratory, and was of the opinion that the green fireballs were not meteorites. Their green colouring was too vivid, their trajectories were too flat, they were not accompanied by the sound and shock waves of natural meteorites, and, finally, they were simply *too big*.

The worst row of Dwight's marriage to date had erupted when, after ten more nights of green fireball sightings, he came under pressure to find out what was causing them. Not considering the time of year, he asked for permission to establish three cinetheodolite stations near Albuquerque, in hopes of ascertaining the altitude, speed and size of the UFOs. Unfortunately, permission came in the form of a formal, written order stating that the stations could only be set up and manned for a period of a fortnight, beginning in December and ending January – in other words, over the Christmas and New Year period. Cursing his own stupidity, Dwight was then cursed out by Beth when he told her that he wouldn't be home for Christmas. Her Irish temper finally exploded and they had a dreadful row. Were this not torment enough, Beth then took Nichola to have Christmas with her folks in Dayton while Dwight and his three unhappy sighting teams set up their cinetheodolite stations in the desert around Albuquerque.

To make matters even worse, nothing was spotted.

In truth, Beth had never really forgiven him for their lost Christmas and New Year – particularly since no green fireballs or other UFOs materialised and it all seemed a waste of time. Now, here he was again, a mere four weeks later, in February 1949, in the middle of what he hoped was the most foolproof plan yet devised for the study of UFOs.

This time, Dwight had put together a dozen separate four-man sighting teams, with a radio operator, an instrument man, a timer, and a recorder. All the teams would be assigned a special radio frequency through which they could keep in touch with one another without being heard by outsiders. When a green fireball, or any kind of UFO, was spotted, the radio operator would immediately relay its presence to the other teams to enable them to track it simultaneously. While he was doing so, the instrument man would be measuring the UFO's angles of elevation and azimuth, the timer would be calling out the time, and the recorder would be writing the details down. By then comparing the records of the many different teams, the speed, size, altitude and flight characteristics of the UFO could at last be accurately ascertained.

Dwight was pleased with himself.

Nevertheless, he was also cold and depressed. Cold because the desert, so hot during the day, was as chilly as Antarctica by night – or seemed to be so. Depressed because the stormy waters of his marriage had not exactly been calmed by this latest trip and, even worse, because, yet again, they had been here for four nights in a row and nothing had shown up.

Dwight was even more depressed because he was head of Project Sign and yet had never seen a UFO in his life.

Sensibly, once it became apparent to Dwight's team that nothing was happening, they decided to take turns at guard to ensure that all of them would at least get some sleep, even if only for short periods. Now it was Dwight's turn, it was four in the morning, and he had another two hours to go before he could waken one of the others.

There they were scattered around him, three men in sleeping bags, looking as dead as the flat plain of the desert and the vast, starry cosmos. Dwight's eyes felt like lead and he had to fight to keep them open, which he did by concentrating on the sky while praying for something odd or exciting to materialise.

It could be an eerie experience. The nocturnal sky played many tricks. You looked up at the stars, many of them already dead, in the past, and you couldn't believe they weren't all really there, they seemed so damned real. Then, of course, the sky kept changing. Things were constantly on the move. Even a trained observer could be fooled by shooting stars, comets, meteors, lenticular and noctilucent clouds, dust and ice crystals, temperature inversions, corona discharges, plasmoids, ball-lightning, parhelia and paraselenae, or mock suns and sundogs, mock moons and moondogs, and even the ever-deceiving planet Venus. In ancient times such phenomena had been viewed as mystical visions or visitations by the gods of the sea or sky. In modern times they were often mistaken for UFOs, even by trained observers.

Just like me, Dwight thought bleakly.

Sighing, trying desperately to stay awake, he was just about to fall asleep when he thought he saw something.

He rubbed his eyes and sat up straight, preparing himself for another trick. What he saw was a streak of light, very low on the horizon – impossible to tell the altitude from here, but it was definitely moving.

Left to right – no: up and down – a streak of white light, then two lights. Perhaps two lights blending into one and advancing towards him.

He rubbed his eyes and looked again. Maybe just a shooting star. No, it was too low for that, so it had to be something else. Perhaps a temperature inversion. Lights from somewhere far away. The headlamps of a car that was moving uphill, its lights beaming into the sky, hitting a temperature inversion, and being sent on for miles to another temperature inversion which bent it again and relayed it back to earth to form what Dwight was seeing . . .

No, not that. Not mock moons or moon dogs either. The light, maybe two lights – sometimes two, sometimes one – was growing longer and thinner, stretching out like chewing gum, as it advanced across the desert floor at very low altitude.

'Jesus Christ,' Dwight whispered, wondering if he should waken the others. 'What the hell . . .?'

No, not low altitude. Not a single light either. Two separate lights, now bobbing erratically, beaming down on the desert floor.

Damn it, they were close. Too close to be high up. They were only a couple of feet above the ground, maybe not even that. Approaching. Coming towards him. Not accidentally at all. Not bobbing – bouncing – a sort of rattling in there, too . . . Then settling down and beaming over the track that led right to Dwight.

A car engine and squeaking springs.

'God damn it!' Dwight whispered.

His three companions sat up. 'What the hell— ?' a dim voice queried. 'I'll kill the bastard in that jeep,' Corporal Mathers said. 'Thought we had us a UFO.'

The jeep took shape in the night, even blacker than the darkness, its headlights blinding Dwight as it turned off the road again and headed straight for him and the others. He was shading his dazzled eyes with his hand when the jeep squealed to a halt right in front of him, churning up clouds of sand.

His friend and sidekick, Air Force Captain Bob Jackson, waved at him and jumped down to the sand.

'Hi,' he said. 'How's it going?'

'You came at four in the morning to ask me *that*?'

'Not exactly,' Bob said. He glanced down at the others, all sitting upright in their sleeping bags. 'Okay,' he said. 'Go back to sleep. This is not for your ears. Happy beddy-byes, kids.' When they had moaned and cursed and were settling back again, Bob looked directly at Dwight and said, more seriously: 'I'm sorry, but this can't wait.' He took Dwight by the elbow and walked him away from the others, out of earshot. 'You look cold,' he said. Before Dwight could reply, he withdrew a hip flask from his flying jacket and unscrewed the cap. 'Brandy,' he told him. 'You're going to need it . . . And not just for the cold.'

Grateful, Dwight had a good slug of the brandy and felt it burning down inside him. He had another slug, felt it going straight to his head, took note of the wondrous lustre of the stars and handed the flask back.

'Okay,' he said. 'What the hell is this?'

'Your official Estimate of the Situation,' Dwight replied.

Dwight nodded his understanding. The UFO-related death of Air Force pilot Captain Thomas E. Mantell over Godman AFB, Kentucky, on January 7 last year, combined with the extraordinary UFO sighting made by Eastern Airlines Captain Charles S. Chiles and co-pilot John B. Whitted near Montgomery, Alabama, on the evening of July 24, had prompted Dwight, as head of Project Sign, to write an official, top-secret Estimate of the Situation. That Estimate had outlined the whole history of UFO sightings, including the fireballs, Scandinavian 'ghost rockets' and American sightings before 1947. It had concluded with Dwight's earnestly held conviction that the UFOs were of extraterrestrial origin.

'So why the brandy?' Dwight asked, gazing with instinctive growing despair over the starlit, barren desert.

Bob sucked his breath in, then let it out again. 'Our venerable Chief of Staff, General Hoyt S. Vandenberg, has rejected the report.'

'What?'

'On the grounds that it lacks proof.'

Dwight was stunned. 'Lacks . . .*proof*?'

Bob shrugged and spread his hands in the air as if about to surrender. 'That's what he said. It's an official, top-secret memorandum. That . . . and something even worse.'

'What could be worse?'

Bob took another deep breath and let it out slowly. 'There's to be a whole new policy at Project Sign. In the future, Sign personnel are to assume that *all* UFO reports are hoaxes. Not only that, but we're to check with FBI officers, and with the criminal and subversive files of police departments, looking into the private lives of the witnesses to see if they're – quote, unquote – *reliable*.'

'By doing that,' Dwight said angrily, 'we'll be shifting the investigations away from the actual UFOs and on to the poor bastards who report them.'

'You've got it, buddy. That's absolutely correct. As for your official Estimate of the Situation, it's going to be incinerated and our project will be renamed Project Grudge.'

'Is that a sour joke?'

'No, it's not – though it may be a sign of General Vandenberg's displeasure with us.'

'What he's saying in effect is that we're to discourage further UFO reports and keep a low profile.'

'Right.'

'We now exist in name only – and that name is Project Grudge.'

'How bright you are,' Bob said.

He handed Dwight the hip flask. Dwight took it and walked out into the darkness and sat on the sand. He had a stiff drink, then another, trying to still his racing heart. Then he looked up at the vast, starry sky, which reduced him to nothing. Eventually, Bob came to sit beside him, trying to give him some comfort.

'What the hell's going on?' Dwight asked him, unable to keep the bitterness from his voice.

'It doesn't need spelling out,' Bob said. 'It's fair warning to us all that it's no longer wise to open your mouth too wide about UFOs.'

'Why?' Dwight asked, feeling increasingly confused and nervous, looking up at the night sky.

'You tell me,' Bob replied.

CHAPTER NINE

With some native guides and a modest contingent of General Stroessner's armed *Federales*, an unhappy Ernst Stoll had endured a seemingly endless journey from the dusty streets of Asuncion, along the Paraguay river by gunboat, to this jetty looming out over the muddy water. His guide, a young, gap-toothed Paraguayan called Juan Chavez, pointed proudly at the jetty and the cleared compound behind it, as if that motley collection of thatched shacks and muddy enclosures would actually bring a smile to Ernst's face. Instead, Ernst removed his hat, wiped the sweat from inside it, spat on the deck near Chavez's feet, then put the hat back on and wiped his face.

'*Scheisse*!' he exclaimed, 'what a filthy hole!'

'Have a beer, *señor* Stoll. It will help to cool you down. You must not let the sun dry you out. You need plenty of liquid.'

Juan Chavez was smiling, a wily grimace, his dark, youthful eyes bright with mischief and the urge to be sly. Ernst nodded and took the beer, the bottle cold in his sweaty palm. He drank, wiped some beer from his lips, then glanced over his shoulder. A group of captured Ache Indians were at the aft end of the deck, all small, emaciated, their narrow eyes dulled by fear, dressed in rags and huddling close to one another as if for protection. Two *Federales* were guarding them, wearing jackboots, holding rifles, both gaunt-faced and bored, chewing gum, their eyes hooded beneath tatty peaked caps, their uniforms threadworn. Ernst studied them at length, feeling only contempt, recalling his own disciplined, immaculate SS troops during the recent war. These *Federales* were not like that. They were a bunch of murderous morons. Corrupt and led by a corrupt leader, General Stroessner, they were men whose only purpose was survival in the most expedient manner. The scum of the earth.

'This is your first time in Paraguay, *señor*?' Chavez asked, smiling crookedly to reveal his missing front teeth.

Ernst stared coldly at him. Chavez was still a teenager, but he looked twice his age. This was due to his missing teeth, the scars on his cheeks, and the cunning in his old-man's brown eyes. He would clearly make a good pimp.

God, Ernst thought, these people!

'Yes,' he said. 'I have never been here before. This is the first time.'

'You will have to get used to it, *señor*. Strangers often go crazy here.'

Ernst had another drink, cooled his forehead with the bottle, then surveyed the widening clearing as the boat inched towards it. This was actually a waterside village, its jetty thrusting out from the tangled shrubs and liana at the edge of the forest, where the banks of red mud angled down to the dark, muddied river. Some men were waiting on the jetty, wearing filthy shirts and pants, nearly all with cigarettes in their mouths, not one of them smiling.

'Heaven on earth,' Ernst said sarcastically. 'I'm sure I'll be happy here.'

'You are staying long, *señor*?'

'Unfortunately, yes.'

'A lot of Germans, former soldiers, live in the jungle, so you may find some company.'

'That's nice,' Ernst said, though he wanted no German friends, having been warned by Wilson to avoid them and keep to himself. What would happen here must remain a secret, no matter how much that cost him in emotional terms. His own regular company could only be the scum of this village; his only form of relief the occasional visit from those in Antarctica. He would live here as if in a monastery, though with some compensations.

'I trust there are some women here,' he said.

'Ah, yes,' Chavez replied, grinning lasciviously. 'You can take your pick, *señor*.'

The gun-boat growled and shuddered, turning in towards the bank; it inched forward and then bounced against the tyres along the edge of the jetty. Ernst glanced back over his shoulder. One of the Ache women was wailing. A *Federale* slapped her brutally across the face and screamed a torrent of abuse. The woman's wailing became a whimper. Ernst yawned and turned away. One of the crew had thrown a rope to a man on the jetty who was tying it around an upright, bending low, shouting inanely. The boat's engine cut out. A crew member removed the gate. A plank was thrown across the space between the deck and the jetty, then tied to some uprights to form a crude gangplank. Ernst moved towards the plank, wanting desperately to get off, but Chavez tugged at the sleeve of his shirt and motioned him back.

'No,' he said. 'First the Ache.'

Ernst stopped and stared at him, repulsed by that gap-toothed grin, but he stepped back as Chavez went to the *Federales* and bawled his instructions. The *Federales* were quick to move, venting their boredom on the miserable Indians, screaming abuse and kicking them to their feet, herding them towards the gangplank. The Indians were not so quick, weak from hunger, confused, so the *Federales* encouraged them along with vicious blows from their rifles. The women wailed and held their children, cowering from the swinging rifles, while their menfolk, uncommonly small and frail, tried in vain to protect them.

It was a familiar sight to Ernst. He recalled similar scenes from the war: the night they had left Kummersdorf and herded their slave labour, mostly wailing Jews, onto the trains in Berlin. He smiled at the recollection, feeling a stab of nostalgia, but managed to suppress it as the first of the Indians stumbled across the gangplank with their hands on their heads. Chavez was leading them down, his shirt unbuttoned and flapping loosely, his broad hat tilted over his old-man's eyes as he gave his instructions.

Ernst felt the sun's fierce heat as he studied the village, a drab collection of leaning huts made from palmetto trunks and vines, dogs and goats sniffing lethargically at the dust, babies lying on corn shucks. The poverty was total, the old and young emaciated, sunlight falling on scattered gourds, woven baskets and banana leaves, on the giant rat that raced across the clearing and vanished into the forest. Ernst looked along the jetty. The Ache Indians had just left it. They were now at the edge of the clearing with the *Federales* surrounding them. Chavez was waving his hands, telling Ernst to disembark; so Ernst finished his beer, threw the bottle overboard, watched it glinting as it bobbed along the river and was swept out of sight. Then he went to the gangplank, crossed without enthusiasm above the muddy, oil-slicked water, and finally stepped onto the soil of what would be his new home.

God, he thought, what a piss-hole!

Chavez, an adolescent martinet, was standing beside an emaciated native in short pants and a torn, filthy shirt. Chavez waved Ernst forward. When he reached the pair, he noted that the man was elderly, had rheumy eyes, and seemed slightly nervous.

'This is Salano Valentinas,' Chavez said. 'The head of the village. Anything you want, you ask him. He is here as your eyes, ears and hands.'

'Welcome, *señor*,' Valentinas said, his voice as rough as sandpaper. 'I trust you had a good journey.'

'Never mind my journey,' Ernst said. 'Just show me where I'll be staying.'

'Yes, *señor*, of course.'

He turned away to lead Ernst and Chavez across the clearing, past the captured Ache Indians, who were now being herded up into the backs of two trucks, the men being punched and thumped with the butts of rifles, the women and children all wailing.

'What happens to them?' Ernst said.

'They will be sold as workers and whores to those living in compounds in the jungle – mostly Germans, of course. Some of them are being taken to your compound. You can do what you want with them.'

'Does President Morínigo know about this?'

'I don't know. Maybe not. The *Federales* who collect them are controlled by Morínigo's hatchet-man, General Stroessner. General Stroessner knows everything.'

More than you can imagine, Ernst thought as they crossed the clearing, surrounded by the huts of palmetto leaves and vine, scattering goats and chickens, passing Indians roasting sweet potatoes, and eventually stopping at a small, badly battered, open-topped truck that was parked at the edge of the narrow track that snaked into the forest.

'I'm not staying here?' Ernst asked.

'No, *señor*,' Chavez replied. 'Your compound is ten kilometres away, hidden deep in the forest. There, even aircraft cannot see you. You will feel very safe there.'

The head-man, Valentinas, climbed up into the open-top of the truck, Chavez took the driver's seat, and Ernst climbed up beside him. Chavez turned on the ignition, accelerated inexpertly, and the truck lurched off into the forest, where the trees kept the sun out. Ernst had thought it would be cooler and was shocked to find that it wasn't: the humidity was much worse, overwhelming him, almost making him gag. Feeling ill, he glanced about, taking in the riot of vegetation, tangled vines and soaring trees in the chattering green gloom relieved only by shafts of sunlight beaming down on the steaming banana leaves. The narrow track was very rough, hacked out by hand and pitted with holes, coiling snake-like between the trees and disappearing ahead of them. Chavez was beaming with pleasure, clearly enjoying the drive; this made him look more like his proper age, which was, Ernst surmised with disbelief, not much more than eighteen. The truck growled and kept going, bouncing roughly over potholes, racing through the shafts of sunlight that beamed down through the trees and illuminated the steaming vegetation. Ernst was suffocating. He was sweating and felt feverish. Glancing over his shoulder, he saw the old man in the back, leaning forward with his chin on his raised knees, his rheumy eyes fixed on nothing.

My new companions, Ernst thought with revulsion. I'll go mad in this hell-hole!

The drive seemed to take forever, an endless journey through heat and gloom, but eventually the truck burst into the sunlight of another cleared area. Lines of barbed wire formed a fence around an expansive wooden building, its sloping roof supported by tree trunks and covered in woven vines and banana leaves. Chavez drove the truck through the open gates in the fence and braked fiercely inside the compound, creating a cloud of dust.

'*Scheisse!*' Ernst barked, coughing to clear his throat of the dust as he climbed down from the truck. 'Are you trying to choke us, you fool?'

Chavez just laughed, then led Ernst and Valentinas across the clearing towards the big house with the open verandah running all the way around it, under the roof raised above the top rooms, which were open at the sides to the elements and obviously used only by the servants. The compound was busy, filled with men, women and children, most of whom were gathered around open fires, roasting sweet potatoes. Though watching Ernst's arrival with nervous curiosity, they made no move towards him.

'The barbed wire is electrified,' Chavez informed him. 'Make sure you don't touch it. So, *señor*, here we are!'

They climbed the steps of the verandah and stopped under an awning of vine and leaves. There was a table and chairs near the entrance to the house and a native woman, too stout to be healthy and as ugly as a bat, stood by the table, wearing a white blouse and long skirt, a towel draped over her right arm. She bowed to Ernst. He simply grunted and glanced about him. On the table was a bottle of brandy, a tray of glasses, and a cup filled with fat, white, wriggling worms.

Seeing what Ernst was looking at, Chavez grinned and picked up a worm. He watched it wriggling between his fingers for a moment, then bit off its head, spat it out and swallowed the rest of it. 'Koro worms!' he explained, picking the cup off the table and holding it out to Ernst. 'Try one, *señor*!' When Ernst shuddered with revulsion, Chavez chortled and put the cup back down. 'You will soon learn to enjoy them,' he said. 'You will learn to enjoy many strange things here. Please, *señor*, take a chair.'

When Ernst took one of the wooden chairs by the table, placing his pistol and holster upon it, the native woman knelt in front of him and laboriously pulled off his boots to wipe his feet with the towel. When this was done, she shuffled backwards, not getting off her knees. Only when Chavez barked at her did she do so; then, obviously obeying his command, she filled the two glasses with brandy and handed one each to Ernst and Chavez, ignoring Valentinas, who was standing just behind Chavez, studying the floor.

Chavez offered his gap-toothed smile and held his glass up in a toast, but Ernst ignored him and just sipped his brandy, then put the glass down again. Casting his gaze over the compound, which resembled an untended farmyard covered in smoke and filled with undesirable human livestock, he realised that he was not thrilled to be here.

'So,' he said, not trying to hide his bitterness, 'this is it: my new home.'

'Yes, *señor*,' Chavez said.

'And this so-called head-man' – Ernst indicated Valentinas with a contemptuous wave of his hand – 'now works for me.'

'That is correct, *señor*. He will translate and tell you all you need to know. He will also take care of the supplies, which will be shipped in from Ascuncion every month. He already has his instructions, *señor*, and will not let you down.'

'I hope not,' Ernst said.

Chavez finished off his brandy and placed his glass back on the table. 'Now, *señor*, I must be off. I go back to Asuncion. I work on a gunboat that sails regularly between there and here, so we will meet quite a lot. If you need me, just call. Goodbye – How you say it? *Auf Wiedersehen*! Until the next time, *señor*.'

Chavez waved, sauntered in a leisurely manner back to the truck, climbed in and drove out of the compound with a lot of rattling and banging.

'*Dreck*!' Ernst muttered, feeling tired and impatient. After having another stiff brandy, he ordered Valentinas to gather together on the verandah the women selected as potential household staff. Valentinas brought a dozen of them, some young, others old, and after examining them as he had often done in Nordhausen – pinching here, prodding there, having a good look at their teeth – Ernst rejected the eldest and most ugly, picking mostly the young to serve him, with one middle-aged crone to be in charge of them. Those chosen all bowed, very solemn, even fearful, then were ushered by the old crone up the stairs at the side of the house, to sort themselves out on the top, open floor beneath the raised roof. Until Ernst decided otherwise that's where they would now live, separated from family and friends, working only for him.

After having another drink, which charged his blood and increased his alertness, Ernst strapped his holster back on and stepped down off the porch, followed by the obedient Valentinas, to inspect the cluttered compound. Disgusted by its mess and lack of organisation, he barked a series of instructions at Valentinas, who nodded vigorously and kept them all in his head, probably not able to read and write.

Among the things planned by Ernst, and relayed to Valentinas, was the need to remove the open fires and move the natives back into the ramshackle, cell-like living accommodations located on both sides of the compound. The natives so housed would then be used as the labour force needed to dig out the centre of the large compound and turn it into a reinforced, concrete landing pad for the flying saucers. Last but not least, though the barbed wire fence was already electrified, Ernst wanted to erect watchtowers on the four corners of the compound and have them manned with round-the-clock machine-gun crews.

Ernst barked all these instructions with renewed, drunken vigour while Valentinas, always standing in his shadow, kept nodding affirmatively.

'Any mistakes,' Ernst informed him, 'and you'll be dealt with personally, harshly, by me. Understood?'

'Yes, *señor.*'

The sun had started sinking when Ernst returned to the house, this time letting Valentinas lead him inside to show him around. There were two floors beneath the open floor at the top, both in the form of four-sided balconies overlooking the large ground-floor living room. The beds in the rooms along the balconies were imported four-posters covered in mosquito-nets, and the bedroom furniture, Ernst noted, was mostly imported German antique. The downstairs living room, however, was filled with well-cushioned bamboo chairs and sofas, bookcases of waxed pine, and low tables carved from local woods. All in all, it was surprisingly comfortable, if a touch too exotic.

Satisfied, Ernst tackled a light supper of bread, cheese and fresh fruit, all washed down with an intemperate amount of brandy. Now more drunk than he had been since leaving Germany, he thought of his homeland, grew unexpectedly maudlin, and had vivid recollections of the women he had known during the war: that lascivious stripper, Brigette, who had performed in the Französischestrasse; that Polish woman, Kosilewski, who had pleasured him to betray him; even Ingrid, his wife, who had loved him, but came to hate him before dying in an air-raid. Those and the others, some willing, some not, some whores and some unfortunate camp inmates used in military brothels. So many women. So many ways.

Ernst remembered and was inflamed, wanting to have them all back, and so barked for Valentinas to bring him a girl – the youngest and prettiest of those upstairs. His wizened servant soon did so, fetching one from the top floor, then he beat a hasty retreat when Ernst glared fiercely at him.

'Yes, *señor*. Of course, *señor*! I will be on the verandah if you need me. I'll sleep out there, *señor*.'

Satiated with food and drink, Ernst tried to undress the young girl, a mere stripling, and beat her badly when she tried to resist. Then, when even the beating didn't work, but simply reduced her to tears, he threw the sobbing creature onto the floor and stormed out to the verandah.

'I will show you what discipline is,' he said to Valentinas, 'and you can tell all the others. Bring in the girl's mother.'

When the girl's terrified mother was brought into the living room, Ernst again told the sobbing girl to remove her clothes. When the girl refused to do so, Ernst unholstered his pistol and placed it to the head of her mother, who was now also sobbing.

'Tell her that if she doesn't do as I say, Valentinas, I'll blow her mother's brains out.'

'Yes, *señor*. Of course *señor*.'

Valentinas relayed the message and the sobbing girl, staring at her fearful mother, nodded agreement. The mother, still crying also, was led out by Valentinas as Ernst ordered the trembling girl to strip and lie back on the floor. When she did so, he removed his own clothes, then stood over her, legs outspread, and told her to get onto her knees. Trembling, with eyes as big as spoons, she did as she was told.

'You will do everything I tell you,' Ernst said. 'Do you

understand what I'm saying?'

'Yes,' the girl whispered, speaking English, which Ernst understood.

'Your fear excites me,' Ernst told her. 'Your degradation is my joy. Now dry your damned eyes.'

Placing his hands on the back of her head, he pulled the girl towards him, closing his own eyes in expectation, making the most of his new life.

The days would be long here.

CHAPTER TEN

The saucer was one of the early models, a mere thirty feet in diameter, descending vertically, silently, towards a dark field in Virginia, its lights flashing on and off, the seamless surface a silvery white, gleaming in a vast sea of stars, level with a Gorgonzola moon. Reaching the ground, it didn't touch it, but merely hovered just above it, swaying slightly from side to side, until its four hydraulic legs emerged obliquely from its base and dug into the soft earth beneath the grass. The saucer's lights blinked out, its silvery-white sheen turned to grey, then its steps angled down from the base and two men in black coveralls marched out, followed by Wilson.

Straightening up, Wilson glanced around him, taking in the grassy hills, the empty fields, the shivering trees. Then he walked across the grass to the unfenced road, where a jet-black limousine was parked. Its windows were tinted and the headlights turned off, but its rear door was opened by someone inside when Wilson approached.

As Wilson slipped inside the car, the flying saucer in the field took off again. It rose slowly, almost silently, to a very great height, its lights flashing on and off around the rim to form a kaleidoscope. Eventually it became dime-sized, then a mere spot of white light. That light hovered in the air, as if just another star, then it suddenly shot away and disappeared.

Wilson closed the limousine door as he sat in the rear seat. Beside him, Artur Nebe was wearing a grey suit with shirt and tie, looking uncomfortable out of uniform.

Too many years in the SS, Wilson thought, with a pistol always holstered on his waist. He must feel naked without it.

'*Guten tag*, Nebe,' Wilson said. 'How is life in the real world?'

'I don't like all the politics,' Nebe said. 'I should be back in Antarctica.'

'You will be. Today. Once we get this meeting over with. After that, you'll have no reason to stay here. You'll come back with me.' He noticed that Nebe was staring too intently at him. 'What is it? My face?'

'Sorry. Yes, it looks different. You look twenty years younger.'

'Not like an eighty-two-year old?'

'More like sixty-two.'

Wilson smiled. 'Plastic surgery and skin grafts. Dr King is doing a good job of preserving me in particular and researching longevity in general. I've also had certain joints replaced with artificial ones, steel and fibre, which King produced during his on-going cyborg research.'

'He seems to be doing well.'

'The knowledge that he can experiment without restraints of any kind has sent his imagination soaring and filled him with energy. He's become a man obsessed with his work and now cares for little else. He doesn't have to be watched any longer; his love of work has enslaved him. He's all ours, Nebe. Completely.'

'And his other needs?'

'We've given him total freedom when it comes to the comfort girls. The sex is all he really wants when he's not working. The needs of most men are basic.'

Nebe offered a rare, chilling smile, being himself addicted to the abducted young women used as whores, or 'comfort girls', in the brothel in the Antarctic colony. 'I'm sure he didn't get sex like that in Hendon, England. That alone should enslave him.'

'It's certainly helped him to forget his wife and children. Family love treads on thin ice.' Wilson rolled his window down and gazed out at the moonlit fields. The trees were silhouetted against a star-filled sky and the wind scarcely stirred. 'When is General Samford coming?' he asked.

Nebe checked his wristwatch. 'In five minutes. He was told to be punctual.'

'Who arranged the meeting?'

'A CIA agent, Jack Fuller. I'd heard he was on your trail. He was in charge of disinformation regarding the Socorro crash – remember? Back in 1947 – and he went to have a talk with that Mike Bradley.'

'The one who pursued me during the war?'

'Yes. Wounded at Kiel Harbour. The explosion set by Ernst Stoll. You paid him a visit the night of the Socorro crash and put a stop to his UFO investigations.'

'Ah, yes, I remember. Have you any idea what he told Fuller?'

'According to Fuller, nothing – but just knowing that Fuller had been to see him made me suspicious. Then, when he also went to see von Braun and Miethe, I knew it was us he was after.'

'So?'

'I contacted him in Washington DC. A meeting was arranged. Same place – right here – and same time. When we met, I told him I knew what he was after and that we were responsible.'

'Did you tell him where we're located?'

'I confirmed it. He already knew, of course, though not in too much detail. He'd interrogated Captain Schaeffer of U-boat 977, the one that took us to Plata del Mar, Argentina, and worked the rest of our route out from there. So he knows we're in Neu Schwabenland, though he still doesn't know the exact location. First US confirmation of the existence of our flying saucers came, he said, through the investigations of Operation Paperclip at the close of the war. Mike Bradley also worked on that, which is why he turned up at Kiel and later became obsessed with UFOs. That knowledge, as well as Bradley's turnaround after the Socorro crash, explain why Fuller went with First Lieutenant Harris to see him in Socorro. Now a select few in the White House, the Pentagon, and the CIA, including Fuller, know we're hidden somewhere in Antarctica. They also know we have flying saucers more highly developed than those being constructed in the United States and Canada.'

'What made General Samford change his mind about meeting us? When I personally tried to set up this meeting, his minions said "No deal".'

'Because you were using a pseudonym then – calling yourself Aldridge – and they didn't relate the name to Wilson, which is who they were looking for. Also, though they knew we were in Antarctica, they didn't believe how advanced our saucers were and assumed we were just a bunch of fanatical Nazis not much different, though possibly crazier, than those who had fled to Paraguay. Reportedly, Samford, protective of his position as US Head of Intelligence, was outraged that his minions would even consider such a meeting. I believe he described us as a bunch of escaped war criminals and demanded that an expeditionary force be sent to Antarctica to get us out and bring us back to the United States to be tried as war criminals.'

'Rear-Admiral Byrd's Operation Highjump.'

'Correct.'

'Which we put to rout. Byrd's expedition was then cut short. The official explanation was hurricane winds.'

'Also correct. But Samford still refused to believe that we were that advanced technologically and asked for Byrd to be psychiatrically evaluated and all his references to our flying saucers excised from his report.'

'So what made the morally outraged US Head of Intelligence change his mind?'

'I arranged for one of our saucers to hover right over

his house one evening in the middle of a party he was giving in the garden of his home in Alexandria, Virginia. A lot of other top brass and their wives or mistresses were in attendance and all of them saw the saucer – it was hovering right over them, casting its shadow on the lawn. *That's* what changed the stubborn General Samford's mind. He's a man who sees reason.'

Wilson smiled. 'It must have come as quite a shock to Samford's guests.'

'It certainly did. All of those present were sworn to secrecy. When a couple of the wives felt unable to do so, their husbands were transferred to Alaska, which was fair enough warning to the others. No-one's talked since.'

'Who would believe them anyway?' Wilson asked. 'Project Grudge is now treating all those who report UFOs as cranks. Witnesses are afraid of public ridicule, so those best equipped to confirm the reality of the saucers – radar operators and pilots – are learning to keep their mouths shut. We have little to fear.'

'There they are,' Nebe said softly.

Looking past the back of the driver's head, Wilson saw the headlights of another car approaching along the dark road. The car slowed down and pulled into the verge, then stopped about twenty yards from the limousine. Another set of headlights appeared behind it, stopping further away. When the lights of both vehicles went out, Wilson saw that the other vehicle was a troop truck.

'Did you know about this?' he asked Nebe.

'I told him he could bring some protection. I didn't mean a whole troop-truck.'

'No problem,' Wilson said.

He stepped from the limousine as the troops were spilling out of the truck to form a cordon across the road. All of the troops were armed. General Samford, in uniform, followed by a man in plain clothes, got out of the other car as Nebe joined Wilson. The two groups approached one another, stopping about three feet apart.

General Samford had a long, lean, almost ascetic face and did not look like a man to take fools lightly. Fuller, on the other hand, was darkly handsome, clearly cynical, slyly watchful and deceptively relaxed. He looked like a man who could handle trouble and probably relished it. Four of the armed troops came up behind Samford and Fuller, stopping a few yards farther back.

Nebe glanced at Fuller. 'So, we meet again.' Fuller just nodded. Nebe indicated Wilson with his finger. 'This is him,' he told Fuller. 'Herr Wilson, this is CIA agent Jack Fuller, and . . .'

'General Samford,' Fuller confirmed. 'Head of US Intelligence.'

'I believe you wanted a talk,' Samford said, sounding like a man suppressing anger. 'Well, here I am.'

'Are you nervous, General Samford?'

'What?'

'You seem to have brought a lot of armed troops to what I'd hoped would be an informal, friendly meeting.'

'I don't have friendly meetings with escaped war criminals. Nor do I like traitorous Americans and their Nazi cohorts.'

Wilson was amused. 'You wrong me,' he said. 'I'm not a man who changes sides. I've always been exactly what I am, which is a man on his own. I can't be a traitor because I've never been a patriot. I go where my work takes me, whether it be here, Nazi Germany, or the Antarctic. You're a soldier, General Samford. I'm a scientist. That's the only difference between us.'

'You're just a goddamned Nazi,' Samford said. 'You and your whole bunch.'

'I am not, and never have been, a Nazi, General Samford. I have no political allegiances, no religion, no belief in any government, left or right. I live for my work, which is science, as you live for the army. You've chosen what you want to be, General, and I've done the same. We're two sides of the same coin.'

General Samford was obviously outraged by the very suggestion, but before he could explode, Fuller said soothingly, 'Okay, you've got us both here. Now what do you want?'

'Can I take it you're both here with the full knowledge of the head of the Air Matériel Command?'

'General Vandenberg knows we're here,' Samford said, practically gritting his teeth. 'Now *what do you want*?'

'We want to trade,' Wilson said.

For a moment even Fuller looked dumbfounded, but General Samford could barely contain himself.

'*What*?' he asked, as if choking on a bone.

'You heard me,' Wilson said. 'As you clearly know, we're not the only ones with flying saucers, though ours are certainly the most advanced. The US and Canada are both involved in similar projects and have already had plenty of test flights. The Harold Dahl and Kenneth Arnold sightings of June, 1947, over the Cascades, were actually of crude US-Canadian saucers being constructed in secret in the wilds of Canada. *Your* saucers, General Samford, not ours. Nevertheless, no matter how long you take or how much you spend, your saucers can never be that advanced without further knowledge of my technology. I, too, have certain needs, General, so I'm willing to trade.'

'I don't—'

'Why would you do that?' Fuller asked, his gaze ever watchful and direct. 'I mean, that would be inviting our technology to catch up with yours, and then . . .' Fuller shrugged and grinned. 'We'd be evenly matched. Then we'd come in and get you.'

Wilson smiled. 'Not quite true, Mr Fuller. In return for what I need, I'll trade certain secrets of my technology, but I'll be doing it a little at a time and never until I've already surpassed what I'm giving to you. Though this will benefit you greatly, you'll always remain behind us, which ensures that we'll retain the advantages we have at this time.'

'A balance of power,' Samford said.

'You might call it that,' Wilson replied.

'A see-saw arrangement, right? A tricky manoeuvre.'

'That's right, Mr Fuller.'

'And just what are we supposed to hand over for all this?' Samford asked, still sounding choked.

'I'm in constant need of various mass-produced components and equipment, as well as food and other supplies. We shipped in a tremendous amount throughout the war years, but it's finally beginning to run out and our saucers are not yet large enough to bring in the bulk we need. You'll do that for us.'

General Samford was red-faced, clenching and unclenching his fists, but Fuller seemed merely intrigued. 'If we do that for you,' he pointed out, 'we'll find out exactly where you are.'

'I don't care,' Wilson replied. 'That information won't help you. You can't get conventional aircraft anywhere near us and your saucers have a long way to go before they can be used to combat us, either with troops or with weapons.'

'So if we can't get in with conventional aircraft, how will we get the supplies to you?'

'We're located at the base of a deep, hidden gorge in Neu Schwabenland, or Queen Maud Land, which isn't accessible by conventional aircraft. You'll be given a location at the other side of that mountain range. There we've already hacked storage spaces out of the base of the mountain and will soon have them manned all the year round. You will drop the supplies, and we will then pick them up and transport them back here in our saucers, as required.'

'But eventually,' Fuller said with a smile not reflected in his cold, steady gaze, 'with the technological information you'll be feeding us in return, bit by bit, our technology, if never quite matching yours, will still be enough to give us saucers capable of flying down into your hidden base.'

'By which time,' Wilson replied, 'we'll have developed some highly advanced form of defence to keep out unwanted saucers – infrasound barriers or heat shields. We're already working on them.'

'You may not succeed,' General Samford said hopefully, 'in which case we could eventually get at you.'

'That's a chance I'm willing to take,' Wilson said. 'And I don't take chances lightly.'

Samford and Fuller glanced at one another, the former outraged, the latter cynically amused.

'What if we reject your proposal?' Samford said. 'Seems to me, we can just leave you in the Antarctic and forget your existence. A few saucers flying here and there aren't going to give us much trouble. Most folks already think the saucers are piloted by Little Green Men or only witnessed by cranks. What can you do to us?'

'Remember the Mantell crash?' Nebe asked, breaking his icy silence. 'The first US Air Force officer to die chasing a UFO?'

'Yes,' Samford said, 'I remember. He either died chasing a Rawin weather balloon or because of lack of oxygen when he foolishly climbed too high.'

'It's a well-known fact,' Nebe said softly, chillingly, 'that Mantell's last words were about something metallic and tremendous in size. That was our saucer.'

Samford glanced at Fuller, then at Wilson. 'I don't believe you're that far advanced,' he said. 'I think Mantell died from lack of oxygen, maybe chasing Venus, so I'm calling your bluff.'

'You reject my proposal?' Wilson asked.

'Yes.'

'Then I'll give you proof, General Samford. I'll give you, the Pentagon and the White House the kind of proof you won't easily forget. Later this month my flying saucers will surround Washington DC. Some will be piloted; others will be small, remote-controlled devices of the kind called Foo Fighters during the war. For your entertainment, we'll even fly around the White House. We'll cause chaos on every radar screen in the area. If your aircraft try pursuing us, we'll play cat-and-mouse with them. Should that not make you change your mind, we'll repeat the performance a week later. I think, General Samford, that your superiors, including the President, will think differently after this demonstration.'

'I'll believe that when I see it,' General Samford said. 'Now go to hell, Wilson.'

Wilson smiled tightly, then returned with Nebe to the limousine. As he was slipping into the rear seat, he glanced back over his shoulder and saw Samford in angry consultation with Fuller. Fuller was shaking his head, as if saying, 'No,' but Samford was obviously overruling him. As Wilson closed his door, Samford shouted at the armed soldiers. Instantly, they readied their weapons and raced forward to surround the limousine.

'Too late,' Nebe said.

Suddenly, a great pyramid of dazzling light beamed down over the advancing soldiers and a bass humming sound, shaking even the limousine, was accompanied by a fierce, swirling wind that bent the trees on either side of the road and bowled the advancing soldiers over. Their weapons fell from their hands as they were swept across the tarmac, bellowing with fear and pain as what seemed like a tornado slammed them into one another or against the trees at the side of the road.

Wilson caught a glimpse of General Samford crouching low, holding his peaked cap on with one hand, shading his eyes with the other, squinting up at that dazzling, descending, pyramidal light as Fuller tugged him back to their own car, just outside the roaring whirlpool of wind, now filled with flying leaves, blades of grass, pebbles and dust.

'Let's go!' Nebe snapped.

The driver of the limousine reversed away from the tornado created by the descending saucer and headed back across the field. There, a second saucer, also thirty feet across, had descended and was resting on its four hydraulic legs, gleaming in the moonlight. The driver stopped about twenty yards from the parked saucer, letting Wilson and Nebe climb out, then he reversed again and bounced back across the field to the road.

The first saucer was now visible, hovering high in the sky, its base spinning and emitting that great pyramidal light, creating the hurricane-like wind that was slamming the soldiers against the trees or causing them to roll between them, across the grass verge beyond the road.

The limousine raced away as the dazzling light winked out, returning the night to darkness. Then the saucer ascended vertically, rapidly, until it was just a pinprick of light high in the sky, one star amongst many. Then the swirling wind settled down, letting the bruised, dazed soldiers stand up again.

They all looked up in awe as the second saucer, containing Wilson and Nebe, ascended vertically, hovered briefly in the night sky, then also shot off abruptly, heading south, and suddenly winked out.

'We've got problems,' Fuller said.

CHAPTER ELEVEN

The telephone call came during supper. Nichola, now four years of age, still blonde and more beautiful than ever, was no longer in her high chair, but sitting instead with Dwight and Beth at the table, having cookies and milk while her parents contented themselves with coffee. It was the month of July in 1952, and although it was pretty late in the evening, the sun hadn't quite sunk yet and the velvet sky was still streaked with pink where the stars didn't show. When the telephone rang, Beth stared at it but made no move to pick it up.

'Okay,' Dwight said, feeling guilty and tense when he saw the look on her face. 'It's for me, right? I'll get it.' Though Beth was sitting beside the phone, he got up and walked around the table to pick it up, which placed him practically up against her shoulder and made her lean away from him. 'Hi,' he said. 'Capt'n Randall.'

'Hate to call at this time of night,' Bob said, 'but you have to come over here. They want you right now.'

'Over where? To ATIC?'

'Yeah, right. That's where I'm calling from. They want you right now.'

'You already said that – but now? This minute? Who the hell are *they*?'

'Members of the Technical Intelligence Division, Air Matériel Command. They want to talk to you about what we've been doing since Project Sign was dissolved and replaced with Project Grudge.'

Even though now well prepared for the unexpected, Dwight was astounded at this. 'Now? At *this* time?'

'Yeah. They practically got me out of bed. They appear to have a very urgent need for some detailed case histories. They've also come to discuss your complaints about how they've been treating us.'

'Shit!'

'No shit, baby.'

'Okay,' Dwight said, 'I'm coming.' He dropped the phone and stared at Beth, trying to hold her gaze, though he couldn't help shrugging forlornly. 'Top brass,' he said. 'I swear, I wasn't expecting this. Apparently they want to interview me – right now, in ATIC. They're waiting over there right now.'

'Right now? This evening?'

'Unbelievable, right?'

Nichola was breaking up a couple of cookies and spreading the crumbs out on the table.

'Why don't you tell them to go to hell? Tell them you have a right to your own life, even if you are in the Air Force.'

'I can't, Beth. It's top brass.'

'That doesn't give them the right. Lord knows, they're working you into the ground already; you have a right to your own time.'

'It must be something special, Beth.'

'Oh, yeah,' she replied. 'Something special. Every time we try to plan something, get together, something special comes up. This marriage won't last the course, Dwight.'

'Nonsense.'

'No, it's not. You work night and day for those people and get no thanks for it. They've even consistently denied you promotion, which is practically punishment. So what's the point, Dwight?'

Not knowing what to say, Dwight glanced down at his daughter. She was licking her index finger and drawing funny faces in the crumbs from the cookies, her brow wrinkled in deep thought. She was also whispering words he couldn't hear and perhaps wouldn't understand.

'Promotion's not the point,' Dwight said. 'I do this because it's my job and that's all there is to it.'

'Promotion may not be the point, but punishment is. They've consistently denied you promotion and you know why that is. It's the UFOs, Dwight. They don't approve of what you're doing. It's a pure PR exercise and someone had to be landed with it. You got the job, but they don't want you to succeed and so they're making it hard on you. God, Dwight, you're a fool!'

Dwight knew it was true. He just didn't know the reasons. On the one hand, the UFOs were treated as a threat to national security, on the other the reporting of them was discouraged. It just didn't make sense. No more than it made sense to establish a UFO programme and then block every move its members made. Beth was right – it was a goddamned PR exercise – and maybe he was the fall guy. He might find out tonight.

After kissing Nichola on the head, making her giggle and squirm, he went to the closet and pulled out his light jacket. He was wearing civilian clothes, his home clothes, and didn't intend changing into his uniform at this time of night. Let the bastards see that at least. Putting his jacket on, he went to the door, opened it, but then turned back to Beth.

'I used to count on your support,' he told her, 'but now I only get flak. What happened, Beth?'

'You traded me in for your work.'

He stared steadily at her, feeling dreadfully hurt, then stepped out onto the porch, letting the door snap shut behind him. The pink sky was turning darker, letting the stars come out, and he stood there for a moment, gazing across the airstrip, taking comfort from the aircraft hangars and the many parked planes silhouetted in the twilight. Seeing them, he was reminded of how much simpler life had been when he'd been flying the B-29s over India, China and the Pacific during World War II. Now the US was fighting a war in Korea. Dwight sometimes wished he could take part in it, instead of remaining here to chase UFOs and dodge flak that came from his superiors and Beth instead of the enemy. Sighing, still feeling wounded and hurt, he started down the steps to the yard.

The door opened and snapped shut behind him and he heard Beth call out to him. When he turned back, she hurried down the steps to cup his face in her hands.

'Oh, honey,' she said, shaking her head in a woeful manner and letting her thumbs slide down to his lips, 'I'm so sorry. I really am. It's not you, sweetheart – it's what they're doing to us. To us. The three of us. We're a family, a good family, a team, and they could tear us apart. That's what frightens me, Dwight.'

'There's no need,' he replied. 'There's no danger of that, Beth.' He removed one of her hands from his cheek and pressed his lips to it, moved by a rush of emotion that brought tears to his eyes. 'We'll be okay. I promise.'

'I worry,' she insisted. 'There's more than one kind of danger. There's the threat to this marriage – that's one – but we're okay if we know that. What we can't fight, what I think we can't defeat, is what happens to so many of those who do the work that you do. That's what worries me most, Dwight.'

He knew what she meant and was troubled to be reminded of it. Too many Air Force officers involved in UFO investigations ended up with career problems, broken marriages and ill health. Too many were denied promotion, punished for cooked-up misdemeanours, or posted to inhospitable climes, often away from their families. Too many for comfort. And it happened too often to too many to be considered an accident. Beth had cause for anxiety.

'I love you,' Beth said. 'You know that, honey. I'm just concerned for you.'

'I love you, too, Beth. I can't help your concern.'

She sighed. 'No, I guess not. I'll just have to be stronger.

We're a family, right, Dwight?'

'Yeah,' he said. 'A real family.'

'Then that's all that matters.' She embraced him and kissed him, clinging passionately to him, then let him go and wiped tears from her eyes. 'You hurry on, now. Take no mind of me. I'll be warming the bed, Dwight.'

'That sounds nice,' he said, then turned away, wiping his own eyes, and hurried along the sidewalk, now deserted at this late hour, past the other houses of the officers' quarters, heading for Wright Field, not looking forward to the meeting, but feeling protected by Beth's love.

CHAPTER TWELVE

The atmosphere in the ATIC operation's room was decidedly tense. Three US Air Force generals were sitting around Dwight's desk, all with thick wallet folders in front of them. Dwight's friend, US Air Force Captain Bob Jackson, had placed a second chair beside Dwight's, behind the desk, and was sitting in it, facing the three generals. Seeing Dwight, he stood up and introduced him to Generals Lamont, Conroy and Hackleman. After exchanging salutes, Dwight took the chair beside Bob, facing the generals over his own paper-littered desk.

A brief, uncomfortable silence ensued, until General Hackleman, silvery-haired, deeply suntanned and lined, coughed into his clenched fist, clearing his throat, then said, 'Sorry to call you out at this time of night, Captain, but this matter is urgent.'

'Yes, sir,' Dwight said.

'It's come to our attention that contrary to Air Force policy, as laid down for Project Grudge, you've been openly supporting the UFO hypothesis and insisting that you have evidence for the physical reality of the phenomenon.'

'I think it's important, sir. And I should remind you that Project Grudge was replaced in April by Project Blue Book, for which there's a more positive policy.'

'I know all that,' General Lamont said testily, 'but we still want to hear what evidence you're basing your assumptions on.'

'Analysis of the photos of UFOs, done in the specialist

Photo Reconnaissance Laboratory, here at Wright Field, have confirmed the saucer-shaped configuration of the sighted UFOs.'

'We know all that as well,' Lamont interrupted rudely. 'We've seen the photographic evidence. What we want to know is what convinces you they're real, solid objects.'

Dwight refused to be bullied. 'With the saucer-shaped configuration and manoeuvring capabilities of the UFOs verified, what we needed was confirmation of what appeared to be their unusually large size and remarkable top speeds, as well as the fact that they appear to be able to hover, almost motionless, in the air. Regarding this, we received a report from Navy Commander R. B. McLaughlin, who'd worked throughout 1948 and 1949 with a team of engineers, technicians and scientists on a classified Skyhook balloon project, located in the Navy's top-secret guided-missile test and development area in the White Sands Proving Ground, New Mexico.' Dwight took his time leafing through one of his wallet folders, before pulling out a report and speaking while glancing repeatedly at it. 'According to that report, on April 24, 1949, at ten o'clock on an absolutely clear Sunday morning, when McLaughlin and his team were preparing to launch one of their big Skyhook balloons – a hundred feet in diameter – the whole crew saw a UFO which, though high up, was clearly elliptical in shape and had a whitish-silver colour.'

'Could have been another Skyhook balloon,' Hackleman said. 'Or maybe even Venus.'

'No, sir,' Dwight replied. 'Neither. With a theodolite, stop-watch, and twenty-five-power telescope, Commander McLaughlin's team was able to track the UFO as it dropped from an angle of elevation of forty-five degrees to twenty-five degrees, then abruptly shot upward and disappeared. Even after putting a reduction factor on the data recorded on the theodolite, Commander McLaughlin estimated that the UFO was approximately forty feet wide and a hundred feet long, had been at an altitude of fifty-six miles, and was

134

travelling at seven miles per second, or approximately twenty-five thousand miles per hour.'

'That's impossible!' General Conroy snapped angrily.

'I'll admit, sir, that there's some legitimate doubt regarding the accuracy of the speed and altitude figures that Commander McLaughlin's team arrived at from the data they measured with the theodolite. This, however, doesn't mean much in the sense that even if they're off by a factor of one hundred per cent, the speeds and altitude of the UFO would be extraordinary. I'd also remind you that various members of McLaughlin's team studied the object through a twenty-five-power telescope and swore that it was a flat, oval-shaped object.'

'And I'd remind *you*, Captain Randall, that Commander McLaughlin had no right to release that report, let alone write the article he published in *True* magazine in March the following year. Small wonder he's been transferred back to sea.'

'With all due respect, sir, matters of naval discipline are not my concern. I was sent the report to read and analyse, which is just what I've done. In my view it confirms that the UFOs, or flying saucers, can fly at extraordinary speeds and reach remarkable altitudes.'

'You say these cinetheodolite cameras aren't always accurate,' General Conroy said. 'Just what are they and how do you use them, Captain?'

'A cinetheodolite is similar to a thirty-five-mm movie camera, except that when a moving object is photographed with it, the developed photograph will also contain three readings that show the time the photo was taken, the azimuth angle, and the elevation angle of the camera. If two or more cinetheodolites photograph the same flying object, it's possible to obtain rough estimates of the object's size, speed and altitude. I stress *rough* estimates because cinetheodolites don't give totally accurate readings.'

'Nevertheless, you insist that the UFO tracked by McLaughlin's team was moving remarkably fast.'

'Yes, sir.'

'How fast?'

'A lot faster than any jet plane we know about.'

The generals glanced uneasily at one another, then returned their attention to Dwight.

'Okay, Captain, that accounts for configuration and speed. What's convinced you that these craft are real, solid objects?'

'Two incidents.' Dwight glanced at Bob, received a slight, knowing smile, then flipped over more pages in his folder and spoke as he read. 'On April 27, 1950, shortly after a guided missile had been fired from the White Sands Proving Ground in New Mexico and fell back to earth, the camera crews of Air Force technicians spotted an object streaking across the sky. As most of the camera stations had already unloaded their film, only one camera was able to catch a shot of the UFO before it disappeared. That photo showed only a dark, smudgy object – but it also proved that whatever it was, it had been *moving*. A month later, during a second missile test, another UFO appeared. This time, two members of the camera teams saw it and shot several feet of film as the – quote, unquote – bright, shiny object streaked across the sky. That film was subsequently processed and analysed by the Data Reduction Group at White Sands. By putting a correction factor in the data gathered by the two cameras, they were able to calculate that the object was higher than forty thousand feet, travelling over two thousand miles per hour, and was approximately three hundred feet in diameter.' Dwight looked each of the generals in the eye. 'I concede that these figures are only estimates, based on the possibly erroneous correction factor. However, they certainly prove that *something* had been in the air and it had been *solid* and moving very fast.'

'Enough to convince you of the reality of the phenomenon,' General Conroy said drily.

'Yes, sir. In combination with the two major flaps that

came the following year: the Lubbock Lights and the Fort Monmouth sightings.'

Again the three generals stared at one another, this time even more uneasily. When General Hackleman turned back to Dwight, his hazel eyes were troubled.

'Ah, yes,' he said. 'We were informed that you'd investigated both cases personally. Kindly give us your report on both events. In precise detail, Captain.'

Dwight began to feel nervous. This was no casual interrogation. These three generals were concerned at what he knew and obviously not pleased with the extent of his knowledge. Nevertheless, they were demanding a detailed report, so, after glancing nervously at the equally concerned Bob Jackson, he picked up another file.

'The Lubbock affair,' he read, 'began on the evening of August 25, 1951, when an employee of the Atomic Energy Commission's supersecret Sandia Corporation—'

'Who?' General Lamont asked abruptly.

'I'm sorry, sir, I can't reveal that. I can only say that he had a top 'Q' security clearance.'

The generals glanced uneasily at one another. 'Okay,' Lamont said. 'Continue.'

'This Sandia employee looked up from his garden on the outskirts of Albuquerque, New Mexico, and saw a huge aircraft flying swiftly and *silently* over his home. He later described it as having the shape of a flying wing, about one-and-a-half times the size of a B-26, with six to eight softly glowing, bluish lights on its aft end.'

General Lamont coughed into his clenched fist.

'That same evening,' Dwight continued, 'about twenty minutes after this sighting, four professors from the Texas Technological College at Lubbock – a geologist, a chemist, a physicist, and a petroleum engineer – observed a formation of lights streaking across the sky: about fifteen to thirty separate lights, all a bluish-green colour, moving from north to south in a semicircular formation.'

'You can't name the four professors either,' Conroy said sardonically.

'No, sir, I'm afraid not.'

'Keep reading, Captain.'

'Early in the morning of August 26, only a few hours after the Lubbock sightings, two different radars at an Air Defence Command radar station located in Washington State showed an unknown target travelling at nine hundred miles an hour at thirteen hundred feet and heading in a northwesterly direction. On August 31, at the height of the flap, two ladies were driving near Matador, seventy miles northeast of Lubbock, when they saw a pear-shaped object about one hundred and fifty yards ahead of them, about one hundred and twenty feet in the air, drifting slowly to the east at less than the take-off speed of a Cub airplane. One of those witnesses was familiar with aircraft – she was married to an Air Force officer and had lived on or near air bases for years – and she swore that the object was about the size of a B-29 fuselage, had a porthole on one side, made absolutely no noise as it moved *into* the wind, and suddenly picked up speed and climbed out of sight, making a tight, spiralling motion. That same evening, an amateur photographer, Carl Hart, Jr., took five photos of a V formation of the same bluish-green lights as they flew over his backyard. Finally, a rancher's wife told her husband, who related the story to me, that she had seen a large object gliding swiftly and silently over her house. That object was observed about ten minutes after the Sandia Corporation executive had viewed *his* object. It was described as – quote, unquote – an airplane without a body. The woman said there were pairs of glowing lights on its aft edge – an exact description of the Albuquerque sightings made by the Sandia employee.'

'Who cannot be named,' General Conroy emphasised sardonically.

Dwight just smiled, then glanced down at his report. 'Subsequent investigation by myself and Captain Jackson'

– he nodded in Bob's direction – 'confirmed that the Washington State radar lock-on had been a solid target – not a weather target. We then calculated that an object flying between that radar station and Lubbock would have been on a northwesterly course at the time it was seen at the two places – and that it would have had a speed of approximately nine hundred miles per hour, as calculated by the radar.'

'Still doesn't prove that much,' General Hackleman insisted with what seemed like hope.

'No,' Dwight said. 'But the five photographs taken by Carl Hart, Jr. were analysed by our Photo Reconnaissance Laboratory. The results showed that the lights, in an inverted V formation, had crossed about one hundred and twenty degrees of open sky at a thirty-degree per second angular velocity. This corresponded exactly to the angular velocity measured carefully by the four professors from the Technical College at Lubbock. Analysis of the photos also showed that the lights were a great deal brighter than the surrounding stars and that their unusual intensity could have been caused by an exceptionally bright light source which had a colour at the most distant red end of the spectrum, bordering on infrared.'

'What does that mean, Captain?' Hackleman's hazel gaze, which was steady, was also too concerned and displeased for Dwight's comfort.

'As the human eye isn't sensitive to such a light,' Dwight explained, 'the light could appear dim to the eye – as many of the Lubbock lights did – but be exceptionally bright on film, as they were on the photographs. While according to the Photo Reconnaissance Laboratory, at that time there was nothing flying that had those particular characteristics, I was pretty startled to discover that the lights on the photos were strikingly similar to those described by the Atomic Energy Commission employee as being on the aft edge of the huge UFO that passed silently over his house.'

'So *did* something solid pass over Albuquerque, New

Mexico,' Hackleman asked, 'and fly two hundred and fifty miles to Lubbock, Texas, at an approximate speed of nine hundred miles per hour?'

'Yes, sir. According to the witnesses, and to the radar and visual-tracking calculations, it did. The Lubbock files were also studied by a group of rocket experts, nuclear physicists and intelligence experts, and they were all convinced that the sightings had been of an enormous, solid object, most probably with a highly swept-back wing configuration and a series of small jet orifices right around its edge.'

There was silence for a moment while the three generals studied Dwight, none of them appearing too friendly, all looking concerned. Then General Hackleman let out a loud sigh. 'So,' he said. 'Who ordered you to personally investigate the Lubbock lights?'

'Major General C. P. Cabell, sir, representing the Director of Intelligence of the Air Force. In a matter of hours of receiving the order, Captain Jackson and I were on an airplane to Lubbock. Once there, we worked around the clock, interrogating everyone involved in the sighting – pilots, radar operators, technicians and instructors. What they told us substantiated the sighting reports.'

'We appreciate the thoroughness of the written report,' General Hackleman said, though displaying impatience. 'Who did you personally report to before writing it up?'

'General Cabell – naturally – and other high-ranking intelligence officers in the Pentagon, where the meeting took place.'

'You reported verbally?'

'Yes, sir.'

'That's what we'd been told,' General Hackleman said. 'But we couldn't find the recording of that meeting.' Dwight glanced at Bob, who was looking more uneasy every minute.

'Every word of that meeting was recorded,' Dwight insisted.

'But the recording was destroyed shortly after,' General Hackleman said. 'At least, so we were informed by the CIA.'

'But—'

'It doesn't matter,' General Conroy said. 'Don't bother asking, Captain. There are good reasons for everything, I'm sure. Now what about the replacement of Project Grudge with Project Blue Book in April this year, with Captain Ruppelt in command? Did you resent being downgraded to second-in-command?'

'I wouldn't be human if I didn't, sir.' Dwight was feeling hot and embarrassed. More so because this very subject had caused more friction between him and Beth, who was convinced that officers involved in UFO investigations always had a hard time from the Air Force and were often consistently denied promotion. Thus, when Project Grudge, which Dwight had headed, had been dropped and replaced with Project Blue Book, with Dwight reduced to second-in-command under the admittedly pleasant, highly effective Captain Edward J. Ruppelt, Dwight's acute disappointment had only been exacerbated by Beth's angry insistence that his 'virtual demotion' was another sign that he should ask to be transferred to another, less controversial, line of work. 'But I should emphasise,' Dwight now insisted to General Conroy, 'that Captain Ruppelt and I have an excellent working relationship.'

'So Captain Ruppelt has confirmed,' Conroy said with a slight, mocking smile. 'Now to change the subject slightly, do you think the stir caused by the Lubbock sightings was responsible for the replacement of Grudge with Blue Book?'

'They certainly helped, sir, but they weren't totally responsible. Though those sightings certainly made the Air Force sit up and take notice, it was the ones that took place a month later that really led to the formation of Project Blue Book.'

'The ones that took place at the Army Signal Corps radar centre at Fort Monmouth, New Jersey.'

'Yes, sir.'

'A top-secret establishment.'

'Exactly, sir.'

'Tell us about those,' General Conroy said.

Dwight opened another file. 'The flap began at eleven-ten in the morning of September 10, 1951, when a student operator was giving a demonstration of automatic radar tracking to a group of visiting top brass – sorry, senior officers.' General Conroy gave a wintry smile, but said nothing, so Dwight, flustered, glanced down at his notes and continued reading. 'After spotting an object flying about twelve thousand yards southeast of the station, the operator switched to automatic tracking, but failed to hold the object. In his confusion, he blurted out to the visiting officers that the object was going too fast for the radar set – which meant that it was flying faster than any known jet. After three minutes, during which the UFO continued to fly too fast for the automatic radar tracking, it disappeared.'

'The weather?' General Lamont asked.

'Checks with the weather department revealed that there were no indications of a temperature inversion.'

'Okay, Captain, go on.'

'Twenty-five minutes later, the pilot of a T-33 jet trainer, carrying an Air Force major as passenger and flying twenty thousand feet over Mount Pleasant, New Jersey, observed a dull, silver, disc-like object below him. It was thirty to fifty feet in diameter. When the object descended toward Sandy Hook, the T-33 pilot went after it. As he approached, it stopped abruptly, hovered impossibly, suddenly sped south, then made a one hundred and twenty-degree turn and vanished out to sea.'

Dwight glanced up from his report, surprised at how breathless and nervous he was. 'The Air Force major in the T-33 confirmed that sighting.' When no-one passed comment, he avoided the three pairs of eyes by looking back at his notes.

'At three-fifteen p.m., back at the Fort Monmouth radar centre, a frantic call was received from headquarters, demanding that they pick up an unknown that was flying very high, to the north, roughly where the first UFO had vanished. A radar lock-on confirmed that the UFO was travelling – I quote – *slowly*, at ninety three thousand feet – or eighteen miles above the earth – and it could also be made out visually as a silver speck.'

'No known aircraft of today can fly eighteen miles above the earth,' Bob said, speaking for the first time.

'Thank you for that observation, Captain Jackson,' General Conroy said drily. 'Okay, Captain Randall, continue.'

Giving Bob a fleeting grin, Dwight said: 'Next morning two radar sets picked up another unknown that climbed, levelled out, dived and climbed again repeatedly, too fast for the automatic radar tracking. When the object climbed, it went almost straight up. The flap ended that afternoon when the radar picked up another slowly moving UFO and tracked it for several minutes, before it, too, disappeared.'

He looked up from his notes. 'Those sightings were witnessed by all the visiting VIPs,' he said, 'and it was they who really got the ball rolling. So, it was the Monmouth sightings, even more than the Lubbock lights, that compelled Major Cabell to order ATIC to establish a new, more serious UFO investigations project. Subsequently, in April, Project Grudge was renamed Project Blue Book.'

'And in contradiction to the policy of Project Grudge,' General Hackleman said, 'Project Blue Book is to work on the assumption that the UFOs, or flying saucers, are real, solid objects.'

'Yes, sir,' Dwight said, sweating too much, his heart beating too fast. When he closed the file, he noticed that his hands were shaking. Not much, but definitely shaking, which really surprised him.

There was a lengthy, tense silence, then General Hackleman leaned forward in his chair and said, 'Anything else, Captain?'

Dwight glanced at Bob and was given a nod of approval

to state what they had both been frightened of reporting. 'Yes, sir,' Dwight said. 'The pattern and nature of a recent build-up of sightings of fiery discs, green fireballs, and large flying saucers, over the past month, along the east coast, indicates something damned scary.'

'Oh?' The general's gaze was steady and intense. 'What's that, Captain Randall?'

Dwight took a deep breath, hardly believing he was going to say it, then let his words come out on a rush of air.

'It seems like some kind of UFO invasion,' he said, 'and it's closing in on Washington DC.'

The silence stretched out forever.

CHAPTER THIRTEEN

The sun was dying. Wilson knew this as he stood in a field of wheat in Montezuma, Iowa, the stalks shoulder-high around him, and gazed across that yellow field to where other green fields met blue sky, then squinted up into the sun's striations, which were silvery and ravishing. Wilson was only ten years old, blond-haired and tanned, but even as the sun's heat scorched his face, he knew the sun was dying. It would take a long time, but die it surely would, and when it died, the Earth would die with it, destroying the great hope of mankind. Wilson, though still a child, was overwhelmed by that knowledge and decided, there and then, without a moment's hesitation, that he had to do something to save mankind and ensure its continuance.

Man's destiny, he was convinced, could only be changed through science and the evolution of a new kind of man, one less prone to mortality.

Even then, as a boy growing up in Iowa, born of God-fearing parents, but unable to accept the idea of Him, Wilson had been convinced that mankind would eventually have to leave Earth and inhabit another, less endangered planet. To do so, he would have to create an extraordinary technology; he would also have to transcend his still primitive nature and escape the physical limitations of his weak, mortal body.

Man would have to turn himself into Superman and then reach for the stars.

Wilson realised this at ten years old as he squinted up

at the sun over Iowa . . . Then he awakened, at eighty-two, to look out over the vast, snow-covered wilderness of Antarctica from his bed near the summit of a mountain in Neu Schwabenland.

Though still groggy from the anaesthetics, the dream, or recollection, had filled him with the awareness of how fragile was mortality and how ephemeral each individual life. From childhood to old age had taken no time at all – the past was virtually in the present – and now he knew with more certainty than ever that no matter what he did to himself, his time would be limited.

Nevertheless, there was still a lot he could do before it ended, so he had to keep that dark moment at bay as long as humanly, or scientifically, possible.

For this reason, he had become his own laboratory animal, experimenting constantly on himself, albeit with the aid of his two specialists: Professor Adolf Eckardt, a former Nazi concentration camp experimental surgeon, and the abducted Dr Paul King, formerly of the Powered Limbs Unit of West Hendon Hospital, London, England. Freed from the moral, ethical and religious constraints of Western surgical research, they were producing between them some extraordinary innovations in prosthetics, organ replacement and skin grafts.

After having some of the latter done successfully to his face and hands, thus making him look sixty instead of eighty-two, Wilson had recently had his weakening heart replaced with the first of Eckhardt's prosthetics and was already recovering from the operation.

Sitting upright on the bed and breathing deeply, letting the cold air clear his head, he called on the phone for Eckhardt and King to come up immediately. He also asked for Hans Kammler and Artur Nebe to come up thirty minutes later, in order to submit their latest reports.

Eckhardt and King entered together, both wearing white smocks, and stood one at each side of Wilson's bed, smiling down at him. King, who had once been devoted to his wife and children in London and terrified of this place, was now devoted to his work and content to take his pleasures with the 'comfort girls' abducted by the flying saucer crews from all over the earth. He was completely reliable. Eckhardt, of course, being a fugitive war criminal, still wanted by the British, not to mention the Jews of Israel, for his so-called 'anthropological' experiments in the Nazi concentration camps, clearly had no place else to go. Nevertheless, he also was delighted to be able to continue his experiments without restraint in the colony's laboratories, using animals and the human abductees being held in appalling conditions in the dank, freezing underground cells. He, too, took his pleasures from the comfort girls and was obsessed with his work.

'So,' he said, lowering his stethoscope to examine Wilson's heartbeat, 'you look good. How do you feel?'

'Excellent,' Wilson said.

Eckhardt listened to Wilson's heartbeat, then straightened up. 'Perfect.'

'It doesn't feel perfect,' Wilson replied. 'It's a little uncomfortable.'

'We'll soon improve on it.' Eckhardt was unfazed by Wilson's cold stare, having known him since the early days in Nazi Germany, way back in 1940, before the dream of the Thousand Year Reich had collapsed into ruins.

As Wilson well knew, Eckhardt and other Nazis were convinced that their Aryan dreams would be resurrected here, which was why they stayed on without persuasion. Wilson knew differently, but was not about to tell them, as he needed to use their insane faith for his own, infinitely more rational, purposes. He also needed them to help in extending his life, even if not indefinitely, as they were doing with his artificial heart and various joint and minor organ replacements.

Wilson's new 'heart', or pacemaker, was a highly advanced device, which, utilizing a piezoelectric crystal and a small balloon filled with water, caused the heart's own pumping to stimulate itself. First created in crude form in Nazi Germany, but recently perfected here in the colony's laboratories, it was more advanced than the one inserted for the first time in a human being in Pennsylvania Hospital, Philadelphia, a few months ago. That recipient, a 41-year-old steel worker, had only lived for eighty minutes after his heart replacement, but Wilson would survive a lot longer.

'The water-filled balloon,' Eckhardt explained, 'will be replaced with something smaller in a few months. Though the pacemaker is already maintenance-free and doesn't require batteries, we'll eventually replace it with a plutonium power source, or nuclear battery, which will weigh practically nothing and last longer. As for the rest of you, that's up to Dr King here.'

Eckhardt smiled thinly, without affection, at Dr King, whom he viewed as a rival for Wilson's attention. King, who despised Professor Eckhardt, politely ignored his smile.

'Your arthritic problems have been cured with joint replacements,' he said, 'but already we have more advanced prosthetics, if you're willing to—'

'Yes,' Wilson interjected without a pause. 'I am. The operations don't bother me.'

'Good.' King smiled like a normal doctor with a normal patient, as if still in the West Hendon Hospital, London, not here in a hidden Antarctic colony from which he would never escape. 'At the moment we're experimenting with artificial knees and elbows of clear acrylic resin reinforced with stainless steel. As for the joints themselves, the main problems have always been corrosion and lubrication, but soon I'll be removing your relatively crude, temporary stainless steel prosthetics and inserting more durable, maintenance-free, one hundred percent mobile joints made of a corrosion-free, easily lubricated, more durable cobalt-chromium alloy. As most of the surgical work on your joints was done for the original replacements, the operations for the insertion of these new prosthetics will be relatively simple.'

'And the rest of me?'

King shrugged and raised his hands as if pleading for clemency. 'It's early days yet, but with human laboratory subjects instead of only animals we should certainly progress quicker than anyone else. That heart will buy you a few more years, but problems with your kidneys and lungs will come soon enough, which is why we're working on those right now.'

'Tell me.'

'Regarding your kidneys, we're experimenting with something first devised by a Dutch surgeon, Wilhelm Kolff, and tested, ironically, on a Nazi collaborator. This involves the use of cellulose acetate film as the filter membrane and heparin as the anticoagulant. Already we have an advanced variation which we think will work, but we also need to find a means of circulating your blood from time to time through the artificial kidney. A cumbersome dialysis machine has been devised, but to avoid having to keep you plugged into it twenty-four hours a day we're working on a six-inch socket which can be permanently implanted in your circulatory system, between an artery and vein, then opened and joined to the artificial kidney. What we've come up with is a six-inch tube of silicone rubber, tipped with polytetrafluoroethylene – an unreactive plastic – with ends that penetrate the skin and are stitched to the adjoining artery and vein. While causing you little discomfort, this will allow you to leave the large dialysis machine for days at a time. Eventually, we hope to have a self-sustaining artificial kidney, but that, alas, will take longer to develop.'

'And my lungs?'

'As those are essentially mechanical, we're looking into prosthetic replacements. However, as the lung is also a membrane of unusually high permeability and, more complex, roughly the area of a tennis court, we need to find a means of imitating it within the confines of the thorax.

This we hope to do with a membrane of exceptionally thin silicone – say, one-thousandth of an inch thick – and with a maximum area of one square metre. This will be placed in the thorax in concentric layers, kept apart and self-supported in a manner that forms minute channels, which in turn form the new blood capillaries. Unfortunately, in this case, the problems are many and the death rate during experiments is high. This is due mainly to our inability, so far, to prevent the artificial membrane from becoming choked by coagulated blood. Nevertheless, I'm convinced that with time, patience, and unimpeded human experimentation, we can produce the required anticoagulant. Then the artificial, implantable lung will be within reach.'

'Good,' Wilson said. He spent a few more minutes discussing the various surgical and medical experiments going on with the abducted humans held in the underground cells, then dismissed his two professors and waited for the arrival of administrator Hans Kammler and chief of security Artur Nebe, both former members of the Death's Head SS. Kammler arrived first, wearing a black coverall, still blond and handsome, but no longer the golden young god of war, now visibly ageing. He took a seat by the bed and nodded at Wilson, not smiling at all.

'You're recovering well?' he said.

'Yes, Hans. No problems at all. I'll soon be on my feet again. So how is Ernst Stoll settling into Paraguay?'

Now Kammler smiled frostily. 'With no great deal of joy, but with dedication – as you had expected. He's greatly increased the defences of the compound, constructed a landing pad for the saucers, and set up a line of communication between himself and General Stroessner, whom he believes will eventually take over as President. As Stroessner is infinitely corruptible, this is all to the good. We will certainly be well protected there.'

'Apart from that, is he doing what he's been sent there for?'

'Yes. The round-up of Ache Indians has begun with the

aid of General Stroessner's *Federales*. For this, Stroessner is being well paid. Stoll claims that Stroessner is using the money to bribe senior army officers and seduce the heads of the Colorado Party. He's buying their support in his bid for the presidency and plans to make his move this year or next.'

'Excellent. We need a man like Stroessner in charge. We also need the Ache Indians – the females as comfort girls and servants, the males as conditioned pilots for the saucers and as experimental surgical fodder for Eckhardt and King. Since even with the abductions, we're running short of human material, a regular supply of the small Ache will be truly invaluable.'

'I don't think Stoll will let you down.'

The door opened again and Artur Nebe entered, small and stout, as solid as a rock, with eyes as dark as his black coverall. His swarthy features, though revealing no emotion, concealed the soul of a monster. As he crossed to stand at the other side of the bed, facing Kammler, Wilson glanced through the panoramic plate-glass window at the far side of the room and saw the vast Antarctic wilderness, its soaring ice-covered peaks and snow-covered valleys stretching out to a dazzling, blue horizon. While the sheer, untouched beauty of it contrasted mightily with the horrors taking place daily in the laboratories and underground cells of this hidden colony, Wilson did not see it that way. The only thing separating man from the beast was mind, and Wilson, all mind, dedicated to the pursuit of knowledge, was embarked on a crusade to redirect the evolution of mankind and turn the thinly disguised beast into Superman. There was no room for emotion in his grand design. His notion of beauty was absolute knowledge and the pure truths of science.

'So, Artur,' he said, looking up into Nebe's dark, fathomless gaze and taking confidence from the murderous well of his nature, 'what have you got to tell me?'

'Everything has gone smoothly. Exactly as we had

planned. The calculated spreading of disinformation has had the desired effect and is leading to confusion, not only with the public, but with military intelligence on a world-wide basis. By now, public opinion is split between those who believe the UFOs are of extraterrestrial origin, those who insist they're misinterpretations of natural atmospheric phenomenon, those who deem them the products of mass hallucination encouraged by too much talk about the subject, and those who believe they're the top-secret experimental craft of their own governments.'

'Official attitudes are equally confused?'

'Yes. The few government, military and intelligence heads who know of our existence here are so concerned about the possibility of public hysteria in the event that the news gets out, they've classified the subject top-secret. They've also classified as top-secret their own race to construct similar saucers in the vain hope of eventually getting us out of here. They're not only concerned with what they see as the new military threat represented by our technology, but by the fact that the Antarctic is Earth's last untapped treasure-house of oil, coal, gold, copper, uranium and, most important, water – the whole world will soon need water – and here we are, threatening to keep them out. That's what concerns them most of all.'

'We can use that when we trade,' Wilson said. 'It's a strong card to hold. But apart from the stubborn General Samford, what do they think of our capability?'

'Deliberately letting the top brass of Fort Monmouth see one of our large saucers finally convinced the Pentagon of our vastly superior capability, though the White House, and Samford, remain unconvinced.'

'They soon will be,' Wilson said.

Nebe didn't return his smile, but continued speaking in his soft, oddly threatening monotone. 'The so-called Lubbock lights, which were in fact the lights on the tail end of an American-Canadian experimental flying wing constructed in secret at the White Sands Proving Ground, has further convinced the American public that alien craft are exploring the earth. The Lubbock lights – that flying wing – also succeeded in further confusing those in military intelligence who do not yet know of our existence and are baffled as to why their own superiors are trying to kill off the sighting reports, even as they say that the saucers are a threat to national security.'

'We couldn't have done better ourselves,' Wilson observed.

'Finally,' Nebe continued, 'the concentrated build-up of flights of our mass-produced World War II *Feuerballs* over the east coast of the United States has been highly successful, leading to nationwide concern and numerous wild stories about green and orange fireballs and extraterrestrial flying saucers, as well as secret speculations in military circles about a forthcoming UFO invasion of the nation's capital.'

'Perfect,' Wilson said. 'We will now proceed to do just that. We'll surround Washington DC in general and the White House in particular with a virtual armada of *Feuerballs*. If that doesn't persuade them the first time, we'll repeat the performance a week later with even more *Feuerballs* as well as some larger, piloted saucers. I think it will work.'

'When will it begin?' Kammler asked him.

'Time is of the essence,' Wilson replied. 'The invasion commences tomorrow.'

CHAPTER FOURTEEN

Just off a flight from Dayton, Ohio, Dwight and Bob Jackson were passing a newspaper stand in the lobby of Washington National Airport Terminal Building when they were stopped dead in their tracks by the headline: INTERCEPTORS CHASE FLYING SAUCERS OVER WASHINGTON DC. Shocked, Dwight purchased the paper and read that the capital was in the middle of the biggest UFO flap of all time.

'The bastards didn't even tell us!' he fumed, folding up the paper and jamming it into the side pocket of his Air Force jacket. 'If we hadn't come here off our own bat, they probably wouldn't have called us. The biggest UFO flap of them all and we weren't even informed!'

'Come on,' Bob said, swinging his briefcase from one hand to the other and heading energetically for the cab rank. 'Let's go and talk to Dewey Fournet.'

Telling the cabbie to take them to the Pentagon, Dwight, still furious, opened the paper again and read the newspaper account of the present flap more carefully, tying the report to what he already knew. He was even more furious about not being informed because he had practically predicted that this flap would occur and, indeed, had informed Generals Conroy, Lamont and Hackleman about it during his recent, unpleasant interrogation.

The Air Force's Project Blue Book was now going strong under the leadership of Captain Edward J. Ruppelt and had received more official UFO reports than it had done in any

154

previous month in its history. In fact, according to Ruppelt, the sheer number of reports was making Air Force officers in the Pentagon frantic.

By June 15, the locations, timing, and sequence of the reports indicated that the UFOs were gradually closing in on Washington DC.

Throughout the afternoon of June 15, reports of 'round, shiny objects' and 'silvery spheres' had come in from all over Virginia, one after the other: 3.40 p.m. at Unionville; 4.20 p.m. at Gordonsville; 4.25 p.m. at Richmond; then 4.43 p.m. and 5.43 p.m. at Gordonsville. At 7.35 p.m. a lot of people in Blackstone, about eighty miles south of Gordonsville, had observed a 'round, shiny object with a golden glow' moving from north to south. By 7.59 p.m. the same object was observed by the people in the CAA radio facility at Blackstone. At 8.00 p.m. a jet from Langley Air Force Base tried to intercept it, but five minutes later the object, moving too slowly to be an airplane, disappeared.

So inexplicable and disturbing were these reports that Captain Ruppelt was called to Washington to give a briefing in the restricted area of the fourth-floor 'B' ring of the Pentagon to General Samford, the Director of Intelligence, some of the members of his staff, two Navy captains from the Office of Naval Intelligence, and some others whom Ruppelt had refused to name for security reasons. That meeting had resulted in a directive to take further steps to obtain positive identification of the UFOs.

Meanwhile, the sightings continued. By the end of June, it had become apparent that there was a considerable build-up of sightings in the eastern United States. In Massachusetts, New Jersey and Maryland jet fighters were scrambled almost nightly for a week, but always foiled when their radar-locks were broken by the abrupt, swift manoeuvres of the UFOs. On July 1, many UFOs were sighted over Boston, then began working their way down the coast. The same day two UFOs had come down across Boston on a southwesterly heading, crossed Long Island, hovered a few minutes over the Army's secret laboratories at Fort Monmouth, then proceeded toward Washington. A few hours later, the first report from Washington was submitted by a physics professor at George Washington University.

For the next couple of weeks, reports about Washington sightings poured in at the rate of twenty or thirty a day and, according to Ruppelt, unknowns were running about forty per cent. Finally, according to the *Washington Post*, last night, July 19, the greatest flap of them all had begun, with UFOs being tracked all over Washington DC and the restricted corridor around the White House filled with interceptor jets trying to chase UFOs.

Immensely frustrated and angry, Dwight finished reading the report, then passed the paper to Bob. By the time Bob finished reading it, he, too, was furious that ATIC had not been informed about the event.

'Damned lucky we were coming here anyway,' he said. 'Otherwise they'd have kept us locked out. Why the hell would they do that?'

'Maybe it was just an oversight,' Dwight replied unconvincingly, staring up at the sunny sky in the vain hope of seeing his first UFO. 'The heat of the moment and so forth. They're probably all frantic by now and just forgot to put the call through.'

'Yeah,' Bob said doubtfully, also glancing automatically at the empty sky over Virginia. 'Maybe you're right.'

When they were inside the Pentagon, that immense five-sided building in Arlington County, Dwight demanded an urgent meeting with Major Dewey Fournet, their UFO liaison man in the capital. Entering his office, located on the fourth floor, they found him in the company of Colonel Donald Bower, the intelligence officer from Bolling AFB, located just east of National Airport, across the Potomac River. Neither Fournet nor Bower looked pleased with this visit.

'Okay, okay,' a harassed Fournet said, waving his hands

as if to defend himself. 'I know what you're going to say.'

'So, what happened?' Dwight asked.

'We've just been too damned busy,' Fournet replied. 'It was an oversight, gentlemen.'

Dwight glanced at Major Bower. 'I don't believe that,' he said. 'Seems to me, you just wanted to keep us out. Why is that, Major?'

'You'd have received a full report in due course,' Major Bower said, his gaze steady and hard.

'Your report, not ours, Major,' Dwight replied. 'It's not the same thing.' He removed his gaze from Bower and fixed it on Fournet instead. 'So what are the facts, sir? Is the report in the *Washington Post* correct?'

Fournet shrugged. 'Yeah, essentially correct. At eleven forty p.m. the ARTC radars at Washington National Airport, about three miles south of the centre of Washington DC, picked up eight unidentified targets near Andrews AFB, Maryland, twenty miles east of National Airport and in direct line with National and Bolling. The objects were flying at approximately one hundred to three hundred miles per hour, then suddenly accelerated to fantastically high speeds and left the area. They soon returned, en masse. During the night, tower operators and the air crews of several airliners saw unidentified lights in the same locations indicated by the radar. Before the night was out, and while interceptor jets tried and failed to catch them, the unidentified targets had moved into every sector covered by the radarscopes, including the prohibited corridor over the White House and the Capitol. The climax came in the early hours of the morning, when the operators in the control tower at Andrews AFB, in response to an ARTC traffic controller's query about a target directly over the Andrews Radio range station, located near their tower, reported that a large, fiery, orange-coloured sphere was hovering in the sky directly above them.'

'Weather?'

'An analysis of the sightings had completely ruled out

temperature inversions. Also, the radar operators at Washington National Airport and Andrews AFB – plus at least two veteran airline pilots – have all sworn that their sightings were caused by the radar waves bouncing off hard, *solid* objects.'

'Oh, boy,' Bob said, glancing at Dwight. 'This sounds really good.'

'That's hardly the right word to use,' Major Bower said. 'It certainly didn't seem good to the top brass of the Pentagon. Nor did it seem good to President Truman, who personally witnessed a UFO skimming right around the White House. In fact, at ten this morning, the President's air aide, Brigadier General Landry, called me, at Truman's personal request, to find out what the hell was going on.'

'Oh?' Dwight said, amused. 'And what did you tell him?'

'I hedged my answers,' Bower replied, 'because truthfully, I couldn't explain the sightings away.'

'On behalf of the Air Force,' Fournet said, 'public relations officer Al Chops has given the press an official "No comment" on the sightings, but the reporters are still massed down there on the first floor, all baying for more. In the meantime, we're investigating the affair. That's all we can tell you.'

'Fine, Major,' Dwight said, taking note of Bob's cynical sideways glance and deciding not to raise any awkward points. 'Have you any objections to me doing my own investigation for ATIC?'

Fournet glanced uneasily at Major Bower, who did not seem too pleased. Nevertheless, he said, 'Of course not, Captain Randall. Why should we mind?'

'Here,' Dewey Fournet said, trying to look helpful as he handed Dwight a manila folder. 'Two of the first reports submitted. One is the unofficial report from the Andrews AFB tower operators; the other is from an F-94C pilot who tried to intercept unidentified lights. I should warn you that these are just off-the-cuff, preliminary reports. More detailed, more accurate versions will be drafted and signed at a later date. But you might find them helpful for the time being.'

'And as I said,' Major Bower added, 'you'll be receiving our own, official report when it's completed.'

'I look forward to it,' Dwight said, then he and Bob saluted and left the office.

'Bullshitter,' Bob whispered as they walked along the spoke-like, windowless corridor in one of the five concentric rings of the building, heading for the small office used by ATIC when visiting here. 'That Bower's the one who stopped us from being informed – maybe because the President is now involved. Whatever was flying around here last night, they sure as hell don't want us to know about it.'

'Well, we're going to get to know about it,' Dwight said determinedly as he unlocked the door of the office at the far end of the corridor. 'We'll complete a thorough investigation and find out just what the hell those interceptor jets were pursuing in the restricted corridor around the White House. No intelligence officer from Bolling AFB is going to stop me – not Bower and not anyone else.' He and Bob entered the office, switching on the light and closing the door behind them. It was a small, square-shaped room with no windows and nothing on the walls. Outside was US Highway 1 and, beyond it, the Potomac River, but they couldn't see either from this gloomy cell. Dwight placed his briefcase on the desk and gazed at the bare wall. 'I want to speak to the chief radar operator at Andrews AFB and the F-94C pilot who put in this report,' he said, fanning himself with the manila envelope. 'Get on the blower, Bob.'

As Bob took the wooden chair beside the desk and picked up the phone, Dwight kicked off his shoes and massaged his hot feet through his socks. Bob flipped open the manila envelope, checked one of the two reports, then asked for the senior traffic controller in the Andrews AFB control tower. After a short wait, he nodded and Dwight picked up the other line.

'Captain Chapman? This is Captain Dwight Randall of the Air Technical Intelligence Centre, Wright-Patterson AFB, Dayton, Ohio. I'm here at the Pentagon with Captain Bob Jackson to check out yesterday's UFO flap. We thought you might be able to help us out.'

'I put in a report to Major Bower,' Captain Chapman responded, sounding uneasy.

'Right. I've got it right here. I believe you were in charge of operations when that huge, orange-coloured sphere was observed right over the Andrews Radio range station, located near the control tower.'

'Oh, yeah . . . that.' Chapman sounded more uncomfortable. 'It wasn't huge; it was large.'

'Says right here it was huge.'

'We were all pretty excited at the time. It was large, not huge.'

'You saw it?'

'Well, yeah, I saw it . . . but when we checked the data later, we realised it was only a star.'

'*What?*'

'It was only a star.'

Dwight glanced at Bob who, holding the phone to his ear, merely shrugged his shoulders.

'I don't get this, Captain,' Dwight said. 'I have your report right in front of me and it clearly describes the object as a – quote – huge, fiery-orange-coloured sphere.'

'It was a large star. I know it was. At the time I submitted the report, we were all still pretty scared and excited. I now regret that description.'

'Okay: it was large. However, I find it hard to credit that seven trained radar operators would mistake a large, fiery, orange-coloured sphere for a star.'

'The heat of the moment, Captain. We all make mistakes. I'm going to change that description when I redraft the report. What we saw was an exceptionally bright star. That's all there is to it.'

Dwight took a deep breath, glanced at Bob, who

shrugged again, then let his breath out in an audible sigh.
'The report also states that you and the six other traffic
controllers on the shift saw this object, or star, hovering
over the Andrews Radio range station, at precisely the same
moment the radar operators at National Airport reported
they had a target over the very same location.'

'I can't account for that, Captain, except to say that the
radars all over Washington DC were going crazy last night
and a lot of atmospheric anomalies are suspected. What
we saw was a star.'

'Okay, Captain, thanks.' Dwight pressed the phone-
cradle down, cutting Captain Chapman off, then said: 'Get
onto that guy in charge of the astronomical charts and ask
him if there were any unusually bright stars in the sky last
night.'

Bob leafed through his notebook, dialled a number and
asked for US Air Force Corporal Alan Collins. After
explaining what he wanted, he sat waiting, drumming his
fingers nervously on the desk and studying the ceiling.
Eventually he nodded, went, 'Mmmmm, thanks Corporal,'
and dropped the phone back on its cradle. 'Nope,' he said.
'No exceptionally bright stars where that UFO was seen.
None at all, Dwight.'

'Damn! Is the pilot of that F-94C available?'

Bob tugged the second report out of the manila folder,
checked it, and said, 'Yeah, he's located at Bolling AFB –
where our good friend, Major Bower, also comes from.
You want me to try him?'

'Damned right, I do.'

Tracking down the pilot took a lot longer, but eventually
Bob nodded again at Dwight and the latter picked up the
phone. After introducing himself as he had done before,
he said, 'I'd like to hear in your own words exactly what
you thought you were pursuing last night.'

'It was a ground light reflecting off a layer of haze.'

'What?'

'A ground light reflecting off – '

'I heard you, Lieutenant, I just don't believe you. I have your report right here and it says that the lights were high up in the sky, in the restricted air corridor around the White House, and that they descended, ascended, hovered, and shot off at incredible speeds.'

'An optical illusion, Captain.'

'But the report—'

'I wrote it in the heat of the moment, right after landing. I was pretty nervous and excited, Captain, not too sure of what was happening, but when I'd settled down and spoken to Major Bower, I realised that I'd misinterpreted what I'd seen.'

Bob silently gave the thumbs-down. 'You spoke to Major Bower?' Dwight asked.

'That's right, Captain. Right after I landed. All of the pilots at Bolling were interrogated about what they had seen by the base intelligence officers.'

'And after interrogation, you were persuaded that what you had seen was not a lot of unidentified lights that made extraordinary manoeuvres over the White House, but simply a ground light reflecting off a layer of haze.'

'That's correct, Captain.'

'If you don't mind me saying so, Lieutenant, that seems a pretty ridiculous statement, given that this report—'

'I'm redrafting it, Captain, to make it more accurate.'

'Given that in this report,' Dwight insisted, 'you say that the lights repeatedly disappeared and reappeared in the sky before eventually shooting away.'

'An optical illusion caused by the layer of haze, Captain.'

'No, Lieutenant, not possible. According to your own statement, the disappearances and reappearances described by you were matched exactly by the radar readings – same location, same time.'

'According to Major Bowers, the radar operatives later said they'd been mistaken. Given that, I can only confirm what I saw.'

'A ground light reflecting off a layer of haze.'

'Yes, Captain.'

'And that's what's going into your redrafted report?'

'Yes, sir.'

'Thanks, Lieutenant.' Angry and frustrated, Dwight dropped the phone, then glared at Bob, who was shrugging and spreading his hands in the air, signifying defeat. 'Major Bower,' Dwight said.

'Intelligence chief of Bolling AFB. He also talked to the Andrews AFB radar flight controllers and radar operatives. Looks like a snow job.'

'Which confirms that they didn't call ATIC because they didn't want us snooping around. They're putting the lid on this thing.' Dwight hammered his fist on the table. 'Well, damn them, I won't let them. Let's get a staff car and travel around a bit – Washington National Airport, Andrews AFB, airline offices, the weather bureau, and anywhere else we can think of. Damn it, let's do it.' Dwight picked up the phone and called the Pentagon transportation section.

'Hi,' he said. 'Captain Dwight Randall of ATIC speaking. I need a staff car for a couple of hours and—'

'Did you say ATIC?' the corporal at the other end of the line asked.

'That's right. The Air Technical Intelligence Centre. I need a staff car to—'

'Just a moment, sir.' There was a pause on the other end of the line, following by muffled whispering, then the corporal came back on. 'Sorry, sir. Did you say Captain Dwight Randall?'

'Yes, Corporal, and—'

'I'm sorry, sir, but I'm afraid I can't help you. Regulations say that we can't make staff cars available to anyone other than senior colonels or generals.'

'Bullshit, Corporal.'

'Sorry, sir, but those are the regulations.'

'Since when?'

'Just recently, sir.'

'Dammit, Corporal, I want that staff car!'

'Sorry, sir, I can't help you. Not unless you get authorization from a senior colonel or general.'

'Alright, damn you, I will.' Dwight pressed the cradle down. 'Can you believe this?' he said to Bob. 'New regulation says we can't have a car unless we're senior colonels or generals.'

'New regulation invented just for us,' Bob said. 'Why not try General Samford? He'll be obliged to help you.'

'Why not?' Dwight said. When he tried to contact the general, however, he was told that he wasn't in his office. When he asked the secretary to track him down, he was told the general couldn't be found. 'To hell with this,' Dwight said, slamming the phone down and putting his shoes on again. 'Let's go down to the finance office and charge a rented car to expenses. They can't argue with that.'

But they did. When Dwight and Bob put in their request to the heavy, grey-haired lady in the Pentagon finance office, she looked embarrassed, checked their names again, then said nervously: 'Sorry, sir, but I can't do that. Policy is that if you don't have a staff car, you use city buses.'

'Ma'm, this is a matter of extreme urgency and one requiring a lot of travelling. We don't know the bus system and it would take us hours to get to all the places we need to visit.'

'Sorry, sir, but I still can't help you. If it's that important, I suggest you use a cab and pay for it out of your per diem.'

'I can't afford to do that, Ma'm. This job is going to take a couple of days and requires travelling all over Virginia. At nine dollars a day per diem, I can hardly—'

'Besides,' the lady said, examining Dwight's papers, 'this travel order only covers a trip to the Pentagon – not Washington, and certainly not a trip around Virginia. In fact, according to this, you're supposed to be on your way back to Dayton by now.'

'Well, I'm not going. This work is more important, and I'm pretty sure—'

The lady sighed and handed back his travel orders.

'Unless you're willing to go through all the red tape of getting these orders amended, you won't be able to collect *any* per diem. Also, you'll be technically AWOL.'

'Are you kidding me?'

'No, sir, I'm not. If you don't head back to Dayton right now, you'll both be classified AWOL. I can't help you, sir.'

Clenching his fist around his damned travel orders, Dwight stormed out of the finance office, followed by Bob. He was just about to head back to his office, when Bob stopped him by tugging at this elbow.

'What?'

'We've gotta leave,' Bob said. 'We can't afford to be AWOL. If they're really trying to stop us, they'll use the AWOL as an excuse to tan our hides. We've got to go back, Dwight.'

'No, damn it, I won't let them give me the runaround this way. I've some friends at Andrews AFB, so let's go there and ask them to call Wright-Patterson for permission to stay in this area for another week or so. That'll enable us to continue our investigations without the help or hindrance of the bastards in here.'

Bob puffed his cheeks out and blew a gust of air. 'I think one of us should go back,' he said. 'Hold the fort, so to speak. The teletype machines are bound to be going mad at ATIC, so one of us should be back there to help Captain Ruppelt. If you want to stay here, go ahead, and I'll go back and clear it with Ruppelt.'

'Great,' Dwight said. 'You smooth matters out with Ruppelt and I'll ring Beth this evening and explain things.'

'One call I wouldn't want to make, partner. Rather you than me.'

'I'll be okay,' Dwight said.

He and Bob returned to their office, closed up their briefcases, switched off the light, locked the door and then left the Pentagon. They took a taxi to Washington National Terminal Airport Building, where Bob was dropped off and Dwight, still boiling mad, took a bus all the way to Andrews

AFB, twenty miles east, in Maryland.

On the evening of July 26, Dwight was having coffee alone in the almost deserted officers' mess of Andrews AFB, thinking gloomily that he had been here for exactly one week to the day, sharing a room with three other officers, phoning Bob Jackson or Captain Ruppelt every afternoon and Beth every evening, when he was inclined to feel most miserable, and had received nothing valuable regarding the UFOs in return for his suffering.

In fact, he was gloomily pondering the ironic fact that he was second-in-command of Project Blue Book and yet had never personally seen a UFO. Every evening since Bob's departure, Dwight had been out prowling around the airstrip of Andrews AFB, scanning the night sky for UFOs, but so far he hadn't seen a damned thing. Nor had the radar operators or pilots – a fact that only increased Dwight's feelings of frustration and inadequacy.

Oddly enough, there had been a flurry of UFO sightings the previous day and evening, though none of them over Washington DC. First, amber-red lights had been observed over the Guided Missile Long-Range Proving Ground at Patrick AFB, Florida. Next, a UFO described as 'a large, round, silver object that spun on its vertical axis' had been seen to cross one hundred degrees of afternoon sky in forty-eight seconds. Then, in the late afternoon, interceptor jets had chased UFOs over Los Alamos and Holyoke, Massachussetts, losing them as they turned into the sun. Finally, that night, F-94s had tried in vain to intercept unidentified lights reported by the Ground Observer Corps in Massachussetts and New Jersey.

But nothing over Washington DC . . .

And not a thing over Andrews AFB where Dwight, after a week on his own, was starting to feel that the whole business was some kind of bad dream which had almost broken up his marriage and might soon break him.

He was gloomily pondering this, at 10.30 in the evening,

when he heard his name being called out over the tannoy system, asking him to report urgently to the control tower.

Dwight jumped up and ran.

The Andrews AFB control tower was in pandemonium, with most of the traffic controllers, eerily shadowed in the night lighting, grouped around the twenty-four-inch radarscopes and staring at rapidly multiplying targets.

'Same as last time,' the captain in charge said, jabbing his finger at the screens, 'but this time they're not just over Washington DC. Those UFOs are spread out in a huge arc from Herndon, Virginia, to here. They're right above Washington National Airport – and also right above us. In other words, they have Washington boxed in.'

'Jesus Christ!' someone whispered.

With everyone else, Dwight glanced automatically at the sky above the darkened, lamplit airfield, but saw only the moon and stars. According to the radar, some of those UFOs were overhead, but they couldn't be seen by the naked eye. To confirm that they actually existed, you had to look at the radarscopes – and there they were: all those white lights constantly on the move, forming a great arc around Virginia and Maryland, but closing in on Washington DC.

'Goddammit!' someone else exclaimed softly, glancing up at the sky. 'Where the hell are they?'

A group of F-94s was already racing along the airstrip and taking off into the sky in pursuit of the targets on the radar screens. Even as they disappeared in the direction of Washington DC, the telephone rang. The chief traffic controller answered it, nodded once or twice, then dropped the phone and said, 'The targets have just left the radarscopes at Washington National Airport, but already people around Langley AFB near Newport News, as well as the radar operators in Langley Tower, are reporting weird lights that appear to be rotating and giving off alternating colours.'

'Jesus Christ!' the same person said again.

Increasingly excited, but also frustrated because he could actually see nothing other than the targets on the radarscopes, Dwight remained in the control tower as the drama unfolded on the radarscopes and by telephone.

By 11.30 p.m. four or five of the targets were being tracked continually over the Capitol. F-94 interceptor jets tried and failed to catch them. Shortly after the UFOs left the sky over the Capitol, more reports came in from Langley Tower, where the operators again described them as unidentified lights that were rotating and giving off alternating colours. Another F-94 was despatched from Langley AFB and visually vectored to the lights by the tower operators. The pilot reported that as he approached one of the lights, it went out 'like somebody turning off a light bulb'. No sooner had this happened, then the targets came back on the radarscopes at Washington National Airport. Again, F-94s were despatched to locate them – but each time they were vectored into the lights, the UFOs disappeared abruptly from the radarscopes and the pilots simultaneously reported that they had visually observed the lights blinking out.

Eventually too frustrated to take it any longer, Dwight tried dialling the Pentagon. Unable to get through because the lines were tied up – or so he was informed by the frantic switchboard operator – he phoned an old reporter buddy, Rex Ginna, *Life*'s UFO expert, operating out of the magazine's Washington News Bureau.

'I can't get through to the Pentagon,' Dwight said. 'What the hell can you actually *see* there, Rex?'

'Fucking fantastic!' Rex exclaimed. 'A real light show here! They could be lights – or silvery discs – it's hard to say what – but they're racing back and forth across the sky right above us. They're also above the Capitol and the White House.'

'Oh, my God,' Dwight groaned, 'and I'm trapped here. What are they doing?'

'They look like bright stars from here. Small lights – or

high up. They're like light bulbs, but they sometimes spin so fast, they become a silvery blur. They're flying in all directions. Sometimes they stop and hover. They rise and descend vertically, shoot sideways, perform all kinds of tricks. Sometimes they're so low, they actually circle the Capitol and the White House, then they shoot up again at incredible speed and just blink out like light bulbs. Damned amazing, I'm telling you.'

That phrase again, Dwight thought. *They blink out like light bulbs.*

'Anyway,' Ginna said, 'they must be taking it pretty serious. All the reporters were ordered out of the radar rooms of Virginia as soon as the interceptor jets went after the UFOs. They told us it was because the procedures used in an intercept were classified, but we know that's bullshit. Most ham operators can build the equipment needed to listen in on an intercept. No, the real reason they threw us out is that some top brass are convinced that this is the night some pilot's gonna get a good, close look at a UFO and they don't want the press to spread the word. So here I am in the news bureau instead, watching the whole show. Too bad you can't see it.'

'Go to hell, Rex!' Dwight hung up on Ginna's chuckling, then tried the Pentagon again. Getting through this time, he asked for Dewey Fournet and was surprised to get him. Fournet sounded harassed.

'Yeah,' he said. 'Right. No point in denying it. Those things are visible overhead and the blips on the radarscopes are being caused by solid, *metallic* objects. They can't possibly be caused by anything else; and whatever they are, they can literally hover in the air, then accelerate to fantastic speeds.'

'And they definitely can't be caused by temperature inversions?'

'No way. We've just checked out the strength of the inversions through the Air Defence Command Weather Forecast Centre – and there's no temperature inversion strong enough to show up on the radar. Finally, no weather target makes a one hundred and eighty degree turn and flies away every time an airplane reaches it. Like I say, those things are solid and metallic. They're also controlled.'

'Any indication of size?'

'We don't think they're that big. In fact, we think they're pretty small. Not big enough to be manned. Some of the ones our pilots are seeing seem much bigger, though we can't be too sure yet. It's the small ones that are coming down real low and winging around the Capitol and . . . Well, I might as well tell you . . . President Truman almost went apeshit when he saw them skimming right around the White House. This whole place is bananas.'

When Dwight put the phone down, he looked up at the sky and was again frustrated to see only stars. Looking at the radarscope, he saw that the screen was literally filled with the white dots, clearly showing that the UFOs were still high in the sky over Andrews AFB.

'Damn it,' Dwight whispered, 'where *are* they?'

Even as he spoke, the lights on the radarscope raced in towards one another, to form a single, bigger light that flared up and went right off the screen.

'What the hell . . .?' the chief traffic controller said, as his men all bunched up closer around the radarscope, wondering where all the targets had gone so suddenly.

At that moment, the floor of the radar tower shook a little.

Everyone looked outside, as if searching for an earthquake, but they saw nothing but the darkened, lamplit airstrip. Then the floor shook a second time, settled down again, and then an eerie yellow light filled the control tower, beaming in from outside, and gradually changed to an amber-orange light that appeared to be beaming down from above. As everyone looked up, straining to see out through the window, the floor shook again, a bass humming sound filled the silence, and the amber-orange light, now clearly beaming down from above, turned into a huge, fiery, orange-coloured sphere that was descending slowly, inexorably, upon the control tower, as if about to land on it and crush it.

With everyone else in the control tower, Dwight looked up at that dazzling apparition, paralysed by amazement and disbelief, his heart pounding dangerously.

Then everything went dark.

CHAPTER FIFTEEN

The so-called UFO 'invasion' of Washington DC led to a secret midnight meeting in the Oval Room of the White House between Wilson and President Truman, General Samford, Head of Air Intelligence, General Hoyt S. Vandenberg, USAF Chief of Staff, and CIA agent, Jack Fuller, through whom the first approach to Samford had been made.

Wilson, wearing civilian clothes and already almost fully recovered after his recent operations, was accompanied by the icy Artur Nebe. Truman was seated behind the ornate oak desk, framed by the Presidential flag and the flag of the United States, with Samford and Vandenberg, both in full uniform, at one side of him and Fuller, wearing a light grey suit, shirt and tie, at the other. All three men were standing just in front of the high French windows overlooking the West Wing's Rose Garden.

Taking a chair at the other side of the desk, with Nebe just behind him, Wilson studied Jack Fuller's cynical, sharp-eyed gaze and the wary faces of the two generals, then he offered President Truman an engaging smile.

'So, Mr President,' he said, 'how did you like our two UFO displays over Washington DC?'

'Very impressive,' President Truman replied, not returning the smile.

'I'm glad you think so, Mr President.'

'I'm sure you are,' Truman said with soft sarcasm.

'I assume you know that not *all* of the saucers were mine.'

172

'Weren't they?'

'No. During the second invasion some of your own saucers, the ones constructed in Malton, Ontario, attempted to intercept, but failed dismally and were pursued back to Canada.'

'We just thought we'd try it on,' Fuller said sardonically.

'Don't do it again,' Wilson told him, then turned his attention on Generals Samford and Vandenberg. 'Can I take it that you gentlemen are now convinced of the superiority of our technology?'

Both men just stared at him, too speechless with rage to speak.

'I take your silence as reluctant agreement. Can I therefore also assume that you will now make no further attempts to thwart us, either in the skies or in the Antarctic?'

'Damn it—' Samford began.

'You can take it that for the time being, at least,' Vandenberg said, sounding choked, 'we accept that such moves would be pointless.'

Wilson nodded, acknowledging the oblique, temporary surrender, then he returned his attention to President Truman. The President did not avoid his gaze, but took his time before speaking.

'Just tell us what you want,' he said.

'The Antarctic is now the most valuable piece of real estate in the world.'

'I am well aware of that fact, Mr Wilson, and also of the fact that you control it simply by being there.'

'The Antarctic is also the greatest natural laboratory on Earth and the West now needs to exploit it.'

'Correct,' the President said.

'You also desperately need its water and mineral wealth, which is why you need me.'

'I am all ears,' the President said when Wilson paused to let the import of his words sink in.

'If you wish to populate the Antarctic with your scientists and research facilities without being harassed by my

173

saucers,' Wilson calmly informed him, 'you'll have to agree to the trade previously discussed that night in Virginia. In return, I'll let those of your people already in Antarctica remain unmolested to engage in reasonable scientific research.'

'What's your idea of reasonable?'

'I'll obviously monitor their activities and put a stop to anything that presents a threat to my colony.'

'You have no right—' Samford began, but was waved into silence by the President.

'In return for the supplies I need,' Wilson continued, intrigued to see how quickly even men of great power and authority could be reduced to petty human behavioural patterns, 'I will pass on valuable secrets of my technology, on a pro rata basis, though only after my own technology has superseded what I choose to give you at any given moment in time. In this way, my technology will turn the US into the most advanced nation on earth, scientifically and militarily, while simultaneously ensuring that it will never become advanced enough to threaten our own existence in Antarctica.'

The President stared steadily at Wilson for a moment, then swivelled around in his chair to judge the reaction of his two generals. Samford looked enraged and helpless at once; whereas Vandenberg, though normally a man of immense authority, was revealing the first signs of shock and disbelief.

'What if we say no?' Fuller asked, his gaze direct and unafraid, his lips curved in a slight, sardonic grin.

This man is like Nebe, Wilson thought. *He thrives on intrigue. Though the one in this room with the least authority, he's the one I must watch the most.*

'Then I'll trade with the Soviets,' Wilson said, 'and maybe even the Chinese. The choice is entirely yours.'

Vandenberg opened and closed his fists, Samford turned a deep red, and the President swivelled back in his chair to face Wilson again.

'You're an American,' he said quietly.

'A goddamned traitor!' Samford exploded.

'Right!' Vandenberg added, almost choking with anger.

'Gentlemen, gentlemen!' the President admonished them, waving them into silence.

Observing the two outraged, high-ranking military officers, Wilson recalled how, all those years ago, the great, innovatory work of himself and Robert H. Goddard had been ignored consistently by the US government and military establishment. He also remembered how their negative reactions to his genius had forced him to destroy his own work, drop out of sight, and spend three decades of his life in lonely anonymity, until he saw his opportunity in Nazi Germany, where his work and that of Goddard had been greatly respected, albeit for the wrong reasons. Now this United States president and his generals and intelligence officers – the same breed of man who had previously tried to stop his work and failed to support Goddard – were accusing him of being a traitor to his country, even as they hypocritically bartered to obtain his technology.

'I'm a scientist,' he told them. 'Nothing more and nothing less. I'm not moved by your patriotism, which is nothing but self-interest, and I won't be a traitor to myself just because you accuse me of being a traitor to my country. You have more blood on your hands than I do – and for less admirable reasons. Now do you agree or not?'

'No!' Samford exploded.

'We've no choice,' Vandenberg argued. 'We can't let the Russians or Chinese get their hands on this traitor's technology. I'm afraid we have to deal with him.'

There was silence for a moment while the President considered. Having previously met Samford and Fuller, Wilson took this opportunity to study General Hoyt S. Vandenberg. The general had been head of the Central Intelligence Group (later the CIA) from June 1946 to May 1947 and his uncle had been chairman of the Foreign Relations Committee, then the most powerful committee in the Senate. Clearly, Vandenberg still had great influence in those areas, as well as all the authority inherent in his position as USAF Chief of Staff. This man, once he had accepted defeat, would be particularly useful.

President Truman was studying Wilson at length, disbelieving, quietly outraged, helplessly intrigued, but eventually he too was forced to raise his hands in surrender. 'I agree with General Vandenberg,' he said. 'We have no choice in the matter. We must deal with this man.'

The ensuing silence was filled with dread and despair, until Nebe, finally speaking for the first time, said in his deadly soft, oddly threatening manner: 'This leads to the delicate matter of security.'

'Ah, yes!' Wilson exclaimed softly. 'I'd almost forgotten.' Studying Fuller, he saw Nebe's murderous double behind his urbane manner and knew that what Nebe was about to say would be understood by him. 'Go ahead, Nebe.'

'Since it's impossible to fly the saucers without being observed,' Nebe said, his voice as chilling as his demeanour, 'whether they be our own highly advanced craft or your crude US-Canadian prototypes, I suggest you implement the widespread use of ridicule, harassment and confusion of UFO witnesses, official and otherwise.'

'We've already done that,' Fuller told him.

'Correct,' Vandenberg added. 'When Project Sign was established in January 1948 it was given a 2A classification and placed under the jurisdiction of the Intelligence Division of the Air Force's Air Matériel Command at Wright Field – later renamed the Air Technical Intelligence Centre, or ATIC. When Captain Dwight Randall of Sign submitted his official, top-secret Estimate of the Situation in July of that year, I personally rejected it on the grounds that it lacked proof, even though the proof was clearly conclusive. I then encouraged a whole new policy at Project Sign: in the future, Sign personnel were to assume that *all* UFO reports were hoaxes. They also had to check with FBI officers and with the criminal and subversive files of police departments, looking into the private lives of the witnesses to check if they were reliable. Most of the Project Sign team took this as fair warning that it wasn't wise to raise the subject of UFO sightings. To encourage this fear, I first leaked the news that Captain Randall's Estimate of the Situation had been incinerated, then I renamed Sign as Project Grudge. As anticipated, this was taken by all concerned as another indication of my displeasure.'

'Very clever,' Nebe whispered admiringly.

'The function of Project Grudge,' Fuller explained, picking up where Vandenberg had left off, 'was to shift the investigations away from the actual UFOs and on to those who reported them. However, since a good twenty-three per cent of their reports were still classified as unknowns, this wasn't easy. For this reason, Project Grudge launched a CIA-backed public relations campaign designed to convince the American public that UFOs did *not* represent anything unusual or extraordinary. As part of this debunking effort, we encouraged the *Saturday Evening Post* journalist, Sidney Shallet, to write a two-part article exposing UFOs as a waste of time; but when that backfired – by increasing public interest rather than diminishing it – we got the Air Force to counteract by stating officially that UFOs were either misidentifications of natural phenomenon or the products of mass hallucination. Project Grudge issued its final report in August 1949 – only six months after its inception. Put simply, its conclusion was that while twenty-three per cent of the UFO reports were still classified as unknowns, most had psychological explanations and the investigation was therefore a waste of time and should be downgraded even further. On December 27, the Air Force announced the termination of the project. Shortly after, the Project Grudge records were stored and most of its personnel were widely scattered.'

'You can do more,' Nebe said, 'to encourage widespread confusion and fear of ridicule when it comes to reporting the UFOs, be they yours or ours. Your Air Force must be seen to be supporting UFO investigations with Project Blue Book while actually hampering them behind the scenes and by otherwise making things unpleasant, or even dangerous, for UFO witnesses and investigators. This can be done through the introduction of some new, restrictive Air Force regulations. You should also form a supposedly secret panel of leading scientists to investigate the so-called UFOs. However, this panel will also include CIA representatives who will ensure that its official report ridicules the whole phenomenon and is leaked to the press.'

'You're asking us to turn our own patriotic pilots and citizens into traitors,' Samford said angrily, 'and, even worse, to do so while we're fighting the war in Korea.'

'A small sacrifice,' Wilson said, 'and one you must make. Otherwise there can be no agreement between us.'

Samford was about to make another angry retort, but was cut short by the stern glances of President Truman and General Vandenberg.

'As Head of Air Intelligence—' Nebe nodded at General Samford – 'and USAF Chief of Staff' – he nodded at General Vandenberg – 'you two are in an excellent position to do this, so please ensure that it's done.'

Vandenberg managed to keep his peace, if with visible effort, but Samford practically turned purple and even took a step forward. 'I'd remind you that the last time we talked you were relatively safe because we were in open countryside with your saucer hovering right above us. This time, however, we're in the Oval Room of the White House, so what the hell can you do to prevent us from arresting you right now?'

Smiling, Wilson told Samford to turn off the lights. When this had been done, the Oval Room was plunged into moonlit darkness. Wilson then removed a pocket-sized electronic device from his jacket pocket and whispered coded instructions into it. A few seconds later, a bass humming sound came from outside, seeming to fill the room, then the room shook a little, as if from an earth tremor, and a dazzling, pulsating, silvery-white light beamed in through the windows overlooking the Rose Garden.

When they all stared at the windows, they saw what appeared to be a row of portholes in a metal body, with the light beaming out of them to form the single, blinding brilliance that now filled the Oval Room.

The row of lights bobbed up and down, as if hovering just above the ground, while the bass humming sound filled the room to exert a subtle, almost palpable, disturbing pressure. Then the humming noise ceased and the silvery-white lights blinked out, plunging the Oval Room back into moonlit darkness.

General Samford switched the room lights back on as Wilson stood up, preparing to leave with Nebe.

'I'll be spending a few days in the capital,' he informed them with confidence, 'so please don't try any tricks while I'm here.'

'We won't,' Fuller said.

General Samford glared at Wilson, General Vandenberg looked stunned, and President Truman simply stared at the windows as if in a state of shock.

Without another word, Fuller led Wilson and Nebe out of the Oval Room, then down to the White House garage, to drive them back to where they were staying, in the excellent Hay Adams hotel.

CHAPTER SIXTEEN

Cold December winds were blowing dust across the desert when Fuller drove up to the house of Mike and Gladys Bradley, near Eden Valley, Roswell, New Mexico. The sun was starting to sink when he got out of his car and walked up the steps of the modest ranch-style house in the middle of nowhere, with only the El Capitán Mountain visible in the distance, beyond the otherwise featureless flatlands.

They sure like their privacy, Fuller thought as he rang the doorbell.

Neither Bradley nor his wife were expecting the visit from Fuller and the latter gazed at him suspiciously through the mesh-wire of the outer door when she opened the main door.

'Gladys Bradley?' Fuller asked.

'If you're here, you must know that already, so why bother asking?'

Fuller had heard she was a tough old bird, so he wasn't too surprised by her tart response. Though now nearing her sixties, Gladys was still as thin as a whip and had a gaunt, suntanned face, under grey hair cropped as short as a man's. She was squinting at him through the smoke from the cigarette dangling down from compressed lips.

'I want to speak to your husband, Mrs Bradley.'

'He may not want to speak to you, mister. Just who the hell are you?'

'Jack Fuller. CIA.'

'Oh, one of those.' She clearly disapproved. 'You got an

appointment?' Fuller shook his head. 'No,' Gladys said, 'I didn't think so. Goodnight, Mr Fuller.'

She was just about to close the main door again when Fuller jerked the outer door open and used his foot as a doorstop on the other one. 'Don't close the door, Mrs Bradley. I might hurt my foot. If I do, I'm liable to get angry and that leads to trouble. You look like a woman of some perception, so you know I'm not lying. Now do I come in or not?'

Still a reporter to her fingertips, Gladys studied him for a moment, then nodded and opened the inner door. 'Okay,' she said. 'I know trouble when I see it. You promise me none of that and I'll let you in.'

'No trouble,' Fuller said.

Gladys nodded again, then stepped aside to let him pass. He entered a short hallway with doors on either side. Gladys closed the door behind him, then skipped ahead to lead him into the large living room, which had an open-beam ceiling, walls and floors of pine boards, and comfortable, old-fashioned furniture on loose Mexican carpets. As they entered, Mike Bradley looked up in surprise, then rose from his armchair in front of the flickering TV set.

'Jack Fuller,' Gladys said, sounding laconic and waving a careless hand in Fuller's direction. 'CIA. He was very persistent. Wants to ask a few questions.'

Bradley nodded, understanding what she meant, then looked directly at Fuller. He didn't extend his hand.

'CIA?'

'That's right, Mr Bradley. I know you won't want to answer my questions, but I'm afraid you'll just have to.'

Just as Gladys had done, Mike Bradley studied Fuller carefully, then glanced inquiringly at his wife.

'It's been years now,' Gladys said. 'It can't make too much difference. This one's trouble and we don't need that at our age. Just answer his questions, Mike.'

Bradley nodded, then held out his hand. 'Hi,' he said as Fuller shook it. 'Can I get you a drink?'

'I could sure do with a beer,' Fuller replied.

'I'll get it,' Gladys said.

As she disappeared into the kitchen, Bradley indicated that Fuller should take an armchair facing the TV. When Fuller did so, Bradley switched the set off – Milton Berle was hamming it up in the Texaco Star Theater – and took the comfortable armchair facing him. At fifty-eight years old, Bradley was still a handsome, well-built, silvery-haired man, though the skin on one cheek was slightly livid from what looked like an old burn.

The explosion at Kiel Harbour, Fuller thought. That's what put him in hospital. Otherwise, the guy looks like Spencer Tracy. Dead ringer, in fact.

'Nice house,' Fuller said, glancing around the living room.

'Yes,' Bradley said, 'we think so.'

The pine-board walls were covered with framed photographs taken from the personal history of the two people who lived here. Apart from early family portraits, the photos of Gladys showed her as a reporter in Roswell in the 1930s, including some with Robert H. Goddard and his rocket team; then the Spanish Civil War, including some of Ernest Hemingway; plus London, England, during World War II; liberated Paris, France; then more journalistic encounters in Roswell after the war. Other photos showed Gladys and Bradley, both in uniform, in London and liberated Paris during the war, or Bradley with other military personnel in France and Germany during the same period. Fuller assumed that the framed photos of a young man and strikingly similar young woman, sometimes alone, other times with children or Bradley, were of Bradley's son and daughter and grandchildren. There were no photos of Bradley's former wife, who had died at Pearl Harbour.

'You two have obviously led quite a life,' Fuller said.

'If you're in the CIA, Mr Fuller, I'm sure you know as much about us as we do.'

Fuller grinned. 'Yeah, I guess so.'

Gladys returned with his beer, handed it to him, then took the chair between him and Bradley. Fuller sipped the beer, which was ice cold, then licked his wet lips.

'Well,' he said, 'times have sure changed since you two got together during World War Two. That was some damned explosion last week, right?'

'It sure was,' Bradley replied, his gaze steady and watchful. 'And so was the one the month before.'

He was referring to Britain's first atomic bomb test in the Monte Bello Islands, off the northwest coast of Australia, which had taken place about eight weeks ago. Fuller, on the other hand, was referring to the obliteration of the whole island of Eniwetok, in the Pacific, by the US hydrogen bomb test of two days ago. 'An awesome sight,' Fuller said.

'Some would call it terrifying.'

'Yeah . . . And now we're being plagued by these damned flying saucers. The world's sure changing, all right.'

'We both know why you're here, Mr Fuller. You don't have to introduce the subject in this roundabout manner. You want to know why I didn't turn up at the Socorro UFO crash site on July 2, 1947, five years ago. You want to know what I know.'

Fuller sighed. 'Yeah, that's it.' Glancing at Gladys, he met a measuring, grey-eyed gaze, so quickly turned back to Bradley. 'Okay, you know why I'm here. From the day you returned from the war in Europe, you were obsessed with UFOs, or flying saucers, and kept in constant touch with the Flight Intelligence Officer of Roswell Army Air Base, First Lieutenant William B. Harris, hounding him for information on any sightings. Yet that night in July, 1947, when Harris called to inform you that a flying saucer had actually crashed on the Plain of Magdalena, near Socorro, inviting you to go and view the crash debris with him, you didn't show up and ever since have refused to say why. You also stopped investigating, or even discussing, UFOs from that night on. What happened, Bradley?'

'What do you know about my activities during the war?'

'You were trying to track down a brilliant American physicist who had once worked with Robert H. Goddard right here in Roswell before absconding to Germany and ending up in charge of a top-secret Nazi research project. He was called John Wilson. Born Montezuma, Iowa, in—'

'You know what the research project was, don't you?'

'We believe it was called Projekt Saucer. We also have grounds for believing that it involved the construction of a highly advanced, jet-propelled, saucer-shaped aircraft.'

'Correct. Then you also know that my reason for being at Kiel Harbour just before the close of the war was to try and capture Wilson before he made his escape.'

'By submarine?'

'You must know that as well.'

'No,' Fuller lied, wanting Bradley to reveal as much as possible from his own knowledge. 'The report on your World War Two activities has been heavily censored. I only know that you made it as far as Kiel, where you were badly wounded in an explosion on the dock. I wasn't sure if you knew what had happened to Wilson.'

'Yes, I knew. Wilson and some of his cronies were taken on board the Nazi submarine U-977, which I actually saw leaving Kiel Harbour. Just before the submarine put out to sea, one of Wilson's Nazi pals, an SS lieutenant, found me lying hurt on the dock, after my car had been overturned. He introduced himself, saying his name was Stoll and confirming that Wilson was aboard the submarine. He also said that Wilson would remember my name. Then he blew up the nearby warehouses, which contained trucks stacked high with slaughtered SS troops: the only remaining witnesses, apart from myself, to Wilson's escape. As you know, I was badly wounded by that same explosion and spent many months in hospital, first in Germany, then back here. When I was released, I became obsessed with flying saucers – not mere UFOs – because I knew damned well that they existed and I wanted to prove it.'

'So why didn't you go with First Lieutenant William Harris when he invited you to the site of the Socorro crash?'

'Initially, I intended going,' Bradley confessed. 'In fact, I left here immediately and was heading for Roswell Air Base, to meet Lieutenant Harris, when I realised that I was being tracked by a flying saucer. It landed on the road ahead and made the engine of my car malfunction; then three men dressed in black dropped out of the base of the flying saucer and surrounded my car. One of them introduced himself as Wilson.'

'Christ,' Fuller exclaimed softly. Glancing at Gladys, he saw that she was still gazing steadily at him, not trusting him an inch. 'So what did Wilson say?' Fuller asked, turning back to Bradley.

'He told me that the world we know is dying – a world of wasteful emotions – and that the new world, his world, was approaching and couldn't be held back. His world, he informed me, would be one of truth, or pitiless logic, and his technology was going to take us there. He then told me to stop pursuing him. He threatened Gladys and my grandchildren. He explained that his flying saucers would fly the skies with impunity and that those who reported them – presumably including myself – would be ridiculed and, where necessary, silenced. He told me again to think of my children. To enjoy my retirement. Then he bid me *Auf Wiedersehen* and took off in his saucer. I was frightened by the advanced capability of that flying saucer, by what Wilson had said, by the knowledge that he had managed to track me down, and so I stopped chasing UFOs.'

Gladys Bradley reached over to squeeze her husband's hand. When he smiled, she let his hand go and sat back again.

Fuller had another sip of beer, then put the glass down. 'The saucer made the engine of your car cut out?'

'That's right. A kind of bass humming sound, almost physical, head-tightening. Then the engine of my car cut out and just wouldn't start again.'

'Why didn't you get out and run for it?'

'I tried, but felt paralysed. It wasn't fear, though I certainly felt that. It was some kind of genuine paralysis.'

'A kind of hypnotism?'

'I was fully conscious, but it could have been something like that.'

'How did you get back to your home when the saucer took off?'

'I just turned the ignition key and the damned thing started up as if nothing had happened, letting me drive home. But no way, after what I'd seen, felt and heard, was I going to go up against that Wilson.'

'Since then, have you ever felt you were being watched? Any contact with UFOs?'

'Yes, on both counts. At least three or four times a year, always when driving at night, my car is paced by lights in the sky – either circular or in a long line, indicating a saucer shape. Also, though less frequently, Gladys and I will be awakened in the dead of night by lights beaming into the house from outside, often accompanied by that familiar bass humming sound. They're keeping their eye on us, Mr Fuller, and they always will.'

'Do you think they know we're having this conversation?'

'I really don't think so. I suspect they keep paying me the unexpected visits just to remind me that they haven't forgotten me. I'm taking a chance by having you here, but if they came tonight, it'd just be a coincidence – an unfortunate coincidence.'

'I'm sorry to put you in this danger.'

'No, you're not,' Gladys said accusingly.

Fuller glanced at her, realised how tough she was, so just grinned and wiped it from his face when he turned back to Bradley.

'So Wilson knew who you were,' he said, 'and also knew that you were there at Kiel Harbour.'

'Absolutely,' Bradley said.

'Do you know where that submarine was taking him?'

'I didn't at the time, but I put it all together later, when I learned through the OSS organization that the submarine I'd seen in Kiel Harbour, U-977, under the command of Captain Heinz Schaeffer, had docked at Mar del Plata, Argentina, a few months after the war.'

'You think they're in Argentina?'

'No. Neither Wilson nor that SS Lieutenant Stoll were found on board. Nor were any of the mechanical parts or drawings relating to Projekt Saucer – so my guess is that they used Argentina as a springboard to the next stop.'

'Antarctica?'

'Yes. The Nazis were obsessed with building underground structures there – just like the enormous underground rocket complexes I saw at the end of the war in Belgium and Nordhausen, Thuringia. Documents found by Operation Paperclip indicated that virtually from the moment the Nazis illegally claimed Queen Maud Land in 1938, renaming it Neu Schwabenland, to the closing days of the war, they were shipping scientists, engineers, architects, builders, slave labour, and the material and plans for various highly advanced projects, including Projekt Saucer, to somewhere there. So it didn't take much to put two and two together and come up with Antarctica. Then, when I read about Rear-Admiral Byrd's aborted Operation Highjump, in 1947, I was pretty much convinced that I was right. Wilson is somewhere in Queen Maud Land, either under or inside a mountain range, building flying saucers and God knows what else. It's a nightmare scenario.'

'Do you think he'd be capable of producing flying saucers with the capability of those being reported?'

'Yes. My bet is that a lot of the saucers are small, remote-controlled machines, which first evolved out of the German *Feuerballs*, better known during the war as Foo Fighters. I certainly think they might be the ones involved in the so-called UFO invasion of Washington DC last July. Other saucers are bigger and piloted – just like the one that stopped me that night on the road to Roswell.'

'What do you think happened to the Projekt Saucer documents and parts divided between the Russians and the Allies at the end of the war?'

'I think it's very likely they now have their own saucers, though they certainly won't be as capable as those created by Wilson and doubtless still being evolved in Antarctica.'

'One last question,' Fuller said, finishing his beer and preparing to leave. 'If we sent an invitation, would you be prepared to return to UFO investigations on behalf of the government?'

'No, thanks, Mr Fuller.'

'Thank *you*, Mr Bradley,' Fuller stood up and turned to face Gladys, who hadn't moved from her chair. 'And thank you, Mrs Bradley.'

She just nodded, not trusting him an inch, letting Bradley walk him to the front door. They shook hands on the porch.

'From what I've read you're a hell of a guy,' Fuller said. 'I mean, you really did some things in your time.'

Bradley smiled in a modest manner, then released Fuller's hand. 'Not really,' he said. 'But I hope that what I've told you helps. I just don't want to be personally involved.'

'You won't be,' Fuller promised.

Walking back to his car, he climbed in and then looked out the window. Bradley was still on the porch, the wind blowing his silvery hair, handsome and invincibly decent in his white shirt and slacks. He raised his hand in farewell. Fuller waved back, turned on the ignition and drove away from the house. When he glanced back, Bradley had disappeared from the porch. The lights of the house beamed out into the darkness, under a vast, star-filled sky. A real picture-postcard scene.

Fuller only drove a short way along the dark road. He stopped when he came to another car that was parked by the side of the road with its headlights off. The man in the other car rolled his window down.

'Well?' he asked.

'He knows all about Wilson,' Fuller said. 'Every damned thing.'

The other man nodded and got out of his car, slinging a canvas bag over his shoulder. He walked back along the dark road, towards Bradley's house. Fuller got out of his car, lit a cigarette and silently smoked it.

When Bradley's house exploded and turned into a distant furnace that lit up the night, turning the sky a bloody red and erasing the stars, Fuller sighed, dropped the butt of his cigarette, ground it into the dust with the heel of his shoe, then climbed back into his own car and drove off.

'Too bad,' he murmured.

CHAPTER SEVENTEEN

Dwight sometimes thought he would never work out just what it was he had seen that night in July 1952, hovering over the control tower of Andrews AFB as if about to descend upon it and crush it. In fact, the object, if such it had been, had merely hovered for a few seconds, dazzling them all with the radiance of what appeared to be its vast, swirling base, before it ascended again, making only a bass humming sound, almost an infrasound, then ascending abruptly and blinking out high above, plunging everyone in the control tower into a brief, blinding darkness.

Normal vision had returned soon enough, bringing the real world back with it, but from that day to this, Dwight had thought constantly, and often dreamed, about that vision of luminous power and wondered just what it was. Now, back in Washington DC, a year later but in the same month, he had to struggle to keep the memory of that night out of his thoughts and concentrate on what he was doing.

He was in the downtown office of the recently formed Aerial Phenomena Investigations Institute, or APII, a civilian UFO organisation, to give a clandestine 'deep background' interview to Dr Frederick Epstein, a forty-one-year old astronomer and head of the institute, who had often been of great assistance to Project Blue Book in its evaluation of UFO reports.

Epstein was short and bulky, with a good thatch of hair, though there were streaks of telling grey in his dark

Vandyke beard, which he tended to stroke a lot when deep in thought.

He and Dwight were facing each other across a cluttered desk, in an office with walls covered by large charts showing the most commonly reported UFO shapes, the most commonly reported UFO formations and UFO manoeuvres, both singly and in formation, the worldwide locations and flight directions of the major UFO waves from 1896 to the present, major UFO events in the United States and overseas, and details of the world's major UFO organisations. The most common flight direction for the UFOs, Dwight noted, was south to north and back again.

'It was the official reaction to the Washington sightings, more than anything else,' Dwight told Epstein, who was recording the conversation, 'that made all of us at Blue Book even more suspicious of the Air Force's stance on UFOs. Too many people were telling us one thing and then changing their stories for their official reports. Also, it became increasingly obvious that the top brass in the Air Force were trying to blind us with some dodgy manoeuvres. After the Washington sightings I became convinced that pilots reporting UFOs were being intimidated into changing their reports or simply remaining silent. I also suspected – and still do – that a lot of information was being withheld from us and that the CIA was stepping into the picture for unexplained reasons.'

Epstein stopped him there, in order to change the tapes. Dwight glanced at the window, but the curtains were drawn, even in broad daylight, and the door behind, he knew, was locked to prevent anyone coming in accidentally. It seemed a melodramatic thing to do and made him feel a little foolish, but when he thought of the mysterious deaths of Mike and Gladys Bradley, whose house had gone up in flames after an unexplained explosion about seven months ago – a tragedy that many thought had been caused by an act of arson – his foolishness was replaced with the fearful conviction that people investigating UFOs were putting themselves at risk.

Dwight was worried not only about himself, but about Beth and their daughter, Nichola. You just never knew . . .

When Epstein had changed the tapes, he looked up and said, 'Okay . . . The CIA was stepping into the picture for unexplained reasons.'

'Right. The person who most worried us was Chief of Staff General Hoyt S. Vandenberg. It was Vandenberg who'd buried the original Project Sign Estimate, caused its incineration, and had the project renamed Project Grudge. We're still not sure just how much Vandenberg was influencing the Air Force or the CIA, but certainly he'd been head of the Central Intelligence Group, now the CIA, from June 1946 to May 1947 and his uncle had been chairman of the Foreign Relations Committee, the most powerful committee in the Senate. Clearly, Vandenberg still has great influence in those areas – and it's from those very areas that pressure's always coming to suppress the results of our UFO investigations.'

'So you weren't surprised,' Epstein said, smiling encouragingly, 'when you learnt that the CIA and some high-ranking officers, including Generals Vandenberg and Samford, were convening a panel of scientists to analyse all the Blue Book data.'

'No. And I wasn't surprised, either, to discover that this panel was to be headed by Dr H. P. Robertson, director of the Weapons System Evaluation Group in the Office of the Secretary of Defence – and a CIA classified employee. The Robertson panel, by the way, was also convened against the objections of the Batelle Memorial Institute.'

'What's that?'

'The private research group used by the Air Force to carry out statistical studies of UFO characteristics and advise them on UFO investigations. Normally the Air Force bows to the Batelle Memorial Institute's every demand, but not in this instance.'

'Certainly sounds like they're determined to form that panel, come hell or high water.'

'Exactly,' Dwight said.

'What can you tell me about the panel?'

'This is strictly deep background. My name's not to be mentioned.'

'You have my word on it,' Epstein said.

Dwight took a deep breath, feeling nervous, but determined to let out what was troubling him, hopefully for future use by Epstein's invaluable organisation. Exhaling his breath in a sigh, he said: 'The Robertson panel was convened in great secrecy right here in Washington DC last January. While some insist that it opened on January twelve, it actually ran from January fourteen to eighteen. Apart from Robertson, the group's panel consisted of physicist and Nobel Prize-winner Luis W. Alvarez; geophysicist and radar specialist Lloyd V. Berkner and physicist Samuel Goudsmit, both of the Brookhaven National Laboratories; and astronomer and astrophysicist Thornton Page, Deputy Director of the John Hopkins Operations Research Office. Other participants included J. Allen Hynek, an astronomer consultant to the United States Air Force; Frederick C. Durant, an army ordnance test station director; William M. Garland, the Commanding General of ATIC; our Pentagon liaison officer, Major Dewey Fournet; my Project Blue Book chief, Captain Ruppelt; two officers from the Navy Photo Interpretation Laboratory; and three high-ranking CIA representatives.'

Epstein gave a low whistle. 'That's some group,' he said. 'Almost impossible to argue with.'

'That seems to be the point,' Dwight said. 'The seriousness with which the subject was supposed to be treated is best illustrated not only by the calibre of the men involved, but also by the fact that the group's report was to be given to the National Security Council, NSC, and then, if the decision was that the UFOs are of extraterrestrial origin, to the President himself.'

'Which may have been so much cotton wool,' Epstein said.

'I think it was,' Dwight told him.

Epstein nodded his understanding. 'So what information was the Robertson panel given?'

'For the first two days of the session, Captain Ruppelt reviewed the Blue Book findings for the scientists. First, he pointed out that Blue Book received reports of only ten per cent of the UFO sightings made in the United States, which meant that in five and a half years about forty-four thousand sightings had been made. He then broke the sightings down into the percentage that was composed of balloons, aircraft, astronomical bodies, and other misinterpretations, such as birds, blowing paper, noctilucent and lenticular clouds, temperature inversions, reflections, and so forth, and pointed out that this still left four hundred and twenty-nine as definite "unknowns". Of those, it was clear that the most reported shape was elliptical, the most often reported colour was white or metallic, the same number of UFOs were reported as being seen in daylight as at night, and the direction of travel equally covered the sixteen cardinal points of the compass. Seventy per cent of those unknowns had been detected visually from the air – in other words, by experienced pilots and navigators; twelve per cent had been detected visually from the ground; ten per cent had been picked up by airborne and ground radar; and eight per cent were combination visual-radar sightings. Ruppelt also confirmed that many UFO reports came from top-secret military establishments, such as atomic energy and missile-testing installations, plus harbours and manufacturing areas.'

'That should have impressed them,' Epstein said. 'They always sit up when their own, top-secret establishments are involved.'

'It *should* have impressed them,' Dwight said, hardly able to contain his lingering bitterness. 'Ruppelt and Major Dewey Fournet had completed an analysis of the *motions* of the reported unknowns as a means of determining if they were intelligently controlled. Regarding this, Major Fournet told the panel of how, by eliminating every possibility of balloons, airplanes, astronomical bodies, and so forth, from the hundreds of reports studied, and by then analyzing the motions of the unidentifieds in the remaining unknown category, his study group had been forced to conclude that the UFOs were intelligently controlled by persons with brains equal to, or maybe surpassing, ours. The next step in the study, Fournet explained, had been to find out where those beings came from; and since it seemed unlikely that their machines could have been built in secret, the answer had to be that they came from outer space.'

'Substantiating evidence?' Epstein asked, distractedly stroking his Vandyke beard and studying the turning spools in the tape- recorder, as if they might reveal something Dwight hadn't told him.

'Yes,' Dwight said. 'The morning after Fournet's summary, the panel was shown four strips of movie film that had been assessed as falling into the definite-unknown category. These were the cinetheodolite movies taken by Air Force technicians at the White Sands Proving Ground on April 27, 1950, and approximately a month later; plus the so-called Montana movie taken on August 15 the same year by the manager of the Great Falls baseball team; and the Tremonton movie taken on July 2, 1952, by Navy Chief Photographer, Warrant Officer Delbert C. Newhouse.'

'Let's take them in turn,' Epstein said.

'Right,' Dwight replied, removing a kerchief from his pocket and wiping the sweat from his face. The room, with its windows closed and doors locked, was unbearably hot.

'One of the White Sands movies,' he said, 'showed a dark smudgy object which proved only that *something* had been in the air and, whatever it was, it had been *moving*. The second movie had been analyzed by the Data Reduction Group at Wright-Patterson AFB, with results indicating that the object had been approximately higher than forty thousand feet, travelling over two thousand miles per hour, and was over three hundred feet in diameter.'

Epstein gave another low whistle and shook his head from side to side in a gesture either of disbelief or admiration.

'The Montana movie showed two large, bright lights flying across the blue sky in an echelon formation. The lights didn't show any detail, but they appeared to be large, circular objects. The Tremonton movie showed about a dozen shiny, disc-like objects fading in and out constantly, performing extraordinary aerial manoeuvres, darting in and out and circling one another in a cloudless blue sky.'

'Astronomical phenomena?'

'No. Any possibility that they might have been that was dispelled when the film clearly showed them heading in the same tight cluster toward the western horizon and, more specifically, when one of them left the main group and shot off to the east.'

'Don't tell me the panel refused to accept *that* evidence!'

Dwight rolled his eyes in disgust, then nodded affirmatively. 'They haven't put out their official report yet, but according to Captain Ruppelt they didn't seem impressed.' He wiped his forehead again, then studied the kerchief. It was soaked with his sweat. 'Yet the Montana movie had been subjected to thousands of hours of analysis in the Air Force laboratory at Wright Field and the results proved conclusively that the objects weren't birds, balloons, aircraft, meteors, clouds, or reflections – in short, they were unknowns. As for the Tremonton movie, it had been studied for two solid months by the Navy Laboratory in Anacostia, Maryland, and their conclusion was that the unidentifieds weren't birds or airplanes, were probably travelling at several thousands of miles an hour, and judging by their extraordinary manoeuvres, were intelligently controlled vehicles. In other words, the evidence was conclusive.'

'But the panel still wasn't impressed.'

'No, damn them. After going over the evidence for two days, the bastards concluded in their initial report that the evidence was *not* substantial, that the continued emphasis

on the reporting of the phenomenon was resulting in a –
quote, unquote – threat to the orderly functioning of the
protective organs of the body politic, and that the reports
clogged military channels, could possibly precipitate mass
hysteria, and might encourage defence personnel to
misidentify or ignore actual enemy aircraft.'

'In other words: the real problem wasn't the UFOs – it
was the UFO *reports*.'

'You've got it,' Dwight said.

Even talking about it could make him feel bad these days,
bringing his buried fears to the surface and encouraging
what he sometimes believed was his growing paranoia.
Yesterday, watching TV, he had seen mud-smeared, weary
American troops celebrating the end of the Korean war – a
sight that had filled him with overwhelming nostalgia for
his own fighting days in World War Two. It was a terrible
truth that war had its attractions, but for Dwight it was
something more than that: it was the desire to escape from
the deepening darkness and dangers of his all-embracing
UFO investigations.

The news of the death of the former UFOlogist, Mike
Bradley, and his wife Gladys, possibly by an act of murder,
had certainly filled Beth with fear and again made her plead
for Dwight to get out of this business. In fact, he had tried,
but the Air Force had refused his request; and now, when
he thought of Bradley's blazing house, he felt trapped and
threatened.

'So what do you think their official report will recommend?' Epstein asked him.

'Nothing honest or realistic,' Dwight replied. 'I think the
whole idea behind the Robertson panel is to convince the
American public that the Air Force has made the definitive
study of UFOs and come up with a negative evaluation. In
other words, their job is to shaft us . . . and I think they'll
succeed.'

'That's why you're giving this information to me?'

'Yes. I think Project Blue Book is going to be restrained

by the recommendations of the Robertson panel. If that's true, you'll be able to use this info' more effectively than us.'

'Thank you,' Epstein said, turning off the tapes. 'Sadly, I think you're right.'

Dwight was glad to make his escape from the airless office in Dr Epstein's Aerial Phenomena Investigations Institute, or APII, and step back into the uplifting sunlight of late July in Washington DC. He caught a cab to the airport.

CHAPTER EIGHTEEN

Marlon Clarke was talking to himself. His guillotined head had been separated from its original body for six years now, but was still functioning in an insane, chaotic manner. Still enclosed in a glass casing with an inner temperature reduced to just above the point of freezing, the head was connected to the two amputated hands and the surgically removed, still beating human heart in the chilled glass case on the desk beside it. Clarke's eyes were still open, but were wide with terror or madness. His dribbling lips were moving rapidly to form a torrent of words that couldn't actually be heard because of the cutting of his vocal chords. Attached by the severed neck to a steel-clamp base enclosing artificial blood vessels and the wiring that connected it to the amputated hands and beating heart, the head was moving slightly, the eyes roaming frantically left and right, as the fingers of the severed hands opened and closed spasmodically, sometimes making the hands crawl across the boxed-in table like large, insane spiders.

'The main problem,' Dr King was explaining to Wilson, Kammler and Nebe, 'is not in perfecting the psycho-physical interaction between head and body, but in retaining the sanity of the severed head. As you can see, Clarke's head is successfully receiving the blood being pumped by the separate heart and has retained its power to agitate the amputated hands, albeit in a chaotic, useless manner. This suggests that while the head still has enough consciousness to send impulses to the severed limbs, it's in a state of delirium, or insanity, caused by disbelief and trauma. It's impossible to ascertain what Clarke's thinking right now – if his thoughts still include self-awareness or not – but his wide-open, wandering eyes prove that at least he's still aware of *something*. We just can't tell how much.'

'So the main problem isn't physical, but psychological,' Wilson said. 'We have to find a way to minimize the shock and retain the severed head's sanity.'

'Exactly,' Dr King said. 'With regard to cyborg development, I believe we can solve this with artificially induced amnesia – chemical or electric stimulation of the relevant areas of the brain. In this case, the severed head, or the beneficiary of a surgically rearranged face, part original, part prosthetic, will assume that it has always been what it is and not suffer trauma. This way, please.'

Leading them across the laboratory, which had walls hacked out of the interior of the mountain and therefore gave no view of the Antarctic wilderness outside, King stopped at a bizarre, headless figure strapped upright to an electric chair that was wired to a large computer console. From the waist down, the figure was a perfectly normal, naked male, though the blood had been drained from the legs, giving them a pasty-white, slightly blue, mouldy appearance. However, from the waist up, the torso was artificial, made from moulded steel plates, with one plate missing, exposing a colourful mass of electric wiring and a narrow glimpse of the original intestines. One arm was missing from the headless torso and the other, Wilson noted, was actually a cobalt-chromium alloy prosthetic.

'The prototype for our first cyborg,' Dr King explained. 'The lungs, kidneys and original intestines will remain, but will be strengthened and supported by a two-chamber pacemaker. Working prosthetic joint replacements have already been perfected and will help defeat the rigours of supersonic flight and space travel. The psycho-physical interaction between brain and artificial limbs will be stimulated by the use of an electronic metal skullplate and the problem of speech for the lower-face prosthetic, including new chin implant, will be solved by using an electronic larynx. Control of the cyborg will be attained by a combination of chemical-electronic stimulation of the brain and computerized, remote-control interfacing between the cyborg and its activating machine, located here in the colony and in the saucers. These are early days yet, but I believe it can be accomplished relatively soon. If we can solve the problem of the sanity of the severed head, we're on our way to success.'

A severed human head was resting on a table beside the electric chair. One eye was missing. An odd-looking eye, rather like a glass marble, was resting on the table beside the one-eyed head.

Smiling, King picked up the loose eye and showed it to Wilson. 'An acrylic eye. We're trying various experiments with them. Unfortunately, so far, when we've implanted them in the heads of living subjects, they haven't worked well. When we replace only one eye, the living nerves of the remaining eye help the replacement to see slightly; but when we replace both eyes at the same time, blindness results. Still, given time and a regular supply of living subjects, we'll get there in good time.'

'There'll be no problem with living subjects,' Kammler said. 'Stoll is doing a good job in Paraguay and the supply of Ache Indians is limitless. You need have no fears there.'

'Good,' Dr King said, glancing with pride around his busy laboratory, which was filled with white-smocked surgeons, bio-engineers, dedicated scientists, headless torsos, amputated limbs, and isolated, still pumping human hearts. 'Please, gentlemen, this way.'

He led them through the nearest door, along a short corridor, and into another, larger laboratory, which contained various chairs, some electric, some normal, all with buckled straps on the arms, and small, dark cells with leaded-steel doors containing narrow viewing panels.

There was a dreadful amount of noise in this laboratory

– and the noise itself, by its very nature, was even more dreadful.

Dr King passed Wilson, Kammler and Nebe over to Dr Eckhardt, the former SS experimental medical unit leader. Eckhardt gave them a tour of his domain.

In a small side chamber, human subjects, male and female, were strapped to heavy chairs cemented into the floor, wearing headphones, bleeding profusely from their nostrils and ears. They were also, in some cases, vomiting into plastic bags taped to their mouths.

'Infrasounds,' Dr Eckhardt explained, raising his voice to defeat the agonized screaming of his victims. 'Sounds just below the level of human hearing – so condensed that they can create physical pressure on the human brain and the body's organs. At the moment, the particular infrasounds being used are bursting the blood vessels in the heads of the human subjects, with the results that you see. We're also experimenting with other infrasound levels to ascertain their potential as surgical tools and beam weapons, which we hope to incorporate in our flying saucers. For this reason, we're also experimenting with strobe lights. Please, come this way.'

In one of the darkened cells, behind the closed, sealed door, a man was being subjected to flickering strobe lights. Viewed through the narrow panels in the leaded-steel door, in the rapidly alternating light and darkness, the man appeared to be writhing and kicking in slow motion, while tearing frantically at his hair or clawing his own naked, bloody body.

'The strobe lights,' Dr Eckhardt explained, 'are flickering in the alpha-rhythm range, between eight and twelve cycles a second, thus causing an epileptic seizure in the human subject – as you can see. Other rhythms produce different results, inducing either drowsiness, full mesmerism, hunger, nausea, and various moods ranging from acute depression to uncontrollable violence. These, also, we are planning to incorporate into beam weapons for the saucers. Come, gentlemen, this way.'

A gaunt, pale-faced woman, wearing a one-piece black coverall, was strapped by her wrists and ankles to the arms and legs of an electric chair. A metal skullcap, wired to the console-control beside the chair, was being lowered onto her shaven head. The woman was sweating, trembling and weeping.

'Please don't,' she whispered.

'A stereotaxic skullcap,' Dr Eckhardt explained, ignoring her as the metal device, containing hundreds of minute, hair-thin electrodes, was lowered onto her shaven head. 'When we can hypnotize or otherwise control human beings by remote control – say, with the use of brain-implants – we will abduct those we want, implant them by means of a stereotaxic skullcap such as this, then return them to the world of ordinary men, to do our bidding as and when required. Eventually, in this way, we'll be able to enslave the world's most powerful men and women without resorting to war and with few aware that they're in our control. In other words, they'll become our brain-implanted robots.'

'You have perfected this?' Nebe asked him.

'No,' Eckhardt confessed, 'not yet. At the moment, most of those subjected to electronic stimulation from the stereotaxic skullcaps become vegetables – but some are keeping their minds longer than others, so we're obviously getting there gradually. The breakthrough will come soon.'

He nodded in the direction of the white-smocked technician at the control console. When the technician flicked a switch, the woman screamed in agony, writhed violently in the chair – or as much as she could with her wrists and ankles strapped – then urinated and collapsed into stillness. The technician turned off the power while a medic examined the woman's pulse and heartbeat. Straightening up, he shook his head from side to side and said, 'Her heart's given out. I think we should try one of the adolescents; they have a much greater will to live.'

'Bring one in,' Eckhardt said.

'The cyborg-and-other experimentation is excellent,' Wilson told King when they had left Eckhardt to his work and were walking back to King's own laboratory, 'but what about human, non-prosthetic longevity? Are you making progress with that?'

'There are still considerable problems, particularly regarding the liver, but eventually even that will be solved. I would remind you that even in the West, some remarkable discoveries and advances have recently been made, including the discovery of DNA, the basic structure of life; the first full chemical analysis of a protein; and the first impregnation of a woman with deep frozen sperm – so the secrets of longevity, and even of life, are now within the bounds of possibility. I would therefore suggest that you arrange for the abduction of some scientists and biologists specialising in these fields.'

'I'll see to it,' Wilson said. 'In the meantime, you're doing very good work here. Keep it up, Dr King.'

Now back in King's laboratory, Wilson glanced once more at the mad eyes and dribbling, silently gibbering lips of the severed head of Marlon Clarke. Impressed, he led Kammler and Nebe out, walking along a recently completed tunnel, past brightly-lit side chambers containing other laboratories, workshops, machine-shops, and rooms containing spare parts and supplies, all guarded by armed men in black coveralls. At the end of the tunnel, in a brightly lit open space carved out of the rock, they took a lift up to Wilson's office, located near the summit of the mountain.

Entering, Wilson was briefly dazzled by the vast, sunlit Antarctic as seen through the panoramic windows that stretched along the full length of one wall, just beyond his desk. He did not sit at the desk, but instead indicated the chairs grouped around a table placed right in front of the window, giving a magnificent view of the white wilderness. The table had been prepared for dinner, with a bottle of white wine being chilled in a bucket. The food, which already was on the plates, consisted of a simple green salad, wholewheat bread and cheese. Wilson liked to eat healthily.

'Gentlemen,' he said, pulling out one of the chairs and seating himself. 'Let's sort our differences out in a civilised manner, over good food and wine.' When Kammler and Nebe were also sitting, both eyeing the healthy food with a visible lack of enthusiasm, Wilson removed the bottle of wine from the ice bucket and filled up their glasses. After toasting one another, they commenced eating, talking as they did so.

'I believe you had a complaint to make,' Wilson said, addressing both men.

'Yes,' Kammler replied. 'While my direct responsibilities are for the scientific aspects of the colony, including labour management and discipline, I believe I should still have a say in other matters.'

'Such as?'

'It's not my belief that we should be negotiating with the Americans in return for their co-operation regarding supplies.'

'How else do you propose obtaining such supplies?'

'The way we've always done in the past: by stealing them and bringing them in on the saucers.'

'The saucers are not yet big enough and our supplies are running out.'

'Nevertheless,' Kammler insisted, glancing briefly at the watchful Nebe, 'I don't believe we should let the West stay in the Antarctic. Even less do I believe that we should give the Americans the slightest knowledge of our technology.'

'We don't have a choice, Hans.' Wilson was very patient. 'We can't wait until we run out of supplies and then make our trade. Once we run out of supplies, the West will have us over a barrel. We can't let that happen.'

'And if the West, particularly the US, uses the knowledge we give them to actually catch up with our technology?'

'That simply won't happen.' Wilson was starting to lose his patience. 'I will only pass on what we've already superseded, which means that no matter how far they advance, we will always be even more advanced – much, much more advanced.'

'I don't think we can take that chance,' Kammler said. 'One of your old Projekt Saucer team, Walter Miethe, is now working for the A. V. Roe aircraft company in Malton, Ontario, helping them to construct some crude flying saucers based on our early designs. Habermohl is doing the same for the Soviets. Wernher von Braun is now working for NASA, reportedly on a long-term moon programme. As for Flugkapitän Rudolph Schriever, he is now back in his home town of Bremer-Haven, West Germany, from where he is informing all and sundry that the Americans have their own saucers and constructed them from his designs, which is partially true. The United States now knows too much, so we should not barter with them.'

'And I repeat,' Wilson said, his patience running out, 'that it can't be avoided.' Disgusted, he turned to the silent, always calculating Nebe. 'And you, Artur, what do you think?'

'I agree with Kammler. We can't take such a chance. If we want supplies, let's go and take them. With our saucers, we can bring the United States to its knees – and from there take over the whole world. Why wait so long?'

'You want power, Nebe.'

'Nothing else in life matters.'

Wilson sighed, despairing of base human nature. 'I'm not interested in power for its own sake,' he explained, 'but want only to guarantee the survival and continuing evolution of this apolitical, scientific community. Eventually, our technology will make us the dominant power anyway, without resort to pointless violence, and in the meantime, we can get what we want with minimum effort. Let the United States bring in our supplies; what we give them in return will serve them well, but not enough to give them an advantage over us. We're safe from attack.'

'I'm a policeman,' Nebe said. 'That's what I'm reduced to here. I'm not a man cut out for peaceful work and long-term commitments. I am being destroyed by boredom. I need something more to do. Let's go to war against the Americans, I say, and prove the worth of our saucers. We will soon rule the world, then.'

'You have the instincts of an animal,' Wilson said, 'and the mind of a cave-man. This subject is closed.'

He saw the flash of anger in Nebe's dark animal gaze and knew that he had struck through to a nerve that would make the man murderous. Glancing at Kammler, he saw that he too was angry, though trying to conceal it with a smile that did not reach his eyes. Wilson knew what they were after: the glory of immediate conquest. He also knew that they now wanted to get rid of him, divide the colony between them, and use the flying saucers to resurrect the Third Reich and ensure that it would finally become their beloved Thousand Year Reich.

It was a pitiful dream, one which filled him with contempt, making him realise that these Nazis had served their only useful purpose and that the time had finally come to put an end to them.

He would do it tonight.

'Well, perhaps you're right,' he said. 'The gamble may be too great. Let me sleep on it tonight and make a decision tomorrow.'

'Excellent,' Kammler responded, smiling, all charm, while Nebe simply stared in a stony manner, which was normal for him.

Wilson raised his glass of wine in the air and smiled falsely at both men.

'I can tell you both miss the war,' he said. 'Peace can often be boring. So – to the war!' They toasted the war by touching glasses. When they had drunk, Wilson said, 'Ah, yes, they were indeed good days.'

As moonlight stroked the frozen peaks in the bright night of Antarctica, Kammler and Nebe nostalgically recalled the days of World War II while Wilson listened, pretending to be interested, but practically twitching with impatience. When, a few hours later, after brandy and cigars, they returned to the subject of how best to deal with the outside world, Wilson pretended to agree with them and promised to let them devise a strategy for war, starting with an immediate attack on the United States, probably targeting Washington DC.

Satisfied, Kammler and Nebe retired to bed.

Understanding that no matter what he agreed to, they would eventually turn against him, Wilson had no intention of doing what they wanted. Therefore, instead of considering their request, he sat at his desk and turned on two TV screens which showed them in their separate rooms, Kammler already sleeping, Nebe naked and straddling one of the comfort girls, his bloated body heaving up and down in a joining devoid of love.

Shaking his head in disgust at what they had forced him to do, Wilson pressed a button located under his desk, releasing jets of lethal gas into their rooms – killing them exactly as they had killed so many others in the gas chambers of the Nazi concentration camps.

Kammler didn't wake up. He died in his sleep. Nebe rolled off the girl, covering his mouth with his hands, tried to open the front door and failed, then attempted to climb through the window as the girl, also realising what was happening, started pounding on the door with her fists, obviously screaming for help. Nebe fell back from the window, rolled on the floor, clambered back up. He grabbed the girl by the hair, jerked her away from the door, then he frantically tried to pull the door open until the gas overcame him. The girl went into convulsions first, writhing naked on the bed, vomiting. Nebe slid down the door, turned away, fell forward, started crawling towards the window on his hands and knees, then collapsed face-down. He went into convulsions as the girl became still, then he too vomited profusely and became still. The dense gas had become a cloud of smoke that obscured his body and made it look like a bloated, hairy animal lying on its side. That carcass did not move.

Wilson picked up his phone and called the Rubbish Disposal Unit. He ordered them to remove the bodies from rooms two and three and incinerate them and all their belongings. Then, immensely relieved and satisfied, he had a good sleep.

CHAPTER NINETEEN

Dwight awoke from a restless, dream-haunted sleep in which he had been pursued by a flying saucer while driving from Wright-Patterson AFB to the town of Dayton. The saucer was immense, with a fiery orange-coloured base, and it came down on Dwight's car, blotting out the whole sky, to make the car's engine malfunction and then swallow it whole. Dwight looked up in terror, his heart ready to burst, as the fiery orange-coloured base, now a bizarre, swirling furnace, spread out all around him and suddenly blinded him.

His scream of fear tore him loose, casting him back to the real world, and he jerked upright on the bed, opening his eyes to the morning sunlight, realising that he was covered in sweat and that Beth and Nichola were in the kitchen, having breakfast already. Breathing deeply, trying to still his racing heart, he slid off the bed, wriggled out of his soaked pyjamas, and gratefully went for a cold shower.

Feeling better after the shower, he put his uniform on and went into the kitchen. Beth and Nichola were facing each other across the dining table, having a breakfast of cornflakes, toast, orange juice and, in Beth's case, black coffee. Nichola was now six years old and as pretty as a picture. Beth, though no longer the young, long-haired beauty he had married, was still, with her short-cropped auburn hair, full lips and slim figure, an exceptionally attractive twenty-seven-year old woman. She was also a woman who spoke her mind, as Dwight knew too well and was reminded of once more when he joined her and their daughter at the table.

'Groaning and tossing in your sleep again,' Beth observed. 'More nightmares, Dwight.'

Dwight sighed. 'Yeah, right.' He helped himself to some cornflakes. 'Sorry if I kept you awake. I wouldn't want to disturb you.'

'No need for sarcasm, Dwight. I was only making an observation. Those nightmares are becoming more frequent and that can't be a good sign.'

'I hate nightmares,' Nichola observed, 'but dreams are okay. Why can't we have ice cream for breakfast? I'm fed up with cornflakes.'

'I'm okay,' Dwight said, spooning his cornflakes up too quickly. 'Everyone has nightmares from time to time. There could be lots of reasons.'

'Like what?'

'What do you mean?'

'What else could be causing the nightmares? Is it us? Something I don't know about? Another woman, perhaps?'

Shocked, Dwight glanced at Nichola, but she clearly wasn't listening. She was running her finger around the inside of her upper lip while lethargically stirring the cornflakes into various shapes. 'A duck,' she said, addressing herself. 'A dog. A . . . Mmmmmm.' Dwight looked back at Beth.

'Are you serious?' he asked. 'Is that what you think?'

She gazed steadily at him, measuring him, then lowered her eyes. 'Well, you haven't exactly been *attentive* lately. Not yourself at all, Dwight.'

'I'm under a lot of pressure,' he said. 'You know that as well as I do. I wouldn't even have *time* for another woman, so it isn't an issue.'

Beth reached across the table to squeeze his hand. 'Get out from under that pressure, Dwight. Neither of us needs it. I know you tried before, but try again to get out of this work. If you can't, leave the Air Force.'

Flushed with guilt and wanting to hide it, Dwight glanced out the window. He was guilty because he understood why Beth would be worried, but when he looked out the window, at the planes parked on the airstrip in the inky shadow of the great hangars, wing-flaps and hangar doors shuddering in the August wind, he knew that he couldn't live without the Air Force and become a civilian. Also – and the thought of this made him feel even worse – though Project Blue Book was certainly putting pressure on and giving him nightmares, it was also exerting a dreadful fascination that he couldn't resist. It wasn't ordinary work, after all.

'I can't eat what's left,' Nichola said. 'They're too mushy and messy.'

'That's 'cause you made them that way stirring them,' Beth retorted.

'I was drawing with my spoon,' Nichola explained.

Dwight placed his free hand on Beth's hand, making a sandwich of it. 'I can't leave the Air Force,' he said. 'What would I do out there? I'm in it for life. Besides, it isn't as bad as you think. Half the things you hear about UFOs are nonsense. Hysteria and wishful thinking have a lot to do with it. You know? The planet Venus, comets, meteors, clouds, plasmoids, corona discharges, parhelia and paraselenae, the sun and moon and stars, even lightning and birds, can all look like bright, solid objects moving at high speed. So people see those, misinterpret what they see, then hysteria or wishful thinking comes into play. As for the UFOs being flown by extraterrestrial beings – well, maybe they're not. Maybe they're just some kind of extraterrestrial phenomenon – a kind of mirage. We're frightened of what we can't understand, so we tend to exaggerate.'

'That doesn't stop your nightmares, Dwight. Also, you're losing weight. We hardly ever see you anymore, and when you're here, you're not here – you're over at ATIC in your thoughts, still working away there.'

'The nightmares will go away with time. I'm pretty damned sure of that.'

'Look, Dwight, I don't know if we're being invaded by flying saucers or not. I only know that my husband is having bad nightmares, losing weight, and is often too exhausted and distracted to even make love to me. I'm worried about that and also about your future. You say you're an Air Force lifer – well, I agree with that – but that being so, what's going to happen to you if, as they seem to be doing, they consistently deny you promotion? We both know why that is, Dwight. It's nothing to do with your competence. It's because most of those who get involved with UFOs are given a hard time. You should have been in charge of Blue Book, but Ruppelt got it instead. Now there are rumours that Ruppelt's in trouble and may get pushed out. That's the way it runs, Dwight.'

'They're just rumours,' Dwight said, though he thought the rumours might be true. 'Some folks just talk too much. We all know that today the official recommendations of the Robertson panel will be released, and that knowledge has encouraged a lot of wild speculation, mostly to do with the fate of Project Blue Book in general and Captain Ruppelt in particular. They're just rumours, Beth.'

'It isn't a rumour that you've been repeatedly denied promotion from as far back as Project Sign. Before that you were everybody's darling; since then they've made all kinds of excuses to put other, less experienced officers in front of you. Those aren't rumours, Dwight. Nor is it just a rumour that a lot of people involved in UFO investigations have had even worse things to contend with, such as being posted to Alaska or even having bad, inexplicable, sometimes fatal accidents, like that World War II hero and UFO expert, Mike Bradley, and his unfortunate wife.'

Dwight gulped the last of his coffee and then put on his Air Force captain's tunic. 'There's no proof for that,' he lied, looking guiltily from Beth to Nichola, secretly convinced that he was placing both of them in danger and

213

feeling guilty because of it. 'It's just more wild speculation.'

'Oh, yeah?' Beth responded. 'Then how do you explain the men in black?'

Dwight had been about to kiss Beth on the cheek, but her words stopped him, making him straighten up again, feeling a chill wind pass through him.

'What do you know about the men in black?' he asked.

'Lots of gossip,' Beth said. 'I prefer to call them stories. Folks are talking about people involved in UFO investigations receiving visits from groups of men dressed all in black. Some say they wear black suits. Others say they're coveralls. Most agree that they're not with the Air Force and though human seem strange. Very pale, folks say. Oddly inexpressive faces. They usually visit in twos or threes, generally arrive in a black limousine, and always warn those they've come to see to stop discussing or investigating UFOs. They tell them that if they continue to do so, they'll find themselves in real trouble.'

'Another tall story,' Dwight said, though in fact he had been receiving an increasing number of such stories, many from reliable sources. 'These tall tales spread like wildfire. You believe all that garbage?'

'I'm only telling you what I heard,' Beth replied cagily, though certainly not joking. 'Most of these stories come from pretty reliable sources – mostly Air Force personnel – and some came from people who had the visitors themselves, ignored what they were told, then got into serious trouble shortly after. In at least one case, the person who received the visitors and told Adele Walters about it – saying he thought it was a hoax – later vanished and hasn't been seen since.'

'If it was a friend of Adele's, it could only have been Ben Little,' Dwight told her.

Little was an amateur astronomer and fanatical UFOlogist, resident right here in Dayton, Ohio, who had frequently, perhaps too loudly, claimed that the flying saucers could be man-made secret weapons of the US and

Canadian governments. After receiving a lot of local press coverage for a couple of days, Little had just upped and disappeared, leaving a wife and three kids. Adele's husband, Ralph Walters, an Air Force Flight engineer, was a close family friend.

'Yeah, that's the one. Obviously, you heard about it, Dwight.'

'Yes. And I also heard that the marriage was in trouble and that Ben Little may simply have fled the coop. I lean towards that hypothesis.'

'I bet,' Beth said. She had his number and he knew it. Though he simply couldn't admit it even to himself, he believed that something bad had happened to the loud-mouthed Ben Little and that the mysterious 'men in black' had something to do with it. He now believed that the 'men in black' existed; he just didn't know who they were. Extraterrestrials? The CIA? Foreign agents? There was no way of knowing.

Trying to hid the shock that Beth's knowledge had given him, he leaned down and kissed her on the cheek. 'See you later,' he said. Then he kissed Nichola on the forehead, tickled her under the armpits, and left her giggling hysterically as he hurried out of the house, to walk the short distance to ATIC, across the airstrip of Wright Field.

The operations room in ATIC was not as spartan as it had been during Project Sign. Now, a lot of UFO photographs and drawings of their 'alien' occupants had been added to the many incident maps, charts and graphs on the walls. The two teletype machines hardly ever stopped working and the single secretarial assistant, WAC corporal Thelma Wheeler, was now a sergeant and had a couple of other secretaries under her.

Though putting on a little weight, Thelma was still blonde and pretty and had eyes only for Captain Bob Jackson, who had somehow managed to carry on an affair with her for years without actually tying the knot, let alone becoming engaged. Even now, as Dwight entered the cluttered room, Bob was sitting on the edge of Thelma's desk, leaning towards her and whispering into her ear. Thelma burst into giggles and slapped Bob's knee, then turned away by swivelling around in her chair and went back to her expert typewriting. Bob looked up, saw Dwight and stopped smiling, so Dwight knew the news was bad.

'Morning,' he said, approaching Bob. 'I take it from the look on your face that the recommendations of the Robertson panel have come through.'

'Yeah,' Bob replied. 'I don't know what's in the report, but Ruppelt doesn't look happy and said we were to go straight in and see him as soon as you got here.'

'Then let's go in, Bob.'

Seated behind his desk, Ruppelt, in his Air Force uniform, still looked like a dark-haired adolescent whose slightly plump, smoothly handsome face showed decency and good humour. Nevertheless, gazing down at the thick folder on his desk, he was clearly not in a good-humoured mood and, indeed, looked decidedly troubled – so much so, in fact, that he didn't notice their arrival and was only distracted from the report when Dwight said, 'Morning, Captain Ruppelt. I believe you wanted to see us.'

Ruppelt glanced up as if confused, trying to collect his thoughts, then he smiled as if it was something of an effort, indicating that Dwight and Bob should take the chairs at the other side of his desk. When they had done so, he glanced down at the Robertson panel report, then looked up again and spread his hands over the file as if casting a net.

'What can I say?' he asked rhetorically. 'Where do I start?'

'Just come out with it, Captain,' Dwight said. 'It'll be easier for all of us.'

'It's not good,' Ruppelt said.

'They've shafted us,' Bob added more bluntly. 'Is that what you're saying?'

'Yes, Bob, I'm afraid it is.' Ruppelt massaged his forehead with his fingers, glanced distractedly at the file, then looked up again. 'I should warn you that this isn't the full report. It's merely a summary of their major recommendations.'

'So when are we getting the full report?' Dwight asked him.

'We're not,' Ruppelt said. 'We're only getting what they want us to know and this is it, gentlemen.'

'What— ?' Dwight began, glancing at the equally shocked Bob.

'Don't ask me,' Ruppelt said. He lowered his head again, to scan the document. 'First, despite the conclusive evidence offered by me and Major Fournet, the members of the panel have concluded that the evidence is *not* substantial, that the continued emphasis on the reporting of the phenomenon is resulting in – I quote – "a threat to the orderly functioning of the protective organs of the body politic" – unquote – and that the continuing UFO reports are clogging military channels, could possibly precipitate mass hysteria, and might encourage defence personnel to misidentify or ignore actual enemy aircraft. In other words: the real problem isn't the UFOs – it's the UFO *reports*.'

'That much I already knew,' Dwight said. 'What bothers me is what they've recommended.'

'It's pretty startling,' Ruppelt said. He glanced at the many posters on the walls around his desk, mostly enlargements of frames from cinetheodolite movies or stills taken with amateur cameras, the UFOs mostly no more than blurred, round-shaped objects. He appeared to be trying to take some solace from them, though not with success. Sighing, he went back to the report. 'As I say, based on the assessment, the Robertson panel has made some unexpected, even startling, recommendations.'

'Ho, ho,' Bob whispered.

'First,' Ruppelt continued, as if not hearing Bob, 'it's recommended that the three major private UFO organizations – the Aerial Phenomena Research Organization, or

APRO, the Civilian Saucer Intelligence, or CSI, and Dr Frederick Epstein's Aerial Phenomena Investigations Institute, or APII – be watched because of what is described as their potentially great influence on mass thinking in the event of widespread sightings. Included in this recommendation is the statement: "The apparent irresponsibility and the possible use of such groups for subversive purposes should be kept in mind." '

'Jesus Christ!' Bob exclaimed.

'Next, it recommends that the national security agencies take immediate steps to strip the UFO phenomenon of its importance and eliminate the *aura of mystery* it has acquired. The means will include a so-called *public education programme.*'

'Mass brainwashing,' Bob translated bitterly.

'Finally, the panel has outlined a programme of public education' – Bob snorted contemptuously – 'with two purposes: training and debunking. The former will help people identify known objects and thus reduce the mass of reports caused by misidentification; the latter will reduce public interest in UFOs and thereby decrease or eliminate UFO reports.'

'Shove it under the carpet,' Bob translated.

'As a means of pursuing this so-called education programme,' Captain Ruppelt continued sombrely, ignoring Bob's outraged interjections, 'the panel has suggested that the government hire psychologists familiar with mass psychology, military training film companies, Walt Disney Productions, and popular personalities such as Arthur Godfrey, to subtly convey this new thinking to the masses. It has also recommended that the sighting reports should *not* be declassified, but that security should be tightened even more while all so-called non-military personnel should still be denied access to our UFO files.'

Ruppelt stopped scanning the report and looked at Dwight and Bob in turn. After a tense silence, he said:

'Interpreting these recommendations the only way possible, it seems clear to me that the whole purpose of the Robertson Panel has been to enable the Air Force to state for the next decade or so that an *impartial* body examined the UFO data and found no evidence for anything unusual in the skies.'

'Damn right,' Bob said bitterly.

'While this is an obvious distortion of fact, it means that the Air Force can now avoid discussing the nature of the objects and instead concentrate on the public relations campaign to eliminate the UFO reports totally. In other words, Project Blue Book is finished. If it continues under that name, it won't be as we know it.'

'No,' Dwight said, 'it won't. Project Blue Book's going to become responsible for a policy of ridicule and denial that'll inhibit the effectiveness of any future study of the phenomenon. It'll now be just another arm of the Robertson panel's CIA-backed propaganda campaign.'

'Those bastards,' Bob said.

Though clearly not happy, Ruppelt smiled at him, then he turned the report over, picked up some other pages, and spread them out on his desk as if they were dirt.

'I'm afraid, gentlemen, that while the deliberately leaked Robertson panel report recommends the dropping of all secrecy and the expansion of Project Blue Book's staff, in the official report, from which this summary has been extracted, they've actually recommended a tightening of security, a mass debunking of the phenomena, a subtle ridicule of witnesses, and . . . the virtual elimination of all the Blue Book staff.'

'Oh, my God!' Bob said, practically groaning.

Deliberately ignoring him, but sounding choked up, Ruppelt said: 'The following are being posted elsewhere.' Lowering his head and sounding even more choked, he read off the list of names of those being posted.

The list included himself. The only people left were Dwight, Bob and Thelma Wheeler.

'The original three,' Ruppelt pointed out. 'You're now in charge, Dwight.'

'Of what?' Dwight asked bitterly. 'They've left me in charge of a pile of shit.'

'It sure smells that way,' Bob said.

Ruppelt stood up and put on his peaked cap. 'I knew this last night and I'm packed already. They told me I had to leave immediately and that's what I'm doing. My bags are out in the jeep and I'm leaving right now. It was my pleasure knowing you, gentlemen. I'm just sorry it's ended this way.'

'So am I,' Dwight said.

They both followed him out of his office and into the main room, where he called the staff together and painfully read out the instructions for their postings. When the shocked staff had taken it in, he walked around shaking hands with each of them in turn, clearly embarrassed when some of the girls shed tears. After shaking the last hand, he indicated that Dwight and Bob should escort him to the front door of the ATIC building. Outside, on the verandah, with the planes taking off, landing, and roaring in low over the runway and hangars, he stared intently at both of them.

'They're trying to grind you down,' he said, 'and they might well succeed, but in the meantime, here are a few questions for you to answer.' He spread his hands in the air and started raising each finger in turn as he ticked off the questions. 'Why, when the Air Force was telling the whole world that the study of UFOs hadn't produced enough evidence to warrant investigation, did they secretly order all reports to be investigated? Why, when all of us had actually read General Twining's statement that the phenomenon was something real, did they deny that such a statement had ever been submitted? Why, when they themselves initiated Project Sign and received its official report concluding that the UFOs were of extraterrestrial origin, did they dissolve the project and then burn the report? Why, when Project Sign was changed to Project Grudge, did they go all out to ridicule the reported sightings and then disperse most of the staff on the project? Why, when the Air Force continued to claim that they had absolutely no interest in UFOs, did they insist that all reports be sent to the Pentagon? Finally, why did the CIA lie to us, why has the Robertson Report been kept from us, and why has Project Blue Book just been destroyed? Those questions need to be answered, gentlemen, and you're the only ones left. Goodbye . . . and good luck!'

He saluted and walked down to his jeep and then drove out of their lives.

'I don't believe this,' Dwight said.

CHAPTER TWENTY

Ernst Stoll was disgusted by the reflection in the mirror. He had aged since coming here, his features now gaunt, skin yellowish from bad food and lack of activity, eyes losing their lustre. Realising just how much the jungle was taking its toll, he cursed under his breath and called for his comfort girl, Maria, to bring him coffee. She did so quickly, padding towards him on bare feet, her face bruised from the beating he had given her last night when his latest sexual innovations had failed to produce the desired result. That, too, was disappearing – his potency, his damned manhood – and when he glanced again in the mirror to see Maria retreating nervously from him, leaving his steaming cup of coffee on the table just behind him, he realised that she knew that all too well and might be talking about it. Feeling even more humiliated, he decided to get rid of her, and started pondering how best to do it as he wiped his face with a towel.

Then the mirror shook a little, bouncing off the wall, making his already fractured image move out of the frame and back in again.

Steadying the mirror with his free hand, Ernst finished drying his face, then put the towel down and felt the floor shaking under his feet as a familiar bass humming sound filled the room, emanating from outside. Realising that they had arrived earlier than expected, he hurriedly buttoned up his shirt, slipped on his boots, and started across the room.

Maria was on her hands and knees, polishing the wooden floorboards with a waxed cloth. A local Indian girl, but the illegitimate daughter of a white man who had discarded her, she had barely turned seventeen, which was the age Ernst now liked them, and her perfect body was visible through the thin cotton dress, where it tightened over her raised rump and curved spine. Ernst felt a wave of the lust that was rarely satisfied these days, so he angrily pressed his booted foot on her spine and pressed her face-down on the floor. The bass humming sound filled the room, making the floors and walls shake, but Ernst could still feel the trembling of the girl under his booted foot. He had the urge to crush her spine, thus releasing his frustration, but instead he took his pleasure from the fear he could hear in her voice.

'Please, master,' she whimpered.

He pressed harder with his boot, heard her soft groan of pain, laughed and removed his boot from her spine, then left the house.

Outside, on the verandah, the bass humming sound was louder, almost palpable, an odd vibration that shook the building, and he looked up to see a three-hundred-foot diameter flying saucer descending vertically, slowly, onto the landing pad that now took up most of the ground in the immense walled enclosure in front of the house.

The craft descending was an object of such beauty, it nearly brought a lump to Ernst's throat, reminding him of what he had lost when sidetracked from aeronautical engineering to become an SS policeman. Still high up in the air and viewed by Ernst from almost directly below, the great saucer was spinning rapidly on its own axis, except for the central part, which was stationary. It was, he knew, constructed like a giant meniscus lens, or like two inverted plates, which were rotating around the dome-shaped, gyroscopically stabilized central fuselage containing the control cabin, passenger accommodations and supplies. Driven by an advanced electromagnetic propulsion system that ionized the surrounding air and created an electrical conducting field, the saucer was not hindered by normal heat and drag; it therefore had remarkable lift while being devoid of sonic booms or other noises, other than a bass infrasound that seemed almost palpable.

The rapid rotation of the great outer rings slowed down as the saucer descended, but its electromagnetic gravity-damping system – which also aided its lift and ability to hover almost motionless in the air – was creating violent currents of air within a cylindrical zone the same width as the saucer, making the grass and plants flutter, sucking up loose soil and gravel, and causing them to spin wildly, noisily, in the air as if caught in the eye of a hurricane.

The native workers who lived in the shacks located around the inner edge of the compound were standing outside their modest homes, untouched by the whirlpool of wind that did not extend beyond the cylindrical zone of the saucer, which made it seem magical. They were looking up in awe as the gigantic saucer descended, its outer rings rotating, its central base motionless, pointing and chattering to express their disbelief, even though they had seen it many times before.

Ernst felt his emotions surge as the saucer descended almost to ground level, filling up most of the compound, its central dome as high as a two-storey building. Composed of an electrically charged, minutely porous magnesium orthosilicate, it had a whitish glow caused by the ionization of the surrounding air, but it darkened to a more normal metallic grey as it hovered just above the ground, rocking slightly from side to side, its massive hydraulic legs emerging from four points around the base to embed themselves deeply into the soft earth. The immense saucer bounced gently on the legs, but eventually settled down and was still. Its rotating rings gradually slowed and then stopped altogether, as did the wind that had been created by the saucer's electromagnetic gravity-damping system. Silence reigned for a moment.

Still standing on his verandah, Ernst was deeply moved and embittered all at once. He should have helped to construct that saucer, flown it, been part of it, but instead he was condemned to this hellish jungle, rounding up Ache Indians and haggling shamelessly with *Federales* instead of using his engineering talents for work in the Antarctic colony. He had been chosen for this and must do it, but it still deeply wounded him.

With the outer rings of the saucer no longer rotating, the bass humming noise faded away and a panel in the concave base dropped down on hinged arms to form a ramp leading to the ground. Armed guards wearing black coveralls emerged to form a protective ring around the ramp, then Wilson appeared, dressed completely in black, followed by more armed guards, dressed in black also.

Ernst stepped down off the porch and went to greet his master. When Wilson shook his hand, Ernst was startled by how youthful he looked. Though now over eighty, the silvery-grey hair was abundant, his skin was smooth on a handsome, ascetic face, and his eyes were as blue and icily clear as the Antarctic sky. The only giveaway, Ernst noticed, was in the slight rigidity to his features when he attempted to smile and, perhaps, a slight stiffness to his movements.

'How are you, Ernst?' he asked, his voice no warmer than his icy gaze.

'I'm fine, sir. And you?'

'All the operations so far have been successful. Doctors Eckhardt and King are making good progress. By having the courage to let them try things out on me, I've kept old age at bay.'

Though aware that the good doctors Eckhardt and King always tried things out on numerous unfortunate live subjects before operating on Wilson, Ernst thought it wise to pass no comment.

'I'm afraid we can't stay for very long,' Wilson continued. 'We'll simply collect the livestock, then be on our way again. You and I can have a quick talk while Porter' – he indicated the armed, black-uniformed brute behind him – 'sees to the Indians. All right, Porter, get started.'

Realising that for the first time Kammler and Nebe were not with Wilson, Ernst waited until the burly Porter had marched off to the cages with a group of his armed thugs before asking about the whereabouts of his former detested World War II comrades.

'They're dead,' Wilson said indifferently, taking a seat at one side of the low table on the verandah. 'An unfortunate accident. They went together in a saucer to collect supplies left by the Americans at the other side of the mountain range. The saucer malfunctioned and crashed, killing everyone on board. Kammler and Nebe are no more.'

Even though he had detested Kammler and deeply feared Nebe, Ernst was shocked to hear of their death. Nevertheless, after calling out for Maria to bring him and Wilson tea, he saw a ray of hope in his darkness. 'So what will you do now that they're gone? Surely you need someone experienced to replace them and help run the colony. Surely, I—'

'No,' Wilson said, quickly crushing his hopes. 'I know what you're going to suggest, Ernst, but it isn't possible right now. I can run the colony on my own. Your work here is more important. We can't do without a constant supply of Ache Indians, so we can't do without your presence here. You have done truly excellent work in opening up and maintaining lines of communication between ourselves and General Stroessner. Those lines must not be broken. As Stroessner will almost certainly become the next President of Paraguay – probably within the next few months – it's important that you remain here to offer him support and strengthen the alliance between us. In time, I promise, you'll return to the colony, but right now your presence here is vital.'

Torn between pride and his suspicion that Wilson was lying and intended keeping him here for ever, Ernst shifted uneasily in his chair. He compensated for his disappointment and deepening depression by barking angrily at Maria who, when she emerged from the house to pour their tea, spilt some into the saucers.

'Her hands were shaking badly,' Wilson noted when Maria had backed nervously into the house. 'Is she frightened of you?'

'Yes,' Ernst said. 'During the war I learnt that fear could work miracles, so I make sure that everyone's frightened of me.'

'Very good,' Wilson said, though it was impossible to tell if he meant it or not, so unemotional, almost toneless, was his soft voice. 'And is the round-up of the Indians trouble-free?'

'Yes,' Ernst replied. 'The *Federales* do it for me. I merely stay in touch with them, tell what I want, haggle like an Arab about the price, then let them get on with it. They know the jungle; also, they've been hunting the Ache for years, so they know what they're doing. Naturally, as you can imagine, they're quite ruthless, which makes them effective.'

'Any problems holding the prisoners in the compound?'

'No. The *Federales* don't bring the prisoners here until I give them a date, which is usually the day before you arrive. If the *Federales* round them up too early, they have to look after them for me and I'm sure they get certain benefits out of that – if you get my meaning.'

'I do,' Wilson replied, not mentioning rape or other forms of abuse, but registering a slight distaste for the low appetites of the still primitive human race. 'So they're only in your cages a short time?'

'Correct.' Even as Ernst spoke, Wilson's black-uniformed troops were opening the gates of the bamboo cages at one side of the compound and starting to herd out the terrified Ache Indians, men, women and children, to march them at gunpoint across the compound and up into the saucer by another, wider ramp that had since been lowered down from the base. Looking up at the towering saucer, some of

the Indians were terrified, started gibbering or covering
their eyes with their hands, then tried either to break out
of the column or turn back. When they did so, however,
Wilson's men in black hammered them brutally with the
butts of their weapons and forced them onward again.

*I seem to have spent half my life watching people being
herded at gunpoint from one form of imprisonment to another,*
Ernst thought, recalling the Jews in the cattle trucks in
Poland and Germany, all fodder for another great dream.
Masters and slaves, indeed.

'The last time we spoke,' Ernst said, 'you were making a
deal with the Americans in return for supplies. I take it
from the fate of Kammler and Nebe that you now have an
agreement with the United States.'

'Yes, Ernst. They drop what we want at the far side of
the mountain range and our saucers pick it up and bring it
home. In return for this, I feed them titbits of our technology
– though never enough to put us in any danger from them.
They've also agreed to the late Artur Nebe's suggestion
for a long-term programme of disinformation based on a
mixture of ridicule and intimidation of UFO witnesses, both
civilian and military.'

'I've been reading about that Robertson panel in
American newspapers and assumed that it might be a threat
to you.'

Wilson gave one of his rare chuckles of pleasure. 'All
part of a planned, CIA-backed programme of disinformation.
Even though the Project Blue Book evidence on UFOs
proved conclusively that the saucers exist, the panel stated
in their report that the evidence *wasn't* substantial, that
the continued emphasis on the reporting of the
phenomenon was resulting in "a threat to the orderly
functioning of the protective organs of the body politic, and
that the reports clogged military channels, could possibly
precipitate mass hysteria, and might encourage defence
personnel to misidentify or ignore actual enemy aircraft."
Naturally, as the United States has just finished fighting

the war in Korea, the Soviets have exploded their first hydrogen bomb, and the Cold War is presently at its chilliest, the American public, and the top brass of the armed forces, swallowed that all too readily.'

This man is truly a genius, Ernst thought, helplessly swelling up with admiration. *There is nothing he can't do.*

'What will the immediate results of this be?' he asked.

'We've already had the results, Ernst. Last August, the Pentagon issued Air Force Regulation 200-2, which the civilian UFO organisations are already describing as notorious.'

'For good reason?'

'Of course. Drafted purely as a public relations weapon, AFR 200-2 prohibits the release of *any* information about a UFO sighting to the public or media, except when the sighting is positively identified as a *natural* phenomenon. In addition, while AFR 200-5, the previous regulation, stated that sightings should not be classified higher then restricted, the new regulation ensures that *all* sightings will be classified as restricted. Then, in December, the Joint Chiefs of Staff followed AFR 200-2 with Joint Army-Navy-Air Force Publication 146, which made the releasing of any UFO information to the public a crime under the Espionage Act, punishable by a one-to-ten-year prison term or a fine of ten thousand dollars. Even better, the most ominous aspect of JANAP 146 – at least from the point of view of those who might fall foul of it – is that it applies to anyone who knows of its existence, even including commercial airline pilots.'

'In other words,' Ernst said, 'to all intents and purposes, and contrary to public Air Force pronouncements, the UFO project has been plunged into secrecy.'

'Correct.'

'It's nice to be protected by our enemies,' Ernst said.

'Very nice,' Wilson replied with a slight, chilly smile, gazing out from the verandah to where the Ache Indians were still being herded at gunpoint from the cages to the great flying saucer. Often they became hysterical when they were actually under its immense base, at the foot of the sloping ramp, but they always scurried up the ramp when they were thumped by rifle butts or, as Ernst now noted, by small metallic devices strapped by the wrist to the knuckles of some of the troops. When the troops merely touched the Indians with such devices, the latter screamed in pain and did as they were told.

'What are they?' Ernst asked.

'Experimental stun guns,' Wilson replied. 'At the moment, they do no more than give severe electrical shocks – not severe enough to knock out, let alone kill, but certainly enough to burn and hurt. But we hope that very soon we'll be able to use them to actually stun, as well as merely hurt, and that eventually, with very fine tuning, they can be used as mesmerizing devices when applied to certain points on the anatomy. Time will bring us everything.'

Ernst felt the great wave of his loss rolling over him to wash him away. Trembling, he finished off his tea, placed the cup back on the saucer, and wiped his lips with the back of his hand.

'I only wish I could be part of it,' he said, secretly wanting to scream for release, but too frightened to do so. 'I mean, being here . . . this jungle . . . these filthy natives . . . I feel like an Arab haggling in a bazaar. I was trained to be an engineer, a scientist, and yet now . . .'

Wilson, in a rare gesture of affection, placed his hand gently on Ernst's wrist. 'No, Ernst, never think that. Such thoughts are for common people. It's vanity that makes you talk this way, and you should be above it. As individuals, we are nothing. Our desires are mere conceits. We only exist to serve the whole, which is past and future combined. You must suppress your own desires, cast off ephemeral needs, and learn to take pride from your small part in life's grander purpose. Man is still essentially animal. His only true worth is in the mind. The mind is the doorway to immortality and the secrets of being.

You are part of that, Ernst. What you do here has its purpose. Like a monk in a monastery, like a hermit in his cave, like a mystic contemplating in his mountain retreat, you will learn to accept this. Discipline brings freedom. Self-sacrifice brings fulfilment. What you lost in the past – your career, your wife and children, your hopes for the Third Reich – and what you feel you're losing now – the comradeship and esteem of your fellow engineers in Antarctica – you'll get back multiplied when what you are doing here has been completed and you see the results of it. Then, and only then, will I bring you back to the Antarctic. When I do, you'll be twice the man you are now – ennobled by knowledge. Believe me, Ernst. Eventually this will come to pass and then you will thank me.'

Desperate to believe him, needing the healing hands of hope, Ernst tried to forget his lost wife, children, early ambitions and dreams – and all else in his dark, squandered history. Trembling, he picked the bell up from the table and violently rang it, calling for Maria.

'Yes,' he said, startled at how deeply he had been shaken by Wilson's softly spoken, unemotional, mesmeric monologue. 'As always, you're absolutely right. All else is vanity.'

When Maria appeared on the verandah, trembling as much as Ernst, he thought of how often he had forced her obedience by threatening to put a bullet into her mother – there and then, right in front of her. Naturally, it had always worked – a child's love knew no reason – but even that threat was unlikely to stop idle gossip. Vanity: yes, it was a dreadful human vice, but one he had not yet learnt to conquer when it came to his potency. To preserve her mother's life, Maria had submitted to all of his demands – unimaginable sexual activities, not mere vice, beyond pornography – and yet none of it, certainly in the past weeks, had helped him to find release. Now, Maria was bound to talk – silence would be impossible for her – and when Ernst imagined the talk spreading around the compound workers, all of whom loathed and feared him, he could not bear the thought of the humiliation he would then surely suffer.

They would thrive on his pain.

'Yes, master,' Maria said, falling to her knees before him, lowering her head, and not daring to look at him without permission. Ernst thought of all she had done to protect her mother and finally knew what would pleasure him. 'Please take her with the others,' he said to Wilson. 'She cannot be trusted.'

'Of course,' Wilson said.

As Maria, sobbing and pleading, was dragged into the great saucer by the armed men in black, and her mother, also sobbing and pleading, was dragged back into her shack by some other Indian women, Wilson stood up and squeezed Ernst's shoulder, then shook his hand.

'Don't worry,' he said, 'we'll put her to good use. Now I must be off, Ernst. Thank you. You are doing excellent work here. Take your pride from that knowledge.'

'I will.'

'Till the next time, *Auf Wiedersehen.*'

'*Auf Wiedersehen,*' Ernst said.

The lump returned to his throat when the great saucer took off, rising slowly, vertically, with a bass humming sound, until it was the size of a silver coin, reflecting the sun. There it hovered for a moment, a silver coin spinning, then it suddenly shot off to the south and vanished in seconds, blinking out like a light bulb.

When it had gone, Ernst looked around him at the immense, walled-in compound, taking note of the shadows being cast by the soaring trees, the awe-struck eyes of the native workers, unwashed, in tattered rags, the pigs in their muddy pens, the chickens frantically flapping wings, the naked children rolling in mud and water silvered by sunlight, the guards at the machine-guns in the towers that looked out over the jungle. Ernst choked up with despair

232

instead of pride and turned back into the house, desperately
needing a drink.

Without Wilson, he took his strength from the bottle
and yearned for escape.

He just couldn't admit it.

Chapter Twenty-One

On the evening of March 7, 1954, Jack Fuller drove along the ten-mile causeway that led from Patrick Air Force Base, Cape Canaveral, Florida, across the Banana River, Merritt Island and the Indian River, to the Starlite Motel in Cocoa Beach, located in the swampy lands around the original village and now a rapidly growing town of ten thousand souls. From here dozens of missiles, as well as Explorer 1, America's first earth satellite, had been fired into space. Many of the motels in the area had been given appropriate names – the Vanguard, the Sea Missile, the Celestial Trailer Court – but the Starlite had gone one better by having a flashing neon rocket as its roadside sign, which made it easy for Fuller to find it. Amused by the sign, he was further amused when shown into his room, where the floor lamp was shaped like a rocket with its nose cone balancing a globular satellite, the walls were decorated with celestial crescents, spheres and orbital paths, and even the towels were embroidered with the legend, 'Starlite Motel.'

'Oh, boy,' Fuller said as he tipped the crew cut kid who showed him to his room, 'it's a whole different ball game here.'

'It sure is,' the kid said.

Fuller had a shower, shaved, changed his clothes and then went to meet Wilson in the Starlite Motel's bar. He was not surprised when it turned out to be a dimly lit, L-shaped room with murals showing the moon as seen through a telescope and Earth as it might be seen from the

234

moon. Nor was he surprised to find that Wilson was already there, drinking what looked like lemonade. He had always been punctual.

Fuller ordered a whisky-and-water from the barman, waited until he had it, then joined Wilson at his table. He was startled to see how young Wilson looked. He seemed to get younger every time Fuller met him, though in this dim lighting it was difficult to ascertain whether or not he'd had more plastic surgery.

He was studying the drinks menu, but when Fuller joined him, he looked up and smiled coldly.

'The town of Cocoa Beach,' he informed Fuller, 'has clearly become obsessed with space. What's that you're drinking?'

'Plain scotch with water.'

'I note that the drinks include a Countdown – ten parts vodka to one part vermouth – and a Marstini. This place is like a movie set, but it's all about space.'

'Yeah,' Fuller agreed, 'I know what you mean. They have a women's bridge club called Missile Misses, a Miss Satellite contest, a fishing boat called Miss L. Ranger, a settlement called Satellite Beach, and even a museum, the Spacarium, that has burned-out components of Cape Canaveral rockets on display. Also, not ignoring the launch of Explorer 1, the Chamber of Commerce is already accepting reservations for space aboard what it's describing as the first globe-circling satellite. That's American know-how!'

'It's always nice to meet a patriot.'

'I'm not ashamed of it,' Fuller said. 'The fact that I have to deal with you doesn't change that one jot. What name are you travelling under this time?'

'Aldridge,' Wilson said. He put the menu down, sipped some lemonade, then added: 'This is certainly an encouraging place for a patriot.'

'Sure is,' Fuller agreed. He had spent the previous night in Patrick Air Force Base, two miles from Cape Canaveral, and was still thrilled by the concept of dozens of Atlas, Thor,

Titan and Snark missiles, as well as the orbiting satellite, being launched from that restricted military zone of about fifteen thousand acres, much of it in uncleared jungle where deer and puma still roamed wild. Now, the formerly untouched land of sand dunes, palmettos, orange groves and swamps had a rapidly swelling population, scores of new businesses, and many new housing developments, containing the fourteen thousand people now employed at Cape Canaveral and Patrick Air Force base.

'Cocoa Beach,' Wilson said, 'was once a small village of a few dozen families. It's now in the process of becoming the US government's largest and most important rocket-launching site.'

'This bothers you?'

'Yes.' Wilson glanced at the cosmic murals on the dimly lit walls, then shook his head from side to side, as if baffled by the childishness of it all. 'Of course,' he said, 'for me there's a certain irony in the fact that most of the rockets being fired from here could not have been constructed without the assistance of Wernher von Braun and his other Nazi scientists, who in turn based their work on the theories of Robert H. Goddard and myself – both neglected Americans.'

'Ah, gee, the man's bitter!' Fuller exclaimed. 'My heart's breaking for him.'

'I could break your mind and body,' Wilson rejoindered, 'and don't ever forget it.'

The icy distance in his voice made the threat even more chilling, but Fuller was not a man to be easily frightened, so he just grinned and sipped his drink. 'So,' he said, placing his glass back on the table, 'why are you here?'

'I thought I'd check on the progress being made here and, if necessary, slow it down.'

'I don't know why you're concerned. As you just said yourself, what we're achieving here couldn't have been done without your assistance.'

'I dole that out carefully. You know why I do so. If NASA

moves ahead more quickly than I deem fitting, I'll take firm measures to slow them down. I won't let you trick me.'

Fuller couldn't hide his pleasure. 'Boys will be boys and scientists will be scientists. You know that if you give us assistance, we're bound to try and exploit it. You've known that all along.'

'Never imagine that you're ahead of me,' Wilson warned him. 'If you do, I'll be forced to prove you wrong – and that could be expensive.'

'I know damned well how ruthless you can be,' Fuller said, keeping his gaze on Wilson's face, though relieved that his remorseless, icy eyes could not be seen too clearly in the gloom. 'You don't have to remind me.'

'I *would* remind you that your own organisation, the CIA, with or without the full knowledge of the government, can also be fairly ruthless – as shown by the murder of various American citizens, such as Mike Bradley and his wife, who know too much about me, my base in the Antarctic, and the US-Canadian saucer projects. Those murders are not committed for my benefit. Nor do I commit them. How ironic that Mr Bradley was frightened of *me* . . . when it was you who murdered him.'

'A casualty of war,' Fuller replied, being proud to have done his duty, 'and not one to give you cause for concern. You didn't come here to talk about that, Wilson – sorry, *Aldridge* – so what do you want?'

'A week ago the United States exploded a thermonuclear bomb over a lagoon at Bikini Atoll, thus dangerously contaminating seven thousand square miles of land and sea, injuring people nearly a hundred miles away from the area, and, even worse, making the world fall-out conscious for the first time. That test explosion, combined with the unseemly haste with which you're expanding Cocoa Beach and Cape Canaveral, makes me suspect that certain people in the Pentagon or the White House are no longer taking my threats seriously. If you don't slow down your rate of scientific progress, particularly regarding the Apollo space programme, I may have to give you another demonstration of my own, still much greater, capabilities.'

'We must be catching up with you,' Fuller replied calmly. 'Otherwise you wouldn't be so damned worried.'

'I don't worry, Fuller. I simply apply reason. And when that tells me you need some kind of warning, I'll make sure you get one.'

'Okay, I've been warned. I'll take your message back to those in charge and I'm sure they'll take heed. Anything else?'

'Not really. I take it that UFO witnesses are still being harassed, ridiculed and thwarted at every turn.'

'Correct.'

'What's the state of Project Blue Book?'

'Not good, you'll be pleased to hear. The project leader, Captain Edward J. Ruppelt, was transferred to Denver and has since left the Air Force in disgust. However, he's now working for the Northrop Corporation and is rumoured to be planning a book that will substantiate the reality of the UFOs, though siding with the extraterrestrial hypothesis.'

'I'm not keen on the idea of a UFO book written by someone with that kind of credibility. Keep your eye on him.'

'I will.'

'And the others?'

'All of the staff, except for the original two officers, have been scattered far and wide, which others obviously view as a form of official punishment, or warning. As for the two remaining officers – Captains Dwight Randall and Robert Jackson – we're keeping the pressure on them all the time and consistently denying them promotion. In fact, by deliberately putting Ruppelt in charge of the former Project Blue Book, instead of Randall, who rightfully should have had the job, we were clearly slighting Randall. By putting him back in charge of the project only when it's been decimated and rendered virtually inoperative, the slight seems even more brutal. To Randall, as well as to those who know of his involvement with Project Blue Book, it must seem that UFO work is the kiss of death. I believe this is already having bad psychological repercussions on Randall. With him as an example, not too many others will be keen to investigate UFOs.'

'He still might need something, another little push, to tip him over the edge. I'll keep him in mind.'

'Yeah, you do that. Anything else?'

'No. Not for now.' Wilson stood up to leave. After studying the cosmic murals on the walls of the bar, he said: 'America is a nation of children – a gigantic nursery. There's nothing worth having here.'

'Rather here than the Antarctic,' Fuller responded. 'What kind of life can you have there?'

'A life of work,' Wilson said. 'And work is the true function of man – the use of the mind. All else is a waste of time.'

'You're not a real human being, Wilson.'

'Nor do I want to be. Now take heed of my warning, Mr Fuller. Tell your superiors not to try upstaging me.'

'I'll pass the message on,' Fuller said.

When Wilson left the bar, Fuller ordered another drink. He took his time drinking it, distractedly studying the crescents, spheres and orbital paths on the walls, thinking of the great dream of space and Wilson's part in it. Fuller was no romantic – he had the instincts of a killer – but even he possessed certain human needs that could not be denied. Wilson was something else: a kind of mutant, without emotion, a creature driven by the dictates of the mind, unhampered by feelings. Even Hitler had been driven by resentment and hatred – recognizable human traits – but Wilson existed outside such emotions, which made him inhuman. Fuller, who was frightened by very little, was frightened by that thought.

He finished his drink, left the bar, and went to look for a whorehouse.

Even whores had feelings.

Chapter Twenty-Two

When Dwight entered the lobby of the airport at Albuquerque, New Mexico, after a commercial flight from Dayton, Ohio, he had been drinking again and was feeling a little drunk, but he knew that it would soon pass away, letting his depression and fear return. He didn't relish that much.

His old friend, Captain Andrew Boyle, was waiting for him in an Air Force uniform too tight for his expanding beer belly, but he seemed as energetic as ever, with a broad grin creasing his good-natured, sun-reddened face. Slapping his hand on Dwight's shoulder, he said, 'Hi, there, partner! Long time, no see. You look like you've lost a bit of weight and could do with some sunshine, but otherwise you're recognizably yourself. Hell, man, it's really good to see you. It's been too long, Dwight.'

'Yeah,' Dwight said. 'Too long.'

They embraced, shook hands, then walked to the car park, Dwight carrying his overnight bag in one hand, Andy dangling his car keys. 'Christ,' he said. 'How long's it been now? Eight, nine years?'

'Nine years, more or less, though it doesn't seem that long. Time moves like the wind these days. We're getting old too fast, Andy.'

'Yeah, and no better for it. Christ, those were the days, man! I still get a lump in my throat when I think of the old B-29s. We did a lot of crazy things in those days. You had to be young to do it.'

Dwight and Andy had flown B-29s over the Pacific during World War II, being shot at by the Japs and having more than one hair-raising escape. That had all ended in 1945, when both were demobilized, and apart from a brief reunion when, a few years later, they served briefly with an Air Force Reserve Troop Carrier Wing, they had only managed to keep in touch through the mail and by phone, united by the kind of emotional bonds that could only be forged in war. They would both go to their graves, Dwight suspected, secretly relishing those dangerous years as the best of their lives. It was a terrible truth.

'Anyway,' Andy said, as they climbed into his well used 1947 Frazer Manhattan in the car park, 'this work you're doing must be almost as exciting – I mean, searching for UFOs.'

'It's not quite the same,' Dwight confessed. 'It's more like a bad dream. Quite frankly, it's pushing me to the limit and I'm thinking of getting out.'

'Out of the Air Force?'

'Right.'

'You were born for the Air Force,' Andy told him, turning on the ignition. 'You're a natural lifer.'

'I used to think so. Not now.'

'I don't believe this,' Andy said. Leaving the airport, he took the road away from Albuquerque, heading into the morning's brightening sunlight, past fenced-in hangars and a lot of warehouses and factories.

As a radar operative at Cannon AFB, Andy had regularly fed Dwight with information on UFO sightings. However, last night he had phoned with more urgency than usual to tell him that the previous evening he had personally witnessed the landing of a flying saucer in the restricted area of the base. That's why Dwight was here.

'I can't believe this business is driving you out of the Air Force,' Andy said, driving with the windows rolled down, letting cooling air rush in around them. 'You thrived on the dangers of the war, so what's happening now?'

'It's not the same as the war,' Dwight said. 'Not the same kind of danger. During the war, we were treated as heroes, doing what our country wanted, but chasing UFOs brings you nothing but flak.'

'Oh? What kind?'

'Antagonistic interrogations. Lack of promotion. Postings to places like Alaska. Accusations of incompetence where clearly there was none. Midnight phone calls from irate superior officers. General harassment of every imaginable kind. Now there's talk of men in black paying visits to UFO witnesses, warning them off. UFO witnesses are also starting to disappear. Dammit, Andy, this isn't something you see. It's not a dog-fight in clear sky.'

'How's Beth taking it?'

'Not much better than me. I'm drinking too much – I know it, but I can't stop it – and Beth's frightened about the men in black, as well as about my drinking and my growing desire to get the hell out of it. It's been eighteen months since Captain Ruppelt's departure from Project Blue Book and, subsequently, the Air Force. Since then, the organisation's been reduced to a mere three members – me, Captain Bob Jackson, and a secretary. To make matters worse, our investigating authority has been passed over to the inexperienced 4602nd Air Intelligence Service Squadron; and most of our projects have been strangled systematically through a deliberate reduction in funds.'

'Jesus Christ,' Andy muttered as the engineering and canning factories on the outskirts of Albuquerque gave way to sun-baked farmlands.

'Obviously,' Dwight confessed, 'I've been badly shaken and disillusioned by what's happened. I'm also unable to comprehend why the Air Force is supposedly concerned with UFOs, yet at the same time is ruthlessly discouraging a proper investigation of the phenomenon. Personally, *I've* been harassed constantly by my superior officers and passed over many times for promotion. Now, I want to get the hell out – but ironically, given that she was the one who first suggested leaving the force, Beth now says it's the drink talking and that there's nothing I could do as a civilian. She thinks I'm threatening our livelihood. She just wants me to transfer out of Blue Book, but I want to get out of the Air Force completely and she simply won't wear that. Frankly, Andy, I don't know *what* to do. I'm just running scared, I guess.'

'I don't blame you, old buddy, but are you sure you're not imagining a lot of this?'

'No, I'm not imagining it. Too many bad things have happened to those involved in UFO research. Also, I'm not imagining the harassment. Christ, Andy, even during that UFO invasion of Washington DC, I was hamstrung and practically ordered back to Dayton. As a matter of fact, I flew here on a commercial flight – at my own expense, Andy – because when I tried to charter an Air Force plane I was refused permission.'

'On what grounds?'

'They said the base was temporarily sealed off because a security exercise was taking place. A *routine* security exercise, they said.'

'This was yesterday?'

'Yes.'

'Then it was bullshit,' Andy said. 'There was no security exercise taking place at Cannon yesterday – and the base wasn't sealed off. Did you tell them why you wanted to come here?'

'No. I just announced myself as head of Project Blue Book. That was enough.'

'But you've visited the base before.'

'That's right. So the only reason they could have had for their lies was the landing you saw. Tell me about it.'

Andy glanced in his rear-view mirror, a reflex action denoting confusion, then he concentrated again on the road ahead.

'Weird,' he said. 'Kinda spooky. Problem is, I'd been drinking, a real bellyful of beer, and that made me keep my mouth shut about it – to everybody but you. It was about two in the morning. I was just returning to the base . . . What the hell! We'll soon be there, Dwight. Let's wait till we get there.'

They arrived at the sprawling Cannon Air Force Base a few minutes later. Driving past the guardhouse and barrier at the entrance, Andy kept going along the fenced-in perimeter lining the road until he came to a place near the outer limits of the base, well away from the airstrip. He slowed down and stopped. Dwight could see the corrugated iron roof of a large hangar beyond the high fence. Andy pointed at it.

'Right there,' he said. 'About two in the morning. I was driving right past there, coming in the other direction – pretty loaded, unfortunately – when I saw that the lights on that hangar were still on. As I was passing, I thought how unusual it was for it to be lit up at that time in the morning. I also noticed that there was a series of arc-lights forming a circle in the cleared area directly in front of it. Then, inexplicably, the engine of my car cut out and I rolled to a halt. Cursing, not too sure of what was happening, thinking that the drink had made me do something stupid, I tried to start the car again, but it just wouldn't spark. Then I heard a kind of noise, a high-pitched whining sound coming from the other side of the fence, and I looked up and saw that . . . that *thing* coming down.'

He shook his head from side to side, as if still not believing it, and looked at the hangar beyond the fence, reliving the night before.

'A domed, disc-shaped aircraft. It was landing about fifty yards inside the fence, in that area illuminated by the circle of arc lights, directly facing the open doors of the hangar. The aircraft, or flying saucer, had no lights – that's why the landing area was illuminated. The circular part around the dome of the aircraft was shaped like two plates, one placed upside-down on the other, and the raised dome in the middle was just like a pilot's nose cabin, made of what seemed like Perspex, with a single pilot in it. The circular plates were revolving around the dome, which seemed to be gyroscopically balanced and, though fixed, was swaying up and down a little as the saucer descended. The closer it got to the ground, the slower the plates rotated and the quieter it became, until the high-pitched whining had become a low whirring sound. The saucer had ball-like landing gear, which I saw being lowered in preparation for touch-down. It was practically hovering in the air, just above the level of the perimeter fence. Then it disappeared below the top of the fence and the sound of it cut out completely. When it did, my car's engine started up again.'

Dwight was hearing all this clearly, but finding it hard to take in. He knew that Andy wasn't lying to him, but it still seemed incredible.

'Any insignia on the saucer?'

'None,' Andy replied.

'And the hangar doors were open?'

'Yes. That hangar, I know, is used for secret aeronautical research projects, so I'm convinced that the saucer was being kept there. Certainly, it didn't take off again. I drove my car off the road, cut its lights and ignition, and sat there for a good couple of hours, sobering up and hoping to see the flying saucer ascending.' Andy shook his head from side to side, as if still finding it hard to accept what he had witnessed. 'But it didn't. At one point I thought I could hear muffled screeching sounds – like clamps or wheels needing oil – then, after a while, I heard the hangar doors closing. The arc-lights above and in front of them were turned off. After that, there was silence.'

'That's a restricted area of the base?'

'Sure is.'

'So what do you think?'

'What do I think?' Andy unconsciously echoed Dwight's words as he glanced up and down the sunlit road that ran past the base. 'I'll tell you. You believe in the extraterrestrial hypothesis, right? Well, let me remind you that most of the best saucer sightings have been over top-secret military installations – in other words, mostly right here in New Mexico. So on the assumption that the saucers aren't piloted by extraterrestrials spying on our military secrets, what else can they be?'

'Soviet secret weapons.'

'Man-made?'

'Right.'

'But not necessarily Soviet. It's highly unlikely that the Soviets could have managed to fly their spy planes over our top- secret military installations without being brought down by us. On the assumption, then, that the saucers are neither Soviet nor extraterrestrial, but are seen over our own top-secret establishments – and, as in this case, have even been seen to land – there's a growing belief among some of us that they're radical new US aircraft prototypes, developed by the Air Force or Navy.'

'I can't really accept this,' Dwight said.

'No? Then let's see if we can get you into the base.'

Andy turned the car around and drove back to the main gate, stopping at the barrier. When he told the armed corporal in the gatehouse who Dwight was, the kid rang through for clearance, then put the phone down and shook his head, looking embarrassed. 'Sorry, sir,' he said, 'but I can't let you bring your guest in.'

'Guest? He's not a guest! He's a decorated US Air Force captain in charge of Project Blue Book. Now let us in, damn it!'

'Sorry,' the corporal said, straightening up, 'but I can't do that, sir.'

'Why not?'

'Because I have my instructions.'

'What reasons were given?'

'No reasons were given, sir. I was just informed by my superior officer that Captain Randall wasn't to be allowed in.'

'And who's your superior officer?'

'Major Shapiro, the base intelligence officer.'

'Anyone else being denied permission to the base today, Corporal?'

'I can't answer that, Captain.'

'Okay, Corporal, thank you.' Andy reversed away from the barrier, then took off in the direction they had come from, back to Albuquerque. 'That's it,' he said. 'Do you get the picture now? The flying saucer I saw last night was certainly no Russian spy plane, since its landing had clearly been prepared for and it certainly spent at least last night in that off-limits hangar. Therefore, it was either an alien spacecraft landing with the full permission of the Air Force or a top-secret Air Force – or even Navy – aircraft. I'd opt for it being one of our own.'

'Oh, my God!' Dwight exclaimed softly, suddenly seeing the implications. 'That would certainly explain why certain members of intelligence don't want us to find out too much.'

'Right. The extraterrestrial hypothesis is a smoke-screen. They're defending their own damned secrets. Those saucers are man-made.' He glanced at Dwight and grinned. 'I've got a bit more for you, but I'll let you have it over a drink. I think you'll need it, old buddy.'

They spent the rest of the drive in silence, which allowed Dwight to think. He was having trouble putting his thoughts in order, but he finally managed to do so. Now he saw, very clearly, the reason behind all the harassment, the smoke-screen of disinformation, the veiled threats from superior officers, the virtual destruction of Project Blue Book: the Air Force was protecting its own while pretending to be concerned with alien spacecraft.

Nevertheless, some nagging doubts remained, mostly to do with the extraordinary capabilities of the saucers reported. Dwight simply couldn't imagine that the Air Force had made such technological advances, not even in secret. Even for him, that was too much to deal with at this present time. It scared him to think of it.

In a roadside bar just outside Albuquerque, they settled into a dimly lit booth, both drinking large bourbons. When they were feeling more relaxed, Andy withdrew an Air Force folder from his briefcase, opened it and squinted down through the gloom at the pages.

'These classified Air Force intelligence documents were leaked to me by a friend. I can't give you his name, but I can verify the authenticity of the documents.' Grinning, he raised his finger like a schoolteacher. 'Okay. Let's try presenting a case for the possibility of man-made flying saucers.' He dropped his raised finger onto the pages opened before him. 'Though it's not widely known, American intelligence has been interested in the possibility of man-made flying saucers for a long time. First indication of this is an old intelligence report – I have it right here in my file – pointing out that a patent for a so-called flying saucer with a circular fixed wing was taken out by an unnamed American citizen as early as March 22, 1932.'

'Unnamed,' Dwight emphasised, sighing with disappointment.

Andy smiled brightly, triumphantly. 'That unnamed citizen was probably Jonathan E. Caldwell. This would explain why, on August 19, 1949, at the height of the immediate post-war UFO flap, the Air Force Command of Baltimore called a press conference to announce that two different types of prototypes which might solve the mystery of the flying saucers had been found in an abandoned farm near Glen Burnie, Maryland. According to the Air Force spokesman, both machines has been designed and constructed before the war by one Jonathan E. Caldwell, with the aid of a local mechanic, and one of the machines had actually been flown.'

'I have that on file as well,' Dwight said.

Andy ignored his disappointment. 'The machines had been abandoned for years and were falling apart, but as they were a combination of airplane and helicopter, with round wings and contrarotating propellers, it was the belief of Air Force intelligence that in flight they'd have resembled flying saucers. So they could have been the prototype of the more advanced UFOs seen in the skies over the past few years.'

'Sorry,' Dwight said. 'That notion was squashed less than twenty-four hours later when, at another urgent press conference, a different Air Force spokesman announced that the Caldwell machines had absolutely no connection with the reported phenomena of flying saucers.'

'Correct,' Andy replied. 'But what the Air Force spokesman *didn't* state is that Caldwell's plane was a craft with a circular wing of the parasol type, or one raised above the fuselage like an umbrella. It was constructed in 1932 and tested the following year by Professor J. Owen Evans in a wind-tunnel in Los Angeles, then flown by the well-known pilot, Jimmy Doolittle, displaying a top speed of ninety-seven mph and a landing speed of twenty-three mph. In 1936, Caldwell produced a modified version of the prototype, but it crashed, killing the pilot, thus putting Caldwell out of business for good.'

'All very interesting,' Dwight said, 'but you're talking about a fairly crude aircraft.'

'All early prototypes were pretty crude,' Andy retorted. 'Nevertheless, it's pretty clear from what I've picked up that US military intelligence continued to be anxious about the possibility of man-made flying saucers, particularly right after the war. They were, as you know, even more concerned because most of the saucer sightings in the US tended to cluster around key development stations such as atomic plants, guided missile areas, and your very own Wright-Patterson Air Force Base.'

Dwight laughed. 'No arguments there.'

Andy turned another page. 'It's clear from remarks sprinkled liberally throughout these documents of the period that US intelligence findings seemed to *exclude* extraterrestrial origin of the saucers. This in turn made them increasingly concerned with the possibility that the saucers were man-made.' He looked up, nodding emphatically. 'More intriguingly, although on the one hand they were concerned with Soviet advances in this field, they soon began suspecting that the saucers might be of US or Canadian origin.'

'You think that's possible?'

'Yes. As the Navy, Army and Air Force are always, and were then, in constant competition with one another, each would have been reluctant to inform the other of any secret projects in the pipeline. So even at the White Sands Proving Ground, used extensively by the Navy for their aeronautical and missile experiments, there are research projects so secret that even the CIA can't learn about them – and given Navy interest in vertical-ascending aircraft, these could have included saucer-shaped prototypes.'

Dwight finished off his bourbon and called for two more. 'I can tell you've got something else prepared. So go on. Lay it on me.'

Andy waited until the waiter had brought their drinks and departed.

'As far as I can tell, the first rumblings about Canadian flying saucer projects were made in a classified CIA memorandum dated August 18 last year – a year after the Spitzbergen flying saucer crash report. The CIA memorandum states: "According to recent reports from Toronto, a number of Canadian Air Force engineers are engaged in the construction of a 'flying saucer' to be used as a future weapon of war. The work of these engineers is being carried out in great secrecy at the A. V. Roe Company factories." He looked up from his notes. 'This report was correct – as were the widespread suspicions that the US Navy was conducting experiments on saucer-shaped, vertical-rising aircraft in secret hangars in the White Sands Proving Ground.'

Dwight gave a low whistle. 'That could make sense,' he said. 'One belief widespread in intelligence circles is that the formation of the lights in the famous Lubbock sightings, and others, aren't indicative of small glowing saucers, but of the many exhaust jets along the edge of a massive, boomerang-shaped aircraft, or advanced flying wing, which would, when viewed from certain angles, strongly resemble a flying saucer, or saucers.'

'Good,' Andy said, then went back to his leaked documents. 'Evidence for United States involvement with disc-shaped aircraft projects surfaced with information about the US Navy's Flying Flapjack, or Flying Pancake. Designed by Charles H. Zimmerman of the National Advisory Committee for Aeronautics and constructed in 1942 by the Chance-Vought Corporation, the Flying Flapjack, or V-173, was an experimental, vertical-rising, disc-shaped aircraft, a combination of helicopter and jet plane, powered by two eighty hp engines and driven by twin propellers, with two fins, or stabilizers, on either side of its semi-circular or pancake-shaped, configuration. Reportedly it had a maximum speed of four hundred to five hundred miles per hour, could rise almost vertically, and could practically hover at thirty-five miles an hour. A later, more advanced model, the XF-5-U-1, utilised two Pratt and Whitney R- 2000-7 engines of sixteen hundred hp each and was reported to be about one hundred and five feet in diameter and have jet nozzles – which strongly resembled the glowing windows seen on so many UFOs – arranged around its outer rim, just below the centre of gravity. It was built in three layers, the central layer being slightly larger than the other two. Since the saucer's velocity and manoeuvring abilities were controlled by the power and tilt of the variable-direction jet nozzles, there were no ailerons, rudders or other protruding surfaces. The material used was a metal alloy that had a dull, whitish colour.'

'In short,' Dwight said, 'a machine remarkably similar in appearance to those reported by so many UFO witnesses.'

'Exactly,' Andy said. 'Now do you remember the April 1950 edition of the *US News and World Report*?'

'Christ, now that I think of it, I do,' Dwight replied, beginning to get excited. 'Information about the Flying Flapjack was released to the public in that edition of the magazine!'

'Correct again, Dwight – and it touched off some interesting speculations. The first of these arose from the retrospective knowledge that the Navy had always expressed more interest in a vertical-rising airplane than the Air Force and had, up to 1950, spent *twice* as much money as the Air Force on secret guided missile research. Also, their top-secret missile-research bases were located in the White Sands Proving Ground – where the majority of military UFO sightings had occurred – and because they weren't involved officially in UFO investigations, they could conduct their own research in a secrecy unruffled by the attentions of the media or the public.'

'Right,' Dwight said, now genuinely excited. 'And according to the Project Grudge report for 1947, the UFOs viewed over Muroc AFB on July 7 and 8 of that year were oscillating objects that flew at remarkably low speed and had tactics unlike an ordinary airplane. Some witnesses, all trained Air Force personnel, observed two discs at an altitude of about eight thoudand feet, both manoeuvring in tight circles with varying speeds and oscillating. Also, just like the XF-5-U-1, both discs had two fins on the upper surface.'

'Go on,' Andy said, grinning at what he had started.

'Another interesting point is that the measurements taken by Navy commander R. B. McLaughlin and his team of Navy scientists of the UFO they'd tracked over the White Sands Proving Ground in 1949, two years after the Muroc sightings, corresponded closely, except for the speed, with the details of the original XF-5-U-1. It's also worth noting that initial reports of the extraordinarily high speeds recorded by McLaughlin turned out to be inaccurate and that later analysis of the data brought the speed much closer to that of an advanced jet-plane . . . or the original expectations for the Flapjack.'

Nodding affirmatively, Andy, now as excited as Dwight, said: 'And the *US News and World Report* also pointed out that the Air Force had called off official inquiry into the UFO phenomenon the previous December, even in the face of overwhelming evidence that the saucers are real. This was seen by many as a clear indication that top Air Force officials now *knew* what the saucers are and where they come from. Therefore, while still denying that the Air Force are involved, they were no longer concerned about the saucers. The article concludes: "Surface indications, then, point to research centres of the US Navy's vast guided-missile project as the scene of present flying-saucer development." '

'In other words, the White Sands Proving Ground and other secret locations right here in New Mexico.'

'Ding, dong!' Andy exclaimed.

'So what happened to the Flying Flapjack?'

Andy glanced at his leaked documents. 'The production prototype of the Flapjack was due for a test-flight at Muroc AFB in 1947 – when the first flying-saucer sightings over that same base and at Rogers Dry Lake, adjacent to Muroc, were recorded. Whether such test flights were actually carried out has never been confirmed or denied by the US Navy. The only official statements given were to the effect that work on the Flying Flapjack ceased the following year – but US involvement with saucer-shaped aircraft didn't end with that prototype.'

Andy had a sip of bourbon and lit a cigarette. After blowing a couple of smoke rings and watching them disappearing, he said: 'At this point, it's worth reminding you of certain facts taken from your own Project Blue Book reports.'

'Always reliable!' Dwight quipped.

'Of course,' Andy responded, then turned serious again as he lowered his eyes to his notes. 'In the reports that started the modern UFO scare – the Harold Dahl and

Kenneth Arnold sightings of June 1947 – both men observed the UFOs in the vicinity of Mount Rainier, the Cascades, in the state of Washington – which separates Oregon and Canada – and both stated independently that the UFOs flew away in the direction of the Canadian border.'

'That's right – towards Canada.'

Andy nodded. 'Shortly after, during the first week in July, there were numerous reports of unidentified, luminous bodies in the skies over the Province of Quebec, Oregon and New England. The next major UFO flap was the so-called invasion of Washington DC in 1952; and while the official flap started on July 19, there was a record, dated June 17, of several hundred unidentified red spheres that flew at supersonic speeds over the Canadian Air Base of North Bay in Ontario, on across the border and then crossed over some of the USA's southeastern states. Finally, nearly all of the subsequent Washington DC UFOs were reported as flying away in a northerly direction; and when they returned, en masse, on July 26, their disappearance in a general northerly direction – towards the Canadian border – also applied.' He looked up from his notes. 'Given this,' he said, 'it's a matter of particular interest that on February 11 last year the Toronto *Star* reported that a new flying saucer was being developed at the AVRO-Canada plant in Malton, Ontario.'

Dwight gave another low whistle, then said, 'Christ, how did I miss that?'

'Because your research team were only looking for UFO reports – not reports about official, saucer-shaped, experimental aircraft.' Andy puffed another cloud of smoke and looked back at his Air Force folder. 'Of course,' he continued, 'the US and Canadian governments both denied involvement in any such projects, but on February 16, after freelance photographer Jack Judges had taken an aerial photograph of a flying saucer resting outdoors in the Avro-Canada plant in Malton, the Minister for Defence Production, C. D. Howe, admitted to the Canadian House of Commons that AVRO-Canada was working on a mock-up model of a flying saucer, capable of ascending vertically and flying at fifteen hundred miles per hour. By February 27, Crawford Gordon Jr., the president of AVRO-Canada, was writing in the company's house journal, *Avro News*, that the prototype being built was so revolutionary it would make all other forms of supersonic aircraft obsolete. That aircraft was called the "Avrocar".'

'Shit,' Dwight muttered. 'Now I remember it!'

'I bet you do.' Andy was amused, but soon went back to his leaked documents. 'Soon the Toronto *Star* was claiming that Britain's Field Marshal Montgomery had become one of the few people to view Avro's mock-up of the flying saucer. A few days later, Air Vice Marshal D. M. Smith was reported to have said that what Field Marshal Montgomery had seen were the preliminary construction plans for a gyroscopic fighter whose gas turbine would revolve around the pilot, positioned at the centre of the disc. Confirmation that the craft actually existed came via last year's April issue of the *Royal Air Force Flying Review* which contained a two-page report on the Avrocar – also dubbed the "Omega" – including some speculative sectional diagrams. According to this report, the building of a prototype hadn't yet commenced, but a wooden mock-up had been constructed behind a closely guarded experimental hangar in the company's Malton plant, near Ontario. The aircraft described had a near-circular shape, measuring approximately forty feet across, and was being designed to attain speeds of the order of fifteen hundred mph – more than twice that of the latest swept-wing fighters. It would be capable of effecting one hundred and eighty-degree turns in flight without changing altitude.'

'Just like a real flying saucer,' Dwight said bitterly.

'Exactly,' Andy said. 'And last November, Canadian newspapers were reporting that a mock-up of the Avrocar, or Omega, had been shown on October 31 to a group of twenty-five American military officers and scientists. To date, nothing else has been reported by the press, but according to these leaked intelligence documents, the US Air Force, concerned at Soviet progress in aeronautics, has allocated an unspecified sum of money to the Canadian government for the building of a prototype of their flying saucer. The machine's been designed by the English aeronautical engineer, John Frost, who once worked for AVRO-Canada in Malton, Ontario, and it'll be capable of either hovering virtually motionless in mid-air or flying at a speed of nearly two thousand miles per hour.'

Dwight gave another low whistle.

'Last but not least,' Andy said, 'according to these documents, the government's hoping to form entire squadrons of AVRO-Canada's flying saucers for the defence of Alaska and the far regions of the North – because they require no runways, are capable of rising vertically, and are ideal for subarctic and polar regions.'

Realising that he had been conned all along by his superiors, who wished to protect their own flying saucer projects, Dwight filled up with rage. With that came the urge for revenge against those who had wronged him. 'All we need is some solid proof,' he said.

'I've got that as well,' Andy responded, grinning like a kid and withdrawing a brown envelope from his Air Force folder. 'When that thing landed last night, I took a photo of it. Naturally, I'm going to keep the negative, but the photo's for you. With my compliments, Dwight.'

Dwight took the photograph and examined it. His heart started racing when he saw the slightly unfocused, but clear enough photograph of a flying saucer hovering just above the fence of Cannon AFB, gleaming in the light from the arc lamps forming a circle around it. His hand started shaking as he took in what he was seeing, but eventually, with his heart still racing too quickly, he slipped the photo back into the brown envelope and put it into his briefcase.

'Thanks a million, Andy,' he said. 'I don't know how to thank—'

'My pleasure,' Andy interjected. 'Now I've got to get home. Back to Cannon AFB, where you're no longer welcome. I'll keep my eyes and ears open.'

'Please do that,' Dwight said.

They left the bar together, embraced and shook hands on the sidewalk, then walked off in opposite directions, Andy clambering into his car while Dwight was carried away in a cab.

He checked into a motel near the airport, went straight to his room with a half-pint of bourbon, drank some of it while endlessly studying that photo of the man-made flying saucer, then lay down and fell into a dream-filled sleep.

Dwight was dreaming of flying saucers that glowed magically in the night and, though serenely beautiful, filled him with fear. That fear deepened as a dazzling silvery-white light filled his vision, gradually surrounded him and then, in an inexplicable manner, pressed in upon him.

The light seemed almost physical.

At first he thought the light was part of his dream, filling up an alien sky, but then he opened his eyes and realised it was real enough: a brilliant, flickering light that was beaming in through the window of the motel room to dazzle him and, in its oddly physical way, tighten his skull and fill it with pain.

Even as he was rubbing the sleep from his eyes, trying to adjust to the unusual, brilliant light and the increasing pain in his head, he heard a bass humming sound, almost an infrasound, and felt the bed vibrating beneath him.

Fully aware that this wasn't normal, and very frightened by it, he was trying to gather his senses together when the room door burst open and two men, both dressed in black coveralls, entered and rapidly approached the bed.

Dwight attempted to sit upright, but before he could do so, one of the men pressed something hard and metallic against the side of his neck. He felt an electric charge course through him, like being struck with a hammer, than he went numb from neck to toe.

Terrified, unable to move a muscle, he could only look on as one of the men picked the manila envelope off the bedside cabinet, tugged the UFO photo out, checked it, then nodded at the other man. The latter leaned over the bed to stare at Dwight with cold, almost inhuman eyes. 'Stop pursuing us,' he said. 'It will only bring you grief. Not only for you, but for your family. You've been warned. *Auf Wiedersehen.*'

The two men left the room, closing the door behind them, leaving Dwight propped up on the bed, still completely paralysed and terrified.

That strange light still filled the room, pulsating, flickering, and at times he thought it might be a line of lights forming the whole. Accompanying the lights was the infrasound – something felt, rather than heard: an almost physical bass humming – and Dwight felt it pressing around him, relentlessly tightening his skull, almost making him black out with pain.

He remained conscious, however, tormented by what was happening. The sweat poured down his face, the visible results of his racing heart, and he felt the panic welling up inside him as he frantically tried to move.

Now his terror was absolute, engendered by the paralysis, and he had visions of the horror of Beth and Nichola when they found him like this. The panic ballooned into mindlessness, stripping his senses bare. He was just about to tip into madness when the pressure of the infrasound decreased and feeling returned to him.

First a tingling in his toes, then warmth in his fingers. He bent an elbow, then a knee, as the brilliant, flickering light outside the window appeared to rise slightly, deliberately, swaying slightly from side to side.

The pressure of the infrasound decreased and finally went away altogether.

Dwight bent and stretched his legs. He flexed his fingers and raised his arms. The dazzling light outside ascended to the top of the window-frame, hovered there for a moment, flared up briefly and then suddenly blinked out.

Dwight knew then that it was actually a line of smaller lights blinking out one after the other, but at very great speed, giving the appearance of one great light popping out.

Darkness rushed back into the room and the sky reappeared outside.

Dwight took a deep breath. He was trembling like a leaf. Sweating profusely, with his heart still racing dangerously, he glanced at the bedside cabinet to confirm that the men in black had actually been here.

The UFO photo was gone.

The men in black had been real, too.

Still in a state of shock, Dwight slid out of bed, hurried across to the window, opened it and looked up at the sky.

There were lots of stars up there. Look too long and they seemed to move. Dwight looked a long time and thought he saw one moving – that big one, almost directly above – but he couldn't be sure. He kept scanning the sky, looking for something unusual, but saw only the glittering lights of that sea of stars in the infinite darkness.

Shivering, though still sweating, trying to still his racing heart, he walked back to the bed, picked up the bottle of bourbon and drank too much of it too quickly.

Now, with his nerve cracking, fearful for Beth and Nichola as well as for himself, he was determined to leave the Air Force for good and put all this behind him.

It was best to be silent.

PART TWO

Chapter Twenty-Three

'I think you all know why we're here,' President Eisenhower said. 'Yesterday, at Cape Canaveral, Florida, Project Vanguard's first rocket, which the American people had been led to expect would put up the first earth satellite in history, blew up on its launching pad. I want to know why.'

Richard Horner, assistant secretary of the Air Force for research and development, coughed nervously into his fist, glanced at the other men in the Oval Room in the White House, then said, 'We still haven't ascertained the exact cause of the explosion, but according to Mr Fuller, here, Wilson was responsible.'

Eisenhower was standing beside his vice-president, Richard Nixon, framed by the window overlooking the Rose Garden and hazed slightly in the incoming morning sunlight. Both men, Fuller knew, were fully aware of the political seesaw arrangement with Wilson. The 34th President of the United States stared directly at him.

'That's correct, Mister President.' Fuller was unfazed by Eisenhower's stern look, which struck him as being that of a bachelor schoolmaster, rather than that of the most powerful man in the country. While admiring Eisenhower as a West Point graduate, renowned World War II military commander, supreme commander of the North Atlantic Treaty Organization, or NATO, and active anticommunist, Fuller viewed his support of desegregation and the Civil Rights Act as unhealthy manifestations of liberal soft thinking. Nor was he keen on Eisenhower's vice-president,

Richard Nixon, whose support for the sleazy Senator Joe
McCarthy and his self-serving witch-hunts had gained even
decent anticommunists, such as Fuller, a bad name. 'Wilson
phoned me an hour before countdown to say the explosion
would occur and he'd arranged it as a warning that we were
making progress too quickly for his liking.'

'Maybe he's displeased with our plans for the creation
of a National Aeronautics and Space Administration,' said
Major General Joe Kelly of the Air Force Legislative Liaison,
or SAFLL.

'He's not,' Fuller informed him. 'That's the first thing I
thought of, but Wilson wasn't concerned about NASA. He's
annoyed by what he described as our increasingly naked
desperation to beat the Russians into space.'

'So he arranged the explosion on Project Vanguard's first
rocket,' Eisenhower said angrily.

'Yes, Mr President,' Fuller said. 'Of course, as soon as
he'd phoned me, I passed the warning on to the launch
team. A last-minute check on the rocket showed no faults
at all, so it was decided that Wilson was bluffing and that
the launching should continue. Then the rocket blew up,
as Wilson had warned.'

'So how did he manage it?' asked Major General Arno
H. Luehman, director of information services.

'With some kind of explosive device,' Fuller replied,
shrugging.

'We can all assume that, Mr Fuller,' Nixon said
disdainfully. 'What we want to know is how he got it aboard.'

'It had to be one of our men,' Richard Horner admitted.
'But with so many working on the project – and nothing
found in the debris that relates to any known explosive
devices – we're having great difficulty in finding out who it
was or how it was done.'

'But we do at least know that Wilson has one, or even
more, of his men planted in our rocket research teams.'

'Looks that way, Mr President.'

'Either he has some planted in our rocket research

teams,' Fuller corrected him, 'or he used some kind of remote-controlled device. Whether one or the other, he proved his point . . . He's way ahead of us and we're still at his mercy.'

That statement led to a brief, uneasy silence and the rising anger of vice-president Nixon. 'It's a public humiliation,' he said. 'Made even more obvious by the fact that it was the Russians, and not us, who inaugurated the space age with their recent launching of the first man-made satellite, *Sputnik 1*.'

'That's old news already,' Fuller responded, enjoying needling Nixon. 'Last month, they sent up that dog, Laika, which orbited the earth in a second Russian satellite, this one six times heavier than the first.'

'Right,' General Kelly said. 'And that *Sputnik* is also equipped to measure cosmic rays and other conditions in space, a good one thousand miles above the earth.'

'That damned dog,' Major General Luehman said bitterly, 'is being tested for its response to prolonged weightlessness, so it's a precursor to future manned spaceflights.'

'They beat us into space,' Nixon said angrily, 'and now this Wilson has deliberately emphasised our humiliation and set the space programme back again. I thought we had a deal with that man!'

'We do,' Fuller said, 'but it's a seesaw arrangement. We give him a little, he gives us a little, but whenever he thinks we've stepped out of line, he also gives us a warning.'

'Like the explosion on our Project Vanguard rocket,' Eisenhower said.

'Right, Mr President. We're only allowed to advance *behind* his technology. If he thinks we're coming close to catching up with him, he pulls these little stunts – and he's very good at it.'

'So we've learned to our cost – as have others. I believe he was also responsible for the crash of the British European Airways Viscount in March this year, for the fire in the Windscale atomic works in Cumberland in October—'

'The Windscale piles are used to make plutonium for military purposes,' Richard Horner interjected.

'Exactly,' Eisenhower said. 'He's also suspected of being responsible for the death of that Royal Navy Commander, Lionel Crabb, found headless in the sea near Chichester Harbour, England, in June this year, after being accused of espionage activities against the Russians. There are even reports that he might have been responsible for exposing the spying activities of Burgess and McLean in 1955 in order to sour East-West relationships.'

'He doesn't like it when we talk to one another,' Fuller explained. 'He prefers us to be in conflict. We're convinced that this deal he has with us he also has with the British and the Russians. He's one real smart cookie. As for causing a little accident each time we advance too quickly – I believe the Russians and Brits have also had disasters caused by Wilson – we'll just have to be more careful about what we're doing in our research establishments, particularly those in the White Sands Proving Ground.'

'You mean our own flying saucers,' Nixon said.

'Correct. However, it's even more important that we continue to keep hidden the fact that the flying saucers most often seen, and also known to abduct people and animals, are in fact man-made by a highly advanced foreign power – which Wilson can now rightfully be called. If the public finds out about Wilson's flying saucers and Antarctic colony, we'll have mass hysteria to contend with.'

'I agree,' Richard Horner said. 'We must continue to encourage a belief in the possibility of extraterrestrials, which is unreal enough to be ridiculed by nonbelievers even as it's being welcomed by believers. It's vital that we prevent the general public from learning that we're being threatened by a totalitarian regime using mind-control, laser-beam technology, and other highly advanced weapons and forms of parapsychological warfare. That knowledge would be more terrifying than the revelation that the saucers have an extraterrestrial source. Distance lends enchantment. The reality of the Antarctic colony would give the populace nightmares.'

'Unfortunately,' Major General Leuhman said, 'stopping speculation about UFOs won't be easy, as there've been more reports this year than any other.'

Fuller knew what he meant. In 1956, ATIC had recorded 670 sightings, but this year, 1957, that figure had risen to over 1,000, with a gradual increase throughout the year, reaching a peak of over 500 for November. Remarkably, in this second week in December, those figures were continuing to climb, making this the biggest year for UFO sightings since 1952.

The sightings, Fuller knew, were caused by a combination of Wilson's saucers, secret Air Force and Navy saucers, and wishful thinking or mass hysteria caused by the launching of the second Russian *Sputnik*. Nevertheless, their crucial factor was that Wilson was now flying more saucers than ever and doing so with impunity. In fact, Wilson controlled the skies.

'UFO speculation won't be lessened,' Major Kelly said, 'by the forthcoming Congressional hearings, brought about by relentless pressure from that former Air Force major, Donald Keyhoe, and his civilian UFO group, the National Investigations Committee on Aerial Phenomena, or NICAP. The problem of handling the hearings and answering congressional inquiries about the UFO programme has fallen to us at SAFLL. So far, by using *Special Report Number 14* for our information, we've been able to insist that there's a total lack of evidence for anything unusual in the skies. However, I don't know how long we can support that claim if we're forced into open hearings on the matter.'

'Congressional hearings on flying saucers!' Richard Nixon exclaimed, aghast. 'I can't believe what I'm hearing!'

Turning to his assistant secretary of the Air Force for research and development, Eisenhower asked, 'Can you help?'

Horner nodded emphatically. 'I've already told sub-committee chairman Donald O'Donnell that hearings aren't in the best interests of the Air Force. He's trying to get the subcommittee to drop the issue, but it's early days yet. Meanwhile, I'll keep stonewalling Keyhoe and NICAP.'

'Anyway,' Major Kelly said, 'if we *are* forced into congressional hearings, we'll simply use the subcommittee as another tool of disinformation.'

'Very good,' Nixon said, flicking beads of sweat from his upper lip and looking shifty as always.

'Meanwhile,' said Major General Luehman, director of information services, 'my department is continuing the education of the public with the use of psychologists specialising in mass psychology. We're also using military training film companies, commercial film and TV productions, such as Walt Disney Productions, and popular radio and TV personalities, including Arthur Godfrey, to put over whatever we deem fitting. We're continuing to disseminate negative literature about the civilian UFO organisations, including Keyhoe's NICAP and Dr Frederick Epstein's Aerial Phenomena Investigations Institute, based right here in Washington DC. Also, we legally harass them on the slightest pretext. Similar treatment is being meted out to Air Force and commercial air line pilots reporting UFOs.'

'Terrific.' That was Nixon.

'It all seems so sordid,' Eisenhower said, looking uneasy.

'But necessary,' Fuller insisted, amused when Nixon smiled encouragingly at him. 'We have to gradually kill off public talk about UFOs and trust that it then becomes a forgotten subject.'

'What about Project Blue Book?' Nixon asked. 'That damned project has done more to stimulate interest in UFOs than any other branch of the services.'

'It's now well under control,' Fuller said. 'Blue Book's been run down and is now under the supervision of the 1006th Intelligence Service Squadron, which knows practically nothing about UFO investigations. As for the vastly more experienced Captains Ruppelt and Randall, both have been pressured into leaving the Air Force for good, ensuring that the UFO projects, our own and Wilson's, won't be discovered by either of them, accidentally or otherwise.'

'Let's hope they're not discovered by someone else,' President Eisenhower said anxiously. 'Gentlemen, thank you.'

Fuller was first to leave the Oval Room, pleased by what he had heard there.

You simply couldn't trust anyone.

Chapter Twenty-Four

Dwight was drunk again. He was in that state a lot these days, but it was always even worse at Christmas, which reminded him of the family he had lost after leaving the Air Force. Now, sitting at the dining table in the untidy clapboard house, by the window overlooking the rusty pumps of the gas station located on a desolate stretch of road just outside Dayton, Ohio, he was listening to the Christmas carols being sung on the radio, sipping from a dangerously large glass of bourbon, and staring out at the dust-covered, dark road.

He was really surprised when a battered Ford pulled up and Beth slipped out.

'Oh, God,' he whispered involuntarily, talking to himself, caught between pleasure and embarrassment that she should find him like this. Sipping more bourbon, trying to calm his agitation, he studied her as she closed the door of the car, smoothed down her auburn hair, then glanced nervously across the yard at the house.

Dwight slipped a little sideways, to ensure that she couldn't see him, then watched her walking up the path to the front door. Wearing a tightly belted overcoat and high heels, she looked as slim and attractive as he'd remembered her. When she approached the house, vanishing from his view, a lump came to his throat. Then the door-bell rang.

Twitching as if whipped, he was about to hide his glass and bottle of bourbon, but realising immediately that he would not get through this meeting without a drink, he just shrugged, had another sip, then went to the door, carrying his still half-full glass. He took a deep breath, opened the door, and looked straight into his wife's girlish, solemn face. She seemed as embarrassed as he felt, but she gave him a nervous smile.

'Well, well,' Dwight said, 'what a surprise! Long time no see.'

'Yes, Dwight, a long time.' The winter wind was howling across her, beating at her, making her seem touchingly fragile against the nocturnal sky. 'Are you going to keep me standing out here all night or can I come in?'

'Oh, sure, Beth. I'm sorry.' He stepped aside to let her in. When she brushed past him, the brief touch of her body sent a shock coursing through him. He closed the door and followed her into the living-room. She was studying the awful untidiness, which embarrassed him even more. 'I guess I'm not too good at housekeeping,' he said. 'And the gas station keeps me pretty busy.'

Beth stared at the glass in his hand. 'That as well, so I've heard.'

'Yeah,' Dwight said, 'that as well.' He defiantly finished off his drink, then topped up the glass. 'You want one?'

'Why not? Just a small one. Let's share a Christmas drink together. Can I sit in this chair?'

'Sure, Beth. Anywhere.'

He poured her a drink as she unbuttoned her overcoat, letting it hang open, then took the easy chair near the fire. She was wearing a white sheath dress that showed off her perfect figure, and when she crossed her long, silken legs, Dwight wanted to stroke them. Instead, he just handed her the drink and took the chair facing her. They raised their glasses to each other in a toast, drank some bourbon and then gazed at one another in silence.

'Who told you I was drinking?' Dwight finally asked, wanting to get the subject over and done with.

Beth shrugged. 'It's all over town. At least among our mutual friends. You've been seen and heard, Dwight.'

Dwight grinned, though he didn't feel good. 'Yeah, I guess I have. It's surprising how these things get a hold. I'm not cut out for a bachelor's life.'

'It's been three years, Dwight. I hear you don't even have a girlfriend.'

'We didn't separate because of that, Beth. I don't need a girlfriend.'

'Just the bottle.'

'That's right, Beth. You've got it. It deadens all needs.'

'And all fears, as well.'

'Those, too, I guess.'

Dwight soothed those fears by having another sip of bourbon, then he held the glass unsteadily in his lap and studied his wife. He had seen Beth only occasionally since their separation, usually when visiting Nichola, but it seemed like he hadn't seen her for years and her presence consumed him.

'You should never have left the Air Force,' Beth said. 'You *needed* the Air Force.'

'Obviously it didn't need me,' Dwight responded, unable to conceal his bitterness. 'You refused to accept it, Beth, but I *had* to get out. They put the pressure on until I had no choice. That's how they stick it to all of us.'

He meant the officers investigating UFOs. First Flight Officer Harris of the Roswell Army Air Base, then Captain Ruppelt of ATIC, then himself. All had been forced to leave the Air Force after receiving too much pressure from above, usually in the form of blocked UFO investigations, unwarranted criticism, midnight interrogations by intelligence officers, unwelcome transfers to bleak spots like Alaska, and even visits from the mysterious 'men in black'. In the end, you couldn't take it any more and just wanted out.

'Yes,' Beth confessed, 'I have to admit that's true. Did you hear about Captain Ruppelt?'

'Yep. After leaving the Air Force he wrote a book, *The Report on Unidentified Flying Objects*, claiming that the

UFOs were real, solid objects. I read it. It was good.'

Beth nodded. 'But have you heard the latest? Ruppelt's done an abrupt about-face. Later this year he's bringing out a new edition of his book, recanting on his former beliefs and insisting that the UFOs aren't real at all.'

'I've heard that,' Dwight said. 'I've also heard that he's not in good health. That isn't uncommon either. Just look at me, Beth!'

Beth ignored the sour joke, instead glancing around the untidy room. Her look of distaste reminded Dwight of his past three years as a bachelor, mostly spent in a fog of alcohol and filled with too many fears and nightmares. It was the drinking, he knew, that had led to the separation. In resigning his commission and leaving the Air Force, he had only given impetus to the break that had clearly been coming. It was hard to recall it clearly now, but he did remember the fear. It was the fear that had led to the drinking, as well as his nightmares. Dwight had once loved the Air Force, lived for it, was proud of it, but when he became involved with Project Blue Book, the Air Force had turned against him, blocking him, chastising him, eventually humiliating him, until his life became a living nightmare from which there was no escape.

All of that came to a head shortly after his visit to Cannon AFB, when he'd had his terrifying experience with the men in black in that motel room outside Albuquerque. That event, more than anything else, had set the seal on his constant dread.

He had started dreaming about flying saucers, alien entities and men in black, and eventually, as his friends in ATIC were attacked one by one – transferred, demoted, charged with spurious offences, haunted by anonymous phone calls – he had become increasingly isolated and then started cracking up.

The drinking came soon enough, leading to many fights with Beth, and when he said he was resigning his commission, that had been the last straw. They hadn't actually divorced, but merely separated, with Beth taking an apartment close to her parents in Dayton and moving in with a deeply upset Nichola. Shortly after that, Dwight left the Air Force, took this job as a gas station attendant, which included the use of the broken-down house, and embarked on the three worst years of his life, trying to deaden his fear and shame with regular drinking.

It hurt just to recall it.

'We may have parted,' Beth said, 'But I'm still concerned for you, Dwight, and naturally Nichola misses you badly.'

'I miss her, too, Beth.'

'She wants you to spend Christmas with us, and I think you should.'

Dwight's instinct was to refuse, but he was stopped by the realisation that Nichola would be hurt if he did. He was frightened of seeing her, of resurrecting buried feelings, but the very thought of her released those emotions and brought a lump to his throat. He was also moved by Beth's presence, still loving her, wanting her, and though feeling awkward with her, embarrassed by his condition, he was moved by a desperate yearning to get back what he'd lost.

'My pleasure,' he said.

During the drive to Beth's apartment near Carillon Park in Dayton, Dwight was increasingly nervous, but the instant Nichola threw herself into his arms, his problems were over. Now twelve years old, with an oval face and long dark hair, Nichola shared her mother's natural grace and beauty. After a light supper and a long talk with Nichola – during which he lied blatantly about the joys of his job at the gas station and then discussed Nichola's progress at school – Dwight retired to the bed in the spare room, where, for the first time in months, he had a sleep undisturbed by dreadful nightmares.

The next morning, Christmas Day, they were joined by Beth's parents, Joe and Glenda McGinnis, whose customary good humour removed the last of Dwight's discomfort at

being back temporarily with his wife and child. Thoughtful
as always, Beth had made Dwight sign the labels on some
of the presents she had bought for Nichola, and when
Dwight saw the delight on his daughter's face, he nearly
choked up. In fact, when he received his own presents, he
had to turn away in order to hide his brimming tears, but
he practically broke down when Beth kissed him lightly,
tentatively, on the lips.

'God, Beth!' was all he could murmur, being practically
breathless.

They had a great Christmas dinner, drank far too much,
revived themselves with an afternoon walk through the
park, then passed the rest of the afternoon in front of the
TV set, which showed snow in many other parts of the
country while Bing Crosby, appropriately, sang 'White
Christmas'. By the early evening, just after Beth's parents
had left, Dwight was in a mellow mood, perhaps
dangerously sentimental, and had to wipe tears from his
eyes a second time when he tucked Nichola into her bed
and returned to the front room.

'God, I miss her,' he said.

'And me, too, I hope,' Beth responded. She was stretched
out on the sofa, wearing slacks and a loose sweater, holding
a glass of wine in her hand, her gaze fixed on the TV.

'Yeah,' Dwight said. 'You, too.'

He had a lump in his throat and wanted to fall to his
knees before her, to thank her for bringing him home, even
if just for Christmas, thus reminding him of what he had
lost by surrendering to fear.

'Beth,' he began, about to pour out his heart . . . Then
the front door-bell rang.

Beth glanced up, blushing a little, then swung her legs
off the sofa and hurried past Dwight, letting her hand slide
across his shoulder as if in encouragement.

'I have a surprise visitor,' she murmured. 'I just hope
you'll be pleased.'

Though initially frustrated at the thought of this

unexpected intrusion, Dwight was at first startled, then delighted, when Beth led former USAF Captain Bob Jackson into the room.

Dwight hadn't seen his old friend for three years, but Bob looked pretty much the same: still sleek-faced and sassy, if a little thicker around the waist. Wearing a plain grey suit with white shirt and tie, he was beaming from ear to ear and looking a lot healthier than the man who had been posted to Alaska just after Dwight left the Air Force. He embraced Dwight, then vigorously pumped his hand.

'Hell, man,' he said, 'it's so good to see you. It's been too long, buddy.'

Stepping away from each other, they both grinned in a kind of dumb disbelief, until Beth said, 'Okay, you two, sit down and I'll get you a drink.'

'I've been drinking all day,' Bob said, 'so a beer would be fine. Christmas Day, don't you know?' He grinned at Dwight and took a soft chair near the fire. 'Had a good Christmas yourself, did you, Dwight?'

'Wonderful,' Dwight replied, sitting on the sofa facing Bob. 'My first Christmas with my family in three years.'

'Yeah, I heard. I only got back yesterday and Beth told me when I called. She also said she was hoping to have you home for Christmas and told me to drop in. Said it might do you good. Am I doing you good, Dwight?'

'Feels just like old times, Bob.' Beth handed Bob a beer, then joined Dwight on the sofa. Dwight was still nursing a glass of wine and letting it last. 'So obviously you know what happened to me. What happened to you?'

Bob sighed. 'Life at ATIC was hell after you left. They kept transferring me here and there, from one lousy place to another. Promotion was refused, I was repeatedly charged for petty infractions, and in the end I just got the hell out. Most of the others on Project Blue Book had similar experiences – just like you and Ruppelt.'

'When did you leave?'

'Two years ago.'

'So what have you been up to since then?'

'Well, you know, Dwight, I just couldn't forget this UFO business. Couldn't get it out of my goddamned head. So after a couple of months just fooling around, including getting married to our former secretary, Thelma Wheeler – remember her?' he asked, briefly changing the subject.

'Hell, yes!' Dwight responded, instantly recalling the sexy blonde WAC corporal from Huntsville, Alabama, with whom Bob had had a long flirtation.

'She got harassed until she left as well,' Bob continued. 'Anyway, when we got married, I wanted to get us out of Dayton entirely, so I took a job as technical advisor for an aeronautical engineering company located in Greenbelt, Maryland. In fact, my job was more like salesman, using my Air Force background to sell the merits of the company to the many military establishments in that area. The job was okay – it got me out and about a lot – but I still couldn't shake off all those questions Ruppelt had raised about the UFO phenomenon. They haunted me night and day. Finally, through one of my acquaintances, I was introduced to Dr Frederick Epstein, a former astronomer who'd become obsessed with UFOs and now heads the Aerial Phenomena Investigations Institute, or APII, a civilian UFO organisation located in Washington DC.'

'I know him,' Dwight said. 'I interviewed him way back in 1953, shortly after he'd formed the organisation.'

'That's right,' Bob said. 'He reminded me of that interview the first time we met. Anyway, I went to work as an investigator for APII, first on a part-time basis, then full time. And that's what I do now.'

Beginning to understand that there was more to this meeting than a casual Christmas visit, Dwight glanced at Beth. She merely offered a slightly teasing smile, sipped her drink, then explained: 'Bob's come to Dayton to make some investigations on behalf of APII. Until this evening, I hadn't seen him for three years either.'

'That's right,' Bob said. 'I'm here to investigate the

growing claims that there's a storage room in Wright-Patterson AFB for corpses found in wrecked UFOs.'

'There was no such room when *we* were there,' Dwight said.

'No, but the base has changed a lot since we left and ATIC was virtually dissolved. There are lots of no-go areas in Wright-Patterson – more now than ever before – and one of them *could* have been a top-secret storage room for crashed UFO parts or even dead crew members.'

'This whole business of alien bodies at Wright-Patterson is based on the notorious Aztec case of 1948,' Dwight reminded him. 'It all began with a book by one Frank Scully, a former Hollywood *Weekly Variety* columnist, who alleged that a saucer crashed east of Aztec, New Mexico, in 1948, and was found virtually intact, with sixteen dead aliens, or UFOnauts, inside. According to Scully, the flying saucer was dismantled and the pieces, along with the remains of the sixteen aliens, were transported in secret to Muroc Dry Lake, now Edwards AFB, California, then on to a so-called top-secret Hangar 18 in Wright-Patterson. Scully also alleged that there'd been three other flying-saucer landings during the same period and that a total of thirty-four dead aliens had been found and were also being preserved at Wright-Patterson.'

'But having been at Wright-Patterson at the time, you didn't believe it.'

'Right,' Dwight said emphatically. 'Precious little substantiation could be found for Scully's claims. In fact, two years later, an investigative reporter, J. P. Cahn, revealed that Scully had received most of his dubious information from Silas Newton and a Dr Gee, later identified as Leo A. Gebauer. Both men were experienced confidence tricksters who'd been arrested that very year for trying to sell worthless war surplus equipment as oil detection devices. They probably based their whole story on the Roswell Incident of 1947, which we both know so well.'

Dwight certainly knew that case well and could still recall

virtually every word of his conversations with Flight Intelligence Officer First Lieutenant William B. Harris, who'd compiled the official report on the Socorro sighting. He also recalled that at the insistence of General Hoyt Vandenberg, then Deputy Chief of the Air Force, the three charred corpses and the debris from the Socorro crash had been picked up by an intelligence team from the 509th Bomb Group and transported under strict secrecy to an unknown destination, though rumour had it as Carswell AFB, Fort Worth, Texas.

'If Scully based his Aztec landing on the Roswell Incident, at least he picked a damned good case,' Bob insisted. 'You and I both know that the crash at Roswell was a real one – just as real as some of the reported landings.'

'What landings?' Dwight asked, becoming interested despite himself.

'One of our leading test pilots, Gordon Cooper, has claimed that while at the Edwards Air Force Base Flight Test Centre in California last year – the same place where Scully's crashed UFO and its dead occupants were reportedly taken in 1948 – a team of photographers assigned by him to photograph the dry lakes near Edwards spotted a strange-looking craft above the lake bed. The object was hovering above the ground. Then it slowly came down and sat on the lake bed for a few minutes. According to the photographers, it was at least the size of a vehicle that would carry normal people and was also a circular-shaped UFO that took off at a sharp angle and climbed straight out of sight.'

'Naturally they photographed it.'

'Yep.'

'So what happened to their film?'

'According to Cooper, it was forwarded to Washington DC for evaluation, but no report came back and the movie never resurfaced.'

'No film, no evidence – the same old story.'

Bob was unfazed by Dwight's cynicism. 'Dr Epstein has

279

shown me the certified statements of two USAF pilots, confirming that UFO landings took place at Cannon Air Force Base, New Mexico, on May 18, 1954, and at Deerwood Nike Base September 29, 1957. He also has CIA-censored reports on another two UFO landings that took place at Holloman AFB. You might be convinced about Cannon AFB, since it was your own experience there, in 1954, that finally encouraged you to get out of the Air Force.'

Shocked to be reminded of that fearsome experience, Dwight glanced at Beth and was rewarded with an encouraging smile. Sipping the last of his wine, he recalled his visit to the road outside Cannon AFB, New Mexico, where his friend Captain Andrew Boyle had given him a good description of his personal sighting of the landing of a saucer-shaped craft outside a hangar in a restricted area of the base. After showing him the specific hangar, Boyle had given him a photograph of the UFO as proof.

Even more vivid and frightening than this recollection was the memory of how, when Dwight had been lying on his bed in his motel room, located on the outskirts of Albuquerque, a dazzling, pulsating light had filled the room, a bass humming sound had almost split his head, and three men dressed in black coveralls had entered. One of them had temporarily paralysed Dwight with some kind of stun gun, another had whispered a warning in his ear, and the third had stolen his invaluable UFO photograph. Shortly after they left the room, the pulsating light and head-splitting noise went away and feeling returned to Dwight's body. What was not to go away was the fear that subsequently drove him to the bottle and out of the Air Force for good.

He felt that fear now.

'Okay,' he said, 'you've got me on that one. What about the other two?'

Grinning, Bob said, 'The first one took place shortly before 8.00 a.m. on an unspecified day in September, 1956, when a domed, disc-shaped aircraft landed about fifty yards from US 70, about twelve miles west of the base. The ignition systems and radios of passing cars went dead and the peak-hour commuter traffic backed up as amazed witnesses – including two Air Force colonels, two sergeants, and dozens of Holloman employees – watched the UFO for over ten minutes, before it took off with a low whirring sound. Shortly after its disappearance, word of the sighting flew from Holloman to Washington DC and the area was soon inundated with Air Force intelligence officers and CIA agents. Base employees who'd witnessed the sighting were sworn to secrecy and the Pentagon's evaluation team wired a report stating that the UFO wasn't any type of aircraft under development by the US or any foreign terrestrial power.'

Bob sipped some beer, then took a deep breath and let it out again. He was clearly enjoying this.

'Then, just this summer, a mechanic at Holloman AFB was working on a grounded Lockheed F-104 jet interceptor when he saw a disc-shaped object hovering silently over the tarmac. After watching the object retracting its ball-like landing gear, he called another mechanic and both of them watched the UFO take off vertically at great speed. During a subsequent interrogation, both men identified the craft type they had seen from a book of over three hundred UFO photographs. They were then informed that the personnel in the base control tower had observed the same object for two or three minutes. They were also warned not to discuss the incident and made to sign a statement swearing them to secrecy.'

'Very persuasive,' Dwight said, impressed by Bob's enthusiasm and responding instinctively to it, feeling more alive than he had done for three years. 'But I still don't believe you'll find a Hangar 18 in Wright-Patterson AFB, let alone alien corpses or crashed UFO debris. What *did* you find there?'

Bob grinned like a Cheshire cat. 'According to my informant, all requests to Wright-Patterson AFB for information regarding Hangar 18 are routinely given the reply that it doesn't exist. However, he insists that Wright-Patterson's top-security Area B contains a building numbered 18-A. In fact, he says he's personally seen it, though never been allowed in. It's a building – not a hangar – with a tall wire fence around it. All of its windows have been knocked out and replaced with concrete.'

'Anything else?'

'Yes. He was adamant that similar storage rooms would be found in the White Sands Proving Ground, Los Alamos, New Mexico, and Carswell AFB, Fort Worth, Texas.'

Dwight involuntarily sat upright at the mention of the latter base. 'And we both know what was shipped to Carswell, don't we?' he asked rhetorically.

Bob's grin widened impossibly. 'Sure do,' he said. 'The corpses and debris from the Roswell crash of 1947. Your eyes are gleaming, old buddy.'

Dwight knew he had been set up, probably for his own good. Glancing sideways at Beth, he saw her widening smile as she reached out to hold his hand and squeeze it. 'Bob called me,' she explained, 'to find out what you were up to. When I told him, he was as upset as me and insisted that we somehow get together to persuade you to help him in his work for APII. I think it's what you need, Dwight, to get you off the drink and give you something to do other than pump gas. Please think about it.'

Dwight thought about it, feeling frightened, but wanting to do it, aware of the warmth of Beth's fingers on his hand, revitalised by her presence.

'You won't have to move to Washington,' Bob explained. 'You can be our Ohio man. Naturally, you'll come and visit us occasionally, but you'll remain based in Dayton. You'll be our eyes and ears here.'

'As far as I recall, Dr Epstein believes the UFOs are of extraterrestrial origin.'

'He's fairly open-minded about it, but he can't think of any other explanation.'

'You know what Andy Boyle told me during my visit to New Mexico,' Dwight said. 'He presented me with the possibility that the crashed or landing UFOs might have been man-made – known to, and protected by, our own military intelligence. Have you told Epstein that?'

'No, I haven't. I don't think the time is right. It's a possibility I'd like you to pursue, but on your own, not through APII. If what Boyle said is true, it'd be too big – and possibly too dangerous – for APII to deal with. We'll have to keep the lid on that, Dwight, until we're sure of our ground.'

'So I investigate general UFO cases for APII while surreptitiously gathering information on the man-made UFOs.'

'That's it, exactly. We keep the lid on the latter cases. They're between you and me, Dwight. In this regard, I've no guilt about using the facilities of APII, since I'll be helping them with what you uncover in all other areas. I need you, Dwight, and you need this work. What do you say?'

Beth squeezed his hand again. 'Please do it, Dwight. It'll help you to find your way back. Your home's here, in this apartment, with me and Nichola, not in that damned gas station. Work with Bob, Dwight. *Come home.*'

'Yes,' Dwight said, feeling renewed and excited already. 'Yes, damn it, I'll do it!'

Grinning from ear to ear, Bob was shaking his hand even as Beth, her eyes brimming with tears, turned into his arms, where she had always belonged.

'Welcome aboard,' Bob said.

Chapter Twenty-Five

Rocking gently in his rocking chair on the verandah of his large house in the enlarged compound buried deep in the jungle near the Paraguay River, Ernst was feeling like an old man as he looked up at the moonlit sky to observe the majestic descent of the biggest flying saucer he had seen so far.

Though an awesome three hundred and fifty feet wide, this transport craft was otherwise like the others: two immense, inverted plates which were rotating around the dome-shaped, gyroscopically-stabilised central fuselage. Though not hindered by normal heat and drag, thus giving off no sonic booms or other noises, other than an almost physical bass infrasound, the saucer was creating violent currents of air within a cylindrical zone the same width as its rotating wing-plates, making the grass and plants flutter wildly, noisily, sucking up loose soil and gravel, and causing them to spin in the air.

As usual, the native workers who lived in the shacks located around the inner edge of the compound were standing outside their modest homes, untouched by the precisely edged whirlpool of wind, looking up in awe and fear as the immense craft descended.

Also looking up, and clearly terrified, were the many captured Ache Indians being held like cattle in the enormous bamboo cages located near the shacks of the compound workers. These unfortunates, who had never seen an airplane, let alone such a gigantic saucer, started wailing and shaking the bamboo bars of their cages, as if wanting to break free and run away. They only quietened down when threatened by Ernst's armed *Federales* and *contrabandistas*. Those that didn't were hammered by rifle butts until either they shut up or collapsed unconscious.

Gradually the great saucer filled up most of the compound. Its central dome was as high as the craft was wide, about the height of a three-storey building. The whitish glow of its electrically-charged, minutely porous magnesium orthosilicate, which was ionizing the air surrounding it, darkened to a more normal metallic hue as it hovered just above ground level, rocking slightly from side to side. Just before touching down, its massive hydraulic legs emerged from six points around the base to embed themselves deeply in the soft earth. The enormous craft bounced gently on the legs, then settled down and was still. Its rotating rings gradually slowed and then stopped altogether, as did the wind that had been created by its electromagnetic gravity-damping system.

Still sitting in his rocking chair on his verandah, Ernst was deeply moved by the sight of the magnificent craft, though he also felt embittered at being condemned to this hellish jungle, rounding up Ache Indians instead of being involved in the great achievements of the Antarctic colony. His feeling of loss was in no way eased by the knowledge that in truth he could never return to engineering because it was now too far behind him and the technological advances of recent years had rendered his old engineering knowledge redundant. Trained as a military policeman by the SS, that's what he would stay: a hunter and warden for Wilson.

Ernst's bitterness was like acid in his stomach, almost making him retch. With the outer rings of the saucer no longer rotating, the bass infrasound faded away and a panel in the concave base dropped down on hinged arms to form a ramp leading to the ground. Armed guards wearing black coveralls emerged to form a protective ring around the ramp, then Wilson appeared, wearing his customary black shirt and pants, followed by some short, nightmarish creatures who had a jerky, mechanical gait and were, Ernst assumed, the first of the promised cyborgs.

Surrounded by his own bodyguard of heavily armed *Federales* and *contrabandistas*, Ernst went to greet his master. Now, when Wilson shook his hand, Ernst was no longer surprised at how youthful he appeared. Though nearing ninety, Wilson looked like a healthy sixty, with a good head of silvery-grey hair and smooth skin on a handsome, though oddly inexpressive face dominated by unusually piercing, icy-blue eyes. Like his facial muscles, his movements were slightly stiff, reminding Ernst that he'd had numerous joint and organ replacements, as well as extensive plastic surgery.

This man, Ernst thought sourly, is a prototype of the creatures gathered around him. Steel-and-cobalt joints, artificial heart and grafted skin. He only *looks* normal.

Ernst shook Wilson's hand and murmured words of greeting while studying the nightmarish creatures spreading out behind him. He realised immediately that they were Ache Indians, which explained their short stature, but that now they were part man, part machine. Their hideous appearance was caused by the fact that their jawbones and mouths had been replaced with metal masks, they were also wearing metal skullcaps, and some of them had prosthetic hands that resembled steel claws. All of them were dressed in tight, one-piece, silvery-grey jumpsuits of a material resembling Thai silk.

They look, Ernst thought, like hideous extraterrestrials: creatures out of a nightmare.

'Your first cyborgs,' he said.

'Yes,' Wilson replied.

'Can they speak?'

'Not yet, but they can function otherwise.'

'Are they still human in any sense that we'd recognise?'

'They still possess fragments of their former memories

and reasoning, but their thoughts and actions, even their emotions, can be remote-controlled by the electrodes implanted in their heads through those stereotaxic skullcaps.'

'The metal caps.'

'Exactly.' Wilson glanced approvingly at the nearest cyborg, then tapped his knuckles against the metal plate covering the unfortunate creature's lower jaw and mouth. 'Deprived of speech by the lower-jaw prosthetic,' he explained, 'they communicate via the stereotaxic skullcaps, which act like miniature radio receivers operated by thought-waves. As an interesting side effect, the lack of speech is gradually producing in them what appears to be a primitive form of mental telepathy, which may soon make even skullcap communication redundant. This is an unexpected, novel development that we must follow through.'

Ernst nodded, intrigued despite his natural revulsion. 'And the metal hands?'

'Myoelectric prosthetics, developed by our excellent Dr King, formerly of the Powered Limbs Unit of West Hendon Hospital, London, England. They're really miniature versions of what we intend developing in larger form for the exploration of the sea-beds, the surface of the moon and, eventually, the planets: remote-controlled CAMS, or Cybernetic Anthropomorphous Machine Systems, of the kind presently being developed by NASA for space exploration. Naturally, we're already well ahead of NASA – indeed, we give them our obsolete prosthetics and CAMS as part of our trade with the US – and we've installed larger versions of these remote-controlled, steel limbs as handling devices in this particular transport craft. Come, let's have a drink on the porch.'

'But how can they stand being like that?' Ernst asked as he and Wilson turned towards the house. 'They're so inhuman. So . . . hideous.'

'I told you. The stereotaxic skullcaps control even their

emotions, so they're programmed to forget everything that went before and to consider themselves perfectly normal. The skullcaps also direct the impulses from the brain to the severed limbs, thus controlling the movements of the myoelectric, prosthetic hands. As we direct those impulses via the stereotaxic skullcap, we can control everything they remember, desire, and fear, as well as their every physical action. I know they look like creatures from another world, but they're very effective as totally obedient slaves and ruthless guards. In the latter context, their ghastly appearance is actually helpful, as it frightens normal human beings to the point of paralysis.'

'I was abducted by aliens,' Ernst said, quoting from a host of recent magazine articles on UFOs and their so-called extraterrestrial occupants.

'Exactly,' Wilson said with a rare display of amusement. 'It's just what we need.'

They returned to the porch and took high-backed chairs on opposite sides of a bamboo table containing a tall bottle of iced white wine and two glasses. A bare-footed servant girl, Rosa, dark skin gleaming with beads of sweat, poured the wine, then stepped back into the shadows of the awning while Ernst and Wilson touched glasses.

'Skol!' Ernst said by way of a toast. After drinking, he wiped sweat from his forehead – how he hated this constant heat! – then cast his gaze over the immense saucer, which practically filled the whole clearing and towered above him like a cathedral of pure, seamless steel. He then studied the nightmarish creatures forming a cordon just below him, facing his armed *Federales* and *contrabandistas*. His native workers, he noticed, were also staring at the cyborgs, their eyes wide with fearful fascination.

'They're merely prototypes,' Wilson explained, noting Ernst's interest. 'Soon they'll be even more advanced. As far as these cyborgs go, what you see is what they are: restructured breathing and digestive systems, implanted skulls and myoelectric hands. They're fed intravenously, which gives us yet another hold over them. However, in later models, to be used for long-term undersea and space exploration, while the kidneys, lungs and original intestines will remain, they'll be strengthened and supported by a two-chamber pacemaker. Advanced prosthetic joint replacements have already been perfected – indeed, I have some myself – and will help defeat the rigours of the ocean bed and extended journeys through outer space. Soon, with our latest innovation – an electronic larynx – they'll be able to speak as well. As for the larger CAMS installed in this transport craft: watch!'

Wilson aimed a small, hand-held device at the front of the enormous saucer, then pressed a button. A bass humming sound emanated from the craft and the ramp leading from its base to the ground was pulled up automatically to form a sealed door. As soon as the door had closed, another section of the base was lowered on hydraulic supports to form a much wider, brilliantly illuminated ramp between the interior of the saucer and the ground. Suddenly, two smaller panels hidden in the otherwise seamless upper surface of the saucer opened to emit beams of an even more dazzling light that converged on Ernst's jeep, parked close to the saucer's outer edge. The beams of light flickered so rapidly they hurt Ernst's eyes, but then, to his amazement, the parked jeep was pulled forward, as if the beams of light were chains. When the jeep was about ten yard from the wide ramp, a CAM consisting of extendable arms and steel platform emerged from inside the saucer to pick up the vehicle and draw it up the ramp, into the saucer. When the jeep had vanished inside, the beams of light blinked out, the small panels closed, and the large ramp withdrew until the base of the saucer was sealed again.

'A form of magnetism created by powerful electrical forces in the laser beams drew the car towards the remote-control grips of the CAM,' Wilson explained, 'allowing it to take hold of the vehicle and draw it up into the saucer.

When the unitiated see this happening to their own cars, they assume it's some kind of miracle – or the highly advanced parapsychological activity of extraterrestrials. As with the appearance of the cyborgs, their terror makes them easier to handle if we wish to abduct them. Do you want your jeep back?'

'Yes, please,' Ernst replied, suitably impressed.

Wilson pressed a button on his hand-control and the process was reversed, with the wide base of the saucer dropping down to form a ramp and the CAM pushing the vehicle out on its extending arms and steel platform, to deposit it back on the ground. Then the ramp was withdrawn back up into the saucer and again became a sealed door in the base.

'We've made even greater advances in our strobe-light and laser-beam technology,' Wilson said, speaking academically, without the slightest trace of pride in his voice – just doing his job. 'Now we're using wave-lengths and rhythmic patterns that temporarily freeze skeletal muscles or certain nerves, thus producing either paralysis or a trance-like condition. Observe!'

Some of the captured Ache Indians were still wailing in terror in the cages near the shacks of the compound workers. When Wilson activated his hand-control, another small panel facing the cages opened in the sloping top-body of the saucer. A dazzling beam of light shot out, like a spotlight, and wandered across the clearing until it illuminated the cage where most of the wailing was coming from. Once caught in the beam of light, the captured Indians became even more vocal in their panic, but when the beam of light started flickering on and off rapidly, turning the clearing into a bizzare, slow-motion film, the Indians caught in it not only fell silent, but began collapsing and falling against each other, until eventually all of them were unconscious. When Wilson turned off the flickering strobe light, the Indians regained consciousness, picking themselves up and glancing around them as if in a daze.

'As we learn more about the wave patterns of the brain,' Wilson explained, 'so we learn that most emotions – fear and anger, docility and aggression, even self-hatred – can be released by exposing the subject to the stimuli of strobe lights flickering in one of the four basic rhythmic patterns: alpha, beta, delta, and theta. In doing this, we can induce just about every kind of condition, from drowsiness, dizziness, mesmerism, or psychological paralysis, to epileptic or other violent seizures. Indeed, by combining strobe lights flickering in the alpha-rhythm range, between eight and twelve cycles a second, with infrasounds, we can cause an epileptic seizure in the human subject – as you can see. Recently we perfected this to the point where we can force a subject to turn against himself in the ultimate manner. Observe, Ernst.'

This time, when the beam of light shot out of the saucer and began flickering on and off at a blinding, disorientating rate while making what was, to Ernst, a barely discernible, but oddly physical throbbing sound, it picked out one of Ernst's compound workers. The man, wearing only a loin cloth and with a machete strapped to his waist, initially stepped back, dazzled, and started covering his eyes with his right hand. However, before his hand reached his head, it started shaking badly, as did his whole body, then he screamed, clasped his head in his hands, and fell to his knees. Trembling even more violently, and shaking his head from side to side as if in terrible anguish, he collapsed to the ground, went into a fit, then managed to get back onto his knees and remove the gleaming machete from his belt.

In the rapid flickerings of the light, all his movements appeared to be in slow motion, as if in devilish pantomime – an illusion that rendered even more horrible what happened next.

Letting out another scream of anguish, the man shook his head violently again, then reversed the machete and quickly slashed his own stomach open. Even as his entrails splashed out, he was hacking at himself again, repeatedly, dementedly, and kept doing so until he toppled sideways, to lie still in the blood-soaked grass.

Some friends, including a woman, possibly his wife, wailed in grief and fear, then bent down to examine the dead man as the flickering strobe light blinked off, returning the night to star-draped darkness.

Within seconds, Ernst's armed thugs were hammering the grieving people with the butts of their weapons, forcing them back, as another two men picked up the dead man and carried him out of sight, to be buried, as Ernst knew, in the unmarked, communal grave outside the compound. When the dead man's relatives and friends continued wailing in grief, Wilson again demonstrated the power of the strobe light by rendering them unconscious with it, after which they too were taken away.

Ernst, feeling nothing for the dead man, was suitably impressed. Though increasingly resenting being kept in this hell-hole, he still had enormous respect for Wilson – and, in fact, practically worshipped him. He often despised himself for this reverence, but could not fight the feeling.

'Finally,' Wilson said, knowing exactly how to impress Ernst, 'look at this.'

Again aiming his hand-control at the immense transport craft, he activated the opening of panels located at half-a-dozen different points, equidistant around the top body, below the level of the mushroom-shaped central dome. With a speed that startled even the expectant Ernst, silvery objects shot out of the open panels and ascended to a height of about a hundred feet, where they stopped abruptly and hovered in the air.

They looked just like the old World War II *Feuerballs*

'They are,' Wilson confirmed when Ernst had made this observation. 'They're highly advanced models based on the originals.'

'How highly advanced?'

'Though still only three to six feet in diameter, they have

most of the capabilities of the larger saucers and are used for reconnaissance and as antiradar and sensing devices. As they can emit strobe lights and laser beams, they're also used as mesmerising or stunning devices, as well as to draw mechanical vehicles close enough to the mother ship to be within reach of the CAMS.'

'In other words, they're used in abductions.'

'Correct,' Wilson said. With what seemed like a soft sigh of regret (Ernst suspected that such an emotion would have been alien to him) he returned the advanced Feuerballs to the mother ship and closed the small panels. He then reopened the wide ramp at the bottom of the transport craft and ordered the cyborgs to start herding the imprisoned Ache Indians up into it. The cyborgs turned away without a word and walked in their oddly mechanical manner to the cages where, with the help of stun guns that clearly stung rather than inducing unconsciousness, they began marching the hurt, terrified Indians towards the big saucer.

'The infrasounds,' Wilson explained, 'are so condensed that they can create physical pressure on the human brain and the body's organs, even bursting blood vessels in the head. They are thus very useful as weapons, which is why we've incorporated them in the saucers. As for the stereotaxic skullcaps, we also plan to use them to hypnotize or otherwise control human beings by remote control. We'll abduct those we want, fill their heads with minute, remote-controlled electrodes, then return them to the world, to do our bidding as and when required. Eventually, in this way, we'll be able to enslave the world's most powerful men and women without resorting to war and with few aware that they're in our control. In other words, they'll become our brain-implanted robots – even those in the highest seats of government.' He offered a smile that failed to warm the Antarctic blue of his eyes. 'So how are you, Ernst? I must say, you look well.'

It was a lie and Ernst knew it, though he was wise enough not to argue. He had aged overnight towards the end of

World War II, when his wife and daughter were killed in an air-raid on Berlin, making him realise he had no-one left but Wilson. At least, he had aged in appearance – he had seen it in the mirror – but since coming to Paraguay he had aged in an even worse way: inside, in his spirit. Now his skin had a yellow pallor, his handsome features were wrinkled, and his body, though bone-thin, felt heavy and lifeless. As for his spirit, it drained out of him with each passing day, leaving nothing but the ghosts of old dreams that were long dead and buried. Ernst knew that he was paying for his sins and that hell was right here on earth.

'I feel fine,' he lied, not yet having the courage to say otherwise. 'How are things in Antarctica?'

'Things run smoothly,' Wilson told him. 'No problems so far. Our secret agreements with the Americans, British and Russians have ensured a constant supply of all the materials we need. As for general man-power and slave labour, we continue to replenish those lost through experimentation or natural causes by simply abducting more people and, of course, by supplementing them with your invaluable supply of Ache Indians. You're still having no trouble in obtaining them?'

'It's easier than it was. With General Stroessner now the President of Paraguay, we have total freedom of movement. The general always needs money.'

'Greed always makes strong men weak, which is what we can utilise. The former war allies are greedy for our technology, which is why I use them.'

'I sometimes worry,' Ernst said, 'that we'll give away too much.'

'You worry too much,' Wilson replied.

'Do I? Please let me remind you that earlier this year Wernher von Braun's first satellite, *Explorer*, was launched successfully into space. Subsequent *Explorer* satellites made the first scientific discoveries of the space age by discovering the radiation belt around the earth. In July, a

US nuclear submarine, *Nautilus*, made a successful four-day journey under the ice of the North Pole. I should also point out that the past year has seen the discovery of electronic miniaturization in the shape of the silicon chip; and that the British and the Americans are both presently involved in Zeta programmes designed to harness the power of the H-bomb. This represents an unprecedented speed of advancement – and it's my belief that it was possible only through the West's access to our innovations, particularly those in the field of electronic miniaturization, which will revolutionise every branch of technology.'

'I understand your concern,' Wilson replied, 'but I think it's misplaced. We can only pass on what we've already surpassed and each time they've tried to trick us, or planned to turn against us, we've easily scared them back into line with a display of our power – as we did with the so-called UFO invasion of Washington DC in 1952 and when we arranged for the explosion in the US *Vanguard* rocket during its launch in December, 1957.'

'I *assumed* that was your doing,' Ernst said admiringly. 'How did you manage it?'

'We abducted one of the NASA engineers, flew him to the Antarctic, implanted electrodes in his head with a stereotaxic skullcap, and programmed him to forget his experience with us while doing exactly as he was ordered. He planted one of our own explosive devices in the rocket – a device so minute it leaves no traces after it's exploded. Naturally, the Americans don't know who he was – since they would never think to examine the heads of their engineers for electronic implants – and so he's still there to do our bidding when we think it's required. The seesaw arrangement is working, Ernst, and we're in control of it. I have to go now.'

The abruptness was typical of Wilson. It was not a sign of rudeness, but of his impatience and inability to sit still and do nothing

As Wilson pushed his chair back and got to his feet,

Ernst saw that the last of the terrified Ache prisoners had been herded up into the transport craft by the stun-gun toting cyborgs and that the saucer was therefore ready to depart. Swelling with a sudden, startling desperation, Ernst followed Wilson across the clearing, through his own armed *Federales* and *contrabandistas*, as well as Wilson's grim, black-clothed guards, before stopping at the brilliantly lit, sloping ramp leading into the saucer.

Glancing up, Ernst caught a glimpse of brilliant white, curving walls, a stretch of glittering, steel-railed catwalk, and figures silhouetted in dazzling light. A lump came to his throat when he thought of how all this had begun – thirty years ago when some primitive, liquid-fueled rockets were shot up from an abandoned three hundred-acre arsenal in the depressing Berlin suburb of Reindickerdorf. Ernst had been there at the beginning, but not for too long. Each time he had been side-stepped, which had happened too often, he had lost another piece of his soul and hope for the future. Now he wanted that back, to return to his lost youth, and so he turned to face Wilson, his master and idol, with tears in his eyes.

'I lied to you,' he confessed. 'I'm not feeling fine at all. In fact, this place is driving me mad and I yearn to escape it. This jungle compound is a pestilence. These stupid natives are my despair. I have no-one to talk to, no-one educated; and now pressure from the West to find and punish former Nazis has made it too dangerous for me even to visit Asunscion, which I used to do regularly to get a break from here. I repeat, Herr Wilson, I'm going mad in this place. Please take me back with you. Replace me with someone else. Give me a respite from this hell-hole and let me do more important work. Let me work on the saucers.'

Wilson stared steadily at him, his blue gaze intense, revealing neither sympathy nor contempt, but merely the icy-bright gleam of pure pragmatism. When he then placed his hand on Ernst's shoulder, Ernst felt his heart sinking, knowing what the answer would be, not able to challenge it.

'I'm sorry, Ernst,' Wilson said, 'but the time isn't right yet. I understand your frustration, but I have to be hard with you, to keep you doing what you must do until this job is completed. Your time will come soon, Ernst. Soon, you won't be needed here. In the meantime, you just have to be patient and do the best that you can. You have to stay, Ernst.'

'But I'm going mad here!' Ernst blurted out, ashamed of the self-pity in his voice, but unable to hide it. 'There's no-one for me here. I can't go to Asunsion. If I can't get away now and then, I will truly go crazy.' Wilson squeezed his shoulder. 'Don't worry, Ernst. The next time we come, which will be in a fortnight, we'll bring you a thirty-five foot, single-pilot saucer – solely for your personal convenience. You can use it to make trips away from here when it becomes too much for you. This small craft will take you just about anywhere you could possibly want, allowing you to avoid Asunscion. It possesses all the capabilities of the larger saucer and is easy to fly. Compared to this, driving a car is complicated.' He squeezed Ernst's shoulder again. 'The next time we visit, Ernst. In two weeks. I can offer you nothing else for the time being, so I trust you'll accept.'

'Yes, Wilson. Thank you.'

Yet even as Ernst said this, unable to meet Wilson's gaze and so lowering his own eyes, he was filled with the chilling conviction that his idol was toying with him, not telling the whole truth, hiding something, planning something else for him, perhaps something not good.

When he raised his eyes again, to search for the truth in Wilson's gaze, Wilson had already turned his back to him and was entering the saucer. The cyborgs and armed guards followed him in, the ramp made a low humming sound and turned back up into the saucer, and Ernst beat a hasty retreat, back onto the porch.

He sat in his rocking chair, started rocking automatically, looking up as the mighty saucer ascended slowly to high above the canopy of the trees, hovered majestically, silently, for a moment, then shot off as a streak of light that shrank at great speed.

Soon it became just one of the other stars above the jungle, then it blinked out, as if it had never been.

Lowering his gaze and glancing around his jungle compound, Ernst saw the high walls of wood and thatch, the guards in machine-gun towers, the open fires smouldering outside the shacks of the native workers, the bamboo cages for the Ache prisoners, the flogging posts and coffin-shaped, windowless boxes used for punishment; the dogs, goats, chickens and pigs, the shit and piss in the open latrines. All was shadowed in the day by the soaring, tropical trees; wrapped most nights in a suffocating humidity; attacked night and day by every imaginable kind of insect and reptile, half of them venomous, others carrying vile diseases. Surveying it all with his weakening eyes, through senses jaded and increasingly numbed, he realised that he really was in hell and receiving God's punishment.

When he thought of World War II and his early days as an engineer, then of Himmler and Kammler and Nebe and the SS, then of his wife and children – both betrayed by him before dying in an Allied air-raid – and finally, of what he was now doing in this jungle, he understood why he was being punished and knew that he deserved it.

Ernst shed sentimental tears, then called out for his servant-girl. When Rosa stepped out of the darkness, on bare feet, looking frightened, Ernst knew that he would make her suffer as he was suffering, easing his pain by inflicting it.

He had created his own hell on earth and now had to rule it.

The devil, he knew, did not need disciples; he just needed victims. Ernst now needed a lot of those.

'Tonight we will do things you can't imagine,' he said to

Rosa as she knelt obediently, fearfully, in front of him. 'Now go into the bedroom, take your clothes off, and lie down on the floor. Don't move a muscle, don't make a sound, until I come to you. Do you understand, Rosa?'

'Yes, master,' she whispered.

Ernst burned in the radiant light of his sick desires and sad self-destruction. Waving Rosa away and glancing up at the stars, he wondered which one of them was actually Wilson's transport craft. Then he filled up with fury and pain.

'I won't stay here,' he whispered. 'I won't! *As God is my witness!*'

So saying, he stood up and entered the big, eerily empty house to take out his frustration on Rosa in ways unimaginable.

Chapter Twenty-Six

Flying into Washington DC at the end of January, 1959, Dwight was picked up at the airport by Bob Jackson and his wife, Thelma, the sexy blonde WAC corporal who had acted as secretary to both of them during the good days at ATIC. Though not quite as slim as she had been when Dwight had last seen her, Thelma was still a very attractive, good-humoured woman.

'A matinee idol!' she exclaimed as she gave Dwight a hug. 'You haven't changed a bit, sweetheart.'

'If we weren't in a public place,' Dwight replied, 'I'd throw you on this floor and try my best.'

'Which wouldn't be good enough,' Thelma said.

Dwight laughed. 'Don't you know it?'

The ice was broken as easily as it can be only with true friends and they left the airport, driven by Thelma in a battered old Ford, like folk who had never been parted.

'A damned mess,' Dwight observed.

'My car?'

'Yeah, Bob, your car. Sooner or later we all accept the hearse, but it doesn't have to be *this* bad.'

'In American society,' Bob retaliated, 'a man's judged by his automobile or his woman. Given this, though my wheels aren't of the best, I'm still on top of the heap.'

'Now you know how he suckered me,' Thelma said, lighting up a Camel and blowing a cloud of smoke. 'I couldn't resist his Irish blarney. He made me feel like a queen.'

'Which you are,' Dwight said.

'You're so straight-laced, Dwight,' Thelma replied teasingly, 'that hearing those words coming out of your mouth makes me melt and have wicked thoughts.'

'Sorry.'

'Don't apologise,' Bob said. 'Instead, take her words as words of wisdom. Never ignore a good woman.'

'I won't,' Dwight promised.

He said it without confidence, even as his chest heaved with an uncontrollable spasm of overbrimming love. It was love for Beth, stabbing through him like a knife, opening him up with a surgeon's precision to all the pain, joy and uncertainty of being back with her.

Getting together again had not been all that easy, though it had certainly been worth it in the end. At first, when Dwight moved back in, he and Beth were awkward with each other, no longer protected by the ease of familiarity and having to inch slowly towards one another. As with most such relationships, their greatest difficulty was in approaching each other in bed after having spent so much time apart. The first night had been bad, an embarrassed, tentative touching that had filled Dwight with the shock of renewed desire, yet simultaneously frightened him, making him feel like an inexperienced schoolboy who didn't know what to do. Giving up, they had slept in each other's arms and awakened self-conscious with each other – though the rest of that day Dwight felt extraordinarily alive, skin glowing with the indelible touch of Beth's own soft skin on his. It had made him feel exalted.

The next night, however, was the breaking of the ice, with Beth taking the initiative, exploring him with her hands and lips, finally taking his hardness into her mouth and exciting him to the degree where he forgot the inhibitions he had developed over the barren years of separation. Set free by her equally shy, caring administrations, surrendering to the ecstasy of pure, sensual pleasure, he had lain there, breathing heavily, his body on fire, as she sat up and straddled him, her naked body pale in the moonlight, beads of sweat glistening on her breasts and thighs, running into her pubic hair.

It was possibly a tribute to the depths of their love that even now, at his age, Dwight was convinced that he would never forget that image of Beth for as long as he lived: naked, sweat-slicked, her hair falling across her face, legs spread and spine curved, full breasts thrusting out, emphasizing the hardened nipples, as she moved up and down on him, turning this way and that, kneading his chest, belly and thighs with electrified fingers and an instinct that seemed to anticipate his every need and desire. He had stared up at her, wide-eyed, running his hands frantically over her, squeezing her breasts, stroking her belly, gripping her hips to let their movement excite him to the limit; then thrusting up with his groin, trying to penetrate even deeper, to bury himself so deeply inside her that he became a part of her – all of that in beams of moonlight that fell on the bed they had purchased two days after returning from their honeymoon in Niagara Falls, thirteen years ago, when they were younger and a lot less complicated. For that reason, when Beth came, her body shuddering astride him, and he followed closely, feeling as if he was dying, he knew that their love had a solid basis that could see them through. That thought, also, exalted him – though even now, almost choked up with love, he could not shake off the anguish and uncertainty caused by the knowledge, gained painfully through the separation, that nothing was permanent.

'So how's Beth?' Bob asked, as if reading Dwight's mind.

'She's fine, Bob. So's Nichola.'

'God, Nichola!' Bob exclaimed, shaking his head in wonder. 'When I saw her at Christmas I nearly freaked. They grow up so fast.'

'How old is she?' Thelma asked, having not yet been to Dwight's place.

'Twelve,' Dwight told her.

'Oh, boy!' Thelma exclaimed, driving the car in a

distracted, deceptively careless way. 'I can't believe you have a kid that age already. She was just a *baby* in Dayton.'

'Born there,' Dwight explained. 'When you and I were young, Thelma.'

She laughed at that and puffed a cloud of cigarette smoke. 'Yeah, right, back in ATIC at Wright-Patterson AFB. Weren't those the days?'

'Good days,' Bob said. 'You used to let me feel your leg beneath your desk, right there in the ATIC office, and my car was our regular passion pit when the sun had gone down. Now we only get together in bed, which shows how much we've aged.'

Thelma laughed again. She had an infectious 'dirty' laugh. 'True enough,' she confessed without blushing. 'But you've got your times mixed up. You were feeling my leg under the desk in 1948, Bob. The passion pit entered the vernacular about 1955, along with Elvis the Pelvis. God, I love Elvis!'

'Elvis killed us all,' Dwight replied. 'He had the voice, the looks and the swinging groin; we've only got the latter.'

'I'm sure Beth's perfectly happy with that,' Thelma said, puffing another cloud of smoke from brightly painted, grinning lips. 'I know that deep down *I* am.'

'Deep down,' Bob said mournfully. When Thelma squeezed his arm affectionately, he grinned and glanced sideways at Dwight. 'So the reunion's working out okay so far?' he asked. 'You and Beth are okay?'

'Yes, Bob, we're fine.'

'Are you sure?'

'Yes.'

'You seen a bit down there.'

'I'm just a bit nervous, that's all. Meeting this Dr . . .'

'Epstein.'

'Right, Dr Epstein.'

'Nothing else?'

Brushing his windblown hair from his eyes, Dwight glanced out of the open window of the car. They were

303

crossing the Potomac, on Memorial Bridge, and Dwight could see all the way along the Mall to the Capitol building. Washington DC always made him think of London, England, though he had never been there. He'd only seen it in books.

'Well,' he confessed finally, 'there *is* something else. The reunion's been fine – I mean physically and emotionally – but something's a bit off with Beth. I don't mean her and me – something else . . . I mean . . .'

'Out with it,' Bob said.

Dwight nodded. 'She's having bad dreams. Nightmares, in fact. Even when we've had a good time together, making love, once asleep she often wakes up screaming.'

'UFO dreams?'

'Yep.'

'Men in black?'

'Yep. All the things she's read about and been told about, not only when we were at ATIC, but since I left home and went on the bottle. Thing is, she never had those dreams, or nightmares, until I returned home. We're happy being back together – I swear it, folks, and I think I can speak for Beth – but she only started having those dreams when we got back together. I guess that's what's bothering me.'

Even Thelma, normally so ebullient, was silent for a moment, her lips slightly open, exhaling a stream of smoke, eyes focused on the buildings slipping past as the car cut into New Hampshire Avenue, heading towards 21st Street.

'These dreams?' Bob finally asked, as if reluctant to do so. 'That's all they are? Dreams?'

'What do you mean?'

'She dreams of UFOs and men in black?'

'Right.'

'Has she said she's had actual contact? I mean, any experiences *other* than dreams?'

'No,' Dwight replied emphatically. 'Definitely not. I specifically asked her those very questions and she was adamant that she was only having dreams and . . .' He shrugged. 'Feeling . . . *haunted*. She says she *feels* she's being watched, but that's all it is – only a feeling. She thinks the feelings might be related to the dreams – a kind of hangover from them – so she's not worried about that aspect of it. It's the dreams, specifically, that are bothering her. What do *you* think, Bob?'

Bob took his time replying as Thelma, still puffing clouds of cigarette smoke, turned the car into 21st Street.

'Well,' Bob said carefully, 'obviously the dreams are related to all she's heard from you, me and others during our years of UFO investigations – the very investigations that broke up your relationship.'

'Agreed,' Dwight said.

'On the other hand,' Bob continued, speaking even more carefully, 'I'm concerned that she didn't have similar dreams when you and I were actually at ATIC – and, in fact, didn't have them during your three-year separation – but has only had them since you returned home.'

'That's my concern,' Dwight said.

'So given that your reunion has been successful—'

'Which it has been – wonderful for both of us.'

'— I can only say that I'm concerned that your return home and, more unfortunately, my visit to your home, has possibly put you back, as it were, in the spotlight – which would of course include Beth. Jesus H. Christ, I certainly hope not, but that could be the case.'

Dwight felt the darkness moving in to enclose him in daylight. 'You mean the people who stole my UFO photos – the men in black – might be back on my trail?'

'Yes, Dwight, I do.'

'And you think they can affect people's dreams?'

'Affect their minds, yes. And since it's known that I'm now working for APII and have been to see you . . .'

'Oh, my God,' Dwight whispered.

Thelma braked to a halt outside the Hampshire Hotel, smiled as brightly as she could manage, and said: 'Here you are, Dwight. Your overnight stop. I'm going shopping

305

while you book in and then go with Bob to see Dr Epstein. Just remember that after I've been shopping, I'll be coming right back here – so no belly-dancers with walnuts in their navels; no bored business ladies in your bedroom. You can go see Doctor Epstein, then come back here and read the Gideon bible until I return. You got that?'

'Absolutely,' Bob said.

He and Dwight clambered out of the car, removed Dwight's luggage from the trunk, and entered the Hampshire Hotel as Thelma drove away.

Driving back to Carillon Park in Dayton after dropping Dwight off, Beth felt good for five minutes – the frost gleaming everywhere, the sky blue and brilliant, the air sharp and invigorating, Dwight's smile as he waved goodbye before disappearing through the departure gates – but within seconds of leaving the airport, even warmed by Dwight's smile, she was attacked by that dreadful feeling of being . . . *pursued.*

It was a feeling that had dogged her every day since Dwight had, to her unquestioned delight, returned home: the feeling that no matter how good they were together, they were being threatened by something that neither could see or identify. That suspicion, which was based on all the things that had caused Dwight harm before – mainly reports of UFOs and stories about men in black – had led Beth, by night, to a succession of frightening dreams and, by day, to this feeling that she was never alone, that she was being watched somehow.

Now, as she drove along the stretch of road that passed the gas station where Dwight, when drinking heavily, had lived his bachelor life, she recalled the Dwight she had met for the first time as a fellow sophomore at the University of Dayton. Though notably handsome and a member of the baseball team, therefore highly desirable to the other female students, he had been surprisingly reserved and even, as some put it, old-fashioned in his general beliefs, which included respect for his parents, the family unit and the Roman Catholic church, a non-fanatical but genuine patriotism, and the general conviction that a man must do what a man must do. These slightly chauvinistic but otherwise admirably virtuous views he had picked up as one of the four children of Ralph Randall, an aeronautical engineer working as a freelance consultant for some of the many experimental aviation laboratories in the area, and his wife, Barbara, a public relations writer for the Miami Conservancy District flood-control project. Both were church-going Roman Catholics highly active in the community, but possessed of a healthy sense of humour. Beth, whose own Roman Catholic parents shared similar views, was absolutely charmed by Dwight and fell in love with him shortly after meeting him at the college Prom, to which she had been taken by another young man, now scarcely remembered.

Bound by convention and being typical of their times, Beth and Dwight had dated formally, swooned together numerous evenings in Dwight's car, usually at drive-in movies, but did not actually consummate the relationship, agreeing that they should wait until they were married, which they planned to do shortly. This plan, however, was thwarted by the Japanese bombing of Pearl Harbour. Almost immediately after that shocking event, with America entering the war on the side of the Allies, Dwight, who had inherited his father's interest in the aviation history of Dayton, was drafted into the Army Air Force and served as a B-29 bombardier and radar operator, flying to India, China and the Pacific with the original B-29 wing. Returning to college at the end of the war, four years later and a lot more mature, he was convinced that he had found what he wanted to do in life – be a full-time member of the Army Air Force – and so kept up his reserved status, flying as a navigator in an Air Force Reserve Troop Carrier Wing while working day and night to gain his degree in aeronautical engineering. He also married Beth, finally consummating their relationship during their honeymoon at Niagara Falls.

Though their initially shy sexual explorations gradually blossomed into an even more deeply satisfying emotional relationship, Beth knew that Dwight could not forget his wartime experiences and would not be kept at home by love alone. She was therefore not surprised when, after gaining his aeronautical engineering degree, he applied to go back on active duty. Luckily, he was posted straight to the recently formed Air Technical Intelligence Centre, located at Wright-Patterson, right here in Dayton, and he and Beth moved into married quarters on the base.

Driving past the garage where Dwight had worked during his period as an alcoholic 'bachelor' – the darkest days of their marriage – Beth was reminded of how, while loving Dwight, she had resented being an Air Force wife, loathed the insular life of the married community in and around the base, and had made her resentment known to him – too loudly, too frequently. To make matters worse, her resentment had become most vocal even as Dwight was suffering from the problems created by his UFO investigations for ATIC. She therefore blamed herself, at least in part, for his plunge into alcoholic despair and subsequent departure from the Air Force he had once loved so dearly.

Now reunited with him, her residual guilt made her work even harder at keeping him happy and providing a certain degree of protection from the troubles which would, she was convinced, come about from his return to UFO investigations. She also knew, however, that only by returning to that work would Dwight fully regain the pride he had lost by leaving the Air Force.

For that reason, and that reason alone, she had asked his friend and old Air Force buddy, Bob Jackson, to persuade him into going to work as the Dayton stringer for Dr Frederick Epstein's highly respected Aerial Phenomena Investigations Institute, based in Washington DC. It was Beth's belief that the many trips Dwight would be compelled to make to APII, which would also give him the opportunity to visit Bob and Thelma, would be good for him. It was also her belief that Dwight was still obsessed with solving the mystery of why the Air Force was harassing UFO investigators, even to the point of ruining their lives, and that he could only do so through a dedicated, well funded civilian UFO organisation like APII. On both counts, then, she felt that his teaming up with Bob and Dr Epstein, while certainly inviting trouble of one kind, would in the end be good for him. Whether right or wrong in that assumption, it was a chance they would both have to take.

So thinking, Beth glanced out of the open window of the car . . . and saw that she was still passing the garage where Dwight used to work.

Startled, she then realised that she was not in fact driving, but had pulled into the side of the road and parked, almost opposite the garage in this otherwise desolate stretch of road. Not remembering having done so, she felt disorientated and checked the time on her wristwatch.

The hands had stopped moving.

Shocked, suddenly frightened, she glanced left and right, behind the car, to the front, hardly knowing what she was looking for. The fields on both sides were empty, as was the road front and rear, but Beth was convinced that something was nearby and was exerting some kind of force against her.

She tried the door of the car, but found that it was jammed. When she tried turning on the ignition, the car would not start.

Trapped, feeling oddly violated, she just sat there, gazing about her, trying to see what it was that she could feel as an invisible . . . *presence*.

Nothing unusual was out there – only the flat fields, the straight, empty road, and the garage across the road.

There was something strange about the garage. Its front door was open, swinging in and out with the wind, and banging repeatedly against its frame. There was no sign of the new owner, Frank Bancroft, neither inside at the cash register nor outside by the gas pumps. Beth thought that was odd.

Something else was odd . . . When she looked more carefully, she noticed that the tall grass around the garage was quivering and being bent as if by the wind – but in an unnatural manner. Behind and at both sides of the garage, the tall grass of the fields was virtually motionless, as if no wind was blowing there. The grass was only bending in a long, narrow line that formed an immense semi-circle, enclosing the garage and stopping at the verge where the field met the tarmac road.

At least Beth thought it stopped there . . . until she noticed that the dust on the road was also being whipped up – again, only in a fine line that ran across the road to the front and rear of her car, the same distance away in both directions, about one hundred and seventy-five feet in both instances. Within and outside those two fine lines of spiralling dust, no dust or debris was stirring.

Feeling increasingly unreal and frightened, Beth glanced in the opposite direction, at the fields on the other side of the road – the side she was parked on – and saw that the two lines of dust curved into that field where the grass was also bent and quivering, forming another large arc that ended on both sides by the road.

The lines of dust across the road, in front of, and behind, the car joined the two arcs of bent, quivering grass to form an immense circle that enclosed the car and garage. Outside that circle, the grass was not moving at all.

Even as Beth studied that huge circle, she saw the tips of the grass slowly turning black and smoking a little. The car suddenly started shaking, as if on a conveyor belt. Startled, Beth grabbed hold of the steering wheel. The car continued shaking – even though it was not moving – and Beth watched, disbelieving, as the bent, quivering grass turned blacker and formed a great dark circle covered in smoke. Just as she thought the smouldering grass was about to burst into flames, it crumpled into black powder and the smoke started drifting away. Soon there was nothing but a great circle formed by the ashes of grass, dead and charred black.

The car stopped its unnatural shaking and the locks, which had been jammed in the closed position, suddenly clicked free.

When Beth turned the key in the ignition, the engine kicked into life instantly.

Impelled by a combination of terror and curiosity, Beth turned the engine off, then opened the door and leaned out of the car to glance along the road in both directions. No other cars were approaching and the road was completely empty, running as straight as an arrow under a sky filling up with low clouds.

Looking across the road, Beth saw that the door of the garage had stopped its banging, though it was now hanging open and there was still no sign of Frank Bancroft.

Taking a deep breath, she looked directly above the car. At first she saw nothing but the gathering clouds, pregnant with rain . . . Then, above the clouds, she saw what looked like a circular light, about the size of a dime but shrinking rapidly, though still casting its striations through the clouds. Even as Beth studied that light, trying to ascertain if it was a separate entity or merely an illusion caused by a combination of cloud and striated sunlight, it shrank to no more than a gleaming speck, then abruptly blinked out.

Without thinking, though with racing heart, Beth clambered out of her car and crossed the road to the forecourt of Frank Bancroft's garage, where Dwight had once lived and worked. When she had passed the gas pumps and was approaching the open front door of the shop, she slowed down, feeling more frightened than ever by the unnatural silence and realising that sweat was pouring down her face.

Stopping by the open door, she glanced up at the sky again, checking that the strange, circular light had indeed disappeared. Satisfied that it had, she glanced across the flat field and saw that the great circle of black ash was still clearly visible.

Shivering, though sweaty and flushed with dread, Beth reached the open door and glanced tentatively into the shop, scanning the shadowy space behind the cash register for a sign of Frank. He was nowhere to be seen. The shop, though empty, seemed untouched.

With her heart now racing so fast she thought it would burst, Beth entered the shop and glanced about her. All the stock on the shelves – cans of oil, cleaning solvents, light bulbs, tools, maps, floor mats, seat coverings and other automobile and driver products – was as it should have been. The cash register, Beth noticed, was firmly closed.

No sign, then, of a hold-up.

Relieved just a little, but with her heart still racing, Beth advanced farther into the shop and stepped around the far edge of the counter containing the cash register.

There she gasped instinctively and froze in horror.

Frank Bancroft had fallen out of his chair and was lying flat on his back, but in a dreadfully contorted position and with his eyes wide and staring at something that had clearly terrified him. He had foamed at the mouth, evacuated his bowels, and fallen out of his chair as he collapsed.

Beth didn't need a doctor to tell her what had happened. This man had died of a heart attack brought on by terror.

Now terrified herself, Beth gasped, covered her mouth with her hand, then ran back to her car. She turned on the engine, which started up with no trouble, and raced on along the road, not stopping until she came to her local police station, near Carillon Park. There she informed the police about Frank Bancroft's death. She did not tell them about her blackout, the stopping of her wristwatch, the malfunctioning of her car, nor of that great circle of black ash. Convinced that they would think she had gone mad, she decided to keep her mouth shut and only relate the details concerning her finding of Frank Bancroft's dead body.

When the report was completed and the police had made
arrangements to have the body collected and the garage
closed up, Beth left the station and drove on home. She
was still terrified.

Chapter Twenty-Seven

Once booked into the Hampshire Hotel, downtown, Dwight and Bob walked the short distance along 21st Street to the Aerial Phenomena Investigations Institute – the same modest, Federal-styled building located just off Pennsylvania Avenue where, six years ago, Dwight had given a deep background interview to the well-known astronomer and astrophysicist, Dr Frederick Epstein, Fellow of the Royal Astronomical Society, member of the American Association for the Advancement of Science (AAAS), and now the dedicated, hard-working head of APII.

Epstein, he noted, hadn't changed much in the intervening years. Back in 1953, because of his rather old-fashioned prematurely greying Vandyke beard, he'd looked older than his age; now, though still only forty-seven, but with his beard even greyer, he looked ten years older than that. Nevertheless, he had good-natured, distinguished features, lively hazel eyes, a ready smile, and a tendency to stroke his beard when thinking. Slightly dishevelled, he seemed right at home in an office cluttered with filing cabinets, loose files, heaped reports, old newspapers, magazines and photographs of UFOs.

The walls, also, were covered in photographs of UFOs, as well as with a lot of poster-sized charts. One showed the most commonly reported UFO shapes, grouped into flat discs, domed discs, Saturn or double-domed discs, hemispherical discs, flattened spheres, spherical, elliptical, triangular and cylindrical. Another chart was broken into two illustrated sections, one showing the most commonly reported UFO formations, the other showing UFO manoeuvres, both singly and in formation. Other charts showed the worldwide locations and flight directions of the major UFO waves from 1896 to the present; major UFO events in the United States and overseas; the major areas of alleged magnetic deviation around the world, including the North and South Poles; and the names, addresses, and telephone numbers of the world's major civilian UFO organisations.

'A major problem we're having,' Epstein was saying as Dwight removed his distracted gaze from the wall charts, 'is that the checking of UFO reports is being made more difficult by the man-made satellites circling the earth in increasing numbers and now, in the case of the unmanned Soviet *Lunik*, passing the Moon to go into orbit around the sun.'

'Which it did only yesterday,' Bob reminded them as he unwrapped a stick of gum and popped it into his mouth.

'Correct,' Epstein said, stroking his beard and looking distracted. 'For that very reason, Dwight, I'm really glad you're considering getting back into this business. We could certainly do with all the expert help we can get. You remember the Levelland sightings?'

'Yep,' Dwight said, feeling comfortable in this company, particularly since Bob Jackson had been indirectly responsible for reuniting him with Beth and Nichola, thus giving him back his sense of purpose. 'Texas. November 1957. The sightings caused quite a stir.'

'Correct,' Epstein said, picking a report off his desk and studying it thoughtfully. 'I've been studying this case in detail, Dwight, so let me refresh your memory by reading from my completed report.'

As Epstein read from the report, it all came back to Dwight. The events in Levelland, Texas, had formed the spectacular climax to the biggest year in UFO reports since 1952. The sightings had begun at 11.00 p.m. on November

2 and ended at 2.00 a.m., the following morning. All the reports were of glowing, yellow-white, torpedo- or egg-shaped objects, approximately seventy-five to 200 feet long or in diameter, that had landed on the roads around Levelland, forcing oncoming cars to brake, stopping their ignitions and emitting quite a bit of heat before taking off again, after which the cars' ignitions had restarted.

The first sighting was at 11.00 p.m. on the night of November 2, just north of Levelland, when one of the objects flew towards the automobile of two witnesses, causing the motor and lights to fail. When the witnesses got out of the vehicle to view the object more clearly, it came so close they were forced to hit the ground. Considerable heat was felt as the object passed over them. When the object left the area, the automobile's ignition and lights came on again.

An hour later, at midnight, a driver four miles east of Levelland was stopped by a brightly glowing, egg-shaped object, about two hundred feet in diameter, that was resting in the middle of the road. As the driver approached the object, his car's engine and lights failed. When the object took off, rising vertically to a height of approximately 200 feet, then shooting off rapidly, the witness's car started up again.

Five minutes later, another witness, driving eleven miles north of Levelland, called the police to report having exactly the same kind of sighting and experience.

Five minutes after midnight, a witness driving nine miles east of Levelland got out of his car when the engine and lights failed. He was about to look under the hood when he saw an egg-shaped object sitting on the road ahead. He described it as about seventy-five to one hundred feet wide, made of what looked like aluminium, and giving off a white glow with a greenish tint. Frightened, he got back into his car and watched the object for about five minutes, after which it took off and disappeared. When it did so, the witness's car started up again.

Fifteen minutes later, nine miles north of Levelland, another car stalled as it approached a similar object sitting on a dirt road. When the object ascended vertically to an altitude of about three hundred feet, then shot off and disappeared, the car's engine and lights started up again.

After this report, Levelland Patrolman A. J. Fowler sent two deputies out to investigate. They reported seeing bright lights in the sky, but had no engine problems. However, several minutes after they had called in, a witness driving just west of town saw a 'large orange ball of fire' coming towards him. It settled on the highway, about a quarter of a mile ahead. When he approached it, his car's engine and lights failed. When the object ascended a few minutes later, the car started up again.

Thirty minutes later, a truck driver informed the police that as he was driving northeast of Levelland, his truck engine and headlights failed when he came to within two hundred feet of a two hundred-foot wide, brilliantly glowing, egg-shaped object on the road ahead. When he got out of his truck to investigate, the object shot up vertically with a roar and flew away. The truck's ignition and lights then came back on.

By this time, other deputies in the area had received similar reports and were out on the roads, frantically investigating. While driving about five miles outside the city, a sheriff and his deputy saw a 'streak of light' with a 'reddish glow' on the highway about three or four hundred yards ahead, lighting up the whole area. A few miles behind the sheriff and deputy, on the same road, two patrolmen saw a 'strange looking flash' that appeared to be close to the ground about a mile in front of them. The last sighting of the evening was by another police constable, who saw an object travelling so fast it looked like no more than 'a flash of light' shooting from east to west.

'In other words,' Epstein now summarised from his own report, 'twelve drivers, including police patrolmen, reported seeing an object and three more reported an unusual flash

317

– all in a single, three-hour period covering the midnight of November second and third.'

'Forming a kind of grand climax to the biggest UFO flap since 1952,' Bob picked up, 'the sightings caused the Air Force a lot of embarrassment. They only investigated the affair days after it had happened, only sent one man to do the job, failed to interview nine of the fifteen witnesses, and stated falsely that lightning had been in the area at the time of the sightings. Under pressure from the public, the assistant secretary of defence insisted that ATIC submit a preliminary analysis to the press. When Captain George Gregory – head of our once beloved, now relatively useless Project Blue Book – did so, he claimed that the evidence was too limited for proper investigation, that only three witnesses could be located, and that contrary to reports, the object, or objects, had only been visible for a few seconds. He also reiterated that the sightings had been caused by lightning and storm conditions in the area – none of which were actually present at the time. Nevertheless, the Air Force's final report blamed the sightings on unusual weather phenomenon of electrical nature, suggesting ball lightning or St Elmo's Fire, and again dragged up stormy conditions, including the non-existent mist, rain, thunderstorms and lightning. With the aid of Donald Menzel, they then tried to blame the recent wave of UFO sightings, including the Levelland affair, on the launching of the second Russian Sputnik. However, when this failed to wash, the public uproar became so loud that the National Investigations Committee on Aerial Phenomena, or NICAP, was able to push for congressional hearings.'

'Yeah, I read about that,' Dwight said, 'but I haven't heard much about the hearings since then.'

'No, you wouldn't have,' Bob informed him. 'In August last year, John McCormack's House Sub-Committee on Atmospheric Phenomena requested a week-long hearing in closed, secret session, but any hope that the hearing would be a fair one was destroyed when the House Sub-

Committee decided to take no further interest in the matter.'

'However, what we discovered right here at APII,' Epstein interjected, 'has given us even more cause for concern. Last December, the Air Force published a staff study that came down heavily on the three major civilian UFO groups, accusing us of being biased and sensationalist. To make matters worse, we also learned that the Robertson Panel, in making their recommendations back in 1953 regarding civilian UFO groups, had used the chilling phrase . . .' Epstein paused for a moment to pick up another much thumbed sheet from his desk and read from it. ' "The apparent irresponsibility and the possible use of such groups for subversive purposes should be kept in mind." ' He dropped the sheet back on the desk as if it was contaminating his fingers. 'We've also discovered recently that the FBI and the CIA are keeping extensive records on people involved in UFO investigations, including the members of this very organisation. Should you be considering joining us, I feel it's only fair that you should know this. You've already had a lot of trouble with the Air Force; you'll get more if you join us.'

Recalling his own dire experience with the Air Force, due to his involvement with UFO research, Dwight knew exactly what Epstein meant. Nevertheless, he said, 'I'm willing to take that chance. Now that Bob's got me interested again, I won't rest until I find out why the Air Force, which so clearly was concerned about UFOs when we were with Project Blue Book, went to such lengths to frustrate our investigations and turn Project Blue Book into a farce. It was, and remains, a contradiction that still keeps me awake at nights.'

'That's exactly why we want you,' Epstein said, standing up and coming around his desk to shake Dwight's hand again. 'Welcome aboard.'

Chapter Twenty-Eight

Even before opening his eyes in his bed in his suite of rooms near the summit of the mountain in Antarctica, Wilson recalled his dream and realised that it had *not* been a dream, but a powerfully vivid, telepathic exploration of his colony.

Having practised meditation and astral projection for years, he had at last developed the ability to see with his 'inner eye'. This morning, in a state of half sleep, just before awakening properly, he had roamed from this room near the summit, down through the hacked-out interior of the mountain to the various layers of the colony: the guard rooms just below him, then the computer rooms; then, further down, the laboratories and surgeries, the machine-shops and storage rooms; then the slave accommodations, dining rooms and ablutions; and finally, at the very bottom of the mountain, the great landing pads and repair shops for the flying saucers. He had made that journey in his mind, seeing everything clearly.

Even as his body was rotting with age, with its various organs being replaced one by one, his Extra-Sensory Perception, practised daily for about seventy years, was increasing dramatically.

Opening his eyes, he gazed through the panoramic windows of his suite at the vast, snow-covered wastelands of the Antarctic. All white. Everything. Except for the sky. The gleaming mountains and valleys stretched out to where that sheet of sheer blue met the white horizon, though that, too, was often rendered a silvery white by wind-swept snow and frost. Light. Lots of light. A unique and dazzling vision. The light flashed off the mountain peaks and glaciers as snow broke up, rolled down the mountain sides, or drifted like powder on the wind, reflecting and bending the rays of the dazzling sun. The Antarctic was vast, supremely beautiful and empty. There were no people out there. No noise. It was the end of the world.

Sitting up in bed, Wilson glanced around the bedroom. It was a functional room with walls of pine-board, clothes closets and a couple of chests of drawers. There were no paintings on the walls, no decorations or ornaments of any kind. There was, however, a series of TV monitor screens banked along one wall and controlled from the control panel on his bedside cabinet. Though Wilson was now able to use his ESP to scan the colony, he could more easily do so by means of the spy cameras located in most areas of the underground complex and transmitting back to the TV monitors in his bedroom and study.

Switching on the monitors, as he did every morning before getting out of bed, he used his hand-control to flick from one screen to the other and check that everything was in order: the great saucers on their landing pads in the cavernous space hacked out of the rock of the mountain; the massive workshops where the saucers were constructed; the laboratories where surgical experiments were conducted on human beings and animals, some dead, others alive; the storage rooms for the collection of frozen human heads, limbs and organs; the slave accommodations where the nightshift workers were sleeping; and the dormitory-styled quarters for the comfort girls. Everywhere he checked, he saw hundreds of people at work, including white-coated scientists, technicians and surgeons; slave workers in grey coveralls; and the flying-saucer pilots in their black flying suits – all illuminated in the arc lights powered by self-charging generators and fixed high on the walls of solid rock, as were the spy cameras. The underground colony was a hive of activity and everything seemed in order.

Satisfied, Wilson slipped out of bed and padded on bare feet into the adjoining bathroom where he attended to his toilet, then had an invigorating cold shower. After drying himself, he put on a silk dressing gown and returned to the bedroom where he sat on the bed, again facing the panoramic window. Telephoning through to the quarters of the comfort girls, he asked the matron to send him one trained in electronic stimulation. When the matron confirmed that she would do so, Wilson dropped the phone back on its cradle and waited patiently.

The girl arrived shortly after, entering via the elevator in the study and coming into the bedroom from there. Wilson's taste in comfort girls changed from time to time – sometimes he liked Eurasians, other times black, then some of the Ache women sent from Paraguay by Ernst Stoll – but his present taste was for slim white girls, preferably no younger than eighteen and no older then twenty. The girl who entered fitted the bill exactly, being slim, blonde, eighteen years old, and dressed in a long flowing robe that emphasized every curve of her body with each step she made. Though subdued with a constant supply of Valium and other sedatives, she was still a little nervous of Wilson and kept her head bowed.

'Your name?' Wilson asked.

'Clare Collins.'

'Where are you from?'

'Albuquerque, New Mexico.'

'When were you abducted?'

'I think about eighteen months ago.'

'You don't know the precise date?'

'No, sir, I've forgotten.'

'Have you forgotten a lot about your previous life?'

'Yes, sir, a lot.'

'Forgetting more every day?'

'Yes, sir.'

'Good. Soon you won't remember a thing about it. Then

you can come off sedation. Do you know what I want?'

'Matron said the stimulator.'

'That's correct. You've used one before?'

'Yes, sir.'

'On me?'

'No, sir. On some others. This is my first time up here.'

'Take your robe off,' Wilson said.

The girl nodded, then took hold of the hem of her garment to tug it up her beautifully shaped legs, then off her perfect body, and finally over her head. Letting the garment fall to the floor, she stood there with her hands by her sides and her head slightly lowered. She had long legs, broad hips, a slim waist and firm, perfect breasts. Her skin, which had been suntanned when she was abducted, was now milky white.

Seeing her, Wilson wanted her but could do little about it because he could no longer obtain an erection without special help. Nevertheless, for the good of his mental health he required sensual stimulation and the sight of this beautiful, naked girl was an aid in obtaining it.

'The stimulator is in there,' he said, pointing to a closet. 'Bring it out and proceed.'

Opening the closet door, the naked girl wheeled out a mobile electronic console. After pushing it to the side of the bed, she raised its lid and lay it backward until it formed a tray. Withdrawing vibrating pads and electrodes fixed to cables from inside the console, she laid them side by side on the tray. She then glanced at Wilson, received his nod of consent, and reached out to untie the belt of his dressing gown. After slowly drawing the robe off his shoulders and down his body, she started when she saw the many lengthy scars crisscrossing his flesh – the visible signs of his many surgical operations.

'Don't worry,' Wilson reassured her. 'None of them hurt.'

Without thinking, he lightly touched the most recent scar, which ran across his left breast. This was from an operation to replace his old piezoelectric crystal pacemaker with a new model. Eventually, so he hoped, he would have a pacemaker with a plutonium power source, thereby weighing practically nothing and lasting a lot longer, but a successful model had not yet been developed.

The girl nodded, relieved. 'You want oil, sir?'

'Yes,' Wilson said, stretching out on his back to let her commence.

She poured slightly heated olive oil onto her hands, then rubbed it into his skin, starting with his chest, moving down to his stomach, then sliding her fingers through his pubic hair and around his penis. Once down there, she rubbed the oil in around his scrotum, onto his inner thighs, then around his hips, back over his belly and down again to the genital area. Taking his penis in her oil-soaked right hand, she massaged it slowly, expertly, managing to raise it a little.

Watching her with his unblinking gaze, taking in the rise and fall of her breasts, the full nipples, the flat belly running down to blonde pubic hair between perfectly formed, exquisitely smooth thighs, he recalled how, even in adolescence, though helplessly aroused by sexual thoughts and feelings, he had translated his desire into a set of equations that enabled him to disassociate himself from the fallacy of romantic love and treat sex as a physiological necessity, like shitting or pissing. Now, even as his 'comfort girl', the abducted beauty Clare Collins, released his half-erection from her oil-soaked fingers and instead used the electric vibrating pads on the most erogenous parts of his body, he was caught between his human need to surrender to pure sensual feeling and his intellectual's need to transcend those same feelings and remain in control.

Yet sensual feeling, he knew, was inextricably linked to mental health and so, when the comfort girl dabbed paste on his temples and fixed electrodes to him, he closed his eyes, shutting out the real woman, and let himself surrender to the voluptuous visions created by the stimulator. The

Theta rhythms being passed through his brain at a rate of four cycles per second altered his mood and, in conjunction with the comfort girl's expert massaging, both with her oil-soaked fingers and the exquisitely soft vibrating pads, replaced his icy intellectualism with temporary desire. As the Theta rhythms increased gradually to a rate of seven cycles per second, filling his head with voluptuous visions worthy of an adolescent, the comfort girl massaged his stomach, loins and inner thighs with the vibrating pads, manipulated his hardening penis with her oil-soaked fingers and finally, when she sensed that he was coming, covered him with her mouth and let him come into her. Without sex, or at least without penetration, Wilson shuddered, orgasmed, found physical release and was returned to the shelter of his intellectual concerns, above petty desires.

Opening his eyes, he watched the comfort girl wiping her lips dry with a tissue, turning off the vibrating pads and removing the electrodes from his temples. Her naked body now seemed offensive to him and he wanted no part of it.

'Put your robe on immediately,' he told her, 'then return the stimulator to the closet and take your leave.'

'Yes, sir. Thank you, sir.'

Backing away from him and keeping her head bowed, the girl put her robe back on, returned the electronic console to the closet, then left the bedroom. Wilson heard her crossing the lounge. He waited until the doors of the elevator had opened and closed, then he put on his dressing gown and picked up the phone to order breakfast.

'I'll have a fruit and nut cereal,' he said. 'And a glass of white wine. Very dry. Very cold.'

Wilson had one glass of dry, white wine with every frugal meal of his day, including breakfast. Apart from those three glasses of wine, he did not partake of alcohol. Nor did he eat meat or fish.

His breakfast was delivered by an Ache Indian who had been lobotomized to render him passive, totally obedient and easily trained. He was dressed in a pair of grey coveralls and soft felt slippers. Knowing better than to speak to Wilson, he simply placed the tray on a table that wheeled over the bed – a steel-framed hospital serving table – then he left the suite and took the elevator back down to the slave quarters located near the bottom of the mountain.

When the waiter had departed, Wilson had his breakfast while watching the world news on his satellite-dish TV receivers. He flicked repeatedly from one screen to another, one country to another, one news item to another, impatient with the triviality of human concerns and their idiotic conflicts, most of which were based on primitive notions of blood or ideology.

Finishing his frugal breakfast, he pushed the wheeled table back along the bed, then swung his feet to the floor, shucked off his dressing gown, and proceeded to dress in his standard working outfit of black coveralls. Leaving the bedroom, he passed through his immense, dome-shaped steel-and-concrete study, which also offered a stupendous view of the Antarctic, and took the elevator down to the parapsychological laboratories.

Like most other experimental areas of the underground colony, the laboratories had been hacked out of the interior of the mountain, with the exposed rock face covered in black pitch. Nevertheless, the irregular shape of the walls gave an even more cavernous and gloomy appearance to them, only slightly relieved by the arc lights powered by self-charging generators and fixed high above the stone-flagged floors. Though the laboratories were heated by phase-change solar-heat pumps located outside the mountain, the irregular walls of pitch-covered rock made it look colder than it was.

While not quite as horrific as the laboratories where Doctors King and Eckhardt kept their Frankenstein's collection of severed human heads, limbs and internal organs, the parapsychological laboratory now contained its fair share of similar horrors, including electric chairs with buckled straps on the arms and head-braces with microphones, used for experiments with infrasounds that could cause haemorrhaging from the eyes, ears and nose, as well as inducing cardiac arrest or bursting the blood vessels of the brain, leading to madness or death; water tanks used for sensory-deprivation experiments on human subjects; and small, dark cells with leaded-steel doors, used for a combination of sensory-deprivation experiments and even more hideous experiments with strobe lights flickering at a rate that could cause drowsiness, nausea, acute depression or fear, absolute obedience, uncontrollable violence and epileptic seizures.

The most notable of the horrors in this laboratory, however, was the severed human head of the unfortunate Marlon Clarke which, almost thirteen years after Clarke's abduction, was still functioning in an inhuman way with the aid of a special stereotaxic skullcap and numerous electronic hairpin implants. At one stage Clarke's severed head, then kept in a glass casing with an inner temperature reduced to just above the point of freezing, had been recording dying brain-waves on the EEG machine to which it had been wired. However, before those brain-waves died out completely, Dr King had used a combination of electronic implantation and injections of chemicals to revitalise them enough to keep the brain functioning.

By that time, Clarke's brain, though certainly functioning again, was doing so in an insane, chaotic manner, but eventually, when attached by the severed neck to a steel-clamp base containing artificial blood vessels and wired to the still beating human heart in a temperature-controlled glass case nearby, as well as to a pair of amputated hands, it had been able to manipulate the latter in a crude fashion, making the fingers open and close as the hands crawled across the table like large, drunken spiders.

Since then, further advances had been made and now the jaw, mouth and nose of the severed head had been removed and replaced with a metal prosthetic, the neck of which was attached by a combination of electric wiring and artificial blood vessels to the body of a small Ache Indian whose head and hands had been surgically removed, the former to be replaced with Clarke's head, the latter to be replaced with myoelectric hands that looked like steel claws.

Clarke's eyes, which once had been filled with unutterable incomprehension and dread, were now unseeing and could only be revitalised by the carefully controlled input from the electronic implants of his stereotaxic skullcap. With his metal claws, metal lower-face prosthetic and bizarre metal skullcap, the formerly normal human being looked like a monstrous creature from outer space.

'He seems pacified at last,' Wilson said, speaking fluent Russian, to the head of the laboratory, Dr Nikoloi Tugarinov, world-famous physiologist and former Vice President of the Academy of Sciences of the USSR. Listed officially in the Soviet Union as 'missing', Tugarinov had actually been abducted by one of Wilson's saucer teams, 'indoctrinated' with a combination of drug therapy and hypnotic suggestion that did not otherwise impair his faculties, and then became a willing – or, rather, helplessly obedient – member of the parapsychological laboratory, working hand-in-glove with Doctors King and Eckhardt in the adjoining laboratories, where the development of cyborgs and much larger Cybernetic Anthropomorphous Machine Systems, or CAMS, was racing ahead, regardless of the cost in human suffering.

'Yes,' Tugarinov confirmed, also speaking Russian. 'As you know, Dr King's main problem was not in perfecting the psychophysical interaction between head and body, but in somehow retaining the orderly functioning of the severed head – given that it was in a state of delirium, or insanity, caused by disbelief and trauma. Having revitalised the head's dying brain-waves, which potentially opened the brain up again to shock and insanity, we solved the problem by inducing amnesia with a combination of chemicals and electric stimulation. Hideous though Mr Clarke now looks, he has no recollection of himself ever looking any different and, indeed, thinks of himself as being perfectly normal. Mr Clarke is now a prototype cyborg who, when activated, will have no recollections of his former life, will therefore think of his controller as a god, and subsequently will do exactly what he is told.'

'Excellent,' Wilson said. 'But his focus seems turned inward at the moment. What's happening to him?'

'Amazing,' Dr Tugarinov replied. 'What we are finding through the parapsychological experiments relating to cyborg mentality is that being deprived of most of their senses – the loss of a sense of smell because of the lower-face prosthetic; the breathing with lungs created artificially to enable them to withstand the extreme pressures of outer space or the sea bed; the inability to speak because of the severing of their vocal cords; and the general loss of their past memories and emotions – this particular form of deprivation has heightened their mental processes in another manner, enabling them to communicate telepathically, often over very great distances. Clarke appears to be focused inward at the moment because he's been programmed to cast his thoughts elsewhere.'

'I've developed such talents myself,' Wilson reminded him, 'by the ruthless suppression of all redundant emotion and feelings.'

'True, but look!' Dr Tugarinov pointed up at a row of monitor screens that were tilted just above the encased, severed head of the surgically mutated, partial cyborg, Marlon Clarke. The screens showed a series of different images, cloudy but distinct enough, of barbed-wire fences, military installations, aircraft on the ground or in flight, and long-distance views of immense parabolic radar dishes. They were, as Wilson knew, all located in the United States, mostly military establishments chosen by Clarke's 'controller', Dr Tugarinov, and being telepathically relayed to the TV monitors wired up to the cyborg's stereotaxic skullcap and keyed into a highly advanced computer.

In the West, electronic miniaturisation with an integrated circuit using a single tiny chip of silicon had been demonstrated for the first time the previous year, but Wilson's scientists, unrestrained in every way, were already well advanced in computer technology and had, in fact, used their first crude silicon chips as part of their secret barter with the US.

'I know what you're showing me,' Wilson said. 'But what's so special this time?'

'Watch closely,' Tugarinov said, using the computer keyboard to increase or decrease the basic rhythmic patterns of Marlon Clarke's brain while flooding it with other impulses from the implants of the stereotaxic skullcap. The eyes in the severed head now attached by the neck to a cyborg torso – half man, half machine – suddenly widened, moved left and right above the hideous metal lower-face prosthetic, then seemed to lose focus as the mental impulses thus agitated leaped over time and space. The screens above Clarke's head, which had previously shown a series of murky monochrome images, now clarified to show what Wilson recognised instantly as first the exterior, then the interior, of one of his own large flying saucers. This, however, dissolved almost immediately and was replaced by the image of a smaller, less sophisticated saucer ascending vertically from what appeared to be part of the White Sands Proving Ground.

Surprised, Wilson practically stood on tip-toe to check the images more clearly. The flying saucer on the screen wobbled in an ungainly manner from left to right, trying to find its centre of gravity, then it ascended vertically, languidly, above the doors of what were plainly aircraft hangars. Soon it passed off the monitors, leaving only the ghostly image of the aircraft hangars, beyond which was a barbed wire fence and a vast stretch of desert.

'That wasn't one of our saucers,' Wilson said. 'Is that

the White Sands Proving Ground?'

'Yes, sir.'

'So what's so unusual about this transmission? We've managed to project to there before.'

'I didn't programme Clarke to telepathically leap to that area. I programmed him to track one of our own saucer flights – which you saw – and then he tuned in by himself to that new image – or, to be more precise, someone tuned in to *him*.'

'So where are the images coming from?'

'Please observe. I am going to key in a non-verbal request to Clarke to identify the source of his present images. Though unable to speak, he can show you on the screen just what's going on.'

Tugarinov tapped his request into the computer keyboard, then stepped back and waited. After what seemed like a long time, but was actually less than a minute, a murky image of a city skyline appeared on the monitor screens.

'I recognise it,' Wilson said. 'Portland, Maine.'

Once Wilson had identified the location, Tugarinov tapped it into the computer to let the cyborg, Clarke, know that they had received the information. When he had done so, the image changed to an apartment block in the same city, then this dissolved to the inside of an apartment in the same building. A middle-aged woman with black hair and a look of pain on her face was tossing and turning on her bed. There were tablets on her bedside cabinet and she appeared to be having a migraine.

'She's in a telepathic trance,' Wilson said.

'Yes. And she's obviously suffering severe stress. That suggests she's tuned in accidentally to someone else, somewhere else. We have to know who and where that source is.'

Tugarinov keyed another request into the keyboard and watched as Marlon Clarke's eyes, framed between the metal band of the stereotaxic skullcap and the top of the metallic lower-face prosthetic, turned left and right, desperately

331

searching for something, then rolled up and went out of focus again, like the eyes of someone lost in their own thoughts.

On the monitor screens above, the woman from Maine gradually faded out and was replaced by a repeat of the crude flying saucer ascending above the aircraft hangars of what was clearly a US Air Force or Navy aeronautical establishment in the arid wasteland of the White Sands Proving Ground.

'Back where we started,' Wilson said impatiently.

'No, wait,' Tugarinov said, tapping a few more instructions into the computer keyboard. 'He'll now find the source for us.'

In less than a minute, the aircraft hangars dissolved and were replaced by the exterior of a clapboard building that had barbed-wire fences visible beyond it and was guarded by US Army Air Force soldiers. A closer image of the same building showed signs clearly marked 'US Air Force' and 'Top Secret'. These signs dissolved to make way for an image of a man wearing army dungarees sitting on a chair in a booth, wearing earphones and either writing notes or drawing sketches of what he was seeing.

The telepathic communication was not sharp or close enough to reveal what those drawings showed, but Wilson had no doubts at all.

'That man is an ESP-trained soldier tuning into the US-Canadian flying saucer we just saw taking off from the White Sands Proving Ground. As that building, also, is in the White Sands Proving Ground, he obviously can't transmit that far yet and is practising on reasonably local subjects. The woman from Portland, Maine, is obviously a psychic who tuned in accidentally to him, just as our cyborg picked up on her thoughts, confusing the US-Canadian saucer for the one he was tracking – namely, our own.'

'The accident doesn't matter,' Tugarinov said. 'What matters is that the Americans, like my Russian friends in the Parapsychology Laboratory of the University of

Leningrad, are now experimenting with ESP.'

'Correct,' Wilson said. 'They thought they could keep it secret, but there are no secrets any more. I think my American friends might need another hard lesson, so keep monitoring that woman from Portland, Maine.'

'Yes, sir,' Tugarinov said.

Wilson glanced briefly at the hideous, surgically mutated head of the former Marlon Clarke, then nodded approvingly at Dr Tugarinov and left the laboratory.

Chapter Twenty-Nine

For the first six months of 1959, Dwight commuted on a regular basis between Dayton, Ohio, and Washington DC, investigating UFO sightings in the former and personally delivering his own reports to Dr Frederick Epstein's Aerial Phenomena Investigations Institute in the latter. As Beth had anticipated, the frequent trips to the Capital were a welcome break from the previous monotony of his life in Dayton and rendered even more appealing because they offered him frequent contact with Bob and Thelma Jackson, both resident in Greenbelt, where Bob had gone to work after leaving the Air Force and before joining APII. When not at APII, he had many a good lunch or evening with Bob and Thelma, who had lost neither their good humour nor their warmth.

Returning to the investigation of UFO sightings in Dayton was indeed an experience for Dwight, not only because of his ongoing fascination with the subject and the many people he was meeting again, but even more so because of his shock at the lack of cooperation he found from his old friends at Wright-Patterson Air Force Base. Not that there were, in truth, many old friends left there, since most had been transferred out of ATIC even before his departure. Nevertheless, the few still working there were singularly unhelpful, claiming that the Air Force no longer had any interest in the matter and viewed civilian investigators as a nuisance.

Apart from those who worked for Dr Epstein's APII, the

other reliable civilian investigators came from the many different UFO organisations now scattered widely across the whole country. The most notable of these was the National Investigations Committee on Aerial Phenomena (NICAP), founded in 1956, headed by former Marine Corps Major Donald Keyhoe, and also located in Washington DC. Though these two major Washington organisations frequently were in competition with one another, it was from NICAP that Dwight had gotten a lot of the mainly young, sometimes eccentric, but always lively UFO investigators who had made his life more interesting during the past six months.

They had a language all their own, being fond of the use of acronyms such as CE1 (Close Encounters of the First Kind), being phenomena that cause a transient effect on the witness, such as time loss or radio interference; CE2 (Close Encounters of the Second Kind), phenomena that cause effects that are semi-permanent and observable by those who did *not* share the experience; CE3 (Close Encounters of the Third Kind), phenomena that include animate entities such as extraterrestrials or robotic crew members; and CE4 (Close Encounters of the Fourth Kind), events that cause the witness, or witnesses, to have unnatural or seemingly impossible experiences, such as psychic interaction, levitation and paralysis; or which affect the witness, mentally or physically, for a long time after the event occurs.

Spouting such scientific-sounding phrases and armed with survey maps, binoculars, theodolites, tape recorders, cameras, notebooks, drawing pads, pencils and pens, these enthusiasts swarmed across the country, mostly to desolate wastelands such as those in New Mexico and Arizona, to visit the site of a UFO sighting and take measurements and photographs; interview witnesses, getting written statements and sketches from them; contact weather centres to check for temperature inversions or other atmospheric phenomena that could be misinterpreted as

UFOs; check local civilian and military airports for information regarding general air traffic and weather balloon launches; and approach local police stations for facts regarding related sightings or witnesses not already interviewed. Considered by many, especially those in authority, to be a great nuisance, they did in fact turn many a UFO (Unidentified Flying Object) into an IFO (Identified Flying Object) while also supplying invaluable written and visual material to the major civilian UFO organisations.

Apart from their contribution to APII, Dwight enjoyed meeting them because so many of them were young, optimistic and enthusiastic in a manner that was both contagious and encouraging.

He needed the encouragement because Beth had told him about her inexplicable blackout and CE1 experience on the road opposite the garage where Dwight had once worked – and where the new owner, Frank Bancroft, had experienced something so terrifying it had caused him to die of a heart attack. Beth's story had only reinforced Dwight's belief that he – and perhaps other UFOlogists – were being watched and were also, almost certainly, in constant danger.

While Dwight's brief with APII was restricted solely to an investigation of UFO sightings as potential extra-terrestrial visitations, he was also secretly keeping his eyes and ears open for any further information on the possibility that they, or other UFOs, were man-made.

This possibility had remained with him ever since his old friend, US Air Force Captain Andrew 'Andy' Boyle, had told him about spherical-or-disc-shaped experimental aircraft, notably the Avrocar constructed at the A. V. Roe aircraft company in Malton, Ontario. Though reportedly this man-made 'flying saucer' had failed to fly with any great degree of efficiency, the fact that its existence had been officially denied until it was photographed on the ground by a press photographer lent some credibility to the notion that the same project, or similar projects, but of a much more advanced kind, were still being undertaken, either in Canada or in the top secret military research establishments of the White Sands Proving Ground, New Mexico.

As long as he lived, Dwight would not forget his experience with the men in black in that motel on the outskirts of Albuquerque in 1954, five years ago – the event that had finally made him decide to leave the Air Force for good. The description given by Andy Boyle of the dome-shaped 'aircraft' he had seen landing outside a secret hangar at Cannon Air Force Base was also an indelible memory for Dwight, since the 'aircraft' as described by Andy was almost certainly a flying saucer: its fuselage formed by two plates, one placed upside down on the other, with a raised Perspex dome in the middle – obviously the pilot's cabin – and circular, gyroscopically balanced plates revolving around it. Whether extraterrestrial or man-made, that flying saucer had undoubtedly been kept for an indeterminate period in that heavily guarded hangar at Cannon AFB.

Later, after his terrifying experience with what may have been a flying saucer hovering outside his motel window, followed by a frightening encounter with a group of men dressed all in black, who had threatened him and stolen Andy's invaluable UFO photo, Dwight had tried to contact Andy again to find out if he'd had a similar experience. First he learnt that Andy had been transferred to Alaska with hardly any notice at all. A week later, he learnt that Andy had died in an unexplained helicopter crash over Mt McKinley. Neither his body nor that of the pilot was ever found.

From that moment on, Dwight had been haunted by Andy's contention that the flying saucers could indeed be man-made. It was not a hypothesis he had dared to raise so far with Dr Frederick Epstein at APII, since he had not come across any supportive evidence for what Andy had told him before his death. He had, nevertheless, asked one of his NICAP researchers, Tony Scaduto, to bring him anything he happened to find along those lines. Now, he was on his way to meet Tony in a bar in Georgetown, to hear what Tony had sworn on the phone was a fascinating story relating to man- made UFOs.

Dwight and Tony Scaduto met in an Irish pub in Connecticut Avenue. Downstairs the bar was packed with drunken marines from Quantico; upstairs, where Dwight and Tony met, it was even more packed, but with a mixed crowd joining in the songs being played by a four-piece Irish band – autoharp, fiddle, flatpick guitar, mandolin – while turning red-faced from Guinness Stout, Harp on tap and very large whisky chasers. Tony was a twenty-five-year old Brooklyn boy, still single, who loved rock 'n' roll music and dressed like Marlon Brando in *The Wild One*. A good-natured, fun-loving young man, he was also very bright, if slightly self-destructive when it came to drinking, smoking and women.

'This is a good place to meet for a talk,' Dwight informed him, glancing at the energetic, noisy Irish band. 'I can hardly hear myself speak.'

'They go off in a minute,' Tony said. 'Then we can talk. What can I get you?'

'I haven't been in an Irish pub for years, so make it a Guinness. Anyway,' he added as Tony ordered the drinks, 'I thought you were a rock 'n' roll fan – not a lover of *this* kind of music.'

'This is the year the music died,' Tony replied laconically. 'Buddy Holly, the Big Bopper and Richie Valens – all killed in a plane crash. Meanwhile Elvis, *sans* sideburns, is serving out his time with the goddamned US Army in West Germany, leaving us with Pat Boone, Frankie Avalon, Bobby Rydell and all the other puke-making mother's boys. No wonder I'm listening to Irish music! It's all we've got left.'

The barman brought two more glasses of Guinness just as the band on the stage took a break to noisy applause.

'They'll be off for forty minutes,' Scaduto told Dwight. 'That should be enough for us.'

338

'So what's this fascinating story you've got for me?'

'Pretty bizarre, to put it mildly,' Scaduto replied, 'so I couldn't resist it.'

'Stop teasing,' Dwight told him.

Scaduto grinned, sipped some Guinness, then wiped the foam from his lips with the back of his hand. 'I picked up this story from one of my informants: a civilian secretary at the Office of Naval Intelligence.'

'Sounds well placed,' Dwight said.

'Yeah. Anyway, according to my lady friend – a great lay, incidentally – a woman psychic in Portland, Maine, recently informed the CIA that she'd had telepathic contact with extraterrestrials in what she thought was a space-ship.'

'A crank,' Dwight said, sounding disappointed.

'Not necessarily, though that's exactly what the *CIA* thought at first. Since to them it seemed like a classic scam – a woman, a supposed psychic, using automatic handwriting for communication with extraterrestrials – the CIA gave it a miss. However, the Canadian government got their hands on the CIA report and, instead of dismissing it, which would seem logical, they sent their leading UFOlogist to interview her where she lived. According to the Canadian government UFOlogist, the woman, in a hypnotic trance, correctly answered highly complex questions about space flight, about which she had formerly known shit.'

Scaduto had another gulp of his stout and glanced at the women scattered around the bar as he licked the foam from his lips.

'Not surprisingly,' he continued eventually, 'when the US Navy learned about this, they sent two intelligence officers to talk to the same woman. During the subsequent interrogation, one of the Naval intelligence officers, who had, please note, *been trained in ESP*, tried to tune in to the woman's contactee. When this experiment failed, he and his colleague returned to Washington DC and informed the CIA at Langley.'

Though the Irish band had stopped playing, a few of the older patrons of this generally youth-orientated pub, their faces flushed with drink, began rocking from side to side and tearfully singing, 'I'll Take You Home Again, Kathleen'.

'Someone should take *them* home,' Scaduto said, then he turned back to Dwight. 'So, where was I?'

'When the ESP-trained Naval intelligence officer failed to make contact with the woman's contactee, he and his friend returned to report their failure to the CIA. How did they react?'

'Well, instead of expressing their disappointment, the CIA – possibly impressed because the Navy had gone to so much trouble for a case they had ignored – displayed more interest than before and arranged for the ESP-trained intelligence officer to try making contact from CIA headquarters at Langley Field, Virginia. Six witnesses – two of them CIA employees, one of whom was agent Jack Fuller, the others from the Office of Naval Intelligence – got together in the office in Langley to observe the results of the experiment.'

Trying to ignore the tuneless singing of the maudlin drunks nearby, Dwight, becoming fascinated despite his reservations, leaned closer to Scaduto and asked, 'Well?'

'This time, when the ESP-trained intelligence officer went into his hypnotic trance, he made contact with *someone.*'

'Was the identity and whereabouts of that someone made known?'

'Not at first. When the intelligence officer, in his trance condition, was asked if he was in contact with ordinary men, spirit beings or extraterrestrials, he said it was the latter. When one of the men in the room then demanded some kind of proof for his assertion, the intelligence officer, still in his hypnotic trance, said that if they looked out the window they would see a flying saucer high in the sky over the Capitol building. When the men went to the window and looked out, that's just what they saw: a large flying saucer hovering silently in the sky, approximately over Capitol Hill.'

'Did they have the sense to try for confirmation of their sighting?'

'Surprisingly, they did. A quick phone call from one of the CIA men – almost certainly Fuller – to Washington National Airport established that at that very moment the radar centre there was reporting that its radar returns were being blacked out in the direction of the sighting over Capitol Hill.'

Dwight gave a low whistle. 'So what happened then?'

'The operator at Washington National Airport had no sooner finished complaining about his blacked-out radar returns when the flying saucer shot up vertically and disappeared – reportedly like a light bulb blinking out.'

'What was the saucer like?'

Scaduto shrugged, sipped some Guinness, then placed his glass back on the counter. 'That's the problem,' he said. 'No description of the flying saucer was released. A lid was slammed on the whole thing.'

Dwight shook his head in despair. 'Damn!' he exclaimed softly, lowering his head. Then he looked up again. 'So how did your friend, the great lay, come to hear the story?'

'Good one!' Scaduto said, grinning from ear to ear. 'Major Robert J. Friend, present head of the increasingly impotent Project Blue Book, was informed of the events by the CIA and arranged for Duke University's parapsychology lab to investigate both the psychic from Maine and the ESP-trained intelligence officer. That led to the mistaken declassification of the original reports – and those reports passed through the Office of Naval Intelligence, thus through my friend's hands.'

'Then on to you.'

'Right. When we were sharing her warm bed.'

'She didn't give you the original reports?'

'No, of course not!' Scaduto was mock affronted, before

grinning again. 'She just whispered the info lovingly into my ear.'

'Before sticking her tongue in it, no doubt.'

'A gentleman never tells.'

Dwight grinned and nodded. 'So what were the results of the Duke University's parapsychology lab investigations?'

'God knows. Their report never materialized, Project Blue Book released no analysis of the sighting report, the government did nothing about the inexplicable Washington radar blackout, and the origins of the flying saucer seen over the Capitol remain a secret to this day. As for the men present at the hypnotic trance session, the CIA took "punitive" action against them by transferring them to other positions – with the single exception of CIA agent Jack Fuller.'

'So why didn't you ask Fuller what happened?'

Scaduto grinned and tapped the side of his nose with his index finger. 'I did. He denied any involvement in such a matter, then laughed and cut me off.'

'He's a sharp man, that Fuller. Sharp and hard.'

'He is that,' Scaduto replied, automatically influenced by the pub and sounding rather Irish.

Dwight had another gulp of his drink, licked the foam from his lips, then stared down thoughtfully at the counter. 'A nice little story,' he said, 'but it seems too far-fetched to be true.'

'Well, it may seem that way to you,' Scaduto replied without pause, 'but the incident – or something very like it – must have occurred, because Major Friend wrote about the whole affair in an official Memorandum for the Record. That Memorandum has since been filed in the Air Force Archives at Maxwell AFB, Montgomery, Alabama – but it wasn't filed until a copy found its way into the hands of a few UFOlogists. The Memorandum is genuine – either that or Major Friend, the present head of Project Blue Book, is submitting fiction in official reports.'

Dwight nodded, acknowledging this undeniable truth.

'So just what are you trying to tell me, Tony?'

'You want another Guinness?'

'No. I'm catching a plane back to Dayton when I leave here. Home sober to greet Beth and Nichola, then have my dinner.'

'Yeah, I get the picture.' Only twenty-five years old, still single, and filled with sexual vitality, Scaduto glanced along the bar to where an attractive raven-haired girl in tight blue jeans and sweater was studying him slyly in the mirror angled over the bar. More wily than the girl would know until it was too late, Scaduto had ascertained her interest and was about to move in on her.

'Okay,' he said. 'Before I offer that little sweetheart a couple of drinks – one from a glass, the other from down below – I'll tell you exactly what I think.' He smiled at the girl, then lowered his eyes as if really shy, concentrating on Dwight. 'I've always been intrigued by the unusual amount of official interest paid to the so-called Woman from Maine – a civilian female with supposed telepathic abilities. I am, however, wise to the fact that both the Russian secret police – the KGB – and the CIA have, for years, been investigating the espionage potential of telepathy, psychic photography, and other forms of parapsychology. I'm therefore starting to wonder if there could be any connection between that fact and the psychic from Maine.'

'What kind of connection?'

'Since communication by telepathy has already been attained with some success in Soviet *and* American laboratories, and between submarine and land bases, it's possible that the CIA was genuinely concerned with that technologically ignorant woman's inexplicable knowledge of the more complex aspects of space flight. As the CIA are interested in the espionage potential of telepathy, it stands to reason that they'd have certain men trained in ESP and would send one to attend the trance session. If we then accept that telepathic communication was made with *someone* in that office in CIA headquarters, Langley,

Virginia, and that the agent in a trance, if not actually
making that UFO materialize, had at least been informed
telepathically of its existence, it then seems possible that
the woman from Maine had been in contact with a
telepathically trained *government* employee, albeit by
accident.'

'Are you suggesting that the UFO over Washington was
a *government* saucer?'

'Yes,' Scaduto said emphatically.

'Man-made?'

'Exactly. The more I investigate these damned things,
the more I'm convinced that the White House, the Pentagon
and certainly Army, Navy and Air Force intelligence of the
White Sands Proving Ground and other top secret areas,
are deliberately causing confusion, doubt and fear
regarding UFO sightings because they're protecting their
own. While the more technically advanced saucers might
indeed be extraterrestrial, I think the US Army, Navy or
Air Force have their own versions. I don't know – but I
think so.'

'Have you raised these beliefs with Dr Epstein or anyone
else at APII?'

'No. This theory goes completely against the grain of
most of the UFO organisations, including APII and NICAP,
so I'm keeping my big mouth shut. You're the first person
in the business who's told me he's interested in the same
theme, so that's why I've told you this.'

'And you're still interested?'

'Damned right I am.'

'It could be a dangerous thing to pursue,' Dwight told
him.

'I don't scare easily,' Scaduto said, then he turned his
head to smile deliberately at the raven-haired girl along
the bar. She crossed her long, blue-jeaned legs on the stool
and returned Scaduto's winning smile.

'You're in like Flynn,' Dwight told him, slipping off the
bar stool and taking his brief case in his hand. 'If you come

across anything else, please give me a call.'

'I will,' Scaduto promised, already sliding off his stool to approach the lovely girl further along the bar.

'And try to stay out of trouble, Tony.'

'The only trouble I'm going to get into,' Scaduto said, 'will be found between that girl's legs.'

Dwight sighed, recalling the days of his own youth. Then he left the bar.

Chapter Thirty

The biggest flying saucer to date, the *Goddard*, named after Wilson's only hero, the American rocket genius Robert H. Goddard, was known as the 'mother ship' because it was three hundred and fifty foot in diameter, a hundred and fifty foot high at the central point between dome and base, built in three layers, and carried not only a crew of over a hundred men, but also the smaller manned saucers, those the size of the original *Kugelblitz*, the even smaller, three feet to twelve feet diameter, unmanned, remote-controlled probes, and a variety of large and small CAMS – Cybernetic Anthropomorphous Machine Systems – either piloted by small, surgically mutated Ache Indian cyborgs, remote controlled from the mother ship, or programmed to react robotically to certain stimuli for the exploration of the sea bed. Technologically even more advanced than its predecessor, *Kugelblitz III*, the gigantic *Goddard* was powered by a combination of a highly advanced electromagnetic propulsion system that ionized the surrounding air or sea, an electromagnetic damping system that aided the craft's lift and hovering capabilities, and bodywork composed of an electrically charged magnesium orthosilicate so minutely porous that it managed to be waterproof while ensuring, when airborne, an absolute minimum of friction, heat and drag.

It was Wilson's intention to have even bigger 'mother' ships for sea-bed exploration and flights in outer space, but at the moment this three hundred and fifty foot craft, submerged deep in the Sargasso Sea between Florida and Bermuda, was the best he could manage for the most ambitious series of underwater experiments he had so far attempted. These had so far included the capturing of underwater beasts and fish never before seen by man, a general exploration of the sea-bed and the collection of samples from it, the abduction of the crew members of boats afloat in the area known as the Bermuda Triangle, and, in two instances, the capture of whole motor launches, complete with their terrified passengers.

'A truly great achievement,' the new Flight Captain of the mother-ship, Vince Whitaker, said as he gazed through the viewing window – he was standing between Wilson and Sea Captain Ritter Dietrich – at the artificially and naturally illuminated wonders of the deep, including all kinds of plankton, bizarre fish, and other creatures never before seen by man and either extremely beautiful or, by human standards, hideous. 'Absolutely magnificent!'

Wilson did not bother explaining to the chemically 'indoctrinated' former NASA astronaut that the colony's great advances in submersible technology had only been made possible because of the many undersea prototypes tried out in Antarctica with living crew members, none of whom had volunteered, many of whom had lost their lives when the prototypes leaked in the ice-covered sea or broke up underwater. However, *Goddard* was the magnificent result of those experiments and could be used either under the water or in the stratosphere. For this reason it had a Sea Captain, Ritter Dietrich, for undersea voyages, as well as a Flight Captain for atmospheric and stratospheric flight. As the last pilot, another abducted USAF officer, had never managed to learn the complexities of stratospheric flight, he had recently been terminated and replaced by this new man, Vince Whitaker, who, the previous month, had supposedly crashed in the sea near the Bahamas, three hundred and sixty miles from Cape Canaveral, during a fifteen-minute sub-orbital test flight of NASA's new Mercury spacecraft.

The three men were standing at one of the many windows of the control room, which had about a dozen reinforced viewing windows around its circular wall and a dome-shaped ceiling of heat-resistant, reinforced Perspex over which was what resembled a great umbrella of seamless steel, though it was actually minutely porous magnesium orthosilicate, like the rest of the hull. In fact, the dome-shaped steel covering on the Perspex ceiling – actually the central dome of the flying saucer – was divided almost invisibly into two concave sections that could slide apart in opposite directions and curve back down into the floor, thus giving the crew members a three hundred and sixty degree view from any part of the flight deck.

The latter was composed of what looked like the standard hardware for a normal airliner, including switch panels, pitch trim controls, autopilot engage switch, inertial navigation, navigational radio selector, weather radar, radio equipment, intercom switches, an unknown brand of ADF (automatic direction finder), computer selection switches, and an unusually small but exceptionally powerful computer that controlled most of the flight-deck functions and could be activated by an electronic 'voice' composed of minute vibrations transmitted at varying speeds and frequencies.

Such orders were conveyed by the small Ache cyborgs who, though having had their vocal cords severed as part of their lower-face surgery, including the removal of the nose, mouth and jaw, communicated electronically from their metal prosthetics to the electronic-voice activated computer. Instructions to the cyborgs were communicated via a pinhead microphone strapped to the throat of a human superior, such as Sea Captain Dietrich or Flight Captain Whitaker, and activated by an on/off switch built into his international date-time wristwatch. As Flight Captain Whitaker had already learned, the flight deck did *not* contain such standard aircraft controls as thruster reverse lights, nose gear tiller, speed brake handle, or even brake pressure or aileron and rudder trims, as these were not required for the unique propulsion system of the *Goddard*.

Dubbed the 'mother ship' because it was actually a carrying ship, the *Goddard* used its wide variety of large and small CAMS to pick up exotic marine life, valuable lost treasure, and a wealth of normally unavailable minerals from the ocean-bed and from Earth – notably, in the latter case, the bodily parts of animals, which were required for the continuing medical experiments in the Antarctic colony.

The mother ship could also release, and receive, highly advanced versions of the original *Feuerballs*, the latest models being used mainly as spy-satellites and radar-blocking devices, but with the added capability of laser-beam technology that could make the engines of automobiles and aircraft malfunction, as well as stunning or hypnotizing human beings.

Looking at the battery-charged lights beaming out through the murk of the ocean, revealing ever more as the great craft surfaced, Flight Captain Whitaker said: 'Aren't you frightened that the lights, if seen by the crews of ships or aircraft, will give your presence away?'

'No,' Wilson replied with confidence. 'USOs, or Unidentified Submarine Objects, are even harder to identify than UFOs because of the diversity of marine biology, which includes a surprising amount of phosphorescent plant and animal life. Look!' He pointed through the window at what appeared to be unusual plants that were drifting through and around the beams of the *Goddard*'s lights, giving off their own eerie illumination. 'Single-celled luminous planktonic organisms. They glow even brighter when near the surface of the sea, being stimulated by the movement of the waves. Others, such as the *Cypridina Noctiluca*, actually *respond* automatically to beams of light, such as searchlights, by ejecting a luminous cloud in the water. Luminous crustaceans, such as copepods, some living on the water's surface, some in the ocean depths, can be found in seas all over the world. Then, of course, you have jellyfish and other coelenterates and ctenophores, which also create patches of light in the water – some very large. So, as you can appreciate, experienced sailors or pilots who see our lights under the water aren't likely to be too concerned. That only comes when we surface. Which, in fact, we'll be doing very shortly. Come with me, Flight Captain.'

Leaving Sea Captain Dietrich to supervise the surfacing of the *Goddard*, Wilson led Flight Captain Whitaker out of the flight deck and along a curving, steel-walled, white-painted corridor (for it was, in fact, circular, running around the inner rim of the giant saucer, as did the corridors on all levels) until they came to a closed door, which opened automatically when Wilson aimed his hand-control at it. The doorway lead to the top level of an immense, silvery-grey dome filled with ladders and catwalks. Below were glittering floors and platforms, modules of steel and glass, shining mazes of pipes coiled around generators, bright lights flashing off more white-painted walls. There were people down there, looking tiny and far away, climbing ladders, crossing catwalks, moving up and down that one hundred and fifty foot drop in elevators constructed like steel cages.

About halfway down, fifty feet above the lowest floor, on a centrally placed, circular-shaped, third-level platform, in the exact centre of the lowest, largest workshop, the smaller man- made saucer, *Kugelblitz II*, which Whitaker estimated was one hundred and fifty foot in diameter, was resting on its launch pad, surrounded by four even smaller, unmanned flying-saucer probes, each about fifteen feet wide.

'This way,' Wilson said, leading Whitaker across the catwalk, above that dizzying drop, until they arrived at the cage-like elevator that descended through the very centre of the *Goddard*, from just under the floor of the flight deck to the third level platform. Once down there, Wilson led the way to the lowered ramp of the *Kugelblitz II*.

Just as they reached the saucer, the *Goddard* broke the

surface of the Pacific Ocean, with the sea suddenly roaring
and pounding as water parted around the protective steel
covering of the dome and rushed down its sides. The great
mother ship rocked gently for a moment as it floated in the
turbulent waves created by its own surfacing, but
eventually, when the sea's surface had returned to normal,
the rocking stopped and the metallic dome divided in two,
forming separate concave plates that moved away from each
other, then sank back out of sight, leaving only the great
dome of special heat-resistant, reinforced Perspex, through
which sunlight beamed down to form a dazzling web of
silvery-white striations that illuminated the gloomy interior
of the mother ship.

Glancing up, Wilson and Whitaker saw the different
floors with men in grey or black coveralls hurrying across
catwalks, clambering up and down ladders, or moving back
and forth in the glass-panelled offices located around the
curved inner wall of the mother ship.

'What a sight!' Whitaker whispered, despite himself.

Even as he was speaking, immense panels in a section
of the circular wall of the mother ship slid apart like the
doors of an aircraft hangar, offering a view of the vast, sunlit
sky and a glimpse of the sea below.

'The level upon which this landing pad is located,' Wilson
explained to Whitaker, 'is approximately fifty feet above
the sea. Come. Let's go in.'

They entered the *Kugelblitz II* by walking up the sloping
ramp that would, once they were inside, be retracted to
form the underside of the bottom disc. This is exactly what
happened: the ramp moved back up into the loading bay of
the saucer on thick steel hinges until it formed part of the
wall, slotting back where it belonged with such precision
that the joins around its edge could scarcely be seen and
formed a perfect waterproof, airtight seal.

The loading bay was actually a space in the revolving
lower disc used only as a passageway for men and
equipment; in other words, anyone, or anything, entering

the loading bay from outside had to continue on until they were in the non-rotating main body of the ship. For this reason, Wilson and Whitaker hurried through the loading bay, which could have been that of any large aircraft, and emerged in the central, non-revolving main body, which also was circular, being the bottom of the large dome-shaped superstructure. After following the corridor around for a few feet, they stepped into an elevator that took them up nearly fifty feet, past the engine rooms, storage rooms, barred cages for abducted people, a surprisingly large surgery where those abducted could be medically examined or even dissected during flight, latrines, foodstores, a small recreation room containing books, maps, and a recently invented video-TV set which could show films on tape, and finally into the circular flight deck.

For the time being the meniscus-shaped, porous-metal covering for the Perspex dome was open, giving those on the flight deck a three hundred and sixty-degree view of the interior of the mother ship, though from their position on the landing pad they could only see the third-floor level and most of what was above it. The flight deck was, at that moment, being prepared for take-off by another crew of surgically mutated and robotised Ache Indians who, being small, and with their lower-face metal prosthetics and myoelectric metal claws (actually small CAMS), looked even more frightening than they would have had they been taller.

No sooner had Wilson and Whitaker entered the flight deck than two massive plates in what had appeared to be the seamless facing wall of the mother ship slid apart with a bass humming sound discernible even from in here and kept opening until they formed a rectangular space about the same size as the entrance to an aircraft hangar. That great space framed a sheer blue sky, the clear horizon, and a strip of green-blue sea.

As Wilson and Whitaker strapped themselves into seats at the control panel – between the busy cyborgs whose metallic throats were making infrasounds that enabled them to electronically 'talk' to the computerised controls – the *Kugelblitz II* throbbed with a bass humming sound, almost an infrasound, then vibrated very slightly, swayed from side to side, and lifted a couple of feet off the landing pad. While it was still hovering, Wilson nodded to Flight Captain Whitaker who, now taking command, spoke his instructions, in plain English, into the pinhead microphone strapped to his throat, as part of a communication system that included a covert ear piece for receiving. Those spoken instructions would be converted by the computer into an electronic language understood by the saucer's control console, which would react accordingly.

Because the saucer utilized a gravity shield which came on automatically when required, its passengers needed no protection against the pull of gravity or increasing outer pressure and were only strapped into their chairs during the initial stages of take-off. Now, under Flight Captain Whitaker's command, the hovering saucer advanced horizontally to the large opening in the sloping side of the mother ship, hovered again halfway across the lip of the opening, then moved outside altogether and stopped again, hovering just a few feet from the *Goddard*, but a good fifty feet about the surface of the Sargasso Sea. There, at a command from Flight Captain Whitaker, the meniscus-shaped, metallic outer casings of the dome emerged from the floor at both sides of the flight deck and curved up and inward to meet at the top of the dome, forming what looked deceptively like a seamless whole. Matching windows in the lower half of the metallic casing ensured that the flight crew still had their three hundred and sixty-degree view, though they could no longer look directly above them.

As the dome was being sealed, the four fifteen feet-diameter, unmanned probes also emerged from the mother ship to surround the *Kugelblitz II* and prepare for take-off.

Being already in the air, the five craft did not follow the usual two-stage pattern of flying saucer take-offs: a tentative, vertical rise of between fifty and one hundred feet, then a spectacular, remarkably quick blast-off, either vertically or at a sharp angle. Instead, they hovered beside the mother ship until the gravity shield had come on, then abruptly shot off to the west, heading for Florida.

Protected by the *Kugelblitz II*'s gravity shield, those inside had no need to keep themselves strapped to their chairs. There was absolutely no sign or feeling of movement. However, as the journey from the Sargasso Sea to the Florida Keys took no more than a few minutes, neither man thought it worth while unbuckling his safety belt. Indeed, so fast was the saucer flying that at first, when the passengers looked straight ahead, they saw no more than what appeared to be a rapidly whipping, frantically spiralling tunnel of shimmering white light streaked with silvery blue, a vertiginous well of brightness which gave no indication of what direction they were actually flying in: up, down or straight ahead. It was, of course, the latter. Flying at a speed well beyond the sound barrier, Mach 1, over fifty miles up, on the very edge of space, they appeared to be suddenly blasted through the very sky itself, a giant envelope tearing open to reveal a vast azure sea which convulsed and turned purple and then, just as abruptly, actually being the same sky, filled up with the dazzling radiance of a gigantic sun, even as the moon and stars also came out, clearly visible in the middle of the day, now visible, with the sun, in an atmosphere so thin that even dust particles could not exist.

Seconds later, the *Kugelblitz II* and its four surrounding probes all slowed down to hovering speed, then hovered directly over Bimini, which could be seen as glowing dots on the radar screen and as it actually was on the TV monitor wired to a high-powered aerial camera. What the TV monitor showed, in fact, was a photomosaic of the western end of the Bermuda Triangle, the Gulf Stream flowing northward between Florida and the Great Bahama Bank, and, in the exact middle of the picture, Bimini itself, here in monochrome, but in actuality a ravishing tapestry of green and blue streaked with so-called 'white' water, containing sulphur, strontium and lithium, which often made it glow eerily.

'Send the probes down,' Wilson ordered into his throat microphone.

Within seconds, the four unmanned 'probe' saucers had shot out horizontally in the four directions of the compass, stopped abruptly, hovered briefly, then shot down towards the sea off Bimini, moving so fast they looked like no more than tiny lights, then disappearing completely as they plunged into the water and descended, still fully operational, to the sea bed. There, under robotic control and with the use of their CAMS, they would explore and collect samples of rock, stone, soil, plants and plankton from what might be the remains of the cyclopean walls, truncated pyramids, carved pillars, causeways and stone circles of a lost civilisation, possibly Atlantis. While Wilson was not quick to embrace this theory, his encyclopaedic knowledge of ancient history impelled him to explore the possibilities and see what could be learnt from them. This was the job of the four small 'probe' saucers that were almost certainly, right this minute, extending their spider-like metallic claws to start picking up things from the sea bed between Bimini and Andros.

'So,' he said when the probes had disappeared into the sea, 'let's head for Cocoa Beach.'

When the relevant instructions had been transmitted, the saucer ascended vertically about fifty feet, then shot off in a blur of speed towards Miami. With its gravitational shield also functioning as an inertial shield, the mass of the UFO with regard to gravity was reduced to a minute fraction of its former value, permitting exceptional buoyancy in the atmosphere, extremely high accelerations (so fast, indeed, that the human eye could not see the saucer's take-off and would imagine it had abruptly disappeared) and the capability of coming to a remarkably fast stop or going into abrupt, right-angle turns without harming those inside, they also being protected by the inertial shield.

Now on programmed autopilot, the saucer knew where it had to go; upon approaching the mainland, it suddenly stopped, made an abrupt turn, and then shot off north, automatically following the topography of the land by means of a control system that bounced radar-like signals off the ground and back to the saucer for instant computer analysis and constantly changing flight directions. Because of this, as well as the weakening and strengthening of the gravitational pull of the earth when the saucer dropped low enough, the saucer appeared to be bobbing repeatedly as it sped on a horizontal flight path towards Cocoa Beach.

It stopped abruptly and precisely over the prearranged meeting place in a field in a protected area just outside Patrick Air Force Base, two miles from the village of Greater Cocoa Beach and Cape Canaveral, the swamp-land from which dozens of Atlas, Thor, Titan and Snark missiles, as well as America's first earth satellite, *Explorer 1*, had been launched.

As the *Kugelblitz II* hovered high above the normal civilian and Air Force flight paths, waiting for the fall of darkness, Wilson and Whitaker partook of a light meal – the usual fruit and nut cereal with a glass of dry, white wine – and discussed the many changes that had taken place down there on the east coast of Florida, where Whitaker had also trained and flown as a budding astronaut, before being abducted by Wilson.

'When I first went there,' Whitaker said, 'about seven years ago, Cocoa Beach consisted of a couple of dozen families strewn amongst the sand dunes and palmettos. Strangers rarely turned up and the villagers did little other than fish for their food and swim for their leisure. Now it's called Greater Cocoa Beach, which includes the original village and its environs, and it has a population of approximately ten thousand souls, including astronauts, aircraft pilots, scientists, rocket engineers, ballistics experts, and a local community obsessed with making money out of the space race. Some amazing things are happening down there.'

'Only amazing relative to the accomplishments of the rest of the West,' Wilson noted. 'Only amazing because of what we *let* them do. But we're now so many light-years ahead, they'll never catch up with us.'

'Jack Fuller thinks differently,' Whitaker said. 'And that man's no fool.'

'He's not a scientist, either, Flight Captain. That's his major weakness. His others are vanity, material greed and excessive patriotism, all of which can be used against him if necessary. We've no cause for concern there.'

Feeling nervous, as he always did when outside the colony, this being part of the chemical 'indoctrination' process undergone upon his arrival, Whitaker checked his wristwatch. 'Maybe we should have arranged the meeting somewhere in Cape Canaveral,' he said. 'It's now a restricted military zone of about fifteen thousand acres, including a lot of uncleared jungle. We might have been more secure there.'

'Or we might have been eaten by a puma,' Wilson retorted, knowing that those animals still roamed wild there. 'Besides, these days the Cape is crawling with tourists – even around the restricted zone, which they try to spy upon with binoculars and cameras. Also, most of the military personnel in that zone still don't know about us, so they could prove to be troublesome.'

'What about those on Patrick AFB?'

'The US-Canadian saucers are tested there,' Wilson explained, 'and kept hidden in secret hangars in a heavily guarded, top secret area – pretty much like Wright-Patterson's notorious Hangar 18. For this reason we trade with them and deal only with those on the base who take part in that trade.'

'Like that CIA agent, Jack Fuller.'

Wilson smiled. 'Jack Fuller trades all over the place –

where we go, he goes. So, yes, like Jack Fuller.' Glancing through the curved viewing window at the other side of the flight deck console, he noticed that the sun now looked like blood pouring along the great bowl of the silvery horizon. 'The sun's setting. They should be there by now. Commence the descent.'

The saucer vibrated slightly, wobbled a little, then, with its circular 'wings' rotating and their flashing lights forming a kaleidoscope, it steadied and descended vertically, first through the civilian and military flight paths, its radar checking for oncoming aircraft, then through the clouds, and finally all the way down to a great circle of lights that marked the LZ, the landing zone, in the middle of a vast field that was encircled by electrified barbed-wire fences and further guarded by fifty well-armed US Marines, spread equidistant around the perimeter.

Mere feet above the ground, whipping up dust, loose soil and leaves, the flying saucer bobbed a little and swayed gently as its short, thick, hydraulic legs emerged obliquely from its convex base and dug into the earth. The bass humming sound faded away, the flashing lights blinked out in sequence, and the saucer came to a rest and was still.

A brief silence reigned.

Beyond the circle of upward-facing marker lamps in which the flying saucer had landed, nothing was visible except that broad, dark field and the starry sky above it. Neither the electrified barbed-wire fence nor the Marines placed around the perimeter were visible. For a while the saucer just sat there like a silvery-grey enigma, making no movement, no sound. Eventually, however, the sound of a coughing engine broke the silence and a US Army jeep materialised out of the darkness to stop just outside the circle of marker lamps. The jeep's ignition was turned off, then its lights were extinguished, thus plunging it back into the darkness just outside the illuminated LZ.

In that darkness, Jack Fuller, wearing a light grey suit

with shirt and tie, clambered out of the jeep, followed by two Marines armed with 0.3-inch M1 Carbine semi-automatic rifles and carrying spare thirty-round detachable box magazines on the webbed belts strapped around their chests. After glancing carefully at the flying saucer, Fuller nodded to the two soldiers, indicating that they should follow him at a reasonable distance. As they spread out behind him, he stepped over the marker lamps and walked slowly, carefully towards the saucer.

Even as Fuller was advancing towards that immense, silvery-grey discus, a bass humming sound emanated from it and the top of a large plate, which before had formed part of the apparently seamless outer surface, moved away from the lower body, opening just enough to let out a long, thin blade of subdued whitish light. The top of the plate kept moving away from the wall, swivelling on hinges along its bottom end, falling backwards all the way to the ground until it formed a broad ramp, eerily illuminated by the pale light pouring out from the loading bay of the saucer.

Three figures were silhouetted in that deliberately reduced lighting: a tall, slim man and two child-sized, oddly shaped creatures whose features could not immediately be defined. Only when Fuller had stopped near the base of the ramp did he recognise the three figures as Wilson and two unfortunate Ache Indians who had been surgically mutated to be fitted with metal prosthetics, including the replacement of the lower face, jaw and hands, thus turning them into robotic cyborgs, half man, half machine. The hands of these creatures were actually small CAMS – (or hideous metal claws, depending on one's knowledge of cybernetics) and their faces were rendered dreadful by the fact that the only human aspect of them were the oddly glassy eyes that turned this way and that between the metal band of a studded stereotaxic skullcap and the metal nose of a prosthetic that had replaced the lower half of the face, including the mouth, jawbone and throat. Even Fuller, who took certain horrors for granted, shuddered when he saw these pitiful, terrifying creatures.

No wonder UFO contactees keep babbling about alien beings, he thought. What else could they possibly think?

The cyborgs stood well apart and a little distance behind Wilson as the latter walked away from the ramp and stopped in front of Fuller. Glancing at Fuller's two armed Marines, he said: 'You know that bringing those men here is a waste of time. If you displease me, or in any way go against me, they won't be able to help you.'

Fuller glanced at the two child-sized, hideous cyborgs standing behind Wilson and saw that they were holding what looked like two stun guns in their myoelectric metal hands.

'Laser weapons?' he asked.

'What a bright boy you are, Fuller.'

'I like to keep up to date. So what do you want?'

'Are you still here on behalf of President Eisenhower?'

'Yeah, right.'

'Why doesn't he send someone of more authority? Why is it always you?'

'Because, as you've doubtless noticed before when dealing with the likes of Generals Vandenberg and Samford, I'm a lot less antagonistic to you than are the men of the military.'

'You're antagonistic, all right. You just don't show it so openly.'

'That may be true, but the President still thinks that it's best to keep the military out of it as much as possible. Also, he believes that if the wrong person finds out that the top brass of the White House and Pentagon are negotiating secretly with the likes of you, public outrage could lead to the fall of the whole damned government, including himself. Me, on the other hand – well, I'm small fry and can be made to carry the can if we're found out. I'm not sure that that's true at all, but it's what he believes.'

'You're not sure, but you know it's possible.'

'Right.'

'And you're willing to be sacrificed that way?'

'I love my country,' Fuller said.

'You're a fool.'

'So Fuller's a fool. What the hell? Now what do you want?'

For a moment it looked like Wilson might actually show anger, but he simply stared steadily at Fuller, as if trying to read him. Obviously believing he had done so, he smiled slightly and said: 'As best I recall, when last you met my requirements for mass-produced components and other items, it left me owing you something.'

'True enough,' Fuller said. 'You've come to pay off your debt to the US government?'

Again Wilson refused to rise to the bait by showing anger over Fuller's bland mockery. Instead, he just said: 'Yes.'

'What is it? Obviously not more scientific information or I wouldn't be here alone. You'd have requested someone who could assess what you were offering. If not that, then it must be something else – something to do with intelligence.'

'You're a fool, but you don't lack common sense. That's exactly it, Fuller.'

'So *what* is it?'

'I note that NASA has finally named the test pilots it's selected for its first manned space project.'

'Yeah, right: Project Mercury.'

'I thought I should warn you not to let NASA become too complacent.'

'Why?'

'Almost certainly the Soviets will succeed, this September, in landing their *Lunik 2* spacecraft on the moon.'

'This is definite?'

'Yes. Over the past two years I've been abducting a variety of Soviet scientists, engineers, academics and cosmonauts, to brainwash them with chemicals, take control of their minds with minute brain implants via stereotaxic skullcaps, and send them back to where they

361

belong as my spies. Right now I have such spies in the Moscow headquarters of the Academy of Sciences, where the *Lunik 2* flight was planned; in Moscow University, where the space experiments were carried out; at the cosmodrome living quarters in East Kazakhstan, where the cosmonauts are being trained; in the airfield at Baikonur, two hundred miles north of the Aral Sea, where the launch will take place; and at the radio tracking complex at Burokane, Armenia, where the flight and moon landing will be monitored. So, yes, I know what I'm talking about. I've already beaten the United States to the moon – albeit in secret – and now the Soviets are about to do the same, leaving the US well behind in the space race.'

'That could be humiliating,' Fuller confessed.

'That's why the Russians are working so hard to do it.'

'That's an important bit of intelligence, Mr Wilson, but not exactly repayment for that last shipment of US material to the Antarctic.'

Wilson's smile was bleak. 'No. I'm forced to agree with that. I do, however, bring you something else.'

Fuller glanced at the two cyborgs standing behind Wilson in the eerie subdued lighting emanating from the holding area of the hundred and fifty-feet diameter flying saucer. Wondering what they were thinking, if anything, about what had happened to them, he shivered involuntarily and glanced beyond them to the illuminated holding bay. The light coming out of the saucers was usually dazzling, even blinding, but this light was pale, almost yellow, and not all that bright, which meant that Fuller could actually see more than usual – and what he saw was nothing. Clearly, the holding bay was only an entrance to the main, fixed body around which the massive rings revolved.

Disappointed, Fuller glanced back over his shoulder, first at the two armed Marine guards behind him, then beyond the immense circle of marker lamps. The light of the lamps, however, made it impossible to see as far as the barbed-wire perimeter where the other soldiers would be on guard. It was no comfort to know that Wilson was right: that if he, Fuller, said or did the wrong thing, he wouldn't have a prayer. He'd be paralysed by a stun gun, dragged up into the saucer, and almost certainly never be seen again. It wasn't a comforting thought.

'So what's the offer?' he asked.

'You'll take this to the White House?'

Fuller sighed. 'Yes, Wilson, direct to the President. So what am I telling him, other than what you've already told me?'

'As you probably know . . .' Wilson began.

'Don't tell me what I already know.'

'As you probably know,' Wilson repeated, almost gritting his teeth in the first hint of rage he had ever displayed, 'at the end of this year, in an unprecedented international agreement, a total of twelve countries, including Britain, America and the Soviet Union, will be signing a treaty stating that no country can claim any part of Antarctica as its own and that the continent must be a preserve for scientific research.'

'A noble idea,' Fuller interjected.

'Once that agreement is signed,' Wilson continued, ignoring Fuller's sarcasm, 'scientific and exploratory bases will be springing up all over the Antarctic.'

'Which gives you a problem,' Fuller said.

'Yes.' Wilson's gaze was as icy as the continent he so loved. 'So in return for a guarantee that there will be no attempts to locate or capture my base and that all sightings of my flying saucers over Antarctica will be treated with ridicule or suppressed entirely – as already they are in the United States and elsewhere – I'll guarantee that America will be the first to land men on the moon.'

'Well, we'd certainly appreciate that,' Fuller said, 'but unfortunately the US can't place restrictions on the other nations signing the Antarctic agreement.'

'The US is the only nation with the capability of launching an attack on my otherwise inaccessible part of Neu

363

Schwabenland – still known to the West as Queen Maud Land – so I'm not yet concerned with the other nations, but only with the US.'

Realising that Wilson was as genuinely concerned as his kind could be, which wasn't much, but at least was something, Fuller felt a twitch of joy – though he also knew that the trade, no matter how indecent, could not be refused. Whether or not he – or the White House or the Pentagon – liked it, they could not afford to let the Russians be first on the moon and would therefore have to give in to Wilson's demands – just as they had done so often.

'I'm still not sure that we can do as you ask,' Fuller lied, knowing damned well that his President would, 'but I'll certainly present it with my personal, strong recommendations.'

'Good,' Wilson replied, showing no sign of gratitude.

After a considerable silence, in which Wilson seemed deep in thought, Fuller, losing patience, asked: 'Well? Anything else, Mr Wilson?'

'Yes. There *is* another matter. I'm concerned that a certain Professor Allen J. Hynek, well-known UFOlogist and codirector of The Smithsonian Institution's satellite tracking programme, has been allowed to head an unofficial UFO advisory group recruited by Project Blue Book and including, as well as the redoubtable Hynek, an astronomer, a physicist, a psychologist, and Major Robert J. Friend, the present head of Project Blue Book and a man too co-operative with civilian UFO groups for my liking.'

'Stop worrying about Hynek or his group,' Fuller told him. 'Project Blue Book is practically on its knees and its so-called advisory group is just another red herring for the increasing number of professional and amateur UFO sleuths. The advisory group, believe me, will be disbanded by the end of next year, after serving its real purpose, which is to spread so much doubt and confusion amongst the UFOlogists that most of them will give up completely and go back to playing with toy torpedoes in their baths.'

'And Hynek?'

'What about him? When the group sinks, he'll probably go down with it. As for Project Blue Book, while it's continued to make a strong show of examining UFO cases, it's now under pressure from above – don't look at me – to produce a report stating that after twelve years of analysing and investigating UFO sightings, ATIC has *no* evidence to suggest that UFOs are either space vehicles, a threat to national security, or of any scientific value whatsoever. The same report will describe the UFO programme as a costly and unproductive burden on the Air Force. Finally, it'll recommend that Project Blue Book's staff could be more constructively used on other programmes.'

'Very good, Fuller.'

'I've nothing to do with it,' Fuller lied, though he couldn't resist a grin of pride. 'Anyway, while that report's being prepared, we're still encouraging the public to think of the UFOs in terms of extraterrestrials – your men in black are widely believed to be just that – so all in all, they're imagining everything *except* man-made UFOs.'

'I know you're loath to take credit for this,' Wilson said, 'but I have to tell you it pleases me.'

'Good. So we're even until you next need supplies. Can I leave now, Wilson?'

'Your detestation is too obvious,' Wilson told him, 'if badly misplaced. Look to your own government – the one you love – and then tell me which one of us is truly moral.'

'I'm not up to that, Wilson.'

'No, I don't suppose you are. Morals aren't your strong point.' He glanced across the dark field at the soldiers hidden in darkness. Though he couldn't see them, he knew they were there and was amused by the thought. 'One last thing,' he said.

'What?'

'Have you heard about the woman from Maine?'

'No.'

'Stop lying. If I know about her – and I do – you must

know that I know you were involved.'

Now understanding that Wilson really *did* have eyes and ears everywhere, Fuller, badly shaken, which was rare, simply shrugged as if it was of no consequence. 'Yeah, right, I know about her. So? *What* about her?'

'I'll tell you about her,' Wilson said, suddenly sounding as angry as Fuller had ever heard him. 'I've learned from this case that the CIA, like the KGB, is heavily involved in parapsychological research, particularly the possibilities of telepathic communication for the purposes of spying. Before you deny it, please let me say that regarding the woman in question, I can tell you that she accidentally broke into an experimental communication between a land-based, ESP-trained Naval intelligence officer and his submerged submarine. Any story to the contrary is nonsense.'

That Wilson had found this out was a truly frightening revelation to the normally unshockable Fuller.

'I can't confirm or deny that,' he replied, knowing how lame it sounded.

Wilson shook his head from side to side, as if pitying the petty deceptions of Fuller and his kind. 'You're hoping to reach our level of achievement in this field,' he told him, 'but you're wasting your time. I know about your lady from Maine because I broke into your telepathic communication in that office in CIA headquarters in Langley, Virginia, and arranged for the flying saucer to hover over Capitol Hill as a demonstration of how advanced we've become telepathically. So you see, Mr Fuller, no matter how advanced you think you are, we'll always be at least one step ahead of you – just as we are with our flying saucer technology. Your men are wasting their time.'

'Maybe,' Fuller responded, trying to sound more confident then he now felt. 'Maybe not. You're playing a dangerous game with these trade-offs, so you might slip up some day.'

'I don't think so,' Wilson said. 'Thank you and good night.'

Flanked by his two hideous, deadly cyborgs, he turned away without another word and marched back up the ramp into his towering, hundred and fifty-feet wide flying saucer. Knowing better than to be within that immense circle of marker lamps when the saucer took off, Fuller hurried away with his two armed Marines, clambered back into the jeep, and let himself be driven back to the soldiers massed around the electrified barbed-wire fence.

From the other side of that fence, Fuller and the soldiers looked up in awe as the flying saucer turned into a magically glowing, egg-shell shaped vehicle that had lights of different colours flashing in rapid sequence around its revolving rings. It lifted off vertically, hovered a few seconds above the ground, illuminating the surrounding darkness with its eerie white glow and kaleidoscopic lights, then suddenly shot up vertically, made an abrupt turn to the west about a hundred feet up, hovered again for a moment, then shot off again and dwindled rapidly until it was no more than a glowing light the size of a dime. That light also shrank, merging with the stars, then abruptly blinked out.

Though nothing unusual could be seen up there, Fuller and the many men massed around him kept scanning the night sky.

'Jesus Christ!' a soldier behind Fuller exclaimed in a stunned, disbelieving way.

'No,' Fuller responded, now staring at the sky and accepting that he might indeed be defeated. 'Jesus Christ was in the past, soldier. You've just seen the future.'

He clambered back into the jeep and told the driver to return him to the Vanguard Hotel in Cocoa Beach. He didn't anticipate getting a good night's sleep, but, at least he could be alone there.

Fuller needed a dark cave.

Chapter Thirty-One

'I don't scare easily,' Scaduto told Dwight when they sat down to cold beer in the sweltering heat of an outdoor bar in Carillon Park, Dayton, Ohio in July 1960. 'But I don't mind admitting that this business is starting to put me on edge. Particularly this latest bit of news.'

'What news?'

'Haven't you heard?'

'Heard what?'

'It was in yesterday's newspapers. Your former Project Blue Book boss, Captain Edward J. Ruppelt, has died of an unexpected heart attack.'

Dwight was truly shocked. Captain Ruppelt was even younger than he was. The last time Dwight had seen him was that sad day in December 1953 when he had informed them of the dire results of the Robertson panel report and, even worse, told them that Project Blue Book was being run down and most of its staff, including himself, dispersed to other locations. It had been a sad day for all of them, but Ruppelt had at least been his relatively young, decent, healthy self. Certainly not heart attack material.

'I don't like it,' Scaduto said. 'In 1953, Ruppelt leaves the Air Force. Three years later he writes a book in which he states categorically that UFOs are for real. Three years after that, he revises that book, reversing his previous opinions and insisting that UFOs are probably natural phenomena. And approximately one year later, in 1960, weary before his time, he dies of a heart attack. It sure makes you think, don't it?'

'Yes, it does.' In fact, this shocking piece of news had reminded Dwight not only of the many other people involved in UFO investigations who had died unexpectedly, been killed in surprising ways, or committed 'suicide' for no discernible reason. It had also reminded him of the many other ways in which UFO investigators had been made to suffer, including financial hardship, problems at work, sudden transfers to far-flung locations, actual threats and other forms of harassment from the mysterious 'men in black', and marital breakdowns based on one or other of the former. Something else not easy to forget was the fact that many UFO researchers had disappeared completely, leaving no indication of why and where they had gone. They had simply never been seen again.

Last but by no means least, the news of Ruppelt's unexpected death, added to the mysterious nature of his unexplained reversal regarding the reality of the UFO phenomenon and subsequent slide into depression and poor health after leaving the Air Force, had brutally reminded Dwight of Beth's bizarre, frightening experience eighteen months ago, when she had been driving (or so she had thought) past the garage Dwight had worked and lived in during the days of their separation.

For months, prior to the incident, Beth had been complaining that she was having bad nightmares, relating to UFOs and mysterious men in black, that she felt she was being followed, though had never actually seen anyone, and that she was haunted by the general feeling that something unknown was making her constantly fretful. The day of the incident in question, when she had just dropped Dwight off at the Dayton airport for his flight to Washington DC for his first formal visit to Dr Frederick Epstein at APII, she had imagined she was driving past the garage then owned by bachelor Frank Bancroft, then realised that she had actually been *staring* at it for some time through the window of her car, which was parked inexplicably by the side of the road. She then noticed that her wristwatch had stopped two hours previously – at approximately the time she would have passed the garage after leaving the airport. Her wristwatch was not the only item to have malfunctioned: when she tried to switch on the ignition of her car, it wouldn't start. Presumably, then, it had stopped of its own accord just as Beth was driving past the garage, about ten minutes after leaving Dayton airport. Which in turn meant that Beth – who could not recollect having stopped and had, for some time, clearly been *imagining* that she was driving past the garage, not just parked facing it – had blacked out, either just before or just after the car had stopped, and had then remained unconscious for almost two hours.

It was damned mysterious.

Even worse was what Beth saw when she awakened: the immense circle first created by the unnatural blowing of the wind, then given added definition by the inexplicable scorching of the windblown grass, which ended up charred and smouldering; and, infinitely more terrifying, the discovery of Frank Bancroft, who had clearly died suddenly and in mortal terror.

Since that incident, Beth had been more frightened than ever and Dwight, though he tried not to show it, had become more concerned for her and himself – he had even started worrying about Nichola's safety.

In fact, from that day on he had begun worrying that his UFO investigations were putting them all in mortal danger. However, when he discussed this matter with Beth, she had insisted that no matter the danger, he must continue the work and solve the mystery that was tormenting him, thus ridding himself of the obsession once and for all. Dwight had been deeply moved by her concern and courage.

'This news about Ruppelt is terrible,' he said to Scaduto, 'but obviously it isn't why you called this meeting. You could have told me about Ruppelt on the phone, so what have you brought me?'

'Man-made flying saucers,' Scaduto said.

Dwight glanced left and right, at the other people packed around the trestle tables to take in the sun while they drank and ate. There were really too many people here . . . too many . . . too close to him.

'Finish your beer and let's go for a walk,' he said, feeling paranoid.

'Sure,' Scaduto said. 'I understand.' He hurriedly gulped the last of his beer, threw the can into the rubbish bin near the table, then proceeded to stroll with Dwight through the park, which was, on this sunny day in July, filled with people walking their dogs, teenagers careening about on rollerskates, and younger children playing with bats and balls. 'I think it's becoming more certain,' he began, 'that the UFOs seen over various Air Force installations are actually top-secret, highly advanced US-Canadian aircraft.'

He fell silent for a moment, letting Dwight take this in, but also enjoying the melodrama, then continued talking as they meandered through the park.

'I should begin by reminding you that at least *some* kind of saucer-shaped prototypes had actually been constructed by the US and Canada: first, the US Navy's Flying Flounder and the Air Force's Flying Flapjack – projects reportedly worked on sometime between 1942 and 1947 – followed by the flying saucer that the Canadian government claimed they'd aborted and passed over to the US in 1954.'

'Right,' Dwight said. 'I remember.'

'Now the most interesting thing about those projects,' Scaduto went on enthusiastically, 'is that the US Navy claimed to have dropped their project back in 1947 but were known to be still involved in super-secret aeronautical projects scattered around the White Sands Proving Ground, New Mexico – where so many flying saucers have been reported. Also, the Canadian government, while admitting that the enormous UFO seen over Albuquerque in 1951 was similar to the one they'd tried to build, claimed that they'd passed the project on to the US because they couldn't afford it . . . In other words, the UFO over Albuquerque could have been a US product based on the Canadian designs of 1947.'

'Where's this all leading, Tony?'

Tony stopped to light a cigarette and contaminate the pure air of the park with smoke. Though bright, he had an addictive personality which, so far, had given him a taste for alcohol, cigarettes and women. He had also flirted with marijuana once or twice, but so far had kept a decent distance from it. Inhaling, then exhaling a cloud of smoke, he started walking again.

'Ever since I began this man-made UFO business,' he said, 'I've found myself harping back to the fact that the first major contemporary sightings, the Kenneth Arnold sightings of June 24, 1947, took place near Mount Rainier in the Cascades in the state of Washington – which divides Canada from Oregon – and that Arnold had stated that *nine* silvery discs had disappeared in the direction of the Canadian border. As I've since found out, however, what wasn't so widely known at the time was that on that very same day another man, Fred Johnson, prospecting about four thousand feet up in the Cascades, reported seeing six similar objects; and three days before, on June 21, Harold Dahl, on harbour patrol in Puget Sound – which runs from the Canadian border to Tacoma – was following the coastline of Maury Island when he saw five UFOs manoeuvring fifteen hundred feet above the coast, before disappearing toward the open sea.'

'Right,' Dwight responded, surprised by his own impatience. 'It's true that those facts weren't widely known at the time, but we covered the Arnold case pretty extensively at ATIC, so we learnt about those other sightings a year or so later.'

'Okay,' Scaduto said, not remotely deterred by Dwight's criticism. 'Let's take it from there.'

Two young people were lying in the middle of the field to their right, under the shade of an elm tree. The girl, wearing tight blue jeans and a tight sweater, was practically buried under a young man wearing the same kind of jeans but with his shirt off. Writhing together and kissing passionately, they were lost to the real world – something that Scaduto clearly noticed with envious gaze.

'Throughout that whole month,' Scaduto continued, tearing his eyes away from the couple on the grass, 'there were a hell of a lot of sightings over the northwestern corner of the United States. By the first week in July there were also reports of strange, luminous bodies in the skies over the Province of Quebec, Oregon and New England. The following week, those sightings spread to California and New Mexico. By the end of the year – the same year the US Navy had, reportedly, *dropped* their flying saucer project – flying saucers were being reported from all over the place.'

'And the next major UFO flap was the Washington invasion of 1952,' Dwight said, 'of which I had personal experience.'

'Correct.' Scaduto glanced back over his shoulder at the young couple on the grass, now quite far away. The sight of them gave him distracting thoughts and forced him to concentrate. 'On reinvestigating that case,' he said, 'using your old ATIC reports as my map, I discovered that while the real flap had started on July 19, there was a record dated June 17 of several unidentified red spheres that flew at supersonic speeds over the Canadian air base of North Bay, in Ontario, then crossed over some of the southeastern states. I also discovered that nearly all of the subsequent Washington UFOs were reported as disappearing to the north, and that when the UFOs returned en masse, on July 26, their disappearance in a general northerly direction also applied.'

'All heading towards the Canadian border.'

'Right, Dwight, you've got it.'

'Well,' Dwight said, 'it's certainly true that Lake Ontario

and Lake Erie are as notorious as the Bermuda Triangle for the unexplained destruction of hundreds of aircraft and ships, the failure of gyroscopes and radio instruments, irrational behaviour in normally sane crew members, and, of course, the sighting of numerous UFOs. It's also true that Canada's one of the greatest aeronautical powers in the world.'

'Yeah,' Scaduto said, sounding richly satisfied. 'I never thought of Canada that way until I began my research. In fact, during that research I came across an article, dated 1952 – at the height of the flying saucer scare – describing Canada as the Promised Land of aviation. Considering that I, and a great many other Americans, had always thought of Canada as a kind of No-Man's Land, I was suitably impressed to learn that in fact it was the home, even back in 1952, of a remarkable number of the most famous aircraft development companies in the world.'

'It also had, and still has, vast areas of heavily wooded and uninhabited land – ideal for hiding secret aeronautical research establishments.'

'Just what hit me!' Scaduto exclaimed, clearly thrilled that he and Dwight had been on the same wave-length, great minds thinking alike, as it were. 'So having learnt these interesting facts, I decided to find out, once and for all, whether or not the Canadian saucer project had really been passed on to the US Air Force and, more important, if the Air Force had then really dropped the project, as widely reported.'

'So what did you learn?'

'A lot.'

Dwight really liked Tony Scaduto and was, in a sense, envious of his relative youthfulness, naïve optimism, and Brooklyn-based 'street' wisdom, but sometimes, as he was forced to admit to himself, Tony's flair for self-dramatization could be aggravating. For this very reason he wanted to devastate Tony with an unforgettably cutting remark, which he now tried to formulate.

'Stop teasing,' Dwight said.

'Okay,' Scaduto responded, satisfied with the belief that he had managed to get one up on Dwight, whom he admired and wished to emulate. 'My research revealed that on February 11, 1953, the Toronto *Star* announced that a *new* flying saucer was being developed at the A. V. Roe plant – now Avro-Canada – in Malton, Ontario.'

'This suggests that it wasn't the first one.'

'Right,' Scaduto said. 'Then, on February 16, the Canadian Minister of Defence Production, C. D. Howe, informed the House of Commons that Avro-Canada was in fact working on a mock-up model of a flying saucer capable of flying at fifteen hundred miles per hour and climbing straight up in the air.'

'Really?'

'It's all there in the morgues of the daily newspapers.'

'Christ!' Dwight exclaimed, becoming excited. 'And then?'

'By February 27, Crawford Gordon Jr., the president of Avro-Canada, was writing in the house journal, *Avro News*, that the prototype being built was so revolutionary that it would make all other forms of supersonic aircraft obsolescent. Next, the Toronto *Star* was claiming that Britain's Field Marshal Montgomery had become one of the few people to view Avro's mock-up of the flying saucer. Shortly after that report, Air Vice Marshal D. M. Smith was reported to have said that what Field Marshal Montgomery had seen was the preliminary construction plans for a gyroscopic fighter whose gas turbine would revolve around the pilot, who would be positioned in the centre of the disc.'

'Oh, my God!' Dwight whispered, glancing left and right at the many other people moving in both directions along the path winding through the park. 'The *Omega*!'

'Good man! You remembered! *Yes!* The press dubbed that then legendary machine "the *Omega*" and in 1953 the British *RAF Review* – *the Royal Air Force Review* – gave it a semi-official respectability by reprinting most of the unclassified Canadian research and including censored drawings of the machine.'

'The research and those drawings were actually *published*?'

'Yeah – but only in Great Britain.'

'Wow!' Temporarily forgetting his personal fears, Dwight felt like an excited school kid. 'So what was the *Omega*?'

'According to the sketches, it was a relatively small, horseshoe-shaped flying wing, with numerous air-intake slots along its edge, ten deflector vanes for direction control, a single pilot-cabin topped by a cupola of transparent Perspex, and a large turbine engine that revolved around the vertical axis of the main body.'

'Then it disappeared,' Dwight tried to anticipate.

'Not quite,' Scaduto replied, enjoying Dwight's shock and excitement at his revelations. 'In early November, 1953, Canadian newspapers were reporting that a mock-up of the *Omega* had been shown on October 31 to a group of twenty-five military officers and scientists. Then in March of the following year the American press were claiming that the US Air Force, concerned at Soviet progress in aeronautics, had allocated an unspecified sum of money to the Canadian government for the building of a prototype of their flying saucer. Reportedly, that machine had been designed by the English aeronautical engineer, John Frost – who'd worked for Avro-Canada in Malton, Ontario – and it would be capable of either hovering in midair or flying at a speed of nearly two thousand miles an hour.'

Dwight gave a low whistle.

'This hot bit of news,' Scaduto continued, 'was followed by Canadian press assertions that their government was planning to form entire squadrons of flying saucers for the defence of Alaska and the far regions of the North. This, they claimed, was because the machines required no runways, were capable of rising vertically, and were ideal weapons for sub-arctic and polar regions.'

'Sub-arctic and polar regions,' Dwight repeated, practically in a daze.

'Right,' Scaduto said, glancing sideways and grinning when he saw the growing awareness in Dwight's eyes. 'So, do you want to hear the rest?'

'Yes,' Dwight said.

'On December 3, 1954, the Canadian Minister of Defence announced that *their* flying saucer project had been dropped, since it would have cost too much for something that was, in the end, highly speculative.'

Dwight stopped walking, glanced at the many people criss-crossing on the park and walking their dogs, flying kites, rollerskating and embracing on the green fields of the park, and then found himself glancing more intently at them, wondering if they were really what they seemed. He saw no men in black.

'So what makes you believe the saucer project wasn't dropped completely?' he asked Scaduto.

'Because on October 22 the following year US Air Force Secretary Donald Quarles released an extraordinary statement through the press office of the Department of Defence. Among other things, he said that an aircraft of – I quote – unusual configuration and flight characteristics – would soon be appearing; that the US government had initiated negotiations with the Canadian government and Avro-Canada for the preparation of an experimental model of the Frost flying disc; and that the saucers would be mass-produced and used for the common defence of the sub-arctic area of the continent.'

'The sub-arctic area,' Dwight murmured distractedly. 'We're back with the sub-arctic.'

'Right,' Scaduto said. 'Ice and snow. But it didn't end there . . .'

Now Dwight stopped walking to stare directly at Scaduto. Dwight no longer gave a damn who overheard. Paranoid or not, he was convinced that everything he said and did was being monitored somehow. Given that conviction, whether sane or mad, he could only follow his nose.

'Okay,' he said, following his nose. 'Tell me the rest of it.'

Grinning wickedly, Scaduto took a deep breath, held it in for some time, then let it all out.

'By February last year the press was receiving ambiguous Air Force statements about a revolutionary new aircraft that had been jointly undertaken by the US Air Force, the US Army, and the Canadian government. Then, on April 14, during a press conference in Washington DC, General Frank Britten implied that the first test flight of the aircraft was imminent and that it was destined to revolutionize traditional aeronautical concepts.'

'So when's that test flight going to be?' Dwight asked, now realising that Scaduto's whole spiel had been leading up to this single, crucial point.

Scaduto, wearing his customary Marlon Brando biker's black-leather jacket and pants with matching boots, brushing his ink-black sideburns with self-worshipping fingers, and taking a deep breath of the kind that all born actors love, said: 'The test flight's already been completed. The results haven't been announced yet. But – get this! – the press has actually been invited to look at the saucer on 25 August – next month – at the Army Transport Museum at Fort Eustus, Virginia.'

'What's the bet you don't see much?' Dwight asked.

'I don't bet,' Scaduto said.

Amused despite himself, being otherwise deeply troubled, Dwight walked out of the park with Scaduto, bid him goodbye, then hurried home to take comfort from Beth's embrace, suck the juices from her throat, and finally lose himself in the tangle of her arms and legs, in her centre, her very being, in that bed they had bought many years ago when, in fear and trembling and mutual need, they became man and wife.

Dwight's dark cave was love.

Chapter Thirty-Two

Dwight's dark cave of love was a help, but not a cure, during the nightmarish month that followed his meeting with Tony Scaduto and the press conference arranged for the unveiling of the first officially acknowledged man-made UFO. Already haunted by her frightening experience at Frank Bancroft's garage, Beth had then started experiencing terrifying nightmares about UFOs and faceless men dressed in black. Soon she was also tormented by the feeling that she was somehow being followed and kept under observation. She felt this even when in her car.

'It's hard to explain,' she said, 'because there's nothing I can put my finger on – nothing seen or heard or actually felt. But when I'm driving, particularly when on the roads outside town – empty roads – I have the feeling that something is pressing down slightly on the car, exerting some kind of pressure, and that pressure is also pressing down and around me.'

She and Dwight were sitting in deck chairs out on the back yard on the tract house they had leased just a week ago, having decided that they needed something bigger than the previous apartment near Carillon Park. Nichola, presently playing in the small, pumped-up pool in front of them with a neighbour's daughter, Tanya Harper, was all of twelve years old and would soon be a teenager in need of her own space, so that had been their major consideration when deciding to move. As the sun was now blazing out of a clear blue sky, Beth and Dwight, both in swim suits and

379

relishing the privacy of their own back yard, were trying for a suntan.

'Any effect on the car itself?' Dwight asked. 'Any malfunctioning?'

'No – yes! It doesn't malfunction, but it definitely drags. In fact, I often find myself checking the handbrake, thinking it's on. Then I find myself looking out of the car, trying to see what's around me, what's slowing me down.'

'Ever stop and actually get out of the car to look directly above it?'

'Yep. That shows you how bad it is. I sometimes get out and look up, but I've never seen anything. Strangely, that worries me even more. And I get almost sick with anxiety when Nichola's with me. I even feel that odd . . . *presence* . . . call it what you will . . . when I'm taking her to school.'

'Does she feel it?'

'She's never mentioned it and I've never asked. No, she seems happy enough strapped in there.'

During the last two weeks of that sweltering July, 1960, Beth's nightmares became more frequent and the feeling that she was never entirely alone increased dramatically. She began feeling it while waiting outside Nichola's school, at the supermarket, sometimes even when sunning herself out in the back yard or tending to the lawn.

'I'll be feeling perfectly fine,' she explained to Dwight, 'engrossed in what I'm doing and suddenly – I mean out of the blue – I'll find myself looking up or around me, expecting to see someone or . . . *something*.' She shrugged forlornly. 'It's a feeling so strong that you're convinced someone is staring right at you and they're very close – you know? Like just the other side of the yard fence, just across the street, or only a short distance behind you in the mall. A very *strong* feeling. Shivery. I'm thinking of the shopping, or what Nichola's doing at school, or where we should go on our next vacation – then, whammo! my head jerks around before I even know it and I find myself staring to the side, behind me, wherever, expecting to see . . . yeah, a man, or men, in black. I always expect to see *them*. And of course there's never anyone there and, as I said, in some way that's even worse. 'Cause sure as hell, it makes you think you're losing your mind or having a breakdown.'

By early August, Beth's feelings of being followed were given concrete form when a black limousine started following her, just about every time she went out. At first she thought she was imagining this, but at the end of the first day with that car on her tail – a particularly busy day that had her driving here, there and everywhere, including school in the morning, the supermarket, the houses of a couple of friends, then school in the afternoon to collect Nichola, she realised that the limo was real enough and definitely following her when it stopped everywhere she stopped, then started up again and followed her when she moved off. By the end of the first day of this, she was truly frightened.

It continued through a second day, then a third and fourth. When Beth stopped, the limo stopped as well, always parking within sight, though never close enough for her to see anything other than the figures of men in . . . black suits. As they were always too distant for their features to be made out, Beth was reminded of her nightmares, in which the men in black, albeit one-piece suits, always seemed somehow faceless.

Finally, during the fifth day, when she was waiting for Nichola to come out of school and suffering the dreadful fear that the men in black might abduct her, she got out of her car and hurried along the sidewalk towards the limo parked a good distance away. The limo didn't move until she was approaching it – until she could clearly discern the two men in the front – black suits, black roll-necked pullovers, dark glasses – but could still not make out their features. Just as she was getting close enough to see what they looked like, the limo pulled out, did a U-turn and raced away.

Relieved, Beth returned to her car and waited for Nichola

to come out of school. When she had collected her and was driving back to the house, the black limo appeared out of a side street and sat on her tail again. When she entered the house, clutching Nichola's hand, the limo parked a good way along the street, but close enough for her to see it from the front window. Just as she picked up the phone to call the police, the limo drove off.

'Just like that,' Beth explained to Dwight, snapping her fingers. 'As if they could see exactly what I was doing. The second I picked up the phone, those bastards drove off.'

That, however, was the last time she was tailed by the men in the limo. Unfortunately, during the second week in August, she began to have serious lapses of memory and what appeared to be brief black-outs which, like her experience by the garage, left her feeling bewildered and disorientated. The black-outs were not dramatic and at no point harmful – she never collapsed or lost control of the moving car – but they were of a nature that was just as damaging emotionally.

Preparing dinner in the kitchen, she would, some time later, find herself lying on the bed or the sofa in front of the TV with no memory of having made the move, but vague recollections of the usual nightmares of UFOs and men in black. Packing her shopping into the trunk of her car outside the supermarket, she would suddenly find herself emerging from the usual nightmares of UFOs and men in black, this time slumped over the steering wheel with the trunk still open and the rest of the shopping still in the trolley. Sitting in the car outside the school, waiting for Nichola to emerge, she would suddenly see Nichola standing forlornly on the sidewalk as the last of the other kids either walked off or were driven away by their parents. Though unable to recall the children emerging from the school, she would rush to collect Nichola, her head still filled with a vision of herself being surrounded by the men in black in a circular, brilliantly lit, white-walled room. Such lapses of consciousness, and the nightmares contained within them, made her a nervous wreck.

Beth went to see her doctor and told him she felt tense and couldn't sleep, though without mentioning the actual cause of her problem. Placed on a course of Valium, some of the tension slipped away, but even the sedative didn't help when, watching Nichola playing with Tanya in the park, she lost consciousness again and awakened to see three men in black suits talking to both the children. When Beth hurried towards them, the men, too distant to be recognised, glanced in her direction, then hurried away to disappear into the trees around the edge of the playing field. When Beth, her heart beating furiously, asked Nichola what the men had wanted, Nichola replied: 'They asked if my mother was Beth Randall. I said "Yes" and they just looked at each other without saying anything else. Then you came along.'

'If those men ever come near you again,' Beth warned Nichola, 'you run away and come straight to me. Understood?'

'Yes, Mom.'

Beth's dreams now became more vivid and frightening. She dreamed that the men in black had abducted Nichola. She had another dream about Dwight disappearing and never being seen again. Mostly, however, her dreams were composed of hallucinatory, fragmented recollections of that great circle of black ash around the garage once run by Dwight; the look of stark terror on the dead Frank Bancroft's face; herself stretched out on a cold, metal table staring up at a ring of faces, some human, some part-metallic and dreadful; small creatures with alien faces and steel claws for hands; curving steel-grey corridors; a room filled with severed human heads and other bodily parts; herself strapped to a chair with a metal cap on her head; and, finally, white-painted steel panels sliding apart to reveal panoramic windows and, beyond them, a vast, desolate terrain of ice and snow.

The dreams, though fragmented, were relentless in the

terror they created for her, making her jerk awake, screaming, bathed in sweat, to be held and rocked by a concerned, helpless Dwight.

'It's real!' she once sobbed. 'I know it's real!'

'No, it's not,' Dwight replied. 'You're just having bad dreams, Beth.'

But even he didn't sound convinced.

In fact, Dwight was, at that point, being torn between his deep concern for Beth and his rage against those who were doing this to her. It was a very personal kind of rage, focused on the men in black, because he now believed absolutely that they existed and were responsible for what was happening to her. Yet even as his anger grew and he determined to fight back, he was frustrated because the men in black made no more appearances.

Instead, worse things happened.

The first manifestation was similar to Dwight's experience in the motel outside Albuquerque, only this time it happened right outside his own house.

Beth had taken some Valium and was still having trouble sleeping, with Dwight holding her in his arms, when the latter felt a distinct rise in temperature, heard a bass humming sound from outside, as if directly above the house, then was startled by the violent shaking of the bed as striations of brilliant light beamed in through the window. The bass humming sound increased, turning into a vibrating presence, a faint pressure, as the room shook even more violently, with framed pictures swinging crazily on the walls and ornaments falling off chests-of-drawers and cupboards. Nichola cried out in her bedroom. 'Mom! Dad!' Though sedated with Valium, Beth tore herself from Dwight's embrace and ran into Nichola's bedroom as Dwight rushed to the window to look out.

He stared into a blinding radiance. It was beaming down from above the house. It was so bright he couldn't keep his eyes open and, cursing, blindly fumbled at the window catches to unlock them and open the window. As he was doing so, the bass humming sound cut out, the room stopped shaking, and Dwight, when he opened his eyes, was able to see clearly.

He saw moonlight shining on the untouched back yard. Nothing else. He opened the window as Beth came back into the bedroom, one arm around the sobbing Nichola's shoulder, patting her head reassuringly with her free hand. Dwight stuck his head through the window and looked up as high as he could, trying to see directly above the house. He saw a shrinking light, what might have been a shooting star, then it blinked out abruptly, leaving only the starry sky.

'It's all right, it's all right,' Beth was repeating consolingly to the sobbing Nichola where they lay together on the bed. 'It's all right now, sweetheart.'

But it wasn't all right. In fact, it was just beginning. During the final week before the press viewing of the Avrocar, as if as a warning to Dwight, the visitations occurred every night for five nights in a row, with the house shaking more each time, the noise growing louder, the pressure becoming stronger, and the contents of the house flung about and smashed. As Nichola howled in Beth's arms and Beth shrieked for the manifestations to stop – not knowing who she was shouting at, but staring fearfully at the window – the striations beaming in from outside would start flickering like strobe lights, the rate increasing every second, until Dwight, Beth and Nichola saw each other as bizarre, jerkily moving figures in a disorientating, constantly changing chiaroscuro filled with hellish noise and applying an indefinable pressure upon them, making them feel that their heads and hearts were going to burst.

Sometimes the burners on the oven would come on by themselves; other times water would pour out of the taps, flooding over the rim of the sink and onto the floor; then the electric lights, radio or TV would turn themselves on and off repeatedly, adding to the general bedlam and visual chaos.

Each night was worse than the one before, with the lights brighter and flickering faster, the bass humming sound deeper and increasingly physical – an infrasound – and the pressure around their heads tighter and giving them headaches. Each night, when it had finished, Dwight would either jerk the window up and stick his head out or run out on the front lawn to see what had caused it – and only see what he thought, or imagined, was a tiny light shrinking and disappearing directly above the house, leaving only the stars in the night sky.

By the fourth day of this final week before the press viewing of the Avrocar, while the outside of the house remained unharmed, the grass on the front lawn and back yard was singed. There was no damage to any of the neighbours' houses and tentative enquiries produced no sign that the neighbours – their houses all spaced well apart – had either heard or seen anything unusual.

'If this happens one more time,' Dwight told Beth as they tidied up the mess of broken glass, picture frames and ornaments caused by the violent shaking of the house the night before, 'I'm going to send Nichola and you to stay with your folks.'

'Every night,' Beth whispered as if talking to herself, not really there. 'Why every night?'

'I don't know, honey.'

'They don't attempt to get near us. We never see them. What do they want?'

We don't even know who 'they' are, Dwight thought, though he didn't actually say it.

'One more time,' he said, 'and you're out of here. You and Nichola both. I don't know what it is, how it's happening, but I'm getting you out of here.'

'I'm not going if you don't ,' Beth said.

'Yes, you are,' Dwight insisted.

The fifth night was the worst of all. The visitation came so late that they thought it wasn't coming and Beth was actually slipping gratefully into sleep. It was just before four in the morning and she was lying between Dwight and Nichola, who was now too frightened to sleep in her own bed. Dwight was still awake, looking sideways at the two most important people in his life – his wife and his daughter – choked up to see them sleeping together, when he suddenly turned cold, then hot, and heard that familiar bass humming sound. At first shocked, then plunging into a cauldron of rage and despair, he reached out to Beth as her eyes opened wide, changing instantly from sleepiness to terror. Even as Beth let out a low groan and turned to embrace the awakened, frightened Nichola, the bass humming sound grew louder, becoming an almost physical vibration, and the whole room began to shake, with the framed pictures swinging wildly on the walls and ornaments and other items rattling or falling to the floor. As Nichola cried out, 'Mom! Dad!' and Beth held her close, pulling the sheets over both of them, light exploded through the window, illuminating the whole room, and then turned into a chiaroscuro flickering on and off with a rapidity that disorientated Dwight.

'Bastards!' he bawled.

As if in response, the bottom end of the bed leapt up in the air and banged down again. The lamp on the bedside cabinet became a fountain of sparks and then exploded with the wires spitting flames. Instinctively, Dwight rolled out of the wildly rocking bed, jerked the plug of the lamp from its socket, then smothered the flames with the shirt he had draped over a nearby chair. Nichola was sobbing in terror under the bedsheet, being comforted by Beth, as Dwight crawled on hands and knees across the floor, showered in debris from the plaster exploding out of the ceiling and raining down upon him.

As more cracks spread across the ceiling and the bed jumped up and down like a maddened beast, the floorboards creaked, screeched, then snapped apart under the heaving carpet. Dazzled by the flickering patterns created by what seemed like strobe lights, Dwight nevertheless managed to reach the door of the bedroom. Glancing back, he saw that the bed had stopped rocking and the ceiling above it was no longer cracking and raining plaster and powder. Knowing that Beth and Nichola, no matter how upset, would be all right, Dwight, in a fury that obliterated his terror, jumped up and ran across the living room, heading for the front door.

As he crossed the living room, the cracks zigzagged along the ceiling directly above him, as if tracking his movements, showering him again in broken plaster and powder. Even here, the furniture was jumping, lightbulbs were exploding, and the light was pouring in through the windows, flickering rapidly, the same as in the bedroom. Disorientated by this, Dwight kept bumping into furniture and once turned in the wrong direction, but eventually, by groping his way along a wall, he reached the front door. Without hesitation, not caring if he lived or died, he tugged the front door open and rushed outside.

What he saw there stopped him in his tracks.

The lights beaming in through the windows of the house and flickering on and off rapidly were blazing out of disc-shaped metallic objects no more than three or four feet in diameter and hovering in mid-air by the windows. The instant Dwight, wearing his pyjamas, rushed out of the house and stopped, frozen by shock, on the path, the lights from the disc-shaped objects blinked out, the objects spun at such speed they became silvery-white blurs, and then they shot upwards at tremendous speed.

Looking up, Dwight nearly fell backwards with shock when he saw the small, spinning discs vanishing into what appeared to be an enormous black hole inside an immense circle formed by multicoloured lights that winked on and off rapidly to form a dazzling kaleidoscope. Approximately a hundred and fifty feet wide, that circle was exerting a downward-thrusting pressure that seemed to press heavily upon Dwight.

Glancing about him, he saw that the stars were visible

outside that vast circle of flashing lights and that directly below the lights, on the ground – at least what he could see of the ground where it wasn't broken up by fences and portions of the other houses – the grass or dust was being sucked up to quiver frantically or billow in a curved line that obviously formed another circle matching the one above.

No sooner had Dwight noticed this than the flashing lights blinked out, leaving only a black hole about a hundred and fifty feet wide and definable only by the stars surrounding it. Then, with a speed that confused Dwight's vision, the black hole shrank, letting the stars rush back in, followed by an abrupt flaring of light hundreds of feet up. The flaring light then shrank and vanished altogether, leaving only the darkness.

Now, where that great hole had been, there was only the normal, star-filled sky.

The grass and grit that had been sucked up in a matching circle had settled down and the downward-thrusting pressure inside the circle could be felt no more.

Realising that he had just witnessed the ascent of some enormous, circular craft and that the small discs had flown back into it before it ascended, Dwight rushed back into the house, through the living room and into the bedroom.

He found Beth and Nichola embracing under the bedsheets, both frightened, but unharmed.

Convinced that the visitations were not only a means of warning him off his UFO investigations, but were also related to the forthcoming press viewing of the A. V. Roe man-made flying saucer, Dwight believed that the night before the viewing – tomorrow night – would be the worst of all.

'I want you to take Nichola and go spend the night with your parents,' he told Beth the following morning as they sat side by side on the sofa in the wrecked living room. 'I think you could both be in real danger. The effects of

389

that . . . whatever it is, have been worse with each successive night and I'm afraid that tonight the damage could be even greater – so I don't want you or Nichola here.'

'I don't want *you* here.' Beth replied, rubbing her bloodshot eyes and looking haggard. 'I'm convinced that sooner or later they're going to enter the house and take you away. I'm sure that's what it's all about.'

'If they do, I want to be here, Beth. I want to know who they are. I can't run away now.'

'If they take you, you'll never be seen again.'

'That's a chance I've got to take, Beth.'

She clung to him, sobbing, begging him not to stay, but after comforting her, he made her call her folks and arrange to spend the night with them. She was still sobbing as she packed an overnight bag for herself and Nichola, but she managed to control herself when Dwight led her and Nichola out to the car and kissed them goodbye.

Dwight watched the car move off along the street and disappear around the corner at the bottom. It was six in the evening.

Returning to the house, which Beth had spent all afternoon carefully tidying, Dwight poured himself a bourbon and sat in the lounge, waiting for nightfall. The telephone rang. When he picked it up, Beth told him she'd arrived unharmed and that he was to call her, no matter the time, when the visitation had ended. Dwight promised to do so, then he hung up the phone and finished his bourbon. Two more large bourbons were poured and a few more hours passed before the sun sank and darkness prevailed. Dwight kept the lights out. He waited patiently for the visitation. He sat in that empty room until dawn broke, but there was no visitation.

'Nothing,' he said on the phone to Beth at nine the next morning. 'Not a damned thing. How about you?'

'The best sleep I've had in weeks,' Beth replied. 'I feel like a new woman.'

'It's as if they knew . . .'

'They knew. They know everything, Dwight. I'm convinced I was followed as I drove here, but they didn't do anything. I think they've been warning you off – maybe because of today.'

'The Avrocar.'

'Yes. They were letting you know that they know what you're doing and don't approve of it.'

'But they didn't come last night.'

'The warning's over. I don't think they'll come back. At least not tonight or in the immediate future. They'll do what they want, when they want, but it won't be tonight. If they'd wanted to stop you going to that press conference, they'd have done it tonight. We're coming home, honey.'

'You do that,' Dwight said.

He hung up the phone, leaned against the wall, covered his face in his hands and sobbed tears of relief.

Later that day, Dwight flew to Washington DC, where he was collected by Tony Scaduto and Bob Jackson, then driven to the Army Transport Museum at Fort Eustus, Virginia. There, in a large, gloomy hangar that included no other exhibits, with a whole pack of journalists and photographers, the latter including Jack Judges, who had first photographed the sole exhibit on display by flying illegally over the base, he was shown the formerly secret, now unclassified man-made flying saucer prototype, the Avro Car.

What those assembled were shown was an experimental, piloted aircraft, forty feet in diameter and weighing 3,600 lbs, that combined the characteristics of air-cushion machines: a crude flying saucer based on the principles of the jet ring and, according to the Army press officer, barely able to rise above the runway during its recent test flight.

It couldn't possibly have been mistaken for what had come down over Dwight's house the previous evening.

'This is bullshit!' Dwight whispered. 'Just another red herring.'

'Apart from the disc-shaped platform of this aircraft,' the Army press officer informed them, standing beneath the Avrocar where it was dangling at an angle from the ceiling, 'the most revolutionary feature of the project is the use made of the gyroscopic effect of a revolving power plant to acquire stability. As you can see' – he pointed to the dome-shaped Perspex cabin in the middle of the disc-shaped body – 'the pilot is seated in a central plastic capsule which can be ejected should the aircraft find itself in difficulties. A gas turbine power plant of unconventional design revolves around this capsule at several hundred revolutions per minute. A stationary wing containing a series of slots in the leading edge, which feed air to the turbine, surrounds the rotating power-plant housing and forms the rim of the aircraft. Part of the intake of air is compressed and fed to combustion chambers in the wing and ejected through a series of exhaust orifices lining the outer rim of the disc. The remainder of the airflow is fed over a series of vertical deflector vanes in the flattened trailing edge of the aircraft for control purposes. A tripod-type launching gear was planned to enable the saucer to take off vertically, but with the disastrous results of the test flight, the work never even went that far.'

'What technical details can you give us?' Bob Jackson asked.

'I'm afraid most of those are still classified,' the press officer replied blandly, 'but I *can* tell you that the power house of this particular machine housed three one thousand horse power Continental J69-T-9 turbojets. It was designed to have a maximum forward speed of three hundred mph and a range of one thousand miles; but when test flown last month, it never did more than hover within ground effect.'

'Is this the only such project being developed?' Tony Scaduto asked.

'It's not the first,' the press officer confessed, 'but almost certainly it's going to be the last.'

'Why?' Bob Jackson asked.

'The truth of the matter is although quite a number of aircraft featuring circular, disc-shaped or annular wing forms have been built and flown in the past few years, the aerodynamics of such shapes haven't been fully established. The design problems facing us are therefore formidable and, in the view of the majority of our engineers, probably insurmountable.'

'So what's happening to this project?' Scaduto asked him.

'We'll be dropping it,' the press office told him. 'As for this prototype, to prove that all the talk of flying saucers is bullshit – sorry, gentlemen, ha, ha, nonsense – we're going to leave it here on display for the benefit of the general public, along with everything else in the Museum. We *have* been interested in the possibility of air-cushion machines capable of vertical take-off and landing – or VTOL – to avoid the necessity of lengthy airways. In the event, the most we could come up with was this pretty primitive, so-called flying saucer. As for real flying saucers . . . well, if you want those, you'll have to go buy yourselves tickets to some science-fiction movies, which I'm told are very popular these days. So please rest assured,' he continued when the laughter had died down, 'that the Department of Defence will soon be formally withdrawing from participation in this interesting, failed project and that no other disc or spherical-shaped prototypes are on the agenda. Ladies and gentlemen, thank you.'

'Withdrawing from participation with *whom*?' Scaduto whispered when the press conference was over and they were making their final, careful inspection of the Avrocar.

'Good question,' Dwight said.

PART THREE

Chapter Thirty-Three

Approximately three years after the public unveiling of the Avrocar, which had killed off most public speculation about the possibility of man-made UFOs, Jack Fuller, who had engineered the whole dodge, was having a bad morning in his office in CIA Headquarters, Langley Field, Virginia. This was due mainly to the fact that he was in the middle of an acrimonious divorce from his second wife, Lorraine Sandison, and she was trying to drive him mad on the telephone.

After his disastrous, eighteen-month first marriage to Belinda Wolfe, the ravishing brunette daughter of Georgetown aristocrats, Fuller had vowed never to marry again. He didn't want kids, he didn't believe in fidelity, and he had a low boredom threshold when it came to sex or romantic adventure. Unfortunately, he also had an eye for sophisticated beauties and an inability to take 'No' for an answer. His second wife, Lorraine, another child of wealthy parents, though from Alexandria, Virginia, had resolutely refused to surrender completely to him until he had agreed to tie the knot. As she was stunningly beautiful and an adroit sexual tease, he had finally caved in and convinced himself that this time the marriage would work out.

Once he had bedded Lorraine, however, his desperate need to possess her waned rapidly. Subsequently, he had refused to give her children, returned almost immediately to the pursuit of other women, and beaten her up once or twice when she refused to submit to his more outrageous sexual demands, which included what he thought was only a *modest* brand of sado-masochistic frolics.

Within three months, Lorraine, a notably cool and, in many ways, calculating beauty, was a sobbing wreck who spent more nights sleeping in her parents' mansion house in McLean, Virginia, than she did in Fuller's fancy apartment off Dupont Circle. Two months ago, encouraged by her outraged parents, she had applied for divorce on the grounds of adultery and repeated physical abuse – this after only seven months of marriage. In fact, Fuller had been relieved, wanting out of the marriage, until Lorraine started picking up the telephone to fill his ear with scorn and various legal threats. When Fuller wasn't listening to her, he was listening to her lawyer, which in no way made him feel any better.

Fuller was therefore in a bad mood when his secretary called to say she had a former USAF Captain, Bob Jackson, on the line, wishing to speak to him on behalf of the Aerial Phenomenon Investigations Institute.

Aware that APII was headed by that troublemaker Dr Frederick Epstein, that it was now using the meddlesome Dwight Randall as a freelance stringer in Dayton, Ohio, and that it had recently been kicking up a stink about CIA involvement in the suppression of information about UFOs, Fuller was about to tell his secretary to give Jackson the brush-off. Realising, however, that he needed some distraction from Lorraine and her scavenging lawyer and, also, that he could not resist finding out what Bob Jackson, Dwight Randall's best friend, wanted with him, Fuller told his secretary to put the call through.

'Mr Fuller?'

'Yeah, this is special agent Jack Fuller. Is this a personal call, Mr Jackson, or are you ringing on behalf of APII?'

'On behalf of APII.'

'APII aren't popular with this office at the moment,' Fuller informed him. 'All that talk about CIA suppression of UFO information.'

'That's the impression we get, Mr Fuller.'

'Impressions can be misleading.'

'Actually more than impressions, Mr Fuller. We have a fairly substantial bundle of evidence here to support our contention that the CIA are involved in the suppression of UFO material and the harassment of witnesses.'

'Well, you guys see what you want to see,' Fuller said blandly, 'and what you're reading isn't always what it seems. Your organisation has us all wrong, but this being a democratic society, I guess that's your privilege. So what did you call me for?'

'Because we're not at all sure that this is a democratic society.'

'Oh? Why not?'

'We've come across some old records indicating that you were the CIA officer in charge of the intelligence team that checked the Socorro UFO crash site with local farmer Marlon Clarke, way back in 1947.'

'No secret in that,' Fuller replied.

'According to local newspaper records, Clarke disappeared soon after being interrogated by you and Air Force intelligence about the sighting.'

'If you're implying that the CIA had something to do with his disappearance, I can only say that's paranoid nonsense.'

'I wasn't about to say that, Mr Fuller. I was only going to ask if, since 1947, there's been any new information on the fate of Mr Clarke?'

'The short answer is no. Marlon Clarke disappeared without trace and hasn't been seen or heard from since. We, the CIA, know no more about his fate than you do. But I'm sure that's not what you really phoned me about.'

'No, it wasn't.'

'Get straight to the point, Mr Roberts. I'm here to oblige.'

'Are you willing to tell me, either on or off the record, exactly what you found at the Socorro UFO crash site?'

'I've told this to ATIC and I've told it to NICAP and I've

also told it to your APII investigators a thousand times: what I and the others found at the crash site was the remains of a Rawin weather balloon – no more and no less. As for Marlon Clarke, he was drunk when he saw the so-called UFO flying overhead, drunk when he drove out there to see it close up, and still drunk when we arrived to interrogate him. As for his subsequent disappearance, he probably drank himself to death in the desert and got dragged away by a wild animal. Those things happen to his kind out there. Anything else?'

'Yes,' Bob Jackson said. 'I don't suppose it'll come as any surprise to you that the two biggest civilian UFO organisations in the United States are feeling an unexpected financial squeeze due to a dramatic decrease in press publicity about UFOs and a corresponding wane in public interest.'

'So the membership for your UFO organisations is dwindling,' Fuller said, not trying to hide his satisfaction.

'Yes,' Jackson admitted. 'And it's our belief that this came about because of a deliberate policy of suppression on the part of the government, through the CIA, which was bothered by our joint call for, and support of, congressional hearings.'

'That's some mouthful,' Fuller said, 'so I'm not sure what you mean.'

But of course, he *was* sure. In July 1960, under pressure from the general public and, in particular, APII and ATIC, the Senate Preparedness Committee had demanded briefings and résumés from the Air Force on some of the major UFO flaps, including the famous Washington DC and Levelland sightings. At the main briefing on July 15, the congressmen present did not go easy on the Air Force, practically siding with the civilian UFO organisations and insisting that in future the Air Force had to keep the committee informed of all pertinent sightings. Nevertheless, against the protests of Dr J. Allen Hynek, then a consultant to ATIC's Project Blue Book, but with the firm support of Fuller, on behalf of the CIA and Major General

Luehman, director of intelligence, the call for public hearings was again resisted.

'We weren't in the least bit bothered by the thought of congressional hearings,' Fuller lied blandly, 'and certainly did nothing to head them off.'

'Well, *someone* did,' Bob Jackson insisted. 'Within a few weeks of the committee's request to be kept updated on all sightings and its recommendation that Project Blue Book be given more funds, it became perfectly clear that information on sightings was not being supplied and that the request for more money had been ignored. It had also become clear that the Air Force, despite the disapproval of the congressmen on the committee, was still insisting that it was doing all that was required regarding UFOs, when in fact it was doing nothing at all.'

'Money recommended by congressional committees often ends up being sidetracked – usually to other benefactors recommended by those very same committees. It may not be correct, but it's hardly cause for conspiracy theories. As for the committee not being sent the sighting reports they requested, you'll have to take that one up with Major Friend, the head of Project Blue Book, not with me.'

'There's a rumour that Friend is in your pocket.'

'Unfortunately, the Capitol thrives on rumours and that's what most of these stories are. Friend's not in my pocket.'

'Is it true that you and General Luehman, director of intelligence, were responsible for subverting the committee's proposals?'

'If it were I certainly wouldn't admit it, so why bother asking?'

Jackson actually chuckled at the other end of the phone, before saying, 'May I continue?'

'You may.'

'Why were the congressional hearings slated for 1962 dropped?'

'Because the Chairman decided that there was no justification for continuing them.'

'But the House Speaker John McCormack believed that the UFOs were real, which makes the abrupt turnaround seem pretty odd.'

Jackson was referring to the fact that House Speaker John McCormack, with the encouragement of the troublesome head of NICAP, Donald E. Keyhoe, had started talking – too often, too loudly – about holding another congressional investigation and finally, in 1961, directed Congressman Overton Brookes of the House Science and Astronautics Committee to look into the matter. Brooks did this by appointing Joseph Karth, then head of the Subcommittee on Space Problems and Life Sciences, to hold hearings on UFOs. When news of the proposed hearings was released, Keyhoe promised that NICAP would offer proof of the Air Force's incompetence in dealing with UFO reports. He would also, he threatened, prove conclusively that the Air Force had embarked on a course of 'contradictory, misleading and untrue statements' in order to suppress information about, and kill public interest in, UFO reports.

Neither Fuller nor Major General Luehman, director of intelligence, was thrilled at this prospect.

'McCormack may have believed the UFOs were real, but the other members of the committee were not so impressed when the man sent to gather evidence to be used *against* the Air Force came back to say he now supported it.'

'You mean Richard P. Hines.'

'Yes.'

'We believe the CIA encouraged those statements.'

'Simply not true,' Fuller lied again.

In fact, though the hearings were not scheduled until 1962, in the middle of 1961, while the Office of Legislative Liaison was directing its attention to heading off the hearings, House Science and Astronautics Committee staff member Richard P. Hines visited ATIC, was 'thoroughly briefed' by the Project Blue Book head, Major Friend, and returned to inform his fellow committee members that he was 'favourably impressed' with the Air Force's efforts.

Given this response, it was not surprising that a week after Hines's return to Washington DC, committee chairman Overton Brooks announced that the Congressional hearings were to be dropped and not likely to be an issue in the near future. The following week, Congressman Joseph Karth, slated to head the aborted hearings, publicly attacked Donald Keyhoe and, by implication, the other major UFO groups, including Dr Frederick Epstein's APII, for trying to 'belittle, defame and ridicule' the Air Force. He also accused Keyhoe of being guilty of 'malicious intent towards a great branch of the military.'

While the verbal slaughter of Keyhoe was still continuing, Chairman Overton Brooks died and the new Chairman, Congressman George P. Miller of California, confirmed that there would be no hearings on the UFO phenomenon.

'Listen,' Fuller said, 'neither I personally, nor the CIA generally, can be held responsible for the fact that a Congressman with an open mind goes to collect evidence that could be used against the Air Force and instead comes back convinced that the Air Force is in the right. That just proved how wrong you and the other paranoid conspiracy theorists were.'

'Maybe,' Jackson responded quietly. 'But we now have strong reason to believe that Hines also informed his fellow committee members that Congressional interest in the UFO programme could be blamed on pressure from – I quote – "undisclosed sources on House Speaker John McCormack".'

'Where did you get that statement?'

'Wouldn't *you* like to know!'

Now it was Fuller's turn to chuckle, even knowing that Jackson's story was completely accurate. 'If you don't reveal your source I can't verify the statement. What other surprises have you got up your sleeve?'

'We also have reason to believe that Hines, as well as dropping McCormack in the shit, dropped Donald Keyhoe in it by suggesting that he was the one who placed the so-called *undisclosed pressure* on McCormack. Since Hines and people like yourself viewed Keyhoe as the most vocal of the advocates for Congressional hearings – therefore the man most likely to break the wall of secrecy regarding UFOs – this would have been a good way of dirtying him with the committee, getting the hearings dropped, and discrediting his civilian UFO group and others like it.'

'More paranoid nonsense.'

In fact, as Fuller knew, since he had been the one to plan it, that's exactly what had happened. From the moment the Congressional hearings were dropped and Keyhoe ridiculed, press interest in UFOs shrank dramatically and public awareness followed suit. Within a year of Brook's death and the final cancelling of the Congressional hearings, all the major civilian UFO organisations, including APII and NICAP, were suffering from a severe lack of funds and, even worse, credibility. To add insult to injury, it was happening during a year, 1962, when sightings were three times higher than they had been in the former 'peak' years of 1947–1951. From the point of view of APII and NICAP, it couldn't have been worse. From Fuller's point of view, it couldn't have been better.

'I don't think it's nonsense,' Jackson said, running up his big phone bill. 'I think that you and your friends were behind Hines all the way, engineered the cancellation of the Congressional hearings, went out to get Donald Keyhoe and thus discredit the civilian UFO organisations, and even now, after seriously diminishing public interest in UFOs, are trying to get rid of Project Blue Book altogether.'

'Excuse the language, my friend, but that's bullshit. The CIA has no interest in UFOs one way or the other. Though speaking personally at this moment, I think I can speak for the CIA when I say that very few folk here at Langley Field believe that UFOs exist.'

Which was another blatant lie. In fact, right now, under pressure from the CIA, ATIC was trying to transfer its UFO programme elsewhere and, hopefully, out of the Air Force altogether, to somewhere less visible. Unfortunately, neither NASA nor the National Science Foundation would touch it, which was giving Fuller a headache. Luckily, it had at least been made a part of the Foreign Technology Division (FTD) of the Air Force Systems Command, where it was languishing without the resources once insisted upon by the Congressional committee.

'All I can say,' Jackson continued doggedly, 'is that between the harassment of individuals and the suppression of civilian UFO organisations, the US government has managed to practically bury the UFO question.'

'The UFO question has cost the US government a lot of money, so that may be an understandable reaction. And for that matter, particularly regarding your conspiracy theories, if the US government is so concerned with the UFO question, why would they want to bury those searching for answers?'

'Because they already *know* the answers,' Jackson replied. 'The UFOs are their own.'

Up to this point, Fuller had been quite amused by Jackson, but on hearing the last remark he turned deadly serious without sounding so.

'The man-made UFO theory is bullshit,' he told Jackson. 'The unveiling of the Avrocar proved that much.'

'A red herring,' Jackson said.

'Oh, yeah?'

'Yeah. We have a researcher – I won't give you his name – who came up with some interesting information about the construction of US-Canadian flying saucers.'

'The Flying Flapjack, the *Omega* and the Avrocar,' Fuller said without hesitation. 'They've all been declassified and shown to the press and, therefore, the public. No mystery there, pal.'

'No? We have reason to believe that the saucers you showed publicly are red herrings and that the real saucers are much more advanced and kept in various secret hangars on US Army, Air Force or Navy bases. Certainly, we know for a fact that one of them is housed in a top-secret hangar in Holloman AFB, Albuquerque, New Mexico. In fact, I personally saw it.'

'*You* personally saw it?'

'Yeah.'

'When?'

'May, 1954.'

'Eight years ago. Are you sure you remember that far back? Maybe, like Marlon Clarke, you were drunk that night.'

'No, I remember it well. I was driving to a motel on the road that runs right past the camp and I saw a hangar at the very end of the base, rising up over the barbed wire of a top security area. That UFO, which was no piss-take Avrocar, descended even as I sat there; then it was wheeled into the hangar. It was one highly advanced, saucer-shaped aircraft.'

'This sounds like some story,' Fuller responded, sounding highly sceptical, though in fact he was shocked by what he was hearing. May 1954, as he well knew, was the night the present APII stringer, Dwight Randall, then a USAF captain, had paid a visit to Cannon AFB in the company of fellow USAF captain, Andrew Boyle. Unfortunately, the latter had been observed on camera, a few nights before, watching the descent of a US version of Wilson's *Kugelblitz II* as it did, indeed, descend onto its landing pad at Cannon AFB.

As it was felt that no-one would have believed Boyle's story anyway, he was left alone for a few days. However, when he put through a call to Project Blue Book's Captain Dwight Randall, inviting him to Albuquerque, a close watch was placed on him. Then, when he drove Randall straight from Albuquerque airport to Cannon AFB, followed all the way, and stopped on the road that ran right past the top-secret hangar at the far end of the base, well away from the main gate, it was decided to follow Randall, also.

When Boyle handed over the photo of the US *Kugelblitz II* to Randall, both men were observed by the Air Force intelligence men following them. It was those same Air Force intelligence men, all dressed entirely in black to propagate the myth started with Wilson's original men in black, who burst into Randall's room, scared the hell out of him, and stole the flying saucer photo from him. A few months later, when Randall was going down the tubes from fear, confusion and drink, Boyle, who had been transferred post haste to Alaska, was terminated in an airplane 'crash' over Mt McKinley.

Now Randall's other friend, this Bob Jackson, was claiming that he was the one who had seen that flying saucer descending on Cannon AFB. Fuller didn't think so. He thought that Jackson had heard the story from Dwight Randall and was using it to try and screw information out of him while protecting his good friend. Well, that was his mistake.

'You have anything to add?' Fuller asked, 'before I drop the phone?'

'Yes,' Jackson said. His breathing seemed more nervous now. 'We have reason to believe that the flying saucers are being used mainly for work in sub-arctic areas. Since I personally specialize in the analysis of flight patterns and have worked out that most of the saucers appear to be flying on northern-southerly routes, I believe the saucers are mainly flying between here and Antarctica.'

'Why?'

'I don't know.'

Thank God for that, Fuller thought. He was silent for a moment, then said, quite deliberately: 'This sounds like Jules Verne to me.'

'Don't be facetious, Mr Fuller. You know I can't be *too* far out.'

Still sounding slightly mocking, though in fact he was deadly serious, Fuller said: 'So what if this fantastic story is true? What's it got to do with me?'

'We're going a long way back here, Fuller.'

'So go a long way back.'

'Given all the evidence now at hand,' Jackson replied, 'the Socorro crash of 1947 almost certainly involved a man-made saucer. And if that's true, you knew just what you were doing when you talked to Marlon Clarke before he disappeared. You're in on it, Fuller.'

There was a fairly long silence while Fuller thought of what to do about this man who was trying to be a hero while protecting his friends.

'So what am I supposed to say?' Fuller asked.

'Am I right or wrong?'

'Right *and* wrong,' Fuller told him.

'Will you tell me more?'

'Under certain conditions.'

'What conditions?'

'Let's meet and work out an agreement. I need some protection here.'

'When can we meet?'

'The sooner the better, Mr Jackson. What about this evening?'

'When and where?'

'I know this little bar at the far end of M Street. It's not very nice, but at least no-one from Langley or the Capitol is liable to be there. A bit low life, don't you know. It's called—'

'Wait, let me write it down.'

Fuller waited patiently until Jackson said he was ready, then he gave him the name of the bar in M Street, down near the Canal, and told him to meet him outside at nine that evening.

'I'll be there,' Bob Jackson said.

Dropping the phone, Fuller kicked his chair back, put his feet up on the desk, clasped his hands behind his head and whispered, 'I'll bet you will!'

Arriving home at his flashy Dupont Circle apartment, which had contemporary art on the white-painted walls, expensive, artificial antique furniture, cunningly concealed lighting, off-white carpets and a total lack of welcoming idiosyncrasy or human warmth, Fuller mixed himself a dry Martini, then turned the TV on to the news – he never watched it; he only listened to it and, as he had no ear for music, it was *all* he listened to.

As Fuller was having another sip of his Martini, his cat, a seventy-five per cent Persian blue named Doc Savage, padded into the room, rubbed itself against Fuller's ankles, then stood on its hind legs to gaze into the dimly lit goldfish bowl. Distractedly stroking the cat's head, Fuller reached into the bowl, pulled out a wriggling goldfish and held it just above the cat's nose. When the cat saw and smelt the goldfish he leaped up, snatched it out of Fuller's fingers with his teeth, then ran back into the kitchen with the fish wriggling frantically in his jaws.

Amused, sipping more of his Martini, Fuller entered the subdued lighting of the bedroom from where he could still hear the news on TV. Setting his Martini on the bedside cabinet, he stripped off his clothing, threw his shirt, tie, underclothes and socks in the laundry basket – his housekeeper came every day – and draped his suit with fastidious care over the coat hanger, which he hung to air on the closet door.

Naked, he glanced at himself in the mirror, noticed that his belly was still flat, given his advancing years – he'd soon be all of forty-two – then made his way into the bathroom. After emptying his bladder, he meticulously washed his hands, filled the sink with hot water, and soaped and shaved himself, using a gleaming strop razor. With the remains of the shaving cream still on parts of his chin, he went to the shower, turned the water on, adjusted it until it was steaming hot, then stepped under it. As his skin turned red from the heat, he thoroughly soaped and cleaned himself, taking particular care with his anus and private parts, then he let the scalding water wash the soap away. When he had finished this cleansing process, which had left him with an erection, he turned the water from boiling hot to icy cold, braved it for two minutes, thus losing his erection, then turned the water off and stepped out of the shower.

He dried himself vigorously with a very rough towel which further reddened his skin. Dried, he applied talcum powder to his private parts, anus and feet, then sprayed deodorant under his armpits and patted after-shave lotion onto his chin and throat.

Returning to the bedroom, he sipped more of his dry Martini, then studied his naked body in the full-length mirror. As he did so, his erection rose steadily again and he imagined a woman on her knees, slipping painted lips over it. Proud that he could still manage this at his age, he picked up his glass of Martini, carried it to the artificial antique table containing the telephone, and sat down on a soft, high-backed chair. After setting his Martini glass on the table, he telephoned his latest acquisition, a twenty-five-year old secretary besotted with men of some authority. He thoughtfully stroked his erection while whispering arousing obscenities to her, but finally arranged to meet her at Clyde's, also located on M Street, at 9.30 p.m.

When the girl had rung off, Fuller stretched out on the sofa, half propped up on one arm, sipping his Martini, listening to the babble of the TV and letting his erect penis return to normal, prepared for better things. Finishing off his Martini, he stood up again and returned to the bedroom. There, he dressed meticulously in a fine-cut Italian grey suit, shirt and tie, with black, patent-leather shoes. After transferring his billfold, loose change, keys, notebook, pen and small leather pouch from the suit he had worn that day to his fresh suit, he checked himself once more in the mirror and left the apartment.

Lacking patience for the parking problems of Georgetown, he caught a taxi to the bar located where M Street ran into Canal Road, which was dark at this hour. It was not dark at the front door of the bar, which was brightly illuminated by the streetlamps, enabling him to see the rather plump, middle-aged Bob Jackson standing uncomfortably beside a group of Georgetown University students who were having their beer on the sidewalk.

Disembarking from the cab on the other side of the road, Fuller paid the driver, then stood there for a moment, in the relative darkness by the bank of the Canal, watching Bob Jackson and recalling the many other times he had either personally tailed him and Dwight Randall when they were together or had had them tailed, photographed and recorded on tape. From his personal observations, as well as from the audio and visual material supplied by his fellow agents, he had learned that Bob Jackson and Dwight Randall were indeed very good friends, deeply fond of each other, with wives who also liked each other as well as the two men. They were decent, good-hearted people who had shared much together and would, Fuller knew, be devastated if anything happened to any other member of the group.

Pity about that, he thought.

Crossing the road, Fuller stepped up on the sidewalk and held his hand out to the portly Bob Jackson.

'Hi,' he said. 'I'm Jack Fuller. Have we met before?'

'No,' Bob said. 'So how did you recognise me?'

Fuller grinned and indicated the young students bunched up all around Jackson. 'You're the only person here over twenty-one,' he said, 'so it didn't need much deducing.'

'Oh.' Jackson looked a bit embarrassed, but was also clearly amused by Fuller's comment. 'Right, I see what you mean.' He glanced again at the students, listened to the rock 'n' roll music pounding inside, and said, 'You really think we can talk in there?'

'Not really,' Fuller said. 'This used to be an adults' place. Come on, let's go to this other place I know, just two minutes away. Just up the side of this bar.'

He walked Jackson around the corner and into the road that climbed steeply up the side of the bar. They soon left the lamplight behind and stepped into a short, unlit strip where the darkness was deep.

Maybe Jackson sensed something, because he stopped and turned around to face Fuller, opening his mouth to speak.

He never got the words out.

Fuller brought the hard, cutting edge of his right hand down across Bob Jackson's neck, hitting the jugular vein precisely enough to cut off the flow of blood to his head without actually damaging the vein itself. Instantly unconscious, Bob fell back against the wall and slid down it until he was resting with his back against it and his knees raised in front of his face. After glancing left and right to ensure that no-one was coming, Fuller took the small leather pouch from his suit, opened it, withdrew an already loaded hypodermic, and sank the needle into the back of Bob Jackson's hand. Even as Fuller was placing the emptied hypodermic back into the leather pouch, slipping the pouch back into the jacket of his suit, and walking back to the bar, Bob Jackson was suffering the violent spasms of a drug that would induce heart arrythmia without leaving any traces behind.

As Bob Jackson was going into violent convulsions, Fuller turned the corner of the pub, brushed past the students, and walked along M Street, to enter the noisily pleasant ambience of Clyde's, where he found his latest acquisition waiting for him. A five feet four inch blonde, very slim, in a skintight dress and high heels, she threw her arms around Fuller when he entered and gave him a long sensual kiss.

'A good meal and a bottle of wine,' Fuller said when he had managed to disengage. 'Then we'll make love all night. Life's for the living, right?'

Chapter Thirty-Four

These days Dwight's mood was one of almost constant depression. For three months after Bob Jackson's sudden death by heart attack outside the student's bar in M Street, Georgetown, Dwight had felt himself torn between shock, grief and deep suspicion. The unexpectedness of the death had been bad enough, followed by the usual horrors of seeing the grief of Bob's wife and two kids, not to mention Beth, then the funeral, the wake and the subsequent dreadful days of numbed disbelief. Making matters worse, however, was Thelma's bewildered insistence that Bob wasn't supposed to have been in Georgetown that particular night, that he was supposed to have come home for dinner with friends, but phoned at the last minute to say that something urgent had come up and he would be late home. Added to this, thus to Dwight's deepening depression, was his own fearful conviction that no matter what the coroner said about Bob dying from a heart attack, he had in fact been murdered.

This conviction grew in Dwight over the months as he tried to adjust to life without Bob and spent a lot of time consoling Thelma who, with her blonde hair now streaked with grey strands, her lush body filling out into middle-aged maturity, remained bewildered as to what her loving husband had been doing up a dark alley outside a student bar when he should have been home. This didn't make sense to Thelma; nor could she understand what had made Bob so excited that he would leave a group of friends sitting around his dinner table, rather than hurry home to join them.

'That just wasn't in his nature,' she told Dwight, 'so it must have been something pretty big.'

'Well, nothing was found on him, Thelma, so now we'll never know.'

Another cause for Dwight's deepening depression was the knowledge that ever since last year's cancellation of the Congressional hearings on the UFO phenomenon, which should have opened the whole debate up for the first time, Dr Epstein's APII, along with the other two or three major UFO organisations, had been suffering an unprecedented series of financial and personal catastrophes, including a dramatic loss of paying members due to lack of public discussion of the phenomenon; the abrupt withdrawal of funds from long-standing support groups and individuals; repeated visits from an IRS desperately trying to find discrepancies in the organisation's accounts; and the damaging loss of a large number of staff due to inexplicable illnesses, marital problems, and alcoholism brought on by various kinds of UFO 'hauntings', including the men in black. Through all of this, Dr Frederick Epstein had battled on with admirable fortitude, but the exhaustion was beginning to show on his lined face, in his prematurely greying hair and beard.

Last but by no means least, Dwight's depression was deepening because his increasing work-load for the understaffed APII was keeping him away from home more often and placing the marriage under strain even as Beth, who'd had a couple of years of peace after the terrifying weeks leading up to the public showing of the Avrocar at Fort Eustus, Virginia, had started being tormented as before. Once more she was having dreadful nightmares about UFOs and men in black, actually seeing men dressed in black following her, either in a black limousine or on foot, though always at a safe distance. Also, this time, to add to her growing fear, she was receiving numerous crank calls, some from people who sounded mentally unstable and whispered insults down the line, others from 'heavy breathers' who refused to say anything or simply chuckled before hanging up. Eventually, though no poltergeist manifestations were evident in the house as they had been the week before the Avrocar viewing, Beth became convinced that her car was being tracked by a UFO that often came down practically on top of her, but somehow managed to always stay out of sight.

Dwight could not forget that the previous 'hauntings' had finished the day before the press showing of the Avrocar and had started up again the day after Bob Jackson's death. These facts convinced him that the hauntings, in both cases, were being organized by the same people, human or otherwise.

Interestingly enough, Beth had had no more black-outs, though the lack of proper sleep due to the nightmares was making her otherwise lovely face become gaunt and weary. Studying her with concern, Dwight was startled to realise that Beth was now forty years of age and that they had been married for seventeen of those years, with Nichola already turning sixteen. He and Beth, then, while clambering over that always painful bridge into middle-age, were gradually being aged even more by the trials they were forced to endure at the hand of a malign, unseen enemy. Dwight wanted to give it up, turn his back and run away, but Beth, even in her own dire condition, refused to let him.

'To do so,' she said, 'would probably add a sense of failure to your already chronic mixture of anger, fear and frustration. In short, it would do you no good, Dwight, and might even do you a lot of damage. So never mind me or what's happening to us; you hang in there and fight this thing.'

'I can't help worrying about you,' Dwight replied. 'You're suffering even more than I am – they're getting at you through me – and I can't help worrying about that. Why don't you go away for a while? Take a vacation. Visit your parents. Help them fix up their new place. They'd probably love that.'

Beth's father, Joe McGinnis, had recently sold his downtown car-sales business and retired with his wife Glenda to Westerville, a pleasant small town located in rolling countryside about twenty-five miles north of Columbus, about a hundred miles from Dayton. They had only moved out a week ago and phoned the day before to say they loved the new house but needed some visitors to give it that lived-in look.

'Why not come down?' Joe had asked Beth. 'I know Nichola is still at school but it's not a long way to travel, so you can come on your own. Besides, there are times when it's good to be alone. Might take years off you, gal.'

'I think Joe's right,' Dwight now told her. 'A change of scenery and air, away from it all. It *could* do you good.'

'Do you think I could manage a vacation without . . .?' Beth could hardly utter the words because the thought of a negative reply was too dreadful to contemplate. She wanted to know if she could go away for a short break and not be followed by . . . *them*. Was there anywhere she and Dwight could be private, out of sight, out of mind? If not, then their life together was truly a nightmare from which there was no escape. 'I just thought . . .'

'It's worth trying,' Dwight assured her. 'What can you lose?'

'Okay, then, I'll try it for a week. When should I go?'

'It's only a two-hour drive,' Dwight replied, 'so why not go this afternoon? Leave now and you'll be there in time for dinner – and all mothers love to cook for their daughters, so that'll be a good start.'

'Mom's cooking and a bottle of Dad's beer. Sounds good to me.'

'Can't harm you at all, Beth.'

'Right, Dwight. I'll go call them and check that it's okay, then I'll pack my valise.'

'You do that,' Dwight told her.

After checking with her folks that it was okay, which it was, Beth packed a valise, had a quick shower, then let Dwight walk her to the car. They kissed and embraced on the sidewalk, not caring who saw them.

'You take care now,' Beth said.

'You have a good time for a change.'

'And don't let Nichola get up to any mischief.'

'I'm a very stern father.'

'Okay, I'll see you in a week.'

'Can I wait that long?'

Beth wrinkled her nose and smiled. 'What a sweet-talkin'
man I've got,' she said. 'Here, give me a big one.'

They kissed again, then Beth got into the car and drove
off. Dwight watched her until the car had turned the corner
at the end of the street, then he glanced left and right,
behind him, at the sky, hardly aware of what he had just
done as he returned to his haunted house.

Beth had told Dwight she would ring him when she reached
her parents' place. When she still hadn't called him that
evening, Dwight called his father-in-law and asked if Beth
had turned up yet. Sounding anxious, Joe said she had not.

'But the journey should only take two hours,' Dwight
said, 'and she's been gone for four.'

'Might have stopped for a meal,' Joe suggested hopefully.

'No. She was planning to have dinner with you. Six on
the dot, remember? Besides, if she knew she was going to
be late, she'd have called, sure as hell.'

'Maybe she had a breakdown,' Joe volunteered. 'Let's
give her another hour.'

'Okay,' Dwight said.

An hour later, at nine in the evening, when Beth still
hadn't called either house, Dwight and Joe simultaneously
checked with their local police stations regarding
breakdowns or accidents. Neither station held a report on
anything regarding Beth or her car; they would, however,
get their patrol cars to try tracking her down and would
call back whenever they found her.

By midnight they still hadn't found her.

Distraught, Dwight did his best to look normal in front

417

of Nichola who, at sixteen, was now a tall, slim young lady with long blonde hair and radiant green eyes, dangerously attractive in figure-hugging denims and sweater, already drawing adolescent boys to the front porch, asking could she come out. Lying that Beth was with her parents and would be calling the next day, Dwight bid Nichola goodnight and watched her disappearing into the bedroom. Blessing God for her presence, he cracked a can of beer and drank it while sitting in a chair placed strategically between the table containing the phone and a window overlooking the front yard. He sat throughout the night, until dawn, but Beth didn't show up and neither the police in Dayton, nor those in Columbus, had found a trace of her.

Now almost out of his mind with anxiety, Dwight tried to hide it when he drove Nichola to school, dropped her off, and then, without realising he was doing it, glanced left and right, behind him and up at the sky. Seeing nothing, though hardly aware that he was looking, he quickly drove home.

Beth's old Ford was parked in the driveway.

Parking his own car too quickly, practically banging into the Ford, he hurried into the house and found Beth sitting on the sofa, sipping black coffee. When he entered, she glanced at him, repeatedly blinking her bloodshot eyes, then put her coffee cup down and jumped up to embrace him. Clearly exhausted, she was shivering and seemed on the verge of tears. Seeing the state of her, Dwight made her sit down again, then he put his arms around her and said, 'God, Beth, what happened? We've been anxious as hell.'

'I don't know. I'm not sure. Another one of those blackouts.' She shook her head from side to side, rubbed her eyes, blinked repeatedly, licked her lips. 'I can only remember the journey as far as the other side of Springfield. Somewhere along the road I must have lost consciousness.' She burst into tears, was consoled by Dwight, then tried recollecting the rest of it. 'All I remember is driving out of Springfield, heading for Columbus. It was about five in the evening. I recall this empty stretch of road beyond Springfield, then . . .' She lit a Camel, inhaled like someone drowning, trying to gulp in air, then blew a cloud of smoke and relaxed a little. 'Nothing!' She shrugged. 'Next thing I remember, I was still in the car, still behind the steering wheel, but the car was at the other side of Springfield – *this* side of Springfield – and facing back where I had come from: in the direction of Dayton.'

'Christ!' Dwight exclaimed involuntarily. 'What time was this?'

Beth checked her wristwatch, looked perplexed, then glanced at the clock on the wall. 'Judging by the time now, I must have awakened between eight and nine in the morning. I couldn't tell the time because my wristwatch had stopped at 5.05. That was either 5.05 in the evening or this morning – I can't tell you which – though I'm pretty damned sure it was 5.05 last night.' She squeezed Dwight's waist and laid her head on his shoulder. 'Oh, God, I'm really scared, Dwight. This is worse than before. I feel like I've been to hell and back and I can't tell you why. I'm shattered. I feel bruised inside and out . . . And most of all . . . *God, I'm scared!*'

She burst into tears again, so Dwight hugged her, stroked her hair, kissed the top of her head, then gently rocked her on the sofa until she had calmed down. When she did so, he cupped her tearful face in his hands, then kissed her on the lips.

'Lie down and have a sleep,' he advised her. 'Take some Valium. I don't want to encourage you to take sedatives, but I think sleep's more important right now. I'll be here. I won't be sleeping. I'll be looking after you. You've nothing to fear.'

'You won't leave the house?'

'I promise. Not until Nichola has to be picked up – and you'll be awake by then. Until then, I'm staying right here – so come on, let's tuck you into bed.'

When he led her into the bedroom, she just stared

silently at the bed, not wanting to lie down.

'You don't have to take your clothes off,' Dwight told her. 'Just have some Valium and lie down and you'll go to sleep instantly.'

But Beth shook her head. 'No. I can't sleep in these clothes. I can't wear them ever again. I feel dirty in these clothes – contaminated – *God, I can't stand these clothes!*'

Clearly distraught, she proceeded to frantically tear her clothes off, like someone covered in stinging ants, until Dwight managed to soothe her again and sit her down on the edge of the bed. When he had done so, he made her swallow some Valium, then told her to lie on the bed and relax.

Even with the sedative, however, Beth insisted that she could not relax until she had taken off her clothes and had a hot shower. This she did, turning herself raw-red in water so hot that Dwight was compelled to reach in and turn the tap to mix more cold with the hot, lowering the temperature. Beth, naked and pink from the nearly scalding water, still took a long time to thoroughly clean herself, almost obsessively so, but finally stepped out of the shower, and, like a docile child, let Dwight dry her with a towel. Still naked and shaking her head to say 'No' when Dwight held up her nightdress, she crawled between the sheets and went to sleep instantly.

Making himself another coffee, knowing he could not swallow food yet, Dwight sat at the table between the telephone and the front window, gazing out on the street to where his car was parked practically nose-to-tail with Beth's Ford. He dwelt repeatedly on Beth's tale of driving out of Springfield at five in the evening and awakening the next morning on the Dayton side of town, as if somehow her car had been picked up, transported back the way it had come, and deposited again on the road leading to Dayton and home. Finally, on an impulse, and after checking that Beth was asleep – as he didn't want her to see him – he left the house and went to check her car.

At first he found nothing unusual . . . then, upon closer

inspection, he found four, absolutely similar, scratched indentations, two on each side of the car, placed equidistant between the wheels, just below the front and rear doors.

In a trance of initial disbelief and gradual acceptance, Dwight examined those indentations repeatedly and finally came to the conclusion that his senses were not betraying him . . . The indentations indicated that four clamps of some kind that been tightened on the bodywork, under the four doors, between the wheels, to raise the vehicle off the ground.

Whatever it was that had moved the car, it was at least physical.

For weeks after Beth's baffling, frightening experience, she suffered from blinding headaches and a repeat of the former nightmares. She also became more convinced that her fears about being followed by men in black had been justified . . . and she was seeing those men in her nightmares.

Finally, when she showed no sign of improvement, Dwight insisted that she visit a psychiatrist, if only to confirm that she was indeed sane and had not imagined the whole business. He felt guilty doing this, as he was already convinced – by the indentations on the car as well as by Beth's undeniable sincerity – that the vehicle had indeed been picked up and transported back to the other side of town while she was unconscious.

Nevertheless, he also felt that the psychiatric evaluation was necessary for Beth's peace of mind and would be a validation for what he had proposed should follow it: a visit to a professional hypnotist for the purpose of ascertaining exactly what had happened along that lonely stretch of road between Springfield and Columbus over a period of eighteen hours.

After quite a few consultations with Beth, the psychiatrist, Dr Phillip Dewhurst, an old friend who had served as a medical officer at Wright-Patterson AFB, ascertained that she was not hallucinating and was, indeed, suffering from genuine amnesia regarding the 'lost' period in question. It was the opinion of Dr Dewhurst that this amnesia was Beth's psychological means of obliterating either a real experience or an exceptionally frightening, possibly repellent, fantasy. Dr Dewhurst therefore recommended, as Dwight had hoped, that instead of a course of sodium amytal or Pentothal to break through Beth's resistance to her buried memory, she undergo regressive hypnotism with his friend, Dr Irma Sagan, B.A., M.A., M.D., formerly of the Society of Medical Hypnotists, London, England, and a highly respected psychiatrist in her own right.

Though initially reluctant to let herself be hypnotised, Beth, after a few more 'hauntings' and nightmares, reluctantly agreed to let Dwight set up an appointment. Subsequently, a few days later, they were shown into Dr Sagan's office in downtown Dayton and asked to take the two chairs at the other side of the desk, facing the doctor. In her mid-thirties, Dr Sagan was a slim, extremely attractive brunette with a bright, relaxing smile – certainly not what the nervous Beth had imagined a psychiatrist and hypnotist would be. When Beth released her nervous tension by blurting out what she thought, Dr Sagan just chuckled.

'I know what you mean,' she said. 'It's the curse of my life. Everyone expects me to be old, distinguished, grey-haired and, of course, *male*. They also expect me to be terribly solemn, maybe even intense or half mad – Rasputin; Svengali. Luckily for you, I don't have to be either. This is a job like any other and I do it well. Are you feeling relaxed now?'

'More relaxed for having met you,' Beth said, 'and seeing that you're not Rasputin or Svengali.'

Dr Sagan smiled at that. 'Fine. Now do you have any doubts about hypnotism? By which I mean, do you believe it can be effective in psychological terms?'

'I'm not sure,' Beth said.

'In other words, coming here wasn't your own idea.'

'No.' Beth glanced at Dwight. 'It was my husband's initially. Then our friend Doc Dewhurst recommended it.'

'Do you trust your husband?'

'Absolutely.'

'Good. Now this is very important. Do you believe you can be hypnotized?'

'No.'

'Why not?'

'Because I think it's self-suggestion. I think that if you *want* to be hypnotized, you can be hypnotized. Maybe simple-minded or easily led people can be hypnotized. On the other hand, if you don't believe in it, or don't want to be hypnotized, then it's not going to work.'

'And you neither believe in it nor want it.'

'I'm willing to try it on the chance that it might help me, but I don't think it'll work.'

'Those are very precise answers,' Dr Sagan told her. 'You have a strong personality.' She stood up and came around the desk, sat on its edge and glanced down at Beth. 'Let me assure you, Beth, that any intelligent adult and most children over the age of seven can be hypnotized, that only the mentally retarded and the psychotic can *resist* being hypnotized, and that hypnotizability is in no way a sign of weak will. Indeed, the more intelligent and imaginative the subject, the better a subject he or she will be. You therefore needn't be ashamed. There's nothing *wrong* in being hypnotized. Just think of it as another branch of medicine and try to accept it.'

'Okay,' Beth responded.

Dr Sagan smiled and nodded. 'So how do you imagine I'm going to hypnotize you?'

'You'll make me lie down and use something visual and repetitive – a swinging key chain, a metronome – to focus my attention. Then you'll talk to me as my eyes follow the movement of the swinging object.'

Dr Sagan smiled again. 'You've obviously been reading up on the subject.'

'Yes.'

'What's the time, Beth?'

Beth checked her wristwatch. 'Thirty after eleven,' she said.

'Thank you.' Dr Sagan placed the palm of her hand against Beth's forehead. 'What if I told you to raise your right hand?'

'I'd ask why you wanted me to do that.'

'What if I just replied by telling you to raise your right hand?'

Beth raised her right hand. 'I'd ask you why you wanted me to do that.'

'And if I refused to answer, would you refuse to raise your right hand?'

'Yes,' Beth said, still holding up her right hand.

'Does this kind of conversation exhaust you?' Dr Sagan asked.

'It does a bit,' Beth replied, still holding her right hand up in the air.

'Your eyes are heavy, aren't they? Drowsy and heavy. Very heavy. So heavy you feel you want to close them, but you can't close them just yet.'

'That's right,' Beth said.

'Would you like to lie down and close your heavy eyes and rest them for a moment?'

'Yes,' Beth said.

'Would you like to lower your right hand and walk to the sofa and lie down and close your heavy eyes for a moment?'

'I would,' Beth said.

'Lower your right hand, Beth, and walk to the sofa and lie down and close your heavy eyes for a moment.'

Fully conscious and feeling that this was the correct thing to do, Beth lowered her right hand, walked across to the sofa, stretched out on it and closed her weary eyes.

Dr Sagan followed her across the room and took the

chair beside the sofa. Switching on the tape-recorder on the table beside the bed, she leaned over Beth.

'Do you mind talking to me, Beth?'

'No.'

'Would you mind answering my questions?'

'No.'

'Open your eyes and waken up, Beth.'

Beth opened her eyes. She felt extraordinarily tired, but more relaxed and less burdened then she had been before. Glancing across the room, she saw Dwight sitting at Dr Sagan's desk, looking extremely concerned as Dr Sagan rewound the tape on a tape-recorder and checked her wristwatch. When Beth sat up, yawning, stretching herself, Dr Sagan smiled at her. 'What's the time, Beth?'

Beth checked her wristwatch, expecting to find that five minutes had passed. Instead, she found that two hours had gone by. She had been asleep all that time. 'My God!' she exclaimed. 'Thirty after one! Where did the time go? What . . .?'

She looked up to see Dr Sagan's easy smile. 'Come here, Beth,' Dr Sagan said. 'Sit beside your husband. You've been in a trance condition for two hours and talked through it all. Would you like to hear what you said?'

'I'm not sure,' Beth replied.

'I think you had better come here and sit beside your husband and listen to the tape. Your husband understands it more than I do. Please, Beth, come on over here.'

Beth got off the sofa and walked across the room to take the chair beside Dwight. She stared with widening, fearful eyes at the tape-recorder and found herself mesmerised by the sight of that revolving spool of tape. Her own voice, when it finally came off the tape, practically hypnotized her all over again.

The Beth on the tape, speaking to all those in the room, gave flesh and blood to Beth's nightmares. It was the disembodied voice of a lost soul speaking from hell.

Chapter Thirty-Five

REPORT OF TAPED HYPNOTHERAPY SESSION

BETWEEN: Dr I. Sagan, B.A., M.A., M.D. of the Sagan Hypnotherapy Clinic, Dayton, Ohio, USA, and:-

PATIENT: Beth McGinnis Randall, also of Dayton, Ohio.

PATIENT'S AGE: 40

STATUS: Private Patient (PP).

DATE: November 12, 1963

SUMMARY: Patient presented herself in the company of her husband, Dwight Randall, at the office of Dr Irma Sagan in the Sagan Hypnotherapy Clinic on November 12, 1963, on the recommendation of Dr Phillip Dewhurst, M.A., M.D., for immediate hypnotic regression and, if required, hypnotherapy.

The patient was suffering from repeated migraines, black-outs and feelings of paranoia based upon the conviction that she was being 'haunted' by an unknown person or persons.

The recommendation for hypnotherapy was made by Dr Dewhurst after four consultations with the patient and his subsequent assessment that she was suffering from amnesia relating to a black-out that occurred on October 2, 1963, during a drive from Dayton, Ohio to Columbus, Ohio.

The purpose of the hypnotic session was to regress the patient to the moment of black-out on October 2, 1963, induce a recollection of the event that had traumatised her and decide on a means of curing the trauma based on the nature of the traumatising event.

Penetration of the amnesia was achieved by taking the patient though the three prime stages of hypnotism: light, medium and heavy, the latter being a state of somnambulism.

The total trance session lasted a total of two hours and a complete regression was attained.

At the end of the trance session it was decided by Dr Sagan that the patient, when awakened from her trance, should be made to listen to her own description of the experience and then, in the full awareness of what had transpired during her black-out, undergo a further series of trance sessions for the purposes of hypnotherapy aimed at relieving her stress while also ascertaining the reality or non-reality of the trauma-inducing event.

At the completion of a total of twelve further hypnotherapy sessions, it was the opinion of Dr Sagan, albeit offered with reluctance, that the patient's recollections in the trance state were an accurate recall of a real event.

Transcript of interview with patient in hypnotic trance condition for inclusion in the confidential archives of the Society of Medical Hypnotists, 4 Victoria Terrace, Kingsway, Hove, Sussex, England.

DOCTOR

You are relaxing, relaxing, very relaxed. You are sleeping, deep sleep, sleeping deeper, very deep. You are sleeping, very comfortable, relaxed, very relaxed. You are deeper and deeper in sleep, very comfortable, deeper. You are relaxed and comfortable. You are deep, deep in sleep.

You are relaxed and you will remember everything and you will answer my questions.

PATIENT
  Yes.

DOCTOR
  All right, Beth. You are very relaxed. You have nothing to fear. You are going back to the evening of October 2, 1963. To the moment when you were driving out of Springville. You are going back now.

PATIENT
  Yes.

DOCTOR
  Do you know where you are?

PATIENT
  I'm in the car. I'm driving away from Springville. I'm on the road leading from Springville to Columbus, fifteen miles out of Springville.

DOCTOR
  What do you see, Beth?

PATIENT
  Just the road. The empty fields on either side. Not much traffic on the road. No traffic here. Sun going down. Almost dark. A nice, easy drive. It feels good to be . . .

DOCTOR
  Yes, Beth?

PATIENT
  I don't want to.

DOCTOR

All right, Beth. You are very relaxed. You have nothing to fear. What do you see or feel?

PATIENT

Feels funny . . . Someone following . . . No, there's no-one there. Nothing out front. Nothing behind me. Fields all empty on either side. Nothing in the sky . . . Darkening. The sky's darkening . . . Strange feeling . . . Oh, no, not out here as well! Someone's following me – not behind me – above me. I can't see . . . Damn it, where are you? Oh, God, right above me! I . . . *No, I don't want to*!

DOCTOR

You are safe, Beth. Relaxed. Very relaxed. There is nothing to fear. You are relaxed. You are safe. What's happening, Beth?

PATIENT

Beside me . . . Beside the car. Two of them . . . Flying saucers . . . Oh, God, Dwight, where are you? Come and see them! What you've always wanted to see. Oh, God, Dwight where are you?

DOCTOR

Dwight's beside you, Beth. He's right here beside you. He's fine. He's okay. He wants you to describe the flying saucers. What are they like, Beth?

PATIENT

Not big . . . not like the ones I've heard about . . . small saucers, spinning discs, metallic and silvery-white, glowing oddly in failing light and spinning . . . Only two or three feet wide. Shaped like two plates placed on top of each other, one upside-down on the other . . . All metal. Smooth surfaces. Spherical. Seamless. Spinning like spinning-tops as they fly through the air, pacing the car, one on each side, parallel to where I'm sitting, very close to the windows ... Now they're ... *I don't want to! I don't want to! I don't want to!*

DOCTOR
It's all right, Beth, you're just remembering. It's in the past. You're remembering. It's all in the past. It can't hurt you. You're remembering and it seems to be happening now, but it was all in the past. It just seems like the present. In the present. Right now. It's right now, but you're safe. What's happening, Beth?

PATIENT
Two small flying saucers, one on each side of the car, right by the front windows, pacing the car, keeping up with the car. They seem solid ... seamless. I can hear them – no, *feel* them. They're spinning like crazy, sort of glowing, and I don't know if I can hear them or feel them, but there's some kind of pressure. Something pressing around me, making the car drag, slowing down ... *Oh, my God!*

DOCTOR
Relax, Beth. Relax. No need to worry. Just tell me, Beth.

PATIENT
The flying saucers have stopped spinning. They're still flying, but not spinning. Oh, God, a slot's opening up in both of them – a glass eye – staring at me ... God! What's that? Some kind of light – beams of light! Those things are shooting beams of light into the car – strange light – very bright and flickering on and off, pulsating, making a noise – no, a kind of vibration ... No! Please, no more!

DOCTOR
What is it, Beth?

PATIENT
My head hurts. I can't think. One of the beams of light

is aimed at the hood of the car; the other's right in my face . . . I can't see properly . . . The car's cutting out . . . Oh, God, my head hurts. The light's blinding me. The car's still cutting out. It's stopping!

DOCTOR

It's all right, Beth, no need to fear. What's happening, Beth?

PATIENT

The car's stopped and . . . *No! No! No!*

DOCTOR

Relax. You are relaxed. You are safe. What's happening, Beth?

PATIENT

Oh, God! Straight ahead. It's coming down over the road. Another flying saucer, but much bigger – *enormous* – about the size of an airliner. Lots of lights flashing around it. Descending slowly on the road just ahead. Hovering there – just inches above the road. Now settling down and blocking my path with those flashing lights blinding me.

DOCTOR

Where are the smaller saucers, Beth? Are they still hovering at both sides of the car? Still shining those beams of light in?

PATIENT

Yes – *no!* I mean, yes, they're still there, one hovering at each side of me, but those slits in their sides have closed up and the light's aren't shining any more.

DOCTOR
Yes?

431

PATIENT

I'm trying to start the car. It won't start. I'm trying to get out and run away, but the doors are locked. Oh, God, I'm trapped here and my head is splitting and . . .

DOCTOR

It's all right, Beth. You needn't be agitated. I'm right here. I'm with you. Just tell me what's happening.

PATIENT

I'm trapped. The doors are locked. I can't get the car to stop. That enormous flying saucer is straddling the road – over a hundred feet wide, as tall as an office building and with lights flashing on and off around its rim . . . No! The lights are going out. I think part of the body is spinning and slowing down as the lights flicker out. Now the lights are out and it's sitting there in the darkness. Nearly dark. And . . . Oh, God! It's making a noise. A kind of bass humming sound. I can *feel* it – almost feel the sound, I mean, and . . . It's opening! *It's opening*! A long slit of bright light along the front, along the bottom . . . getting bigger, higher, like a door or panel lifting up. And . . . it's a door in the front – a big door, like the door of an aircraft hangar – just like Wright-Patterson, Dwight – and . . . Oh, God, there are people in there – just standing there, not moving, in the light of what looks like a holding bay . . . Looking at me, I think – I can't be sure – they're silhouetted. *Human* figures – some normal . . . but some . . . Oh, my God, some so small! So small and misshapen about the head and hands . . . The light . . . They must be distorted by the light . . . Oh, my God, *no! no! no!*

DOCTOR

Calm. You are calm. You are not there. You are here. You are here with us and absolutely safe. You are there. What's happening, Beth?

PATIENT
   Lights! Other lights. Two brilliant beams of light coming
out of that big saucer. Beaming right at the car. Flooding
the car with light, flickering on and off . . .

DOCTOR
   It's all right, Beth. What's happening?

PATIENT
   That noise! I can *feel* the noise! I can't think for the noise
and . . . The light in that saucer is expanding – *No!* A ramp
is falling down. The ramp's fallen down to touch the ground
and lead up into the saucer . . . Now – Christ! – something
is coming out, emerging from each side of that holding
bay . . . Large steel claws – clamps of some kind – now
stretching out of the holding bay on hinged arms and
hanging over the end of the ramp . . . They've stopped
moving. They're just hanging there on the end of the hinged
supports, like big steel claws on steel arms.

DOCTOR
   What are the figures in the holding bay doing, Beth?

PATIENT
   Nothing. They haven't moved at all. I can only see the
shape of them – not their faces – because they're silhouetted
by the brilliant, almost blinding light. Also – my eyes hurt
– I'm dazzled by the light filling the car and flickering on
and off so fast it disorientates me . . . making that *sound* –
the sound I can *feel* . . .

DOCTOR
   Yes, Beth?

PATIENT
   They're just standing there – watching me, I think . . .
God, those small ones aren't natural – the wrong shape . . .

And . . . No, I don't believe it! Now the smaller saucers are
shooting their beams of light at me again – no! at the car –
front and rear of the car . . . and . . . *The car's moving!* It's
being pulled forward! Oh, God, I can't hold it back . . . The
handbrake doesn't work and the car is being pulled
forward . . . *by what?* The beams of light! They're pulling
the car forward as the smaller saucers advance, taking me
– I mean the car – towards the steel ramp of the big saucer
and those men in the doorway . . . I want out! I want out! I
can't move! Oh, please God, *let me out!*

DOCTOR
It's all right, Beth. I'll make sure you get out. Just tell
me what's happening.

PATIENT
The flickering light is doing something to me . . .
pressure . . . deadening me . . . paralysing me . . . Oh, God,
I can't move and the car has reached the ramp and those
claws – the big clamps on hinged arms – are moving down
on both sides of the car, two on each side . . .

DOCTOR
Yes, Beth, what's happening?

PATIENT
The car's rocking. The clamps are taking hold, one under
each door, between the front and rear wheels and . . . Oh,
God, I can't breathe! It's just panic. Trying to stop it . . .
Yes, better . . . Can breathe again . . .

DOCTOR
You can breathe again, Beth. You have no panic. You're
very much in control. What's happening, Beth?

PATIENT
Now the lights of the smaller saucers have blinked out

and the saucers have flown into the holding bay and disappeared in the brilliant light . . . Thank God they've gone . . . But . . . Oh, no!

DOCTOR
    What is it, Beth?

PATIENT
    The mechanical clamps . . . they're lifting the car slightly and drawing it up the ramp and into the holding bay, into the brightening light . . . And those figures, they're moving at last, parting, stepping aside to leave room for the car . . . I'm inside the saucer! I'm inside! Let me out! *Let me out!*

DOCTOR
    You are relaxed, very relaxed, deeply relaxed. There is nothing to fear. You are deep, deep in sleep, you are relaxed and nothing can harm you. You are okay. You can answer my questions. You are inside the hold of the flying saucer, but you have nothing to fear. You can answer my questions. What do you see inside?
    (The patient does not respond.)

DOCTOR
    Can you hear me, Beth?

PATIENT
    Yes.

DOCTOR
    You have just been drawn up into the hold of the large flying saucer. What do you see?

PATIENT
    Light. Very bright. The bass humming sound has stopped. The figures are silhouetted by the light but are now on both sides of me, surrounding the car. The clamps

on the steel arms have just been released and the hinged
steel arms are bending, withdrawing the clamps up above
the car. The steel arms are moving back into the hold on
grooved tracks, like railroad tracks, leaving the car just
sitting there . . . Everything echoes. The noise of the steel
clamps on the hinged arms reverberates as the mechanism
moves back into the holding bay and then disappears from
view. The bass humming noise has stopped and my
headache has gone. I can move, but I feel drained of energy
and a little bit dazed. Oh, God, now they're . . . I don't want
to! *I won't!*

DOCTOR
Tell me. It's all right, Beth, you can tell me. You can't be
harmed if you tell me. What's happening now?

PATIENT
The silhouetted figures are surrounding the car. Most
of them look like normal men, all wearing black boiler suits.
Though some of them . . . *Oh, no!*

DOCTOR
Go on, Beth.
(The patient does not respond.)

DOCTOR
Tell me what you saw, Beth.

PATIENT
Some of them – the ones who looked small and
misshapen in silhouette – are alien creatures. They have
hands like the metal clamps that pulled the car into the
saucer – metallic claws with hinged joints. There are metal
caps on their heads, studded with . . . I don't know . . .
electric plugs. Their eyes appear to be normal – not
American . . . Oriental? – but the lower half of their faces

are made of metal – nose and chin, I think. The metal covering the lower part of the face has no lips. They look just like little men from outer space; they look goddamned hideous.

DOCTOR
    Yes, Beth?
    (The patient does not respond.)

DOCTOR
    You can talk about it, Beth. It's okay. I'm beside you and listening. Please describe them more, Beth.

PATIENT
    They're small – about five feet tall. Maybe smaller, not much taller. Like the human beings, they're wearing boiler suits, but silvery-grey instead of black. Now all of them – the human beings and the small aliens – are surrounding the car . . . I'm frightened. Yes! But it's all in my head . . . I don't do anything because, though I'm frightened, I'm also drained and passive. I'm waiting for them to do something or for them to tell me what to do. They're just standing around the car and looking in. They're looking at *me*.

DOCTOR
    Is anyone speaking, Beth?

PATIENT
    No. One of the men in black coveralls is opening the car door and pulling me out. Not *pulling* me out – just sort of helping me. I'm frightened, but I don't try to resist. I don't have the will. He's helping me because I feel weak and a little bit dizzy. I think he knows how I feel.

DOCTOR
    So the man has pulled you out of the car. What's happening now, Beth?

PATIENT

I'm looking around me. The sloping ramp is swinging back up to form part of the wall . . . Now it's closed. It fits so well I can't even see the joins. The walls are white-painted metal. Not walls – one wall – curving around on both sides of me. Part of the circular exterior of the saucer. The roof of the holding bay . . . I call it that because I feel I'm in an aircraft, or, maybe, an aircraft hangar, like the ones they had at Wright-Patterson AFB . . . The roof of the holding bay is dome-shaped. It has that hollow ringing sound, like all aircraft hangars have, but it's shaped like a dome – or only part of a dome – more like a large slice of orange.

DOCTOR

What else do you see?

PATIENT

Machinery! The big machine that lifted my car and carried it into the holding bay, but with its hinged arms now folded and the clamps – like giant versions of the metallic hands of the small aliens – now folded down and tucked against the wall. Machinery. Lots of it. A bit like a garage. I don't know what kind of machinery it is, but I feel like I'm in a garage or an aircraft hangar. I'm seeing all of this in the bright light – it's all bright light and shadows.

DOCTOR

What happened next, Beth? The men have helped you out of the car and the door of the holding bay has been closed, so what happened next?

(Note: When Dr Sagan went into the past tense, so did the patient.)

PATIENT

I became very frightened again. Started shaking badly. I was looking at the small, alien creatures – at their hideous, mostly metallic faces – and I guess that got to me. Then one of them, an alien, passed his hand over my face – he was holding something in it – and I felt heat going into my head and then I felt a lot calmer.

DOCTOR
You weren't frightened anymore?

PATIENT
I went kind of limp. I felt sort of dreamy, not real, removed from it all. It became like a dream.

DOCTOR
Yet you were still awake?

PATIENT
Yes. Awake, but as if I was dreaming. Dreaming though awake.

DOCTOR
Were there any distinct sounds in the hangar? Any signs of movement?

PATIENT
Yes. Shortly after the door closed – I mean, when the ramp was drawn up again to become part of the wall – I felt the floor vibrating – not shaking, just vibrating – and then heard a sort of background humming.

DOCTOR
Humming? The sound of low-powered engines?

PATIENT
No. A kind of bass humming – I can't really explain it – but not a mechanical sound. More like an electrical sound – very faint, but distinct.

DOCTOR

Any sensation of movement?

PATIENT

A kind of floating sensation, but I wasn't too sure. I was still a bit light-headed. It could have been some kind of movement.

DOCTOR

Such as flight?

PATIENT

Could have been.

DOCTOR

And then?
(The patient does not respond.)

DOCTOR

What happened next, Beth?

PATIENT

I can't remember. I think I blacked out. Yes! I see corridors – curving corridors – with portholes along one wall and steel doors – all closed – in the other wall. *Not* all closed – no! Sometimes a door would be open – not many, but some. Then I caught glimpses of what looked like a huge machine-shop: jibs and cranes, catwalks, ladders, machinery, lots of men ... I assume they were men, but they seemed faraway – in grey coveralls. Then ... *Oh, God!*

DOCTOR

It's all right, Beth. I'm still here, right by your side. You have no need to fear. What did you see?

PATIENT

Another room. I was in a different room. Circular, dome-shaped ceiling, white-painted metal walls, men and women in white coats working at long tables beside glass tanks that were covered in frost and ... *Oh, God, no!*

DOCTOR
It's all right, Beth. What you saw was in the frosted glass tanks. What did you see?

PATIENT
Bodies. Naked human bodies. Sleeping or dead. With wires running out of their heads and attached to the inside of the tanks.

DOCTOR
Wires?

PATIENT
Cables. Electric cables, I think. They were fixed to the inside of the tanks and other wires came out of outside and ran up to machines showing zigzagging lines on what looked like TV screens.

DOCTOR
EEG machines?

PATIENT
Pardon?

DOCTOR
Have you ever seen in real life hospitals, or perhaps on television, machines that record brain-waves or heartbeats, indicating if a patient is alive or dead?

PATIENT
Yes.

DOCTOR
Were these machine like those?

PATIENT
Yes

DOCTOR
So the naked people, either unconscious or dead, were in frosted glass cages wired to machines that may have been recording their brain-waves or heartbeat.

PATIENT
Yes. It seemed something like that. I . . .

DOCTOR
Yes, Beth?
(The patient does not respond.)

DOCTOR
You don't want to recall it, Beth, but you can. It's all right. You are safe. What were the people in white coats doing at the long tables?
(The patient does not respond.)

DOCTOR
What are they doing, Beth?

PATIENT
Joining things together. Welding things. Fitting wires into sockets and soldering metallic joints and operating computer consoles and putting things together.

DOCTOR
What things?
(The patient does not respond.)

DOCTOR
What things, Beth?

PATIENT
Severed heads. Amputated limbs. Internal organs – oh, God, a human heart, still beating! Joining them to other human and metallic body parts. *I can't look!* I *won't* look!

DOCTOR
Don't look, Beth. You don't have to look. Look away. What happened next, Beth?
(The patient does not respond.)

DOCTOR
It's all right, Beth, you have passed through that room. You have nothing to fear. What happened next, Beth?

PATIENT
Can't remember. Darkness. Things moving through darkness. Silence and darkness and breathing and the sound of my heartbeat. I'm floating. Can't see. I am where nothing is.

DOCTOR
Did you have a black-out, Beth?

PATIENT
Yes. A black-out. I think so. I know I had a black-out. I awakened in . . .

DOCTOR
Yes, Beth.
(The patient does not respond.)

DOCTOR
You had a black-out, Beth, and then recovered. What happened next, Beth?

PATIENT
I'm somewhere else. Another room. Curved white walls, but I don't think they're metallic.

DOCTOR
An inside room.

PATIENT
Yes.

DOCTOR
And?

PATIENT
I'm looking up at the ceiling. Dome-shaped. It's brightly lit, but I can't see the lights. I think the lights are hidden.

DOCTOR
And?

PATIENT
I'm looking up at the ceiling.

DOCTOR
You're lying down?

PATIENT
Yes. On something pretty hard. Not a mattress. Something cold and hard. I think it might be metallic. When I move, it feels cold and hard.

DOCTOR
You're lying on something cold and hard, which may be metallic, and you're looking up at the dome-shaped ceiling.

PATIENT
Yes. A dome-shaped ceiling. White like the walls. Curved

walls like all the other walls I passed. All curves. All domes.

DOCTOR
And lying on this cold, hard, metallic bed, looking up at the dome-shaped ceiling, you saw . . .

PATIENT
A circle of faces staring down. Light beaming down to blind me. Spotlights, I think, not too bright or big, but beaming down from behind the shoulders of the men staring down at me.

DOCTOR
What kind of men?

PATIENT
Normal men. One handsome and somehow ageless, with very smooth skin, but little movement in his features. Grey hair – no, white hair. I thought the white hair was strange because his face seemed so young, though expressionless.

DOCTOR
Young, but . . . What do you mean by 'little movement in his features' – by 'expressionless?' He looked human and otherwise normal?

PATIENT
Yes. Kind of handsome. Kind of handsome given his white hair and the lack of movement, of mobility, in his features. I think he might have had plastic surgery, though I couldn't see scars or lines.

DOCTOR
Were you strapped to the bed?

PATIENT
Not a bed. A kind of table.

DOCTOR
A kind of surgical table?

PATIENT
Yes, maybe that.

DOCTOR
Let's call it a bed. Were you strapped down?

PATIENT
No.

DOCTOR
Did you try to sit up?

PATIENT
No . . . Yes, I tried, but I just couldn't move. When I tried to move, I felt paralysed and that brought back my fear.

DOCTOR
So did any of the men surrounding you, looking down at you, actually speak to you?

PATIENT
Yes, the one who had a young face, but with white hair, and maybe plastic surgery.

DOCTOR
What did he say?
(The patient does not respond.)

DOCTOR
What did he say, Beth?

PATIENT
Don't worry. You're not paralysed. You're not hurt or damaged in any way. You will come to no harm.

446

DOCTOR
  He spoke English?

PATIENT
  Yes.

DOCTOR
  Accent?

PATIENT
  He was American – I'm sure he was American – but he also sounded kind of European, like those guys in the movies.

DOCTOR
  When he spoke to you, did you try to reply?

PATIENT
  Yes.

DOCTOR
  You could speak?

PATIENT
  Yes.

DOCTOR
  What did you say?

PATIENT
  I asked him where I was.

DOCTOR
  And he said?

PATIENT
  Nothing.

DOCTOR
  Nothing?

PATIENT
  He just smiled and aimed something in his hand at the opposite wall. He pressed a button and two steels panels slid apart to form a big window, letting me see what was outside.

DOCTOR
  What was outside?

PATIENT
  Stars!

DOCTOR
  Pardon?

PATIENT
  Stars! I saw nothing but stars. Then he pressed another button and the light dimmed and the stars disappeared, and then I saw . . .

DOCTOR
  Yes, Beth?
  (The patient does not respond.)

DOCTOR
  What did you see through the window, Beth?

PATIENT
  Earth.

DOCTOR
  Earth?

PATIENT
Not earth – *the* Earth. Just as I'd seen it in those films sent back by the satellites. The globe of Earth. At least, I think it was the Earth. It looked like Earth on the films and photos I've seen. I think it was Earth.

DOCTOR
Did the man showing you this say anything at all at this point? Did he speak?

PATIENT
Yes.

DOCTOR
What did he say?
(Note: At this point the patient, who has no reported interest in, or knowledge of, acting, adapted a surprisingly convincing male voice.)

PATIENT
Beautiful, isn't it? But why look so surprised? The Soviets and Americans have both put men into space – and that's exactly where you are, Mrs Randall . . . above Earth, in outer space, just like Yuri Gagarin, Alan Shepherd, Major Titov and Lieutenant-Colonel John Glenn. Indeed, next month the Russians will be putting what they assume will be the first woman into space – but you've beaten her to it. Don't you feel proud?
(Note: At this point in the hypnotic trance session even Dr Sagan seems so startled that she can think of nothing else to say for quite some time. For this reason there is a large gap on the tape before the question-and-answer session picks up again. When the patient next speaks, her voice has returned to normal.)

DOCTOR
So how did you react when you saw Earth and the stars outside the window?

PATIENT
I was calm. I felt a bit remote. As if I'd been drugged.

DOCTOR
Did the man showing you the stars say any more?

PATIENT
Yes.

DOCTOR
What did he say?

PATIENT
He said . . .

DOCTOR
Yes?

PATIENT
We picked you up by mistake. It wasn't you we wanted.
We thought it was your husband in the car and instead we
got you.

DOCTOR
Anything else?
(The patient does not respond.)

DOCTOR
You're safe, Beth. Nothing can harm you. Did he say
anything else?

PATIENT
He told me I shouldn't worry. That they weren't going
to harm me. He said they were just going to check that I
was okay and then take me home. He said that when I got
back home, I wouldn't recall what had happened to me,
but that eventually I would be the means of warning Dwight

that he was endangering himself, as well as me and Nichola, by investigating UFOs. He said that although I initially wouldn't remember my experience, it would all come out eventually, at the appropriate time, which was his way of warning Dwight.

DOCTOR
  And?

PATIENT
  Nothing else.

DOCTOR
  He said nothing else?

PATIENT
  No.

DOCTOR
  Not another word?
  (The patient does not respond.)

DOCTOR
  Did he say anything else? *Anything*, Beth? You can tell me. It's all right. What else did he say?

PATIENT
  Nothing. He stepped aside. Another man, speaking German, held up a long, sharp-pointed, silvery instrument. Awful! *Terrifying!* The others held my legs apart. The one with the awful instrument leaned over me, looking between my legs, and then ... Oh, please, no! Please! Don't! Oh, God, it hurts! Please stop it! Oh, God, please, God help me, don't, please stop him, I can't ... Oh, God, stop! *No! No! No!*

DOCTOR

Relax, Beth, relax, relax, you are relaxed, you are safe, I am here, you are all right. Tell me, Beth. It's all right to tell me. What else did they do?

PATIENT

No! No! No! No! No!

DOCTOR

Yes, Beth, yes, it's all right, I am here, Dwight is here, you're not alone, you can tell us. You can talk to us, Beth. What else did they do?

PATIENT

Oh, God, the pain! I can't bear the pain. Sometimes pain and then a kind of pleasure that goes beyond pain. Things inside me – in there. Deep inside me – oh, the pain! In my ears, up my nostrils, in . . . I can't accept . . . I refuse to . . . Yes! They did! On my stomach – they turned me onto my stomach and put something in there . . . *Pain.* Please, God, help me! First the back, then the front. Needles under my skin, metallic probes in every orifice, juices sucked out and liquids pumped in and all the pain and even more pain and sometimes . . . Oh, God help me – pleasure. Yes, that as well. They tormented me with pleasure that went beyond the bearable and brought me – my racing heart! – *I can't breathe!* – to the point of . . . Pain – back to pain – experimenting, trying to see what was possible, from one extreme to the other, pain and pleasure combined . . . And all the time looking at me, studying me, as if I was nothing, an insect, something trapped on a slide under a microscope . . . Oh, God help me, please let me go! Please, don't! No more. *Please!*

DOCTOR

Forget it, Beth. It's in the past. It's been and gone.

You are here now. You're safe. You are safe here with me and can't be harmed, you are here in the present. Think of the present without fear and tell me what they are doing, Beth. They have finished and the pain has all gone and I want to know how it ended. No more pain. You can tell me. What did they do when they finished, Beth?

PATIENT
   Nothing. When they finished, they stepped aside. They took the samples they had taken out of me and then went away, leaving him – only him!

DOCTOR
   The one with the handsome features and white hair and lack of expression. The one who spoke American with an accent. What did he say or do, Beth?

PATIENT
   I don't want . . .

DOCTOR
   You are safe, Beth. I am here, you are protected. What did he say or do?

PATIENT
   He . . .

DOCTOR
   Yes, Beth?

PATIENT
   He started lowering what looked like one of the metal caps worn by the aliens onto my head – it was like being in a dentist's chair: the metallic cap was on a hinged arm – and he said he was going to erase my memory of this experience, but leave enough to be revived at a later date

by others. Then he placed the metal cap on my head and somehow made it tighten around my skull. I was frightened. *I'm frightened!*

DOCTOR
Did this metal cap have wires running out of it, attached to some kind of equipment?

PATIENT
Yes.

DOCTOR
Have you ever heard of a stereotaxic skullcap?

PATIENT
No.

DOCTOR
All right. He lowered the wired metal cap onto your head and tightened it around your skull. What happened next?
(The patient does not respond.)

DOCTOR
What happened, Beth?

PATIENT
I'm frightened. Terrified. Don't do it! Please, don't do it! I won't tell anyone. I won't! I promise! Please, don't do it! *Don't!*

DOCTOR
What happened then, Beth?
(The patient does not respond.)

DOCTOR
What happened, Beth?

PATIENT

Pain. Stars. Sparkling lights. Darkness. I am where nothing is, in the darkness, and only know that I don't know.

DOCTOR

Don't know what?

PATIENT

My own name. What I am. Where I am. What is. I am where nothing is, in the darkness, and only know that I don't know.

DOCTOR

You blacked out again.

PATIENT

I awakened.

DOCTOR

Where were you when you awakened, Beth? What did you see?

PATIENT

I was nowhere. I was just awake. I knew I'd awakened.

DOCTOR

Where are you now that you've awakened, Beth? What are you seeing?

PATIENT

I'm still in the car. I feel sleepy . . . must have slept. I'm on my way to Columbus – just left Springfield – and . . .

DOCTOR

Yes, Beth?

PATIENT
Where am I? I thought the sun was setting. I was heading for Columbus. Why's the car . . .?

DOCTOR
Yes, Beth?

PATIENT
I don't believe . . .

DOCTOR
Yes, Beth?

PATIENT
That road sign . . . It says I'm heading for Dayton. I must have been driving home. I fell asleep driving home . . . No, I didn't. I couldn't have done that. I was driving to Columbus, out of Springfield, and now . . . Dayton. The car's parked by the side of the road in the direction of Dayton. It's . . . I can't tell the time. My wristwatch has stopped. It stopped at 5.05, though I can't tell if that's yesterday evening or this morning . . . No, not this morning. It couldn't have been this morning. I was definitely driving out of Springfield, heading for Columbus, at about five yesterday evening as the sun was sinking. Now the sign says Dayton. The car's parked facing Dayton. It's . . . *some* time in the early morning . . . I'd say eight or nine . . . and I'm heading back to Dayton. Oh, dear God, what's happening. Dwight? Where are you, Dwight? Oh, God, what's happening to me? *I don't want to! I don't want to! I don't want to!*

DOCTOR
All right, Beth, that's all we want to know. You have been very good. You have been very helpful. You are in deep, deep sleep, very deep, deep sleep, you are relaxed, you are very relaxed, you are sleeping, deep sleep. In a moment you can waken up. You won't remember what's

been said between us. You won't remember until I ask you to do so, you are asleep, deep, deep sleep. All right, Beth, you are waking up now, you are waking, waking slowly, pleasantly, you are pleasantly waking up. You can waken up, Beth.

TRANSCRIPTION ENDS

Chapter Thirty-Six

'There are now a great number of foreign exploration stations in the Antarctic,' Wilson's assistant, Salvatore Fallaci, said as he sat beside Wilson at the panoramic window overlooking the glittering white wilderness. 'Ever since the International Geophysical Year in 1957–58, the twelve nations have, with your co-operation, been spreading out to set up more and more bases. If they continue to do so, our security is likely to be threatened.'

A former Mafioso with his hands steeped in blood, Fallaci had been abducted and brain-implanted to obey Wilson's every whim as a scout and roving executioner. Otherwise, he seemed perfectly normal. He was now reporting to Wilson after having just returned from a tour of the Antarctic by saucer, checking on the movements and activities of the various nations which now had polar exploration bases here.

'It's been so long since I studied this situation,' Wilson replied. 'What it's like out there nowadays?'

Fallaci glanced down at his notes. 'The US are based at McMurdo Sound and still have their Ronne Antarctic Research Expedition in the old Service East Base camp at Marquerite Bay. Australia has established stations on Heard and Macquarie islands, as well as their Mawson Station on the mainland coast of MacRobertson Land. France has established permanent bases in the Kerguelen and Crozet islands. The Argentines have established General Belgrano Station on the Filchner Ice Shelf. The

458

Norwegians are at Cape Norvegia. The USSR, long active in East Antarctica, now also has Bellingshausen Station in the Antarctic Peninsula, is constructing at Novolazarevskaya, and plans additional stations in West Antarctica. A profusion of British, Chilean and Argentine bases are now located so close together around McMurdo Sound that we must seriously consider the possibility that they're there for intelligence rather than science.'

'You think they'd be foolish enough to try that?'

'Yes, boss. The more you give them, the more confident they'll become – not really able to imagine just how much further you've advanced – and the more confident they become, the more foolish they'll be.'

'That's true enough,' Wilson replied, though he didn't seem concerned. 'Good Sicilian logic. So what else are they up to?'

'Inland stations for the observation of the sun, weather, the aurora, the magnetic field, the ionosphere and cosmic rays include the Byrd Station for the US in West Antarctica; Vostok for the USSR at the south geomagnetic pole and the pole of relative inaccessibility; and Amundsen-Scott Station at the South Pole, also for the US. I should also remind you that a nuclear power plant was set up at McMurdo Station in 1962 and a seawater distillation plant is being installed right now and should be ready by next year. The Antarctic is no longer a safe haven. We're not alone, boss.'

Wilson smiled at that remark. 'We're not alone' was a catch-phrase now widely used in the West about flying saucers, still widely believed to be flown by extraterrestrials.

'So apart from the possibility of intelligence gathering,' he said, 'what else excites their interest here?'

'They believe that western Queen Maud Land, actually Neu Schwabenland, right on our doorstep, could be similar to the gold-producing Witwatersrand beds of South Africa; that the mountain belt of the Antarctic Peninsula could be similar to the copper-rich Andes; that the Antarctic continental shelves near Coats Land and the Adéle and George V coasts could be comparable to the Agulhas Basin off South Africa and the Otway Basin off southern Australia, which are potentially great sources of petroleum. They're also racing to find the metal minerals for chromium, copper, gold, lead, tin and zinc. Even more ominous, their realisation that Antarctica contains nearly ninety per cent of the world's ice has led them to serious discussion and experimentation regarding the possibility of harnessing it as a boundless supply of nonsalt water. Last but by no means least, they're presently investigating the possibility of using the Antarctic as a long-term deep-freeze storage site for grain and other foods; and, even worse, as a site for radioactive-waste disposal and storage.'

'I would never permit that,' Wilson said.

'I needn't remind you of the increasing ruthlessness of the hunters of fur seals and the whaling ships operating around our shores and depleting the waters. I should remind you, however, that tourism, which commenced way back in 1958 with nine-to twelve-day tours of the Antarctic Peninsula arranged by the Argentine Naval Transport command, is now expanding dramatically with hotels proposed for the McMurdo dry valleys and plans already being drawn up for the introduction of various alpine sports, including skiing and mountaineering, as well as commercial tourist helicopter flights over the wilderness. Between the planes of the tourists and those of the various exploration bases, we have a potentially serious security problem.'

'I'm not too concerned,' Wilson replied. 'As long as our mutually beneficial, clandestine trade continues with the various nations located here, they'll keep their aircraft well away from Neu Schwabenland.'

'That's only the United States, Great Britain, Canada and the USSR. The smaller countries aren't included in the trade and therefore don't know of our existence – so they'll continue to fly in this direction and, so far, have only been prevented from seeing us by the relative inaccessibility of the terrain. However, they're developing better aircraft every year – aircraft designed specifically to fly in polar regions – and some day, I believe, they'll be able to reach us. Likewise, the forthcoming tourist flight pilots won't know about us and could choose this area as one of their flight routes. The mountain is, after all, particularly spectacular from the point of view of a tourist.'

'I've anticipated that possibility,' Wilson replied, 'and been working on a means of preventing it. As you just said: the mountain is already an area of inaccessibility. Before the smaller countries or tour operators develop an aircraft that can reach here – and, indeed, before the nations we're trading with grow arrogant and turn against us – we will have developed an invisible force field that will, like the saucer satellites, which in turn were based on our old *Feuerballs*, cause normal aircraft engines to malfunction and force them either to crash or turn back before entering the area. Should anything manage to slip through the force field, we will have by then, as a last resort, a working pulse-beam weapon. So I think we're safe for the foreseeable future. In the meantime, our saucers will continue to haunt the various Antarctic exploration bases by hovering over them, causing blips on their radar screens, or otherwise harassing their aircraft – as, in fact, we've been doing for some time now, to the consternation of the pilots and intelligence agents.'

'That's why they describe a lot of the area in Antarctica as inaccessible.'

'Precisely,' Wilson said.

Glancing through the window, down those dizzying depths between the sheer walls of the mountain where it formed a natural well, he saw the latest two hundred and fifty feet diameter mother ship on its landing pad, surrounded by smaller saucers of various sizes. Seen from above, especially from this great height, they looked like perfectly formed, silvery plates turned upside down. With no protuberances of any kind, no identifying marks, not even a visible seam, they had their own bizarre beauty.

'So what's the general UFO situation in America?' Wilson asked his roving scout and assassin.

'No problem,' Fallaci replied. 'I can confirm that the virtual dissolving of Project Blue Book, combined with the ridicule heaped upon UFO witnesses and the suppression of information or news about UFOs – undertaken by Air Force intelligence and supervised by CIA agent Jack Fuller – has reduced public interest in UFOs almost to zero, removed pressure from the Air Force, and given the civilian UFO organisations severe problems, most of them due to a lack of funds caused by falling memberships.'

'Falling because UFOs have been systematically erased from public consciousness by the choking off of news about the subject.'

'Exactly.'

'This all sounds very good to me,' Wilson said with a thin, almost good-humoured smile.

'It's certainly not bad,' Fallaci said. 'Nevertheless, we must continue to keep a careful eye on the Europeans, Americans and Soviets who have, over the past few years, been co-operating more openly, which isn't good for us.'

'They're co-operating more openly?' Wilson asked. 'That *does* surprise me!'

'Me, too,' Fallaci said, 'but it's true. They've been drawing closer for the past few years, but really huddled together in December 1962 with the formation of a multilateral NATO nuclear force; the signing in July 1963 of a treaty between Britain, America and the Soviet Union, banning nuclear weapons tests in the atmosphere, outer space and underwater; and, finally, the installing on August 10, 1963, of a "hot line" between the Kremlin and the White House to reduce the risk of accidental war. This unprecedented co-operation between these old enemies suggests that they may be hoping to unite into the one, all-powerful force that can eventually be turned against us.'

'Fear not,' Wilson replied with the supreme confidence of a man to whom emotion is alien. 'I'm giving them someone else to worry about. The assassination of President Kennedy – a good job well done, incidentally—'

'Thank you, boss.'

'As I was saying, the assassination of Kennedy has already strained the US-Soviet relationship: as we anticipated, many Americans view his death as the result of a Soviet plot. Also, before this year is out, the Chinese will, with our help, successfully test their own atomic bomb over Sinkiang, a western province bordering the Soviet Union. That will, I think, make the Soviets more concerned with the Chinese than with us; while the Americans, still obsessed with the death of their president and his Soviet-worshipping assassin, Lee Harvey Oswald, will be extremely suspicious of the Soviets and much less concerned with us.'

The intercom on the table beside Wilson rang. Picking it up, he listened intently, then put the intercom down, swivelled around in his chair, and used his remote-control to turn on the twenty-eight inch TV standing across the room. A machine known as a video-recorder was resting on a stand beneath the TV and it came on automatically, to record the programme being shown.

'Intelligence,' Wilson explained to Fallaci. 'They say there's something on CBS-TV that I should see. It's starting right now.'

When the picture on the TV screen came into focus, Wilson immediately recognised the parched terrain of Socorro, New Mexico, where the famous UFO crash had occurred on July 2, 1947. The very same day, Wilson recollected, that farmer Marlon Clarke, who had been unfortunate enough to have seen the debris of the crash and the corpses of the crew, had been abducted by another flying saucer and brought here. Clarke's severed head, which they had managed to keep alive for years, had recently been attached to a combination of human and mechanical parts and was still functioning, albeit programmed by a stereotaxic skullcap, as part of what would soon be a perfect, absolutely obedient, killing-machine cyborg. Now, thinking he was about to see a documentary on that old crash, Wilson was surprised to see a documentary on another UFO crash in Socorro – but one that had taken place just a few days ago.

What he saw enraged him.

On Friday, April 24, 1964, at approximately 5.50 to 6.00 p.m., Opal Grinder, manager of the Whiting Brothers' service station in Socorro, New Mexico, claimed that the driver of a 1955 model Cadillac, which had a Colorado licence plate and also contained the driver's wife and three boys, stopped at Grinder's service station for gas. The agitated driver told Grinder that 'something travelling across the highway from east to west' almost 'took the roof off' his car as he was driving just south of town, north of the airport. He suspected that the object had either landed or crashed, as he had also seen 'a police car head off the road and up a hill in that direction.' Continuing into town, he had met another police car heading in the same direction. To Grinder's suggestion that he might have seen a helicopter, the unnamed man said, 'That sure would be some funny helicopter!'

Subsequent investigations by the police revealed that the object had been observed flying only a few hundred feet to the northeast of the north-bound Cadillac at 5.45 p.m on April 24, and was 'egg-shaped, had a smooth aluminium or magnesium-like surface, and seemed to be a little longer than the four-door Green 1955 Cadillac in which the family was riding.' The craft dropped to barely ten feet above the ground, flew directly at the Cadillac, and passed silently within ten feet of its top, almost touching the tip of the radio antenna. It streaked onward a few hundred yards to the southwest, where it stopped abruptly, hung in midair for about thirty seconds, then descended vertically, silhouetted by the low afternoon sun, to land just beyond a small hill which hid it from the view of those in the Cadillac.

The driver of the Cadillac and his wife then observed a white Pontiac police car as it turned off a north-south road that ran west of US Highway 85, cut across rough terrain, and headed for the rise beyond which the strange flying object had landed. Thinking that perhaps they had seen some 'new type of aircraft' that was being developed in the area, the driver of the Cadillac kept driving toward Socorro, eventually passing another police car. This one, which was from the New Mexico State Police, was moving urgently in the opposite direction, also heading for where the strange aircraft had descended.

Once in Socorro, the driver of the Cadillac stopped at the Whiting Brothers service station on the north side of town, where he told the manager, Opal Grinder, that someone was flying 'a funny looking craft' dangerously low over the highway on Socorro's south side, had landed, and was probably being checked out by the officer of the pursuing police car. Then the driver of the Cadillac continued his journey with his family.

In fact, the man in the white Pontiac police car was Lonnie Zamora, a thirty-one-year old Socorro policeman described in a subsequent report by investigating FBI agent J. Arthur Byrnes Jr as 'a sober, industrious and conscientious officer, and not given to fantasy.'

Zamora's extraordinary experience had begun at approximately 5.45 p.m. when he set off in pursuit of a speeding black 1964 Chevrolet, following it south, after pulling away from the west side of the courthouse. About a minute later, at approximately the same time as the unknown man from Colorado had sighted his UFO, when Zamora was a half mile south of Spring Street, he heard a roar and noticed a brilliant blue 'cone of flame' low to the south-southwest, at a distance of approximately 2,400 feet. As Zamora was wearing prescription glasses with green sunshades, he was at this stage unable to distinguish the difference between the flying object's body and the 'blue cone of flame' shooting out of it. However, as the flame was over the location of a dynamite shack owned by the town mayor, Zamora assumed that the dynamite was blowing up, so instead of continuing his pursuit of the Chevrolet, he turned off the paved road and headed across the rough terrain, toward what now looked like a descending flame and sounded like a 'continuous roaring.'

Because of the position of the speeding Chevrolet, it was assumed by the investigators that its driver would have either seen or heard the descending object.

Zamora drove across the rough terrain, toward the roaring 'flame', for about twenty seconds. By this time he was able to note that the flame definitely was 'bluish, very brilliant, a little orange around the edges, more so near the bottom' and that it was 'sort of motionless, but appeared to *descend slowly*.' He could not see the bottom of the flame, which had just descended behind a hill; not did he notice smoke; but some dust seemed to be moving over the area where it had landed.

The 'flame' disappeared completely behind the hill, but the roaring continued as Zamora tried more than once to make his Pontiac climb the steep, gravel-covered slope. Then, as he finally began to ascend successfully, the roaring of the hidden 'flame' died away.

Turning over the hilltop, Zamora saw a 'shiny type object' down in the ravine, or arroyo, to the southwest, at a distance of about a hundred and fifty yards. He stopped his car for a few seconds, in order to study the object. At first he thought it was 'an overturned white car' with the far end raised higher than the nearest one. Then he saw two people in white coveralls very close to the object.

As if having heard Zamora's arrival, one of the persons turned and looked straight at his car, then jumped slightly, as if startled by seeing it there.

Zamora had only stopped for a few seconds. Now, as he started forward again in his car, he noted that the object was 'like aluminium – it was whitish against the mesa background, but not chrome' and it seemed oval or 'egg-shaped' with support legs extending obliquely from it.

The people in white coveralls looked like normal human beings, but 'possibly they were small adults or large kids.'

As he drove on again, Zamora descended into a dip and temporarily lost sight of the object and the two people beside it. Worried that he might have come across a top-secret experimental vehicle from the White Sands Proving Ground, and wanting one reliable witness other than himself in case of trouble with the authorities, he radioed to the sheriff's office that he was checking a possible 10–40, or accident, down in the arroyo, and wanted New Mexico State Police Sergeant Samuel Chavez to come alone to the location.

As his message was being relayed to Chavez by Ned Lopez, the Socorro chief dispatcher, Zamora stopped his car again and started to get out, still talking on the radio. He dropped the microphone accidentally and leaned down to retrieve it. Even as he was straightening up, he heard 'a heavy slam, metal-like, heavier than a tank hatch . . . then another slam, *real loud*.' He was now completely out of his car and could see the object in clear view, about fifty feet away in the arroyo, with two of its four extension legs extending obliquely down to the ground. He could also see, for the first time, a large, red insignia on one side of the object's otherwise smooth, featureless, egg-shaped body.

The two people in white coveralls had disappeared – a fact which, combined with the metallic 'slamming' noises heard by Zamora, made him assume that they had entered the strange craft by some unseen door.

He had only taken two or three steps toward the object when he heard 'a roar . . . not exactly a blast, very loud roar . . . not like a jet . . . started low frequency quickly, then rose in frequency – a higher tone – and in loudness, from loud to very loud.' At the same time he saw 'bright blue flame' shooting out from the underside of the object and it started to rise vertically from the ground.

Thinking that the object was about to explode, Zamora threw himself to the ground. He felt a wave of heat, but when no explosion came, though the roaring continued, he got up again and ran back to his car. Bumping into it while glancing fearfully back over his shoulder, he lost his glasses and sunshades. Picking them up, and determined to keep the car between himself and the ascending object, which he still felt might explode, he ran north across the mesa, glancing back two or three times to observe that in about five or six seconds the object had risen level with his car, about twenty feet above the bottom of the arroyo, and was still roaring and shooting flame from its underside.

About fifty feet from his car, when just over the rim of the hill, Zamora turned back toward the object, but shielded his eyes with his arm in case it exploded.

At that moment, the roaring stopped and was replaced with a 'sharp tone, a whining sound' that went 'from high tone to low tone in maybe a second, then stopped.' Then there was silence.

Zamora saw that the object was no longer rising, though it *was* still moving: heading away quickly, in perfect silence, west-southwest, passing over, or rather south of, the dynamite shack as it flew away.

Realising that the object was in flight and not exploding as he had feared, Zamora raced back to his car, picked up his glasses from where they had fallen, then once more radioed the Socorro sheriff dispatcher, Ned Lopez.

Lopez later confirmed that he had received the call from Zamora, breathlessly telling him to look out the window of the sheriff's office to see if the object was in sight. As Lopez was at the north window, not the south, and therefore could not see the object, he asked Zamora what kind of object it was. Zamora said, 'It looks like a balloon.'

In fact, even as he was talking to Lopez, Zamora was watching the UFO disappearing in the distance. It stayed about ten to fifteen feet above the ground, following the terrain, until it was near the perlite mill on the west side of US 60, about a mile away. There, it suddenly 'angled up at a steep climb and got small in the distance, over the canyon or mountain that way, *very fast*.' He remembered it as 'a bright, whitish oval getting smaller and smaller as it sped away, upward and over the mountains.'

Approximately one minute and fifty seconds after Zamora had first heard the roar and seen the 'flame' in the sky, the UFO was gone.

Sent urgently to the landing site by the message relayed through dispatcher Ned Lopez, New Mexico State Police Sergeant Sam Chavez reached Zamora just after the UFO had disappeared. Even as Chavez was approaching Zamora, the latter was making a sketch of the red insignia he had seen on the object before it took off. Though he had remained calm enough to do this, he was, according to Chavez, as 'white as a sheet' and in a cold sweat.

Examining the landing site with Zamora, Chavez also saw that the brush was smouldering in several places, after being ignited by the flame, and that there was what appeared to be a 'quadrangle' formed by four heavy, wedge-shaped imprints in the soil.

'So there you have it, folks,' the commentator said breezily, standing in front of the barren landing site in the wastelands outside Socorro with a microphone in his hand and a view of the dynamite shack over his right shoulder. 'A widely respected Deputy Marshal of Socorro, New Mexico, has stated categorically that he's seen a flying saucer and its occupants. Whether or not it's true remains to be seen. We're not alone, folks!'

Wilson used the remote control to switch the TV off. Then, quietly furious, he turned to Fallaci and said: 'The damned fools! That was one of their own saucers from the White Sands Proving Ground. This will probably resurrect worldwide interest in flying saucers. I have to see Fuller.'

'I'll get him,' Fallaci said.

Chapter Thirty-Seven

Wilson was correct. The Socorro Incident of April 24, 1964, soon became the most famous UFO sighting since the original Socorro sighting of 1947, resurrecting widespread public interest in the subject and replenishing the depleted financial resources of the leading civilian UFO organisations by dramatically increasing their membership to what it had been in 1961 before the dropping of Congressional hearings and the propaganda campaign against NICAP's Donald E. Keyhoe had taken their toll.

A few weeks after the Socorro Incident, Randall flew to Washington DC to have a meeting with Dr Frederick Epstein and Tony Scaduto in the revitalised APII organisation headquarters in 21st Street. As Scaduto had just returned from New Mexico, where he had been sent by Dr Epstein to check out the Socorro Incident, the purpose of the meeting was to hear what he had to say. Since Epstein was at that stage convinced that the UFOs were of extraterrestrial origin, Scaduto and Randall had still not confided their belief that at least some of the flying saucers could be man-made. Scaduto was now looking uncomfortable, because he was close to that subject.

'First thing I learned when I got to Socorro,' he reported, 'is that Deputy Marshal Zamora's radio transmissions had been heard by others, including State Police Senior Patrolman Ted V. Jordan, who arrived at the landing site shortly after Chavez, in the company of Socorro Under-sheriff James Luckie. A cattle inspector named White, who had also heard Zamora's radio calls, turned up at the landing site; and just after 6.00 p.m. FBI agent J. Arthur Byrnes arrived to investigate.'

'So what did you find?' Dr Epstein asked in his quiet, thoughtful way, while stroking his Vandyke beard, which now had lots of grey strands.

'I found the burnt brush, which seemed genuine enough,' Scaduto replied. 'I then interviewed every witness I could find – the ones who'd seen the brush when the burning was still relatively recent – and they all confirmed that the brush had been scorched by flames and that the pad prints, or landing imprints, had been made, in the words of one investigator: "by wedge-shaped units being forced by great weight, down into the rather well-packed soil of the ravine." '

'What size would these have been?' Epstein asked, letting the tip of his pencil dangle over his notebook.

'The wedges would have had a horizontal length of twelve to sixteen inches, a horizontal width of six to eight inches, and a vertical wedge-depth of four to six inches. I have to say, though, that this latter measurement was impossible to define accurately because of the inward falling of the soil.'

Scaduto pulled a press-cutting out of his jacket, unfolded it and smoothed it down on Epstein's desk with the palm of his hand.

'According to the detailed account in the April 28, 1964, edition of the local biweekly newspaper, *El Defensor Chieftain*,' he continued, reading from the press cutting, 'the landing gear imprints – I quote: "did not appear to have been made by an object striking the earth with great force, but by an object of considerable weight settling to earth at slow speed and not moving after touching the ground".'

He put the press cutting back into his pocket, then looked up again, glancing first at Dwight, then giving all of his attention to the thoughtful Dr Epstein.

'Though some of the bushes were still smouldering when Chavez, Jordan, Luckie and White were present, they all agreed that there was no odour indicating that combustion of any conventional fuel had caused the burn damage.'

'Very good,' Epstein murmured.

'Jordan was particularly impressed by the fact that the flame described by Zamora had obviously sliced a large greasewood bush located almost centrally in the landing gear quadrilateral, without leaving any signs of turbulence, like the kind that would've been caused by normal rotors or jet exhausts. Jordan also took Polaroid pictures of the landing site and the four imprints within minutes of arriving on the scene.'

'You got copies?' Epstein asked like a stern schoolmaster.

'Yes, boss, I got copies.'

Epstein smiled and nodded. 'Fine, Tony, continue.'

Scaduto glanced at Dwight and grinned, then turned back to Epstein. 'Reasoning that the landing mechanisms of an experimental lunar landing module could have made the depressions in the ground, I contacted NASA, the Jet Propulsion Laboratory, and about fifteen local industrial firms to see if they'd been conducting any experiments with lunar landing modules in the area. In each case, the answer was no. I then established that no helicopters or aircraft were in the area at the time of the sighting and that the direction of the winds ruled out the possibility that the object was a balloon.'

'This sounds too good to be true,' Epstein said, smiling distractedly, as if lost in his own thoughts. 'We certainly appear to be talking about a real, physical object that landed and took off.'

'Well, digest this piece of interesting news,' Scaduto said, no longer looking uncomfortable and instead getting into his stride. 'Just before leaving Socorro I received a call from my set of eyes and ears at ATIC, and he told me that Project Blue Book, even under the leadership of the sceptical Major Quantinilla, is going to list the case as a genuine unidentified: the only combination of landing, trace, and occupant case so far listed in the Blue Book Files.'

'At least Blue Book's still active.'

Epstein gave a soft whistle to express his surprise and pleasure.

'At least they're still doing *something*,' Dwight said sardonically.

'Now, now,' Dr Epstein responded soothingly, knowing how bitter Dwight felt about how he had been treated by USAF. 'Go on, Tony, we're listening.'

'Regarding Blue Book's involvement,' Scaduto continued, 'I found that the case had been examined by Dr Lincoln La Paz, who had worked on the old Project Twinkle, and by NICAP's Dr J. Allen Hynek. The last named was there in his official capacity as consultant to the USAF. I also have it on the best of authority that Hynek has already pronounced it "one of the major UFO sightings in the history of the Air Force's consideration of the subject" and one of "the soundest, best substantiated reports". That was the final clincher when it came to Major Quantinilla's decision to list it in Project Blue Book's files as the first known combination of UFO landing, trace and occupant case.'

'Wonderful!' Dr Epstein exclaimed softly.

'So what did you find out about the landing site?' Dwight asked more pragmatically.

'Examination of the landing site revealed that the diagonals of the quadrilateral formed by the four landing marks intersected almost exactly at right angles. I therefore asked for, and received, Hynek's report, which contains a very interesting notation.'

Scaduto opened the notebook he had been holding in his lap, flipped a few pages over, then read aloud: 'One theorem in geometry states that if the diagonals of a quadrilateral intersect at right angles, the midpoints of the side of the quadrilateral lie on the circumference of a circle . . .' He glanced up from his notebook. 'Here's the important point,' he said, then went back to his reading. 'It is thus of considerable interest that the centre of the circle so formed on the Socorro landing site virtually coincided with the principal burn mark on the ground. Under certain circumstances the centre of gravity of the craft would have been directly over the centre of the circle, hence making the presence of the burn mark more significant.' He closed the notebook and looked up. 'In other words, what Hynek is saying is that the indentations and burn marks on the ground clearly indicated a real, physical object of circular shape. It wasn't a mirage or an hallucination on the part of Deputy Marshal Zamora. That vehicle was real enough – and it was shaped like a saucer.'

'And if the vehicle was real,' Dwight interjected, 'then so were its occupants.'

'Exactly!' Scaduto exclaimed with satisfaction.

'This is sounding better every minute,' Dr Epstein said.

'And it gets even better,' Scaduto told him. 'Get this . . . Checking with a receptionist in the Socorro County Building – a very nice lady, incidentally, who saved me a night's hotel bill – I learnt that by 7.20 p.m. on the evening of the sighting, CIA agent Jack Fuller and US Army Captain Ord/C, Richard T. Holder, up-range commander of the White Sands Stallion Site, met in the Socorro County Building where they proceeded to interrogate Zamora. In the course of this interrogation – according to the tapes heard by this lady and others – Byrnes told Zamora that it would be better if he did not – and I quote – "publicly mention seeing the two small figures in white" – unquote.'

'Two small figures in white,' Epstein repeated.

'Correct.'

'Not black?' Dwight asked.

'No, white.'

'But they specifically told Zamora not to mention the figures seen by the saucer,' Dr Epstein said.

'That's right,' Scaduto replied. 'Which suggests that the figures in white were certainly there.'

'Anything else?'

'Yes.' Scaduto was excited. 'Jack Fuller then recommended that in future Zamora refuse to describe the insignia he had seen on the side of the vehicle to anyone other than official investigators.'

'Insignia?' Dr Epstein asked, leaning forward and staring intently at his young researcher.

'Yeah, there was an insignia on the craft. According to the report witnessed, notarised and filed in the Socorro County Building, it was red in colour and approximately one-and-a-half feet tall. Zamora sketched it for his report. According to his sketch, it was an inverted V, or a vertical arrow, with a line under it, vertical lines on each side, and a parabolic arc over the point of the arrow.'

'Any idea what it represented?'

'Some.' Scaduto grinned like a triumphant schoolboy. 'A computer scientist buddy of mine ran it through his data base and came up with the notion that it's similar to a medieval Arabic sign for Venus. However, another friend, an engineer, insisted that it's confirmation that the UFO was a man-made craft.'

'Man-made?' Dr Epstein asked. 'I don't think I can wear this.'

'I think you might,' Scaduto told him.

'All right, Tony, continue.'

'In support of his claim, this buddy of mine showed me how, by moving and rotating the lines of the drawing, the initials "CIA" and "AD" could be formed, the latter representing the initials of Allen Dulles, present head of the CIA. He also showed me that the parabolic arc above the arrow, or inverted V, could represent a stylized cross-section of the body of the flying saucer – or a pressure wave – while the arrow, or inverted V, with a line under it, could indicate that a vertical thruster is centrally located in the fuselage, or circular wing. Finally, he knocked me sideways by stating that the placing of the symbol on the side of the craft – just above the thruster orifice on its underside – could be a warning that the thruster is located there; while the use of red for the symbol could be a danger sign, just as it is with current aircraft symbols.'

Scaduto straightened up in his seat, looking pleased with himself.

'So where is all this leading?' Dr Epstein asked in his quiet, patient manner.

'The implication,' Scaduto said, 'is that the Socorro sighting was of a highly sophisticated, piloted, man-made craft that had flown from, and returned to, somewhere in the White Sands Proving Ground.'

For a considerable period of time there was silence in the room, broken only by the soft drumming of Epstein's fingers on his desk. Finally, he took a deep breath and said, 'Man-made saucers?'

'Yes. From somewhere in the area.'

'But do you think these saucers can account for all the sightings we've had since World War II?'

'No,' Scaduto said, 'but they sure as hell could account for the many stories of flying saucers being held in secret hangars on US Air Force bases.'

'And the other ones? The technologically advanced ones? The mother ships?'

Scaduto shrugged. 'I don't know.'

'Well,' Epstein said after some thought, 'although APII has, up to now, carefully avoided all so-called "occupant" cases, in this case, given Deputy Marshal Zamora's reliability as a witness, and because Blue Book is listing the case as a genuine unidentified, I think we should – how shall I put it? – *liberalize* the organisation by including occupant cases in the future. I myself will avoid the man-made UFO hypothesis, but if you gentlemen wish to pursue it, please do so. In the meantime, I think we should use the latest Socorro sighting as leverage to press again for Congressional hearings.'

'Good idea,' Dwight said.

Sitting behind his desk, wearing an English tweed jacket and pants, with striped shirt and tie, his hair still plentiful but turning grey, as was his short, pointed beard, Epstein looked older than his age. After massaging his forehead, he sighed and glanced from Scaduto to Dwight.

'Well, gentlemen, I guess that's it for the day. It's a lot for one day.'

'You want to join us for lunch?' Dwight asked him. 'I'm having a light lunch with Tony here, before catching the plane back to Dayton.'

Epstein glanced at the mass of papers on his desk, then raised and lowered his hands in a rabbinical gesture – or simply one of weariness. 'I can't,' he said. 'The Socorro Incident has brought the work in and my desk, as you can see, is already overburdened. Besides, when I get tired I can't eat – and I certainly can't drink a thing at lunchtime, so I'll take a rain check.'

'You're sure?'

'Yes, I'm sure.'

Dwight and Scaduto pushed their chairs back, then Dwight leaned over the desk and shook Epstein's hand. 'Until the next time,' he said.

'Have a good lunch and a pleasant flight back, Dwight.'

'Hopefully without sighting any UFOs around the plane,' Dwight joked.

'That would make your day,' Epstein said.

Scaduto just waved his hand and sauntered out of the office ahead of Dwight. Once on the sidewalk outside the building, they caught a taxi the short distance to Clyde's in M Street, Georgetown, near to where Bob Jackson had been killed. Recalling this dreadful fact, Dwight felt a spasm of grief combined with rage and decided he needed a stiff drink. When they were seated, he ordered a large bourbon. Scaduto had beer. Throughout lunch they talked nonstop about UFOs in general and the recent Socorro Incident in particular, growing more excited every minute, which helped Dwight forget that his dear friend, Bob Jackson, had been murdered just a little farther along the street. No way in the world would

Dwight ever think Bob had died of a heart attack.

Eventually, when they had finished the lunch, settled the check and were leaving, Scaduto said: 'I'm telling you, Dwight, I still believe the UFOs are man-made and probably emanate from both Canadian and American top-secret establishments, probably in the White Sands Proving Ground.'

'I'm still not sure of that,' Dwight confessed, as they made their way out of the packed garden restaurant, through the bar, and out onto the busy, neon-lit sidewalk near the centre of Georgetown.

'Don't forget,' Scaduto continued, unperturbed, as they stood on the sidewalk, watching the passers-by, many of them exuberant students from Georgetown University, 'that the Brits have already demonstrated a proper, highly advanced, vertical take-off aircraft using swivelling jet nozzles – the *Hawker P1127*. And laser-beam technology – often included in UFO reports, though generally treated as pure science-fiction – has been making incredible advances since its discovery four years ago by the Hughes Aircraft company in California. So the capabilities of the flying saucers reported are definitely moving into the area of the possible. The saucers *could* be man-made!'

'But some of the saucers are really so far advanced that I find it difficult to believe they could be man-made.' Dwight glanced automatically along M street, towards Canal Road, and found himself trying to imagine what had happened to Bob Jackson that fateful night of his death. This in turn led him to another line of thought. 'Take Beth's experience, for instance,' he said. 'The one she recounted under hypnosis – that wasn't a dream, it was a real experience, and the technology suggested by her recollections had to be pretty stupendous. The beams of light from the small saucers somehow immobilized her car, then pulled it into the mother ship. The beams of light from the mother ship disorientated her and somehow paralysed her. Then, of course, when she was inside the ship, she was shown . . . *the stars.*'

'Yeah,' Tony replied softly, in wonder. 'She saw the damned stars!'

'That thing was up there in space,' Dwight continued. 'I can't imagine man-made aircraft – flying saucers or other kinds – being capable of that just yet.'

'Why not?' Scaduto replied, grateful to get off the subject of Beth's UFO experience, which he knew still disturbed Dwight greatly. 'The astronauts have been in space, certain of our conventional aircraft now reach the stratosphere – and according to Beth, the guy with the expressionless face told her to warn you off the search for, quote, *man-made UFOs* . . . And now this sighting at Socorro seems to prove conclusively that whatever Marshal Zamora saw, it was certainly real enough, and piloted by two guys in coveralls . . . No planes in the air at the time; no weather balloons . . . It was real, Dwight. It left burn marks and depressions. It was *physical* . . . So where the hell did it come from?'

'I don't know,' Randall confessed. 'I know only this . . . I'm frightened for Beth and Nichola. I'm even frightened for myself. So if I continue to work for Epstein, I've got to do it off the record – and you've got to cover the more public sightings. You've got to cover *for me.*'

'No sweat,' Scaduto said.

The two men shook hands on the crowded pavement, then went their separate ways.

Chapter Thirty-Eight

Stopping his car in the middle of the desert between Las Vegas and Nellis Air Force Base in the dead of night, Fuller lit a cigarette, inhaled gratefully, blew a cloud of smoke and realised that he wasn't looking forward to this particular meeting with Wilson.

For the past year, ever since Wilson had called a meeting to angrily discuss the so-called Socorro Incident, when a USAF flying saucer, based on the *Kugelblitz I*, and its three-man crew had been spotted by Deputy Marshal Lonnie Zamora, Fuller had been having regular, mostly unpleasant meetings with Wilson, who had expressed his concern about the resurgence of public interest in UFOs generated by the Air Force's carelessness in letting one of their two-man saucers from the White Sands Proving Ground be witnessed by a widely respected Deputy Marshal.

Indeed, the Socorro Incident of 1964 had become in the collective mind of the public the most fascinating UFO sighting since the original Socorro case of 1947. Approximately a year later, on June 12, 1965, one of Wilson's own, smaller flying saucers had crashed near Nellis AFB, Las Vegas, Nevada. The saucer and dead crew members had been taken into a top-secret research laboratory on the base for examination. That was two weeks ago.

Demanding the release of the remains through Fuller, Wilson had been refused and, at a later meeting, had coldly told Fuller to inform his superiors at the White House and

480

the Pentagon that he would take 'retaliatory' measures.

Knowing that Wilson was capable of inflicting great damage on the United States, Fuller had conveyed his message to the Pentagon. Unfortunately, because of the speedy advances being made on their own flying saucer projects at Avro-Canada, in Malton, Ontario, and at other top-secret research establishments in the White Sands Proving Ground and elsewhere in New Mexico and Arizona, the top brass of the Air Force were growing arrogant, believing they could outflank Wilson, and so refused to hand over the invaluable debris of Wilson's vastly superior crashed saucer.

Now, as he glanced up and saw what appeared to be a star rapidly growing bigger in a black sky flooded with stars, Fuller was preparing to convey this second refusal to Wilson. He didn't look forward to it.

On the other hand, as he realised when he glanced back over his shoulder and saw the neon spires and minarets of Las Vegas soaring out of the vast desert darkness, this was where Elvis Presley had made his recent movie, *Love in Las Vegas*. Fuller loved Elvis. Elvis was a great American. Fuller also loved Ann-Margret who, when she performed with Elvis in the recently released movie, had almost made Fuller cream his pants.

Amazing, Fuller thought, *the things I get to see doing this job. Here I am, metaphorically speaking, walking in the footsteps of Elvis and Ann-Margret. No wonder I love my country. Where else could you do this?*

Turning away from the sparkling, high-rise, neon splendours of distant Las Vegas, Fuller stuck his head out of the open window of the car and looked up again.

The expanding star grew bigger until it became dime-sized, then like a balloon, and finally, with startling speed, a large, saucer-shaped dark mass surrounded by a pulsating whitish glow. Widening as it descended, until it was immense, almost blotting out his entire view of the night sky, it stopped abruptly, hovered directly above him, and then, as if sensing the presence of his car – which in fact, as Fuller knew, it had – it glided slowly sideways, all two hundred and fifty feet of it, stopped again where it could not damage his car, then descended even more, its whitish glow dimming more with each second of its stately descent.

Eventually, it settled gently on the ground, its nearest edge about fifty yards from Fuller's car. The whitish glow faded away, the lights flashing around its rim then also faded out, and finally it was just a vast, silvery-grey, dome-shaped mass, eerily beautiful in the moonlight.

Fuller, of course, was now used to the sight of Wilson's extraordinary flying saucers (he never thought of them as UFOs) and, to a certain degree, took them for granted. He therefore waited patiently for the invisible panel in the outer body to fall out and backward, forming a doorway into the holding bay and a ramp that led from there to the ground. He did *not* wait patiently when the unmistakable form of the tall, lean, apparently seventy-odd-year-old Wilson was framed in that brilliant light, but instead clambered hurriedly out of his car and advanced to meet him.

The knowledge that he, Jack Fuller, the fearless, could be frightened of Wilson filled him with nausea. Nevertheless, approaching Wilson, meeting him halfway, Fuller was able to maintain his outward appearance of sardonic pragmatism.

'Mr Wilson!' he exclaimed softly, by way of greeting.

Wilson's hair was silvery-white but abundant. His face was lean and handsome, with piercing sky-blue eyes, but also oddly expressionless. That, Fuller knew, was due to plastic surgery, though he wouldn't have dared mention the fact.

Wilson nodded. 'Fuller.' His face was grim. 'Let's waste no time in idle conversation. You know why we're here. Do I get my crashed saucer back or not?'

Fuller spread his hands in the air, indicating that he had come empty-handed.

'They said no?'

' 'Fraid so.'

'That was foolish of them.'

'The military mind can be foolish at times.'

'I do not require your facetiousness, Fuller.'

'Sorry.'

'What else did they find in the wreckage?'

'Crew members. Very strange, I'm told. Someone used the word "cyborgs", which was new to me at the time, though I've since been familiarized.'

Wilson smiled bleakly, There was a certain aspect to Fuller's bottomless pool of corruptibility, cynicism and blind patriotism that amused him. The crass stupidity of the majority of the human race, but in this case combined with a certain low cunning, was exemplified in Fuller. The CIA agent, Wilson realised, had grandiose ideas about himself. Well, time would teach him . . .

'You're not too far from being a cyborg yourself,' Wilson said in a rare demonstration of cynicism which was, after all, a human emotion.

'That sounds facetious, Mr Wilson.'

'You don't like to be put down. You have the need to prove yourself. These are admirable traits in a child, but you should have risen above them. Still, you are what you will be – which is not much at all – and I will therefore, willy nilly, be forced to accept this and deal with it. You're a messenger and I treat you as such by asking one question: Your superiors said no?'

'Yes, they said no.'

'You do realise, I suppose, that I could go into that Air Force base and take what I want without a problem.'

'Without a short-term problem,' Fuller replied, getting as much satisfaction as he could out of this conversation, which wasn't, in his view, that much. 'But in the long term it wouldn't do you much good. By which I mean that the use of force would only draw attention to that secret hangar in the base. And the more – how shall we put it? – the more *unusual* the method of your assault, the more attention it would subsequently receive in the media. Which isn't, if I may say so, exactly the kind of attention you want.'

'What a clever man you are, Mr Fuller.'

'Gee, thanks, Mr Wilson.'

Wilson ignored the nervous sarcasm. 'Why do they want to keep my saucer and its dead crew members?'

'Because your saucer is more advanced than their own and the nearest we've come to workable cyborgs are fairly basic Cybernetic Anthropomorphous Machine Systems, or CAMS.'

'I'm surprised you could pronounce that.'

'I have my moments.'

'So they're no longer satisfied with what I'm already giving them. They think they can *steal* my technology and perhaps catch up with me.'

'I'm afraid that's the case, Mr Wilson. It's the nature of the beast to grow arrogant and turn on its master.'

Wilson almost sighed. 'Well, I'm sorry to hear that, Mr Fuller, because I had hoped to avoid unpleasantness. Now, alas, I'm going to have to teach the White House and the Pentagon a lesson they won't readily forget.'

Fuller, not being as stupid as his superiors when it came to an assessment of Wilson's powers, had feared that this was how he would react and feared even more what he might do. 'What lesson would that be, Mr Wilson?'

Wilson's smile was chilling. 'I'm going to black out most of the east coast. A *total* black-out, Mr Fuller. If, by the first week in August, I do not have my crashed saucer back, I will begin the process of turning out all the lights. I will do this gradually, bit by bit, to give you time to change your minds. But if, by November, you're still holding my crashed saucer, every light on the east coast will go out.'

'Every single light on the east coast of America?'

'Yes. Every single light. Now take that message back to your superiors and, if they still refuse my request, keep your eye on events during the first week in August. Good night, Mr Fuller.'

Fuller sat in his car until the enormous, majestic flying saucer ascended vertically, suddenly shrank and shot off to the east. Then, feeling chilled by Wilson's warning, he drove straight to Las Vegas airport and caught the first plane back to Washington DC.

When he had conveyed Wilson's message to the White House and the Pentagon, via CIA Headquarters in Langley Field, Virginia, they refused to believe that Wilson could do what he was threatening. They all thought he was bluffing.

The following week, the first week in August, 1965, Fuller asked the Langley Field press-cutting department to send him reports on any unusual stories regarding power lines or electricity generators. In fact, even before the first cuttings had been received, he knew Wilson's game was starting when one of his CIA physicists, engaged in an intelligence study of the relationship between UFOs witnessed over power lines and subsequent unexplainable power failures, submitted an unusual report.

During the first week of August thousands of people in Texas, Oklahoma, Kansas, Nebraska, Colorado and neighbouring states witnessed one of the biggest UFO displays ever. Unidentified lights flew across the skies in formation, were tracked on radar, and played tag with civilian and Air Force aircraft. Reading the descriptions given by hundreds of witnesses, Fuller thought the descriptions of the lights were very similar to those he had received about the Nazis' World War II *Feuerballs*.

As Fuller subsequently found out from his daily perusal of the relevant press cuttings, this unexpected major display of UFOs ended abruptly a week later.

That evening of the first day in which the UFOs had not been seen, while in bed with the most recent of his nubile girlfriends – he liked them young these days – Fuller was shocked to receive a personal call from Wilson.

'I didn't know you had my home phone number,' Fuller

said, trying to hide his feeling of violation at close to midnight.

'I have everything on you,' Wilson replied, 'including the details of the blonde creature lying beside you, just about legal age.'

Now practically sweating, wondering where the hell Wilson was speaking from and just what he had seen of his evening frolics, Fuller said, 'So what do you want at this time of night?'

'I want to know if the ambitious morons above you have seen enough and are willing to return my crashed saucer and its dead occupants.'

'I'm really sorry to have to say this,' Fuller replied, feeling more sorry for himself, 'but the ambitious morons above me are acting like just that – morons. They're insisting that the recent UFO flap was purely accidental.'

'Then they are truly moronic.'

'Well,' Fuller said, trying to recover his equilibrium and act cool for the benefit of the naked blonde beauty lying beside him, 'as they said, what you threatened didn't come off: the lights didn't go out.'

'I told you I would give them a chance to change their minds before I went further.'

'They thought you were bluffing.'

'Then I'll show them otherwise,' Wilson said, 'and I'll do it in the middle of winter, to cause even more chaos.'

'That's three months away,' Fuller replied.

'I'm sure you can wait that long. Good night, Mr Fuller.'

Fuller dropped his phone, rolled over to the blonde, and slithered onto her sweat-slicked, naked body. Attaining an instant erection, he slipped it into her and whispered, 'How long do you think we can keep this up? Does three months sound good?'

The remark was, he realised instantly, a very poor joke designed to quell the unexpected, uncustomary fear that was making his stomach churn. He knew the joke hadn't worked when the fear, crawling through him like a malignant, ghostly presence, made him lose his erection before he could properly use it.

This had never happened to him before, but then he'd never known fear before.

He would have to get used to it.

Three months later, on the night of November 9, 1965, hundreds of UFOs, most in the form of darting lights, were reported from Niagara, Syracuse, and Manhattan. That same night, all the lights went out – in Connecticut, Massachusetts, Maine, New Hampshire, New Jersey, New York, Pennsylvania, Vermont and a section of Canada – they went out over a total area of 80,000 square miles and a population of twenty-six million people. The biggest power cut in American history, it caused chaos and panic.

Even while this blanket of darkness was falling over the land – and was already being dubbed the Great Northeast Blackout – Fuller was on the phone at CIA headquarters in Langley, Virginia, trying to find out what had caused it. He learnt that the huge power grid that controlled all of the blacked-out areas – an interlocking network linking twenty-nine utility companies, with hundreds of automatic controls and locking devices – had always been considered to be invulnerable . . . yet the system *had* failed and the cause of the black-out couldn't be ascertained.

The only thing known for certain at this point in time was that the failure had occurred *somewhere* in the flow between the Niagara Falls generators and the Clay power sub-station, an automatic control unit through which the electric power flowed from Niagara to New York.

Shortly after Fuller had digested this report, he received a call from a CIA friend, Dick Lamont, at Andrews Air Force Base.

'There's a UFO connection,' Lamont said.

'What kind?'

'The first report of an unidentified,' Lamont told him, 'was made by the Deputy Aviation Commissioner of

Syracuse, Robert C. Walsh, and several other witnesses, all of whom, just after the power failed at Syracuse, saw what resembled a huge fireball *ascending* from a fairly low altitude near Hancock Airport. Approaching for landing at that time was flight instructor Weldon Ross and his passenger, computer technician James Brooding, both of whom saw the same object. At first they mistook it for a burning building on the ground – something corroborating the fact that the fireball was at low altitude – but then they realised that it was something in the air . . . a single, round-shaped object about a hundred feet in diameter, which they later described as a "flame-coloured globe" . . . And according to Ross's calculations, that object was directly over the Clay power sub-station . . .'

No sooner had Fuller dropped the phone than it rang again. This time it was Wilson.

'Well?' he asked softly.

'I have to talk with the President,' Fuller replied.

'You do that,' Wilson told him.

A few hours later, at 3.30 in the morning, after his urgent telephone chat with President Lyndon B. Johnson, Fuller was landing by helicopter in the most heavily guarded area of Nellis AFB, Las Vegas, Nevada. Two crude coffins and a pile of large wooden crates had already been loaded onto a caravan of army trucks, which were surrounded by a ring of armed troops. Fuller clambered into the back of a diplomatic car and told the driver to go. The car, which had tinted, bullet-proof windows, led the convoy of trucks away from the large, floodlit hangar to a restricted airstrip at the northern edge of the camp.

Climbing out of the limousine, Fuller glanced about him and noted that the whole area was surrounded by barbed wire and protected by more helmeted, armed troops. Satisfied with the security arrangements, he supervised the unloading of the two coffins and crates. When they were unloaded and forming one large, pyramid-shaped heap in the middle of the airstrip, the soldiers were ordered into

the trucks and driven back to camp, leaving Fuller alone
with a high-ranking Air Force officer.

Not intimidated by high-ranking Air Force officers, Fuller
lit a cigarette and waited.

Eventually, one of Wilson's mother ships descended
silently, majestically, a great pyramid of steel cocooned in
a white haze, its multicoloured lights flashing rapidly
around its circular rim, to settle just above the field at the
far side of the runway. When it had landed, the lights
flashing around its rim flickered off, one after the other,
the white haze disappeared, as if the light had been sucked
in through the porous metal of the saucer's body, and then
a large, formerly invisible panel fell out to form a ramp
sloping down to the ground.

At first no more than a sharp-edged silhouette in the
dazzling light of the interior of the saucer's holding bay,
Wilson's assistant, Salvatore Fallaci, became recognizably
human as he walked down the ramp and approached Fuller,
just getting out of his limousine.

As Fuller noted immediately, Wilson was not present.
Instead, Fallaci emerged from the saucer surrounded by
four creatures who easily could have been mistaken for
aliens, or extraterrestrials, but were, as Fuller now knew,
cyborgs surgically mutated from what had once been
normal human beings: the small Ache Indians of Paraguay.
Averaging five feet tall, sometimes even smaller, only
occasionally taller, they'd had facial surgery to replace the
nose, mouth and throat with metal-covered prosthetics.
While this alone would have made them look bizarre, they
were made even more 'alien' by their remote-controlled
metal hands, which were in fact small CAMS of the kind
used for sea-bed exploration.

The children of Frankenstein, Fuller thought. *That's who
I'm dealing with. That fucker Wilson is Frankenstein.*

'Good evening, Mr Fuller,' Fallaci said.

'More like good morning,' Fuller responded.

Fallaci smiled. He had that Italian charm. 'Normal people

489

keep normal hours,' he said, 'and are always boring.' He glanced towards the trucks lined up behind Fuller. 'Is everything there, Mr Fuller? By which I mean the crashed saucer and its dead occupants. Those and every other single item you took into that hangar.'

'Every single item,' Fuller said. 'You're getting everything back.'

'It's nice to know that above and beyond you there are people with common sense.'

'Go screw yourself,' Fuller said.

He had finally come to accept – and it hadn't been easy – that he was frightened of Wilson. He had never been frightened of anyone in his life – not until he met Wilson, who had always been icily polite and civilized. Fuller was frightened of Wilson's steady blue gaze, of his absolute pragmatism, of the way he could look directly at you and reduce you to nothing. Wilson lacked normal feelings. He passed judgement, then acted. What he did was dictated by a logic so pure it had to be inhuman.

Fuller accepted that. He didn't like it, but he understood it. Pragmatism was his own meat and potatoes – a man did what he had to do. That was Wilson. That was Fuller, also. Now he and Wilson were opposite sides of the same coin.

You couldn't believe this shit coming down, but there it was on your plate. You either ate it or you starved to death. That was life in a nutshell. On the other hand, though Fuller patriotically ate this shit, he wasn't about to do so in front of Salvatore Fallaci. The Italian Mafioso was only Wilson's minion and as such could be used as a repository for Fuller's fear and frustration. All the things Fuller wanted to say to Wilson – but did not dare say – he could say to Fallaci.

'I'm not here to be insulted,' Fallaci said, 'so let's do what we have to do. May I start?'

'What the fuck do you think?' Fuller responded, trying to obliterate his fear of Wilson by shitting upon his assistant. 'We didn't come here at this hour to rock and roll. Take what you want and then leave.'

'I will do exactly that,' Fallaci said. 'Thank *you*, Mr Fuller.'

Using what appeared to be a miniature microphone strapped to his throat, Fallaci directed the hideous cyborgs, step by step, as they removed the crates containing the separate parts of the crashed flying saucer and the coffins containing the dead crew from the army trucks and carried them up the ramp, into the brilliantly lit holding bay of the immense mother ship. When this was done, the cyborgs also entered the saucer, leaving only Fallaci outside, still facing Fuller.

'You've shown sound sense,' Fallaci said to Fuller. 'Mr Wilson thanks you.'

'Don't mention it,' Fuller replied, trying to sound sardonic, though his stomach was churning with tension.

Fallaci grinned, turned away and walked up the ramp into the mother ship. The ramp folded back in and the great saucer-shaped craft, now looking seamless, emitted a bass humming sound, gave off a magical white glowing, lifted gently off the ground, like a soap bubble floating on water, then ascended vertically to the heavens and swiftly disappeared.

'Good God,' the high-ranking Air Force officer beside Fuller exclaimed softly, 'I don't believe my own eyes!'

'That's what those bastards are banking on,' Fuller responded. Then, defeated and trying not to show it, he and the officer walked back across the dark, silent airstrip.

Chapter Thirty-Nine

Dwight had begun to feel that he had no real life – out there, where the real world was. He seemed to have spent the past decade indoors, pouring over reports of UFO sightings and UFO photographs, piecing this and that together, trying to make sense of what seemed senseless, trying to find logic in his own nightmares. Those nightmares were, of course, based on what had happened not only to him, but also to Beth, and he had, for that reason, been keeping a low profile with regard to his UFO researches. So low, indeed, that even Dr Epstein and Tony Scaduto of APII had begun sending him letters, asking him what the hell he was doing.

Finally, in November 1966, a year after the Great Northeast Blackout, Dwight pulled himself out of that dark hole in which he lived – not his home, but his bruised and terrified soul – and met Epstein and Tony Scaduto, who'd flown in from Washington DC, in a Chinese restaurant in Dayton for lunch and a talk. The former looked a lot older, with his hair and Vandyke beard now mostly grey, but Scaduto hadn't changed much and still wore his leather biker's gear. They made an unusual team.

'My feeling,' Dr Epstein said as he turned his noodles expertly on his chopsticks, 'is that you've practically given up your UFO research. We're getting nothing back, Dwight.'

Dwight shrugged. 'I won't deny it. I *have* practically given up. Ever since that incident with Beth I've been frightened for her – *and* Nichola – so I decided to keep a low profile and not draw any attention to myself. What the hell, why lie about it? I was so scared, I decided to drop out altogether in the hope that those bastards – the men in black – whoever – would forget us entirely.'

'Perfectly understandable,' Epstein said, nodding sympathetically. 'Had I been in your situation, I'd have been just as frightened.'

'You probably *are* in his situation,' Scaduto said. 'You just don't know it yet. I mean, man, if you're running an organisation like APII, those fuckers are bound to be watching you.'

'But they've never bothered me,' Epstein replied.

'They have their own ways and reasons,' Dwight said. 'But living with the constant expectation of a visitation is just as bad as the visitation itself.'

'So what have you done recently?' Epstein asked.

'Well, believe it or not – and I can't believe it myself – Nichola's turned nineteen and is planning to marry.'

'Nineteen!' Scaduto exclaimed. 'Fucking unbelievable!'

'We age overnight,' Epstein added gloomily. 'So you've been involved in the arrangements for the marriage?'

'Right,' Dwight said.

'And Beth? How has she been coping?'

'You mean the marriage or her CE-IV experience?'

'Both.'

'She's thrilled by the marriage – very romantic that way. I think it's been a great distraction for her, regarding the other thing. It's kept her mind off it.'

'And what about the other thing – the CE-IV experience?'

'Since having her hypnotic treatments, Beth's headaches and nightmares have disappeared, but she's gradually remembering the details of her godawful experience and now lives in fear of the men in black and the possibility of being abducted again. That, in a nutshell, is why I've virtually stopped working for APII. It's for Beth. I'm frightened for her. I think that what they did to her was a warning – and it's a warning I'm heeding.'

Just thinking about it made Dwight feel that a wall of darkness was closing in around him, even in daylight. You were there, in that dungeon of the mind, and you would never get out. That's what they could do to you. Who 'they' were, he still didn't know.

'I don't mind admitting that we're desperate to get you back at work,' Epstein said. 'A recent Gallup Poll has shown that approximately nine million Americans now believe they've seen a UFO. Our input supports that figure. To put it mildly, we're being overwhelmed with reports. So we need all the help we can get.'

'*Nine million*?' Dwight asked, hardly believing what he was hearing.

'Yes. An astonishing figure, right? The Gallup Poll was undertaken in the wake of one of the most widely publicized events in the history of the UFO controversy: the furore over the Dexter and Hillsdale, Michigan, sightings that occurred eight months ago. Did you read about them?'

'Yeah.' Dwight only recalled them vaguely, which made him feel foolish. 'Well, I remember reading about them and seeing some news items on TV. It was at a time when I couldn't face anything about UFOs, so I guess I gave them a miss. I used to just turn my head away.'

'You must've been in a fucking *bad* way,' Scaduto said.

'I was,' Dwight admitted.

'May I refresh your memory?' Epstein asked.

'Sure. Go ahead.'

'On March 20, eighty-seven women students and a civil defence director at Hillsdale College, Michigan, saw a glowing, football-shaped object hovering over an empty swamp a few hundred yards from the women's dorm. It repeatedly raced at, then retreated from, the dorm, dodged an airport beacon light, and flew back and forth for hours before disappearing. The next day, in Dexter, Michigan, sixty-three miles away, five people, including two police officers, reported seeing a large, glowing object rising from a swampy area on a farm, hover for a few minutes at about a thousand feet and then leave the area.'

'An impressive set of witnesses,' Scaduto said.

'Quite so. And within a few days nearly every newspaper in the country and all national TV news shows were carrying reports on the sightings. This placed intense pressure on the Air Force to investigate the incidents.'

'I remember that much,' Dwight said, getting interested despite himself. 'The head of Project Blue Book, Major Hector Quintanilla, sent Dr J. Allen Hynek to investigate the sightings.'

'Right – and Hynek had to virtually fight his way through the reporters to get at the witnesses. Later he stated that the entire region was gripped by near-hysteria. He did, however, manage to complete his investigation and afterwards held what was reported as being the largest press conference in the history of the Detroit Press Club.'

'Hynek's widely respected,' Dwight said, 'so where he goes, the press goes.'

'Knows his stuff,' Scaduto murmured.

'He's brought respectability to the subject,' Dr Epstein said, 'and I'm grateful for that. Unfortunately, in this instance, he fell flat on his face.'

'Oh?' Dwight queried. 'How?'

'He made the simple mistake of not thinking before he opened his mouth. With the news hounds all baying for an instant explanation for the sightings, he suggested – purely hypothetically – that they might have been caused by marsh gas.'

'What the fuck's that?' Scaduto asked.

'It's a phenomenon caused by the spontaneous ignition of decaying vegetation. It produces pretty eerie, glowing lights.'

'Thank you, professor.'

'Anyway, the press latched onto the words "swamp gas" and had a field day making fun of it, with the ironic result that coverage of UFOs reached unprecedented levels during March and April – particularly regarding the Dexter-Hillsdale sightings. So much so, in fact, that Weston E. Vivian, Democratic Congressman from Michigan, and Gerald Ford, House Republican minority leader, formally called for congressional hearings.'

'Oh, Christ, yes,' Dwight said, 'I should've known. I naturally read about those.'

Epstein nodded affirmatively. 'Exactly. You read about them. We *all* read about them. The House Armed Services Committee acted on Ford's suggestion and on April 5 – for the first time in the history of the UFO controversy – Congress held an open hearing on the subject. When the hearings were completed, the Secretary of the Air Force, Harold D. Brown, directed the Air Force chief of staff to make arrangements for a special independent, civilian team to investigate selected UFO sightings. Subsequently, on May 9, the Air Force announced that it was planning to contract with scientists for a UFO investigation.'

'And last month,' Scaduto interjected excitedly, 'the Air Force announced that the University of Colorado had accepted the UFO study project and that Edward U. Condon would be in charge.'

'Who's Condon?' Dwight asked, more intrigued every minute.

'An internationally known physicist and former head of the National Bureau of Standards,' Epstein told him.

'Impressive,' Dwight murmured.

'Which is exactly why they picked that bastard,' Scaduto said sardonically.

'Here's the interesting part,' Epstein said. 'The part not included in the news reports.'

'Go on,' Dwight responded, leaning forward across the table.

Epstein smiled slightly, knowing he'd hooked Dwight again. 'Dr James E. McDonald,' he said, 'a senior atmospheric physicist at the University of Arizona's Department of Atmospheric Sciences and one of the nation's leading scientific authorities on UFOs, had accidentally seen the classified version of the previous Robertson Panel report at Wright-Patterson AFB. This led him to reveal, when speaking to members of the University of Arizona's Department of Meteorology, that the CIA had ordered the Air Force to debunk UFOs, as seen in the uncensored version of the Robertson report.'

'Fucking A!' Scaduto exclaimed.

'The news services picked up this story,' Epstein continued, 'and publicized it widely on the same day that the Air Force announced the establishment of the Condon Committee.'

'Condon was picked,' Scaduto interjected, 'because he's already shown that he doesn't believe in UFOs. He's been picked to help the Air Force deny that they deliberately debunked UFOs and to help them bury this subject once and for all. What say you, Randall?'

'I say you're right,' Dwight replied. 'And what we have to look into is . . .'

He stopped, realising that he'd just committed himself again. When he saw the grins on the faces of Epstein and Scaduto, he couldn't help laughing.

'I don't believe it,' he said, when he had managed to contain himself. 'You pair of bastards came all the way from Washington DC just to seduce me into going back to work.'

'We sure did,' Epstein said.

'So are you in or out?' Scaduto asked.

'Count me in,' Dwight said.

The three of them raised their glasses in the air and tapped them together in a toast.

It was the last of their good days.

Chapter Forty

Sitting on his rocking chair on the verandah, overlooking the fenced-in compound, Stoll watched the arrival of Wilson's flying saucer with no great deal of pleasure. This time Wilson was coming in a medium-sized saucer, a hundred and fifty feet in diameter, and carrying, so Stoll hoped, a thirty-five feet diameter, two-man saucer with a cyborg pilot for Stoll's personal use. Stoll had his own thoughts about that and they were making him nervous.

In fact, as he watched the *Kugelblitz III* descending vertically over the steaming canopy of the jungle, he was torn between his need to escape this filthy hole and his dread of what might happen if he tried. Over the past few months it had dawned on him that he had now been here for years – nearly twenty years, in fact – and that there had been no indications that Wilson would ever let him leave. Stoll was rotting in this jungle; perhaps even losing his mind. With little stimulation, he could not stretch himself and was, he felt, becoming like a vegetable, blending in with the forest. So depleted was he that he could not even enjoy sex with his Ache comfort girls, let alone still be thrilled with the feelings of power he had once received from running the compound like a vengeful god. Now he wanted only to die in the Fatherland, preferably in Mannheim, where he had been born, and rest in the same soil that had taken his wife and children so many years ago.

Naturally, he was nervous about telling Wilson this, but

was determined to do so. A man could only take so much and he, Ernst Stoll, had had enough. He would plead for release.

As the saucer descended slowly, majestically, into the clearing, its familiar bass humming sound grew louder and became almost palpable, an odd vibration that shook Stoll's log-and-thatch house. Looking up, he saw the immense, spherical, seemingly seamless craft blocking out the sky as it dropped lower. Still quite high up, the saucer was spinning rapidly on its own axis, except for the gyroscopically stabilised central fuselage, which was stationary. The rapid rotation of the circular outer wings slowed down as the saucer descended, but the electromagnetic gravity-damping system was creating violent currents of air within a cylindrical zone the same width as the saucer, making the grass and plants flutter, sucking up loose soil and gravel, and causing them to spin wildly, noisily, in the air as if caught in the eye of a hurricane.

As always, the native workers and captured Ache Indians, who either lived in the shacks located around the inner edge of the clearing or were kept in the bamboo cages within it, were looking up in awe as the gigantic saucer descended, its outer rings rotating, surrounded by the whitish glow caused by the ionization of the surrounding air. This glow darkened to a more normal metallic grey when the saucer hovered just above ground level, rocking slightly from side to side, its thick hydraulic legs emerging from four points equidistant around the base to embed themselves deeply into the muddy ground. The saucer bounced gently on the legs, but eventually settled and was still. Its rotating wings gradually slowed and then stopped altogether, as did the wind that had been created by its electromagnetic gravity-damping system. Silence reigned for a moment.

As the bass humming sound faded away and the panel in the concave base dropped down on hinged arms to form a ramp leading to the ground, Ernst got out of his rocking chair, walked down the steps of the verandah, and advanced to meet Wilson. The latter emerged from the saucer, tall, slim, naturally elegant, white-haired, oddly handsome with the aid of plastic surgery, and with a psychic aura as cold as a block of ice. Ernst practically trembled with fear as soon as he saw him.

Wilson didn't shake his hand. He just nodded and said, '*Guten tag*, Ernst. It is good to see you.' Speaking German, he was inclined to become very formal.

'And good to see you, sir.'

'You are well?'

'Yes, sir, and you?'

'I'm in excellent condition for my age, given all the surgical and medical aids I've had. You must try it yourself, Ernst.'

Ernst felt himself smiling nervously. 'I don't think I'm quite ready for that yet. Perhaps a few years from now.'

Even as Ernst was speaking, four of the hideous cyborgs, surgically mutated from unfortunate Ache Indians, came down the ramp behind him, looking even smaller than they were when standing around the tall, lean Wilson.

'I have brought your present,' Wilson said, still speaking his very formal German, 'but let us have lunch first.'

'Naturally. Yes.'

Ernst led Wilson back to the house where, on the verandah, which was pleasantly cool, they had what Wilson considered to be a major meal – fruit and nut cereal, with a glass of cold, very dry white wine. Over lunch, Wilson expressed his concern that the Soviets and Americans were – ironically with his help – progressing technologically much faster than he had anticipated.

'Since Lyndon B. Johnson was sworn in as President,' he explained, 'after the assassination of Kennedy, both the Soviets and the Americans have had men drifting outside their spacecraft; two separate US Gemini spacecraft met in space and flew side-by-side only six to ten feet apart – an achievement requiring astonishing technical accuracy by their modest standards; the first space docking was made by a US astronaut; and, finally, an unmanned US Surveyor spacecraft soft-landed on the Moon.'

'Well, you *did* help them with that,' Stoll dared to remind him, 'albeit indirectly with your supplies of advanced technical drawings and equipment. Which was, as I gather, part of your long-standing agreement with them.'

Wilson sighed. 'Yes. As part of that agreement I promised the Americans, through Jack Fuller, that they would be the first to land a man on the moon. As always, I'd intended keeping that promise. However, the speed with which the Americans are advancing scientifically has made me feel that I must hinder their progress – as well as Soviet and American progress in general. It's clear from my recent conversations with Jack Fuller that they're growing arrogant – believing they can somehow catch up with me – which is why I arranged last year's Great Northeast Blackout as a warning. They cooled down for a long time after that, but already they're growing arrogant again and need another lesson.'

'What have you planned?'

'I've learnt through one of my brain-implanted spies located with NASA that they've a rehearsal for another Apollo launch planned for January 27 next year. The same man – one of NASA's top scientists – will therefore ensure that the spacecraft malfunctions and bursts into flames, killing all three of the astronauts on board. A couple of months later – I believe this will be April – when cosmonaut Vladimir Komarov is due to orbit the earth in a Soyuz spacecraft, we'll attack it with a laser-beam weapon fired by one of our saucers. We'll make the spacecraft crash, killing Komarov. The combined deaths of the cosmonaut and three astronauts will almost certainly cause consternation and result in delays in the space-race between the Americans and the Soviets. I think this will work, yes?'

'I would think so,' Stoll said.

When the meal was finished, Stoll made his usual report

to Wilson – telling him about the negative or positive aspects of the capturing and holding of the Ache Indians and any difficulties presented by his dealings with Paraguay's officials, most as corrupt as their master, President Stroessner. Finally, when he'd completed his report, he glanced across the compound with its mud-and-thatch shacks, goats, chickens, mosquitoes, piles of shit and everything else he detested here, including the native workers, men and women alike, and suddenly blurted out that twenty years here was too much.

'I desperately want to return to Germany,' he said finally.

'Why do you wish to return?' Wilson asked in a surprisingly calm manner, as if he had been expecting the request.

'It is the Reich . . .'

'It is not,' Wilson interjected in his remote, calm way. 'The Reich died with the ending of the war. What you want is no more.'

'Still, my wife and children died there. Everything I had was there. I have been here for two decades and I'm growing old and I yearn for my past. Please, sir, let me go.'

'I didn't realise you were still so sentimental,' Wilson said with a chilling smile.

'Nor did I,' Stoll replied, 'but I am. It's a sign that I'm growing old.'

'I'm sorry, Ernst,' Wilson responded, showing no kind of emotion whatsoever, 'but I'm afraid I cannot say yes to that just yet. We still need you here. You are doing invaluable work here. Rest assured that it will end in a year or two and then we can consider this matter again. But why Germany? There's nothing left for you there. In a year or two, when your work here is finished, you can return to Antarctica for medical and surgical rejuvenation. When that's completed, we will find you something suitable to do there or, if you prefer, somewhere else. But not Germany. There, you could still be picked up as a war criminal and forced to stand trial. We cannot risk that.'

'That's the problem,' Ernst said, already feeling desperate, knowing that he was going to lose out again to Wilson. 'It's not just a matter of getting back to Germany. The fact is, I don't think I can stand it here much longer. This place is driving me crazy. I have to get out.'

'You simply need a break now and then,' Wilson insisted in his cold-blooded, icily pragmatic way. 'You don't need to return to Germany. You just need to get out of here more often, perhaps visit Asuncion.'

'The journey is too difficult,' Ernst replied, his heart sinking with the knowledge that Wilson was going to be unbending about letting him go. 'And besides, it's too dangerous. This compound is in the middle of the jungle and the only way out is by river. That makes short breaks difficult.'

'Which is precisely why I've brought you a gift, Ernst. A small, two-man flying saucer with a totally obedient cyborg pilot. Come and look.'

Even as they stood up and walked down the steps of the verandah, a thirty-five feet wide flying saucer emerged slowly from the holding bay of the mother ship, barely inches above the floor, but certainly floating in the air, and advanced out over the clearing, watched by the awed, terrified natives and Ache Indians. Made, like all of the saucers, from minutely porous magnesium othosilicate and electrically charged, it was surrounded by a whitish glow caused by the ionization of the surrounding atmosphere. With its outer rings spinning around its fixed, cupola-shaped central fuselage, it looked like a giant spinning top. Unlike the bigger saucer, however, it had a visible perspex dome not much larger than the cockpit of a small airplane.

Standing beside Wilson in the clearing as the saucer advanced towards him, Stoll could see, in that small, two-man pilot's cabin, the silhouetted figure of what had to be the cyborg pilot. A lump came to his throat as the saucer settled on the ground, its four hydraulic legs extending to embed themselves in the mud. He was recalling how desperately, when an aeronautical student, first at the Institute of Technology in Munich, then in the rocket technology classes of Professor Karl Emil Becker at the University of Berlin, he had wanted to join the VfR, or Spaceship Travel Club, in the company of the likes of Wernher von Braun, Rudolph Nebel, Willy Ley, and Hermann Oberth, to build rockets that would soar to the heavens. That dream had been crushed when he joined the SS and, eventually, came under the influence of the almost inhuman Wilson who, for the past twenty years, had kept him imprisoned between helpless reverence and dread. Now, when he studied the small flying saucer, he saw the means of his escape and, formulating it, was filled with terror at the thought of what Wilson might do if he failed, was captured and brought back. Thinking about the possibilities, Ernst had to wipe sweat from his brow and control his body's trembling.

'Beautiful!' he exclaimed softly, referring to the small saucer now resting in the middle of the clearing, dwarfed by the *Kugelblitz III*.

'Yours,' Wilson responded. 'It's not stratospheric, but its range is virtually limitless and you can use it for lengthy journeys at an altitude that will keep you well above normal airplanes, out of the range of radar and out of sight. Use it to give yourself some breaks, away from this place. You'll feel better then.'

'It's been so long,' Ernst said hesitantly. 'I don't know how to fly any more. Certainly not . . .'

'The cyborg pilot will do it for you when it's not on autopilot. One of our first fully functioning cyborgs. Look!' Speaking into the pin-head microphone strapped to his throat, Wilson ordered the pilot out. With this saucer being so small, the pilot emerged rather like the pilot of a normal airplane: by opening the dome-shaped perspex hood, which split into two parts, then clambering out and simply slithering down the sloping side to the ground. When, in this instance, the pilot had done so, Stoll looked at him in amazement.

He was amazed because he actually recognised what was left of the original Marlon Clarke, the farmer abducted in Socorro, New Mexico, in 1947 and flown to the Antarctic after witnessing the crash of a flying saucer. Clarke had been turned into a fully functioning man/machine hybrid, or cyborg. His head had been severed, kept in cold storage, then transplanted to the body of a small, headless Ache Indian. Ernst was surprised that he still recognised Clarke, because there was so little of his original face to be seen. His skull was covered in the stereotaxic skullcap that kept electrodes implanted in his head at all times and his lower face – ears, nose, mouth and jaw – had been replaced with an ugly metal prosthetic. The hands of the original Ache Indian had been sliced off and replaced with what would have looked to most people like vicious metal claws but were in fact highly sophisticated Cybernetic Anthropomorphous Machine Systems, or CAMS, capable of highly sophisticated movements. Clarke looked like a monster.

'Plastic artificial heart,' Wilson explained. 'Bionic audio transmitters to replace the mechanism of the inner ear. Plastic arteries. Synthetic bones in both legs and the lower arms attached to the CAMS. The latter, while looking like metal claws from afar, actually have fingertips of polyvinylidene fluoride, which detects alterations in pressure and delivers the appropriate impulses to the nerve ends. Brain implanted, of course, and programmed for absolute obedience – you speak, he obeys. Here, strap this pin-head microphone to your throat.'

Ernst took the tiny mike, wrapped the strap around his neck, and clipped it shut with the microphone resting on his Adam's apple.

'Now identify yourself,' Wilson informed him. 'Tell the cyborg your name.'

'My name is Ernst Stoll,' Ernst said.

'Good,' Wilson said. 'That's all he needs to know. He now knows the sound of your voice and will react automatically to it with total obedience.'

'Amazing,' Ernst said.

'He's a gift for your years of devotion. Use him well, Ernst. Now I must be going.'

Nodding at Ernst – since he rarely shook hands these days – Wilson walked back up the ramp of the hundred and fifty feet saucer, followed by his four hideous cyborg guards. Once they were all inside, the ramp closed and the saucer lifted slightly off the ground. Shortly after it had lifted off, and while it was merely hovering above the ground, its four hydraulic legs were drawn back into the base of the central body and the panels closed so precisely that the joins around them could not be seen. Then the saucer rose vertically, slowly, to just above the canopy of the trees, hovered again for a few seconds, then suddenly shot upward, shrank rapidly, and then disappeared.

The cyborg, Marlon Clarke, was standing silently in front of the small flying saucer, practically brain-dead until activated by instructions from Ernst. Terrified by what he was contemplating, but unable to resist it after too long in this hellish jungle, Ernst hurried back into the log-and-thatch house, to have a strong drink of bourbon, which helped give him the courage he needed to do what he was planning.

Sitting there on a sofa in the middle of the room, he looked around at the photographs that showed his own history: a golden-haired child in the courtyard of his parents' imposing neo-Gothic house in Mannheim; a handsome youth sitting with a pretty young blonde-haired lady, Ingrid, later to be his wife, at an outside table of the Kranzler Café on the Kurfürstendamm in Berlin; clambering out of an army car at Stadelheim Prison, Berlin, in his black SS uniform; posing, already cynical, in the same uniform outside Gestapo Headquarters in the Prinz Albrechtstrasse with friends Brandt and Ritter, both killed in the war; celebrating with the same two friends and some whores at the Schauspielhaus in 1937, all drunk and holding up steins of beer; wrapped in a great coat covered with snow as he planted swastikas in the snow of Neu Schwabenland in 1938, claiming the territory for the Third Reich; already ageing and embittered when with the flying saucer team – Wilson, Rudolph Shriever, Klaus Habermohl and Otto Miethe – outside the hangar of the research centre at Kummersdorf, located at the other side of the firing range separating it from Wernher von Braun's Rocket Research Institute; twice with the Reichsführer, Heinrich Himmler – first looking icily controlled in the SS headquarters in Berlin, then, six years later, looking deranged in the sanatorium of Dr Gebhardt at Hohenlychen; finally, with Generals Nebe and Kammler in the great underground complex of the Nordhausen Central Works in Kahla in the Harz Mountains. And, of course the women, his *few* women – that erotic dancer, Brigette, from the White Mouse in the Französischestrasse; the sensual, treacherous Jew bitch, Kryzstina Kosilewski, from Cracow; and, coming last, but in a framed picture hung on the wall directly facing his desk, his wife, Ingrid, and their two children Ula and Alfred, taken two weeks before they died in an Allied air-raid . . .

Ernst almost choked up then, overwhelmed with emotion, recalling that more human aspect of himself before the war, Wilson and this hellish jungle had eaten up the last of his soul. He was going mad here – he had to get out – and now he was going to attempt to do just that while he had the chance.

He was terrified of what would happen if he failed, but he still had to try it.

Hurriedly packing a shoulder bag with his basic necessities, the photographs he had just been studying and, most important, the great deal of cash he had gathered together over the years from various transactions with General Stroessner's corrupt officials, he left the house for what he hoped would be the last time. Crossing the muddy compound to the saucer, he glanced with distaste at the log-and-thatch shacks, the native men and women kneeling around camp fires, the mangy dogs and chickens and goats, all dwarfed by the soaring trees, and was thrilled at the thought of never seeing them again. Approaching the cyborg, who stared at him with living, though dulled eyes from between the metal skullcap and the metal lower-face prosthetic – a truly hideous sight – he ordered him, by speaking into his throat microphone, to climb up into the saucer. When the cyborg had done so, Ernst followed him, clambering up the gently sloping side and slipping into the pilot's domed cockpit. When both he and the cyborg were strapped into their seats, their shoulders almost touching, which made Ernst feel uneasy, he told the cyborg to take off, ascend as high as possible, then turn towards the sea and set the autopilot for West Germany.

Obeying, the cyborg activated the saucer and soon, after the cupola-shaped cockpit covering had closed automatically, its circular outer wings were rotating around the cockpit and taking on the whitish glow of ionization. The saucer lifted off gently, swayed just above the ground, then ascended in a stately manner until it was just above the canopy of the trees. Ernst, so excited he could hardly breathe, managed to take one last glance at the fenced-in compound, now practically lost in the jungle far below, then the saucer suddenly shot off at startling speed, flying smoothly above the vast, river-divided, densely forested landscape of Paraguay.

He never even got to see the sea. No sooner had the small saucer gone into horizontal flight than Wilson's craft appeared magically out of nowhere to sit on its tail. Horrified by this, Stoll was also terrified when Wilson's voice came out of amplifier vents in the cyborg's steel facial prosthetic, saying in German, 'I know what you're attempting, Ernst, and I'm very disappointed in you. You will now be punished for your betrayal. I'm sorry to have to do this.'

The cyborg suddenly let out a demented, hideously human wailing sound that cut right through Ernst. Smoke poured from behind the mouthless, lower-face metal prosthetic, followed by showering sparks. Then, as the cyborg continued its ghastly, ear-splitting wailing, the steel prosthetic blew off, revealing the surgically shredded bone and flesh around the removed mouth, jaw and nose, with blood squirting out and splashing over Ernst. Even as Ernst looked on, aghast, too shocked to think clearly, the cyborg's head started smoking beneath the skullcap and he made an odd rattling sound – the sound of Marlon Clarke dying – then slumped sideways in his seat, clearly dead.

As Stoll stared at him, paralysed with shock, the saucer flipped over and started spinning rapidly towards the earth. Rendered dizzy and nauseous by the spinning, almost deafened by the hammering of wind against the canopy, not knowing which way was up and which down, Ernst was further punished by the sight of the dead cyborg rocking wildly in its seat with blood still geysering out of the mess of exposed bone and flesh where the metal prosthetic had been. He then saw the spinning jungle rushing up towards him and knew that the saucer was about to crash.

Ernst screamed in terror.

Miraculously, just before the saucer reached the canopy of the trees, Wilson's saucer appeared above it. A pyramid of brilliant light, some kind of force field, beaming out of the base of Wilson's enormous craft, enveloped Ernst's spinning machine and appeared to place it under control again.

Now held in the pyramid of light, Ernst's saucer, though the right way up, raced on a descending trajectory towards the jungle – heading back, as Ernst realised with dread, in the general direction of his compound by the river.

The jungle raced up towards him. The pyramid of light blinked out, then Wilson's saucer ascended abruptly, vertically, and appeared to dissolve into the sun. Ernst covered his face with his arms as he crashed into the jungle.

He survived . . . almost certainly because of Wilson. Though the saucer crashed, it levelled out before doing so, smashing through the trees, hitting the ground the right way up and sliding through the soft mud until it finally stopped.

Though battered, bruised, badly cut and bleeding, the shocked Ernst still managed to crawl out of the saucer, which was dented but still in one piece. Standing upright, almost falling from dizziness, he orientated himself and wiped blood from his eyes. After taking a final look backwards at the crashed saucer, which already was being covered in falling leaves, he began what he knew would be a long, hellish march back to the compound.

He had been punished and sentenced. Now he knew that he would be imprisoned in the compound for the rest of his days.

His hell was right here on earth.

Chapter Forty-One

In October, 1967, Dwight paid a visit to Dr Epstein and Scaduto in the APII headquarters in Washington DC, where he was introduced to two new members of APII, both physicists: a handsome, sardonic young man named Robert Stanford – whom Epstein always addressed as 'Stanford' – and the relatively famous Dr Irving Jacobs. Stanford was pretty flashy, dressed like a Californian in a sky-blue open-neck shirt, denims held up with a fancy-buckled belt, and a windcheater jacket. Dr Jacobs, being older and wiser, was wearing a standard grey suit and black shoes.

'Though he looks like he comes from Malibu,' Dr Epstein joked, 'Stanford actually hails from right here in Washington DC...'

'McLean, Virginia, to be precise,' Stanford corrected him with a shit-ass grin.

'Dr Jacobs, on the other hand, hails from Camelback Hill, Phoenix, Arizona, and has been kind enough to fly here just for this meeting. They've signed up to work for APII and I'm very pleased they're with us.'

'Delighted to have you aboard,' Dwight said, shaking the hands of both men.

'Still got me to deal with, though,' Scaduto interjected, looking even more cocky than Stanford. 'Bet that gives you headaches!'

'Headaches with bastards like you I can enjoy,' Dwight replied. 'At least they keep me awake.'

'Ain't he just the nicest sonofabitch?' Scaduto asked

511

rhetorically. 'Say, hey, let's get cookin'!'

Though he didn't know anything about the flashy, cocky Stanford, Dwight had read about Dr Irving Jacobs in *Who's Who* and knew that apart from working for NASA and the American Nuclear Society, he was seriously interested in the UFO phenomenon. That he was joining APII was therefore good news, since his reputation in so-called 'serious' areas could only enhance the credibility of the organisation.

'Okay, gentlemen,' Dr Epstein said, indicating the chairs around his desk with a wave of his hand. 'now that my good friends Dwight Randall and Tony Scaduto have had their regular little let's-get-together skirmish, please take a seat and let's talk.' When they were all seated, lighting up cigarettes and sipping water or coffee, he said to Dr Jacobs: 'As you still work for NASA, Irving, can I just begin by saying how sorry I was to read about the deaths of those three American astronauts, Grisson, Chaffee and White, in the flash fire that swept through their Apollo spacecraft last January. It must have been a real blow to you.'

'It's been a bad year for the space programme in general,' Jacobs replied. 'I mean, apart from our three astronauts, there was the death of that Soviet cosmonaut, Vladimir Komarov, when his Soyuz spacecraft crashed after coming out of orbit. In neither case – NASA or the Soviet incident – did anyone have a clue as to exactly what happened. God knows, it was certainly a year of disasters that set the space programme back a good deal and could threaten its funding.'

'Which won't help APII,' Stanford said. 'Because when public interest wanes in the space programme – which it always does when funding is cut and there's no media attention fixed on it – it also wanes regarding UFOs. Some people, alas – indeed millions of goddamned people – tend to link the two together. That's one of life's unfortunate facts.'

'The man's a philosopher,' Scaduto said.

'You read me loud and clear,' Stanford replied. 'I have a big mouth.'

'On the other hand,' Scaduto said, 'to get back to the subject of this meeting, it *has* been a wonderful year for UFOs.'

'In what way?' Dr Jacobs asked.

'Biggest goddamned UFO flap since the mid-1950s, including the great March concentration from Montana to Maryland.'

'I was out of the country then,' Dr Jacobs said. 'I did read a little bit about it, but can't remember too much. I was in Paris, France, where the government is seriously discussing the setting up of a UFO programme, but their newspapers don't write too much about this country.'

'No, the Frogs wouldn't,' Stanford said sardonically.

'Literally hundreds of witnesses reported UFOs,' Scaduto told him. 'And there were more UFOs reported from as far apart as Saigon, Vietnam, and Brixham, England. Most notable was a large, saucer-shaped object photographed clearly over Calgary, Alberta. However, the most widely publicised UFO-related incident was the one about a horse called Snippy, found gutted in a surgical manner, with fifteen unexplainable exhaust marks in the earth around its carcass.'

'Fascinating,' Epstein said. 'The Snippy case has reminded us – I mean me and a hell of a lot of other UFO researchers – that over the past few years there's been an increasing number of similar incidents, when animals, including whole herds of cattle, were killed and robbed of their limbs and innards with what appears to be pretty precise, surgical skill.'

'That's one of my specialities,' Stanford said, adjusting his big-buckled belt and looking, with his flashy clothes and matinee-idol handsomeness, not remotely like the very bright physicist that he was. 'I mean, what've we got here? We've got animals being killed, sliced, and gutted where they stand with a precision that can only be surgical. I say it has to be done by extraterrestrials.'

'Why?' Dr Jacobs asked.

'They want the parts for research purposes,' Stanford replied without hesitation. 'Some kind of medical or surgical research. See how we work, right? I mean, see how our bodies function.'

'By why so many parts?' Randall asked.

'That's the million-dollar question,' Stanford replied.

Dwight was just about to reply when Scaduto indicated with a slight shake of his head that he should say nothing more on the subject. Wondering what Scaduto was up to, Dwight went back to more mundane matters, mainly checking the facts and figures regarding recent UFO sightings in his particular area of Dayton, Ohio.

'And how's Beth?' Dr Epstein asked.

'She's improving, but never too settled,' Dwight replied, plunging immediately, helplessly, into a well of fearful memories and dread. 'She still has nightmares, but at least, for the time being, there are no visits from the men in black, either real or imagined.'

'You have to be brave, Dwight.'

'No,' Dwight replied, '*Beth* has to be brave. I can only offer support.'

'She's a strong woman.'

'Yes, I think so.'

'Well,' Epstein said, obviously uncomfortable with the subject and raising his hands inquiringly in the air. 'Anything else to discuss or can we call it a day?'

'No more from me,' Scaduto said.

'You?' Epstein asked of Dwight.

'Not from me,' Dwight replied.

'Anything you two want to ask?' Epstein said to Stanford and Jacobs.

'Not really,' Stanford said. 'It'll take me about a month to check through these APII reports, but once I've done it I'll get back to you.'

'Robert and Irving,' Epstein explained, 'have been taken

on to do a long-term projection based on the flight patterns of UFOs, assessing frequency, direction of approach and retreat, and any other flight patterns that will give us an indication of where they come from. We now have a fairly broad knowledge of their technical abilities and extraordinary flight characteristics; what we don't know is exactly *what* they are and where they come from. That's what Stanford and Dr Jacobs are going to try to assess by analysing every single report in the APII files, going all the way back to 1947. Any help you two . . .' here he nodded at Dwight and Scaduto – 'can give them will be greatly appreciated.'

'Just give me a call,' Dwight said.

'Likewise, guys,' Scaduto added.

'Well, that's about it,' Epstein said. 'You two lunching as usual?'

'Yep,' Dwight replied. 'And as usual you're going to refuse.'

'I'm afraid so,' Epstein said, raising his hands in that oddly rabbinical manner. 'I have a desk piled with work and a lot of business still to cover with Dr Jacobs and Stanford here. So if you'll excuse us . . .'

'We come all the way to Washington DC to be thrown out of his goddamned office,' Scaduto said. 'On the other hand, a nice lunch and some liquor . . . Are you ready, Dwight?'

'I'm right there in your shadow,' Dwight said.

They both stood up, shook hands with Robert Stanford and Dr Irving Jacobs, then left the office.

Soon after, they were having their customary lunch in Clyde's in Georgetown, which Dwight had once enjoyed, but which now always reminded him of the mysterious death of his best friend, Bob Jackson. For that reason, if no other, the lunches were not as joyful as they had once been, though they were always informative.

'Have you mentioned your man-made UFO theory to

Epstein yet?' Dwight asked Scaduto when the food was finished and they were having another beer.

'Nope.'

'Why not?'

'He's a wonderful researcher, but he believes implicitly in the extraterrestrial hypotheses and I think he'd believe that any work I did in that particular direction would be a total waste of the organisation's time and money. So, you know, I don't mention it.'

'Maybe you should.'

'Hey, hold on there, my friend. I get *paid* by APII. Don't wanna lose my income, don't you know?'

'But you still believe in it, right?'

'Fucking A. That's what we're doing here.'

'Thought this was just our normal Georgetown lunch, though I *did* catch your eye back at Epstein's place.'

'Clever man.'

'So what did you want to tell me?'

'I struck gold,' Scaduto replied. 'The fucking mother lode, man.'

'Go on,' Dwight said.

'Get this. One of my buddies in NICAP informed me that the members of the board of governors of that organisation – our lively rivals – had managed to run down one of the CIA agents who'd been transferred – how shall I put it? – *out of harm's way* after the Woman from Maine affair. The agent, who'd been transferred to London before being eased out of the service, was naturally feeling embittered and so was willing to talk off the record, which eventually he did, during a meeting in the Drake hotel in New York.'

'A meeting with you?'

'Shit yes.'

'Okay. Sorry. Go on.'

'Well, according to this guy one of his assignments in the CIA was to undergo specialised training in Duke University's parapsychology lab, a sensory-deprivation establishment at Princetown and the psychology department at McGill University in Canada. The purpose of all this was to open his mind – a highly responsive one – to mental telepathy, sightless vision, and psychokinesis.'

'You want me to ask why. I can tell.'

Scaduto grinned. 'The reason – and I think you've already guessed – is that the Russkies were already employing such skills for espionage purposes.'

'That's only a rumour. Unsubstantiated.'

'Bullshit. It's a fact and you know it. You know damned well that the Parapsychology Lab of the University of Leningrad has been neck-deep in this shit for years.'

Dwight grinned and raised his hands in the air as if pleading for mercy. 'Okay, I know it. Please continue.'

'So this guy,' Scaduto continued, 'after a year of training at both Duke and McGill's parapsychology labs, found that he could, like Ted Serios, cause photographs to appear on a film by merely *studying* the camera. A year after his training, in 1959, he was working with US Naval Intelligence and having successful shore-to-ship telepathic communications with an atomic submarine, the US *Nautilus*. And the same year, when the press exposed the *Nautilus* experiments, he was transferred back to Washington to work with – wait for it . . .'

'Don't tell me.'

'The female psychic from Maine.'

'Oh, Christ.'

'Right.'

'So he made contact?'

'No. At least not straight away. During his first session, in the presence of the female psychic, he couldn't make contact. However, at the second session, in that CIA office in Washington DC, when the woman wasn't present, he went into a trance and made contact with . . . *someone*.'

'Stop tormenting me.'

Scaduto's grin was now like that of a Cheshire cat. 'Well, like the woman from Maine, he was scribbling down, automatically, what it was he was hearing in his trance. However, he never found out what it was he wrote, because before he snapped out of his trance, one of the CIA agents spirited the message out of the office.'

'So they didn't want him to know who he was talking to,' Dwight said.

'Correct,' Scaduto replied. 'And when he finally awakened from his trance, he found everyone at the window, all excitedly scanning the sky over Capitol Hill, where the UFO had been.'

Scaduto paused, grinned, and said, 'You want to hear the rest?'

'You're a natural-born actor, Tony. Just get the hell on with it.'

'Well, you know, this guy's intrigued, right?'

'Obviously.'

'But he's also annoyed because his notes had been taken from him. So later he had a clandestine meeting with one of his colleagues, who'd been present at the time, and asked him if the UFO had been real. His colleague, being drunk and careless with his Irish lip, confessed that it had been, that it was part of a top-secret government project, and that one of the crew on board had been ESP-trained.'

'So the woman from Maine had picked up his thoughts by accident, like someone tuning in to another wavelength.'

'Exactly.'

'Well, I'll be damned.'

'And that wasn't all,' Scaduto continued excitedly. 'According to my drunken colleague – who, once he started talking, couldn't stop – the UFOs reported to have landed at Cannon AFB, Deerwood Nike Base and, apparently, Holloman AFB, were for real – but they weren't extraterrestrial.'

'Man-made.'

'Right. The products of highly secret activity between the Canadian and United States governments.'

'We're back to the Avrocar, which was bullshit. I need another beer, Tony.'

518

'Fuck the beer and listen. These aircraft, flying saucers, call them what you will, in no way resemble the aborted projects that were leaked to, then shown to, the media, us poor shitheads included. In fact, they were highly advanced flying discs of pretty extraordinary capability – and there were a total of about twelve in existence.'

'Only twelve?' Randall asked sceptically.

'Yeah,' Scaduto replied. 'According to my man, his colleague had been seconded to Royal Canadian Air Force Intelligence, where he was given the task of implementing internal security on the flying saucer project. There he discovered that the project was being run jointly by the Canadian government, the US Air Force and Navy, and a few high-ranking Army officers from the Pentagon. Those bastards had managed to maintain secrecy by locating the underground production plants in the deserted regions of southern Canada, between British Columbia and Alberta; by ensuring that the production of the numerous components of the saucers was distributed between hundreds of different, international companies, none of whom could have guessed what the individual components were for; by undertaking the more specialized research in the top-secret military installations of the White Sands Proving Ground at Alamogordo, New Mexico, and similar establishments all over Canada; and, finally, by deliberately confusing the press and public with a continuous stream of ambiguous leaks and misleading statements.'

'In other words . . .'

'They're real flying saucers, they're being produced in Canada, and they're being tested and flown from top-secret American bases.'

'Do you really think this could be true?' Dwight asked.

'It sounds crazy, I know,' Scaduto replied, 'but I'd like to find out. You want to come with me?'

'I want to go back to Beth,' Dwight said.

'Love prevails,' Scaduto replied. He led Dwight out of the bar and stood beside him on the crowded pavement of

519

M Street. 'You'll come with me,' he said. 'I *know* you will. Because you have to find out. You simply have to. You've gone through so much by now, you won't be able to ignore the one opportunity you have of finding out the truth. That's the hook in your throat, my friend. Adios. I'll call you.'

He walked off along the street as Dwight stood there, recalling what he had said and accepting the truth of it.

Dwight just had to find out.

Chapter Forty-Two

In the early hours of February 26, 1968, Wilson was set down in a field just outside McLean, Virginia, by one of his flying saucers and driven from there in a limousine ordered up by Jack Fuller to the Hay Adams hotel, conveniently overlooking Lafayette Park and the White House. When he checked into the hotel, he did so under the name of Mr Aldridge. The real Mr Aldridge was a US citizen who had been abducted many years before, surgically terminated and used as spare parts for the ongoing cyborg programme. Wilson therefore had all of the unfortunate Mr Aldridge's papers, with his own picture replacing the original in Aldridge's passport. The purpose of the visit was to discuss the ongoing activities of the widely publicised Condon Committee. This he did with Jack Fuller over a light lunch in the Tudor dining room of the hotel.

'My so-called Great Northeast Blackout appears to have had the desired effect,' Wilson said. 'The Condon Committee being set up, as it were, by you and your friends at Langley Field.'

'Always pleased to oblige,' Fuller replied sardonically, hiding the fear he now always felt when in Wilson's presence. 'I have to admit that the blackout certainly convinced everyone that your technology is still vastly superior to ours.'

'So they're now willing to play the game my way.'

'Yes. And the Condon Committee, backed by us, is our way of showing you we mean it.'

This was not strictly true and both of them knew it. The Condon Committee merely represented another defeat for the US in its cat-and-mouse game with Wilson – they had been warned and had taken heed – but sooner or later they would try to foil him again; then, if they failed, he would punish them . . . and so it went on.

'I notice that Condon, soon after establishing the committee, started making it perfectly clear that he had little patience with the UFO hypothesis. Was that your doing also?'

'Yeah. Condon also deliberately showed a partiality to obvious crank claims and cases that serious UFO investigators had already dismissed as hoaxes. Eventually he made it clear that he was intent on proving the whole idea of UFOs as nonsense. All that for you, Wilson.'

'But there's a thorn in the side,' Wilson said. 'This Dr James E. McDonald.'

Fuller sighed. McDonald was a senior atmospheric physicist at the University of Arizona's Department of Atmospheric Sciences who had been interested in the UFO phenomenon for years. He was now one of the country's leading authorities on the subject and strongly outspoken in his criticism of the Air Force and the CIA.

'I'm afraid so. McDonald isn't afraid of ridicule and he's got a hell of a lot of energy. In fact, his individual research into UFOs has already far outstripped that of all other researchers, save perhaps J. Allen Hynek and APII's Dr Epstein.'

'How did McDonald get into it?'

'About two years ago, in March, 1966, he obtained the National Academy of Science's approval for a discreet, one-man study of UFOs. But when he heard of the Air Force plans to contract a UFO study to a university, he declined to use the support of NAS and instead used personal finance. That way he was able to investigate scores of sightings and interview hundreds of witnesses. Thrilled by his success, he then launched a crusade to alert the scientific community to the seriousness of the problem. He also took on the Air Force, repeatedly attacking it for its lack of scientific investigation and its pronouncements designed to soothe the public. Finally, he attacked us – the CIA – for our involvement in the Robertson Panel report.'

'A real trouble-maker,' Wilson said.

'Yep. And there's worse to come.'

'I am all ears.'

'In August 1966, the Condon Committee co-ordinator, Robert Low, chosen especially by me and my colleagues, wrote a memorandum to the University of Colorado's administrators expressing his lack of belief in UFOs. For this reason, Low suggested, the Condon Committee's real objective should be a public relations exercise in which the trick would be – and I quote – "to describe the project so that, to the public, it would appear to be a totally objective study but, to the scientific community, would present the image of a group of nonbelievers trying their best to be objective, but having an almost zero expectation of finding a saucer".'

'And how did they recommend that this be best accomplished?'

'To place the emphasis on the psychology and sociology of persons and groups who report seeing UFOs rather than the non-existent UFOs themselves.'

'In other words, place the persons and groups reporting UFOs in the firing line of humiliation and ridicule.'

'Correct. However, Dr McDonald has recently managed to get his hands on that old report – which shows clearly that the Condon Committee had been formed simply to discredit the UFO phenomenon. This has led to a scientific scandal, the firing of a couple of the leading members of the committee, and, worse, a Congressional hearing to begin this July.'

'Never mind the findings of the Congressional hearing,' Wilson said. 'No matter what they say, just make sure that the committee recommends the final, complete closure of

Project Blue Book. As for McDonald, I think I should clip his wings in the fullness of time.'

'You do that,' Fuller said.

He was trying to be flippant, but when he gazed into the icy-blue, penetrating eyes of the silver-haired Wilson, he knew that he was faced with pitiless intelligence. Wilson had cast off all normal emotions as being superfluous to his requirements; now he lived with a logic so rigorous it had made him inhuman. Fuller now thought of Wilson as a mutant. Though born and bred right here in America, he was a true alien being.

'So what about Dr Epstein and our other fine friends at APII? What have they been up to?'

'Epstein has brought in two new men – Doctors Robert Stanford and Irving Jacobs, both physicists – who between them have produced a very large, detailed report showing that most of the more advanced flying saucers, and certainly the big ones, fly on a north-south course – in other words, towards Antarctica.'

'That's too close for comfort.'

'Right. And the publication of the report has led to a whole spate of articles about holes in the poles and hidden UFO bases – just like your own, in fact. Luckily, most of them were of the more fanciful variety and we've used that as the basis for a continuing programme of disinformation. I mean, the more outrageous the theory, the quicker we'll use it. So the APII report, while fairly accurate, is being buried in a whole heap of ridiculous stories.'

'Nevertheless, if they've picked up on that, we better watch them closely.'

'They've picked up on something even more dangerous: the possibility that the UFOs are man-made.'

Even Wilson, who rarely registered emotion, looked a little surprised. 'Epstein?'

'No. Epstein still supports the extraterrestrial hypothesis. It's the other two: Dwight Randall and especially that other kid, Tony Scaduto. He's obsessed with the notion.

In fact, he's taken himself up to Canada and is living there right now, working in Malton, Ontario, to check out the Avro-Canada plant. He has a good nose, that one, and tenacity, so he might have to go.'

'You're having him watched?'

'Of course.'

'Good. Keep me informed of what he and Randall are up to. Is there anything else?'

'No, that just about wraps it up.'

'Then good day, Mr Fuller.'

Fuller pushed his chair back and walked out of the restaurant, slightly cheered by the thought that Wilson would at least be picking up the tab. This was a human reaction.

Chapter Forty-Three

Scaduto dropped in on Dwight in November, 1968, two days after Richard Nixon had been elected as the thirty-seventh President of the United States. Having spent almost a year working as a barman in Malton, Ontario, which had enabled him to make a living while he sounded out the clients about the work they were doing in the local Avro aircraft production company, he was keen to pass on what he had learnt to Dwight.

'I can't believe I'm back in God's country,' he began when he and Dwight had settled in the living room, in front of an open fire, with a couple of beers. 'I feel like I've been in the fucking wilderness. Back in the real world at last!'

'Hardly God's country any more,' Dwight told him. 'At least not this year. One of our spy planes seized by North Koreans, one of our nuclear bombers crashing in Greenland, the most shameful war in our history going on in Vietnam, Martin Luther King assassinated, black riots in most major cities, Bobby Kennedy assassinated, the police indulging in an orgy of Nazi-style violence at the Chicago convention, and now we've got a President that no-one would buy a used car from. God's country no more, I fear.'

'Stop being so pessimistic,' Scaduto said cheerfully, wiping beer from his lips with the back of his hand. 'Next month, I guarantee it, we'll have three American astronauts orbiting the moon in the Apollo 8 spacecraft. Might even find a few UFOs up there. I can't wait to see it.'

'So did you see any UFOs in Ontario, Canada?'

'Not quite, but I got close. See, I got me a job as a barman in Malton, near the Avro-Canada plant, and plying these guys from the factory with drinks I picked up enough idle talk to convince me that Avro had continued to work on saucer-shaped jet aircraft long after the public unveiling of that useless piece of shit, the Avrocar. At the same time, in my spare time, I also drove around a lot of southern Canada, between British Columbia and Alberta, and found a remarkable number of top-security research plants and aircraft factories. And those fuckers, man, they're hidden in the hills and couldn't be seen from the air if you had a giant telescope. Real dense forest up there in Alberta.'

'Well, we *did* know that before, Tony.'

'Nice to be reminded, though.'

'True enough. So what else did you find out?'

'Well, when I was travelling around the place I became bosom pals with a pilot who'd once worked for a Canadian-US company involved in the design and construction of remarkably advanced saucer-shaped aircraft: some piloted and as large as regular aircraft; others only two or three foot in diameter, remote-controlled, and being mass-produced. Both prototypes reportedly based on captured German World War II designs.'

'What makes you think he was telling the truth?'

'The production plant for the saucers was located in a densely forested, mountainous region which protected the plant from the eyes of the commercial airline pilots. But my friend, who now runs a private flight-training school just outside Alberta, knows the tricky flight path that takes you over the testing grounds for the saucers, and he agreed to fly me over them, in the hopes of seeing a saucer on the ground. Unfortunately, he agreed to this just as I had booked my flight back here, but I'm going back eventually to take him up on his offer. I want you to come with me.'

Though instantly excited by the thought, Dwight said, 'I'm frightened of drawing attention to myself or Beth. Particularly as Beth's being plagued again by bad dreams about the men in black. I wouldn't want anyone to know I was doing that.'

'I guarantee that the pilot, Hank Lomax, won't know your real name and all references to the flight booking will be in my name. I don't have a wife and kids, so I'll take my chances.'

'I don't think I can resist it, Tony, but I'll have to ask Beth. She's in a pretty bad way at the moment and has begged me to stay out of the business.'

'But you'll ask her?'

'Yeah.'

'When?'

'I can tell you're keen. I might as well get it over and done with, so I'll ask her tonight over dinner. Did you want to stay, by the way?'

'Nope. Not if you're gonna have your little chat with Beth. Don't think I wanna see that.'

'You're pretty cynical about marriage, aren't you?'

'That's 'cause I'm not married.' He handed Dwight a card. 'Here's the hotel I'm staying in in Dayton. Give me a call when you know.'

'I'll do that,' Dwight said.

Scaduto stood up, finished off his beer, then went into the kitchen-diner to call out a slightly nervous goodbye to Beth. Though she had nothing personally against him – and, indeed, had once found him amusing – she now disliked seeing him arrive because she knew he was bringing news about UFOs and, almost certainly, trying to persuade Dwight to return to UFO work, which she no longer wanted him to do.

In the event, Dwight didn't have to wait until dinner time to broach the subject as Beth, the instant Scaduto had departed, came out of the kitchen, drying her hands on a towel and looking grim. She was still an attractive woman, but she looked worn down by nervous tension. 'So, what did he want?'

'He just wants me to make a trip with him to Alberta,

Canada, then fly over some forested area where we think there may be man-made UFO construction plants.'

Her face went white with barely suppressed fury. 'You promised, Dwight. You said . . .'

Dwight cut her short by holding up his hand. 'I won't go if I don't have your permission, but Tony did insist that he won't be giving my real name to the pilot and the aircraft will be rented in his name. Besides which, I can't see how we would attract much attention by simply flying a chartered plane over the mountains. Lots of tourists do it.'

'You're looking for UFO bases!' Beth snapped vehemently.

'From an airplane, Beth. Not on the ground.'

'I don't give a damn. If they see the plane they're liable to come up and blow you out of the sky. Who knows? And I don't want to be left alone here. You know that. I'm scared!'

'You can spend a night or two with Nichola. She . . .'

'Never mind, Nichola! I don't want you to go. I'll be worried for you and for myself and that's all there is to it. Honestly, Dwight,' she continued, then repeated an accusation she had often made during the early years of their marriage. 'I think you're more concerned with UFOs than you are with me. Well, damn it, go if you want to, but don't expect me to sanction it.'

With that she turned away and stomped back into the kitchen. Dwight followed her in and placed his arms around her. 'It's okay,' he said, 'I won't go. I guess I just didn't think.'

When she turned into his arms, smiling, he was reminded of how lovely she had been when they first married and how, under the beginning lines of middle-age, she had retained that beauty. Touched, he kissed her again and patted her rump.

'Still pleasantly firm,' he said.

She had started to cry and now wiped tears from her eyes. 'You'd have found that out sooner if you'd touched it more often,' she said. 'A woman gets to miss certain things.'

'Well, I guess I'm not as young as I used to be.'

'If you can't manage everything, a little touch here and there can work wonders.'

'I'll bear that in mind.'

'At least you still know how to kiss.'

'It's like learning to swim; once learnt, it's not forgotten.'

'Then plant another one on me, then get out of here and let me get on with the dinner. Nichola's coming to join us.'

'Terrific,' Dwight said.

After kissing her again, then patting her rump once more, he returned to the living room.

He realised instantly, however, that he was extremely depressed at losing the possibility of actually seeing a man-made flying saucer on the ground – more than that: he was crushed. Though he hadn't been drinking since the days when he was separated from Beth and on an alcoholic binge, he now poured himself a tall, consoling bourbon, hoping to drink it before Beth came back into the living room. Unfortunately, at that very moment, Nichola, now twenty-one years old, married, and four months pregnant, opened the front door and walked in, coming to dinner.

She saw the glass of bourbon in Dwight's hand before he could set it down. Still blonde and as pretty as a picture, she frowned disapprovingly.

'What's that, Dad?'

'Only an aperitif.'

'What's the excuse?' Nichola asked, removing her coat and throwing it carelessly over the back of the settee.

'No excuse. I just felt like it. Your husband does this every night before dinner, so why do I need an excuse?'

Nichola's husband was eight years her senior and working as a civilian engineer with the military aviation development branch of Wright-Patterson Air Force Base. A decent, good-natured man, he had a fondness for cigars and his glass of bourbon every night before dinner. Apart from that, he had no drinking problems, so Nichola didn't mind. She clearly did, however, feel troubled to see her father with a glass in his hand again.

'Larry's never had a drinking problem in his life,' Dwight's stern daughter replied, 'but you did.'

'Only once, sweetheart.'

'Once was enough to make you a wreck and force Mom to leave you for a few years. Here, give me that.' She took the bourbon off Dwight, then sat on the settee, crossed her shapely legs, sipped the bourbon, which she liked as much as did her husband, and said, 'So what's happened to make you reach for a drink?'

'I just wanted to give you an excuse for having one,' Dwight replied, unable to resist the gentle sarcasm.

Nichola just smiled. 'I have one every evening with Larry. It slips down real easy.'

'My boozing daughter.'

'So why did I have to stop you from boozing like this loving daughter?'

'He wants to go chasing UFOs again,' Beth told her, coming into the room at that moment, 'and I won't let him.'

'How do you mean, chasing UFOs? He's been doing that for years.'

When Dwight told her, Nichola said, 'You mean there's a real chance you could crack this mystery once and for all? I mean, resolve this business that's been haunting you for years?'

'Yes,' Dwight said. 'If we can find those saucers on the ground, the game is all up.'

'And you can stop feeling that you're being driven crazy by things you don't understand.'

'Yeah, Nichola, right.'

Nichola turned to her mother. 'Then I think you should let him do it.'

'What?' Beth looked shocked.

'I think you should let him do it,' Nichola insisted. 'If a simple flight over the mountains of Alberta is going to resolve years of mystery, then obviously you should let Dad make it and pray that he comes back with what he needs to let him feel at peace. Otherwise, if you tell him that he can't go . . .' She held up the glass of bourbon and tapped it with her fingertips . . . 'He'll be back on this. So let the man go.'

'You don't understand, Nichola, it could be dangerous. It could draw attention to him, and then all that dreadful . . . *business* will start again. I don't think I can bear that.'

'You can if you know that the pain could all end pretty quickly.'

'It's dangerous.'

'But worth the risk. He goes up there with Tony Scaduto, he charters an airplane, and a couple of days later, if things go okay – and that's the chance we've got to take – he's back here and we're all home and dry. For God's sake, Mom, he's been pursuing this mystery since 1947 – you can't make him stop now. He'd certainly be back on the bourbon and he might actually go crazy. So let him take this chance, Mom. And besides, the odds on something dramatic happening to him – like being shot out of the sky by a UFO – are pretty damned slim.'

'At the least, he could end up in prison,' Beth insisted, now clutching at straws.

'You're imprisoning him with your fear,' Nichola told her mother, 'and that isn't right.'

Taken aback by her daughter's forthrightness, but also proud of her, Beth said, 'All right. Okay. You win! I just can't bear the thought of being . . .'

'Alone here,' Nichola finished the sentence for her. 'Well, you don't have to. You can come and stay with me and Larry in Springfield until Dad returns. You can even have a bourbon every night, which is more than he'll get. So are we agreed, folks?'

'Yes,' Beth said.

'Thanks,' Dwight added.

Deeply moved, he kissed both of them on the cheek, then he picked up the phone and spoke to Scaduto in his hotel in Dayton.

'When do we leave?' he asked.

Chapter Forty-Four

On the commercial airline flight to Calgary, Alberta, Scaduto drank a hell of a lot and became quite drunk. When Dwight commented on this, Scaduto said, 'You know this is gonna sound crazy – particularly with what you and Beth have been through – but now I've begun to feel – definitely, absolutely, that I'm being watched, though I can't put my finger on just how. No Men in Black or black limousines – but somehow watched. I don't know if it's real or just goddamned paranoia, but that's what I feel. And so I find myself drinking, trying to deaden it, trying to say: "Go away".'

Glancing through the porthole window of the airplane, Dwight saw a sea of white clouds and, below, great swathes of greenly forested hills. It looked desolate down there. 'I've got to confess,' he said, 'that while out of deference to Beth's fear that I'd bring attention to myself I was reducing my activities for APII, I was intrigued by the revelation that the US-Canadian saucers had been based on World War II designs. Ever since you told me that I've been spending most of my time holed up in libraries – even wrote to England's Imperial War Museum and corresponded with German and American UFOlogists about the subject. I was pretty astonished to learn that it was true.'

'You proved it?'

'Yeah.'

Scaduto sipped more whisky, looking excited. 'So what did you find?'

Though he now practically knew all of it off by heart, Dwight glanced occasionally at his notes to ensure that he made no mistakes.

'According to official reports, Allied aircraft during World War II were harassed by UFOs – mostly in the shape of balls of fire – from as far back as 1944. Shortly after the war, in the summer of 1946, the more familiar types of UFOs, mostly cigar-shaped, swarmed across Scandinavia, seemingly coming from the general direction of the Soviet Union. The conclusion at the Pentagon was that German scientists, seized by the Russians at Peenemünde where the V-2 rocket had been developed, were constructing advanced weapons for the Soviets and that the unidentified, so-called missiles were being launched from the rocket test site of Peenemunde which was then in the Russian-occupied zone of Germany. This suspicion became stronger when the British, who'd also seized and taken back to Britain a wealth of Germany's top-secret scientific and weapons-research material, announced that the Germans had been working since 1941 on extraordinary aeronautical projects and on processes to release atomic energy. Included in the former was a – this is a straight quote from the documents – remotely-controlled, pilotless aircraft and a device that could be controlled at a considerable distance by another aircraft – unquote.'

'Which could account for the fireballs,' Scaduto said.

'Right. Anyway, faced with this, and thinking of the Soviet so-called missiles, possibly more balls of fire, that had been seen over Scandinavia, there was a sudden British-Canadian-United States alliance to beat the Soviets in the race to follow through the German designs and complete their extraordinary aeronautical projects.'

'Which gets us to the man-made UFOs.' Scaduto interjected excitedly.

'Yes. It's true that what they were attempting to build in the underground plants in Canada right after the war – with British and United States back-up – was a machine with the extraordinary capabilities of the machines suggested in the incomplete German material. They wouldn't achieve that goal for another twenty years, but the first, fairly crude versions of their saucers were successfully tested over the Canadian border on June 21, 1947: a total of five disc-shaped aircraft, two of them piloted and approximately fifty feet in diameter, the remaining three remote-controlled by the pilots flying nearby, these three a mere three to six feet in diameter. Those particular flying saucers could reach an altitude of approximately seven thousand feet, could hover uncertainly in the air, and had a horizontal flight speed of about six hundred miles an hour.'

'That test flight,' Scaduto said, 'could account for the Harold Dahl sighting of the same day.'

'Right,' Dwight said. 'However, it was what happened *after* that test flight that really got the ball rolling. On June 24, three days after the first successful test flight of the five Canadian-US saucers, a total of nine, highly sophisticated, *unknown* saucers flew down over the Canadian underground plants, hovered there for about twenty minutes, shot off toward the Cascades where reportedly they circled the test area; returned, circled the plant for another twenty minutes, then shot off at incredible speed. From that day on – the day, incidentally, of the famous Kenneth Arnold sighting – those flying saucers, and others, returned again and again, and eventually spread out across the whole world.'

'My God!' Scaduto whispered dramatically, then hurriedly finished his drink as the airplane came in to land at Calgary. 'Where the hell do the *others* come from?'

'That's the million-dollar question,' Dwight replied, 'and it keeps me awake at night.'

A few minutes later, the airplane landed and Scaduto's friend, the pilot, Hank Lomax, met them. He was a small, feisty character with flaming red hair and a face mottled by a combination of sunshine and booze. He was wearing a logger's red-and-black checkered jacket, oil-smeared blue denims and buckled boots. After being introduced to Dwight, he led both of them from the building to his old Ford car parked outside.

'We're going first to my private flight-training school on the outskirts of town,' he explained when they were driving out of the airport. 'From there we'll fly out in my four-seater Piper to the region you want.'

As Lomax drove them up through spectacular, forest-covered scenery, Scaduto looked around him and said, 'Just look at those hills and peaks. Easy to hide *lots* of things up there!'

'Just wait till we get in my Piper,' Lomax told him. 'Then you'll really see something. We'll be heading for British Columbia.'

During the drive he told them about some of the people he had worked with at the A. V. Roe (Avro-Canada) plant in Malton, Ontario. 'Quite a few of them were Germans,' he said. 'I do remember that much. And one of them in particular, Otto Miethe, claimed to have worked on a programme called "Projekt Saucer" in Nazi Germany. I mean, I couldn't believe it: there we were working with the sons of bitches we'd fought in France and Germany. Anyway, that's exactly what we were working on: saucer-shaped jet aircraft with circular, rotating wings and the pilot's cabin fixed in the middle, based on those old Nazi designs. They weren't as advanced as some of the UFOs you read about, but they were definitely based on the German designs and much more advanced than the original German prototypes. The smallest ones, about three feet wide, were really remote-controlled probing devices that could also be used to block radar and cause other malfunctions in any aircraft they flew near. You could control 'em from the ground or from another aircraft in flight; and they certainly resembled balls of fire when in the air. The larger ones came in different sizes and were all piloted. When I left, the largest was about seventy-five feet in diameter, but I know they had plans for an even larger one.'

'Who ran this company?'

'It was part of the A. V. Roe company, later called Avro, but it was backed by the British, Canadian and US governments and guarded just like a military camp. You had to sign a top-secret clause to work there with imprisonment as just one of the many punishments mentioned if you broke the secret, even after leaving the company. I'm taking one shitty chance with you guys, I can tell you, but what the hell!'

'And other companies like it were, or are, scattered all over British Columbia and Alberta, Canada?'

'Right. See, what they'd do to really keep these constructions secret and help 'em with disinformation, was they'd use a company like A. V. Roe – the main plant in Malton, Ontario – as a front. When something leaked out about what they were doing, or when there was a public outcry, they'd call a press conference and show the reporters and politicians a piece of shit like the Avrocar. Meanwhile, they'd have another factory, run by A. V. Roe or some other big company, but listed as a straight experimental aircraft company. This one would do the real flying saucer construction work in a location hidden well away from view – like the one I'm going to show you. Every couple of years, they'd formally close the factory down, listing it as bankrupt, when in actual fact they were simply moving the programme to a new, hidden location. That way, though you couldn't hide the factories completely from prying eyes, they were all over the place, opening and closing down again, and that made them almost impossible to trace. I mean, this plant we're going to, you can bet your balls it'll be gone if you come back in a year's time. So that's how they operate.'

'Very neat,' Dwight said, forced to admire the faceless men who had made his life a torment.

A few minutes later they reached Lomax's flight-training school just outside of Calgary. There, they squeezed into his four-seater Piper *Tri-Pacer* and quickly took off, heading across Alberta to British Columbia, flying above the spectacular plateau that fell down from the Rocky Mountains and eventually formed the southern part of the boundary with British Columbia.

Though not personally flying the plane, Dwight almost got a lump in his throat, being suddenly reminded of his early days, when he had been a B-29 bombardier and radar operator, flying to India, China and the Pacific with the original B-29 wing; then as a navigator with an Air Force Reserve Troop Carrier Wing. Those days were long gone now.

'Hey, what did you think of the results of last July's Congressional hearings on the Condon Committee?' Scaduto asked Dwight, having to shout against the noise of the wind and the biplane's engine. 'I read that they'd resulted in a resolve to form a proper, official UFO enquiry.'

Scaduto was referring to the end result of the notorious Low Memorandum, which brought enormous criticism down on the head of Edward U. Condon and his committee, most of it levelling the accusation that the committee's work had been either plain shoddy in its investigations and conclusions or, more likely, a snow job for the Air Force or the CIA, designed specifically to kill off the UFO controversy. So loud was the furore that Congressman J. Edward Roush delivered a speech on the House floor, saying that the Low Memorandum and a subsequent *Look* article by journalist John Fuller had 'raised grave doubts as to the scientific profundity and objectivity of the project.' Roush therefore called for a new Congressional investigation under the auspices of the House Science and Astronautics Committee. Scheduled July 29, it was set up more ambitiously as a symposium and included an impressive array of participants, including J. Allen Hynek, astronomer Carl Sagan, the engineer James A. Harder, an astronautics engineer, Robert M. Barker, and even the widely respected, trouble-shooting atmospheric physicist, Dr James E. MacDonald.

Concerning the reality or non-reality of UFOs, some of those men were sceptics, but the deliberations of the hearing-symposium resulted in a general, implied criticism of the Condon Committee and a strong recommendation for the continued study of UFOs. Ironically, the hearings came to an end during a peak period of sightings that resurrected nationwide public and press interest in the subject.

'Well, the hearing-symposium might have made that recommendation,' Dwight responded, also shouting against the noise, 'but personally I'm sceptical that it'll happen. The Condon Report has just been delivered to the National Academy of Sciences for review and it's my belief that no matter what its conclusions are, the recommendations of the Congressional hearing-symposium will be overridden and we'll be back where we started – with no official support for UFO investigations.'

'You're just a cynic,' Scaduto said.

'You're like that about marriage,' Dwight told him, 'so I can feel free to swing that way about official UFO studies.'

'So it goes!' Scaduto quipped.

Glancing down, Dwight saw just how dense and seemingly impenetrable the forested hills and mountain ranges were. Noticing the direction of his gaze, Lomax said, 'You're wondering how they could even transport an aircraft factory into those regions, right?'

'Right,' Dwight replied.

'Well, it looks impenetrable from here but normal men can do anything and down there, spread right across the region from Alberta to British Columbia, there are not only hidden aircraft factories, but also coal mines, the odd oil field, plants for the utilization of natural gas, and even cleared areas for the cultivation of wheat, oats and barley. So though they're all hidden from each other, as well as from us, that place is a hive of activity. And we're just starting to fly over the region you wanted.'

Glancing down again, Dwight saw that they were now flying over snow-covered mountain peaks edged sharply against the blue sky, casting their shadows down the slopes of the dense, tree-covered mountains. They flew east and west, north and south, in a criss-crossing motion, sometimes at high altitude, which gave them great all-over visual coverage; other times at an altitude so low Dwight thought they were going to crash, though they always made it, even if only by a hair's breadth, through the stark-shadowed gorges.

They flew for a couple of hours, until early afternoon, yet saw nothing but the forest and mountain peaks. Eventually, when all were in agreement that they had done enough for one day, they decided to turn back.

Lomax was already at high altitude and was just in the middle of his turn when Dwight saw something glinting in the falling sun. At first he thought it was nothing – sunlight glinting off a patch of ice – but then, as the plane advanced and he saw a bit more of that glinting object, he was certain it was solid and metallic.

'Down there!' he bawled.

Lomax and Scaduto both glanced down and agreed that the object was indeed solid and metallic. Lomax immediately descended to a low altitude that enabled him to fly along a steep-sided gorge that wound dangerously through the mountain until it led to a natural clearing where the ground had been cleared for the construction of corrugated iron buildings, stone-block buildings, wooden administration huts and accommodations, and what were certainly aircraft hangers.

It was an expansive aeronautical establishment surrounded by barbed wire and high cliffs . . . and there, on the ground, some half lost in the shadowy interior of the aircraft hangars, a few sitting on landing pads on the ground, were half-a-dozen solid, metallic, flying saucers.

They were all about one hundred and twenty feet in diameter and had their pilot cabins located at the centre of gravity. None had any markings of any description.

The three men in the plane whooped and hollered with exultation as Lomax flew directly over the flying saucers on the landing pads, then ascended again until the establishment had disappeared from view.

While Scaduto was frantically marking the location on his map, Lomax turned back to make another run.

'I don't think we should,' Dwight said. 'They might spot us next time.'

'We've got to get some photos,' Scaduto said, removing a camera from his satchel. 'We can't miss this one, Dwight.'

'Damned right!' Dwight exclaimed, now just as excited as his friend. 'It's too late to stop now.'

'You sure you want me to go back?' Lomax asked.

'Yep,' Scaduto said, slipping his camera out of its case and screwing on its high-power telescopic lens. 'And go as low as you can.'

'Hold your breath, boys.'

Lomax turned in a wide arc until he was facing the gorge again, then he descended until he was below its sides and began a second hair-raising flight through its narrow, winding course until the flying saucer construction plant had come into view. This time, as he streaked above the saucers parked outside the hangars, he banked sharply to enable Scaduto to aim the camera down and snap as many pictures as the brief time allowed. Scaduto managed to click the lens-trigger four times before, within seconds, Lomax was straightening out the plane and making his sharp ascent out of the gorge.

Still looking back and downward for his last glimpse of the construction plant, Dwight saw one of the parked saucers swaying from side to side, then lifting a few feet off the ground. Even as the hills falling away from the plane cut off the view, he saw the saucer shooting up vertically at tremendous speed. Before he could say a word to the others, the saucer had vanished above the clouds.

'I just saw one take off!' he bawled, then jabbed his index finger at the sky and said, 'It went straight up there!'

Suddenly, with a speed that was terrifying, the clouds directly above were blown apart and a dark pinprick descended in the blinking of an eye to become an immense, circular-shaped, swirling blackness that roared directly above them.

'Oh, shit!' Lomax bawled, automatically covering his head with one crooked arm, thinking that . . . *thing* up there was going to crash down upon him.

'It'll hit us!' Scaduto screamed.

But it didn't. Instead, with miraculous precision, it stopped abruptly, mere inches above the cockpit, and hovered there, now so large that it looked like an enormous, inverted whirlpool or cosmic funnel, swirling and giving off an odd, bass humming sound.

Even though the plane was still flying horizontally, that great mass stayed right above it.

A swirling, circular blackness with a glowing edge.

As the plane continued on its horizontal course beneath that great mass, Scaduto, getting his senses back, raised his camera to shoot into its featureless underside. Instantly, a pyramid of brilliant light shot out of the centre of the swirling blackness, temporarily blinding the three men in the plane. Scaduto, with his eyes closed but still holding the camera up where it had been, clicked off as many shots as he could before the plane started shuddering and then rocking wildly.

'Jesus Christ!' Lomax bawled. 'We're going out of control!'

Then the engines cut out.

'We're going down!' Lomax screamed.

Miraculously, the plane did not go down. Instead, with no sound whatsoever from its own engines and only that strange bass humming sound from above, it kept flying forward, albeit shuddering and rocking wildly, as if held up by the pyramid of light. It flew like this for a few seconds, then, as abruptly as it had exploded over the plane, the pyramid of light blinked out and, simultaneously, with a speed that defied the senses, the swirling black hole edged with light shrank to a dot and disappeared back through the clouds.

Instantly, the plane, with its engines still silent, plunged towards the ground.

'We're going down!' Lomax screamed a second time. But at that moment the engines suddenly roared back into life, as powerful as they had been before, thus lifting the aircraft too quickly and throwing it into a violent spin. As Lomax fought to get back control, the spinning aircraft plunged towards the forested hills of Alberta; but eventually he managed to pull it back up, control the spin, and level out completely.

'That light, whatever it was, cut our engines out,' Lomax said. 'The light, or something above it, also held us up in the air while the engines were out.'

'Amazing precision,' Dwight recalled. 'It came down on us so fast you could hardly see it descending, then it stopped mere inches above the cockpit and moved sideways as we were moving forward, staying in exactly the same position above us. When it left, I hardly saw it going, it ascended so fast. I've never seen anything like it.'

'Why did the – whoever was in the saucer – let us go,' Scaduto asked, 'instead of wiping us out in a crash?'

'Because they know that if we report the sighting,' Dwight replied, 'not a soul will believe us and we'll simply become laughing stocks. If they'd made us crash, on the other hand, that crash would have had to be thoroughly investigated, which could lead the authorities back to them. That's how they've done it for years.'

They flew back to Calgary with all possible speed, stunned by the experience they'd just had.

When they had returned to Dayton, Ohio, a few days later,

they learned, as Dwight had guessed, that the Condon Report, which had just been released, had savaged the UFOlogists, mocked those who had criticised the committee's project before the report was in, vilified the other UFO research programmes and recommended the closing down of Project Blue Book.

They also learned, when Scaduto went to collect the photos he had taken of the swirling black base of the 125 feet saucer, that the film had been lightly scorched and the negatives destroyed when still in the camera.

'It was the light,' Dwight said bitterly.

Chapter Forty-Five

In March 1969, Fuller attended a meeting at Air Force Headquarters in Washington DC, with representatives of the Air Defence Command, Air Force Systems Command, Office of Aerospace Research, Office of Scientific Research, and Office of Information. Not required to be present for the first half of the meeting, which was closed even to him, Fuller arrived just as most of the gold-braids were into their second or third whisky, bourbon or brandy and puffing clouds of smoke from fat cigars, all paid for by the unwitting taxpayer. Looking at the faces of those around the long table, some reasonably decent, most the sagging, untrustworthy masks of those who have told a lot of lies and learned to live with them, Fuller was not overly impressed and thought his own brand of patriotic vice was at least less emotionally stultifying.

'Welcome, Fuller,' an Air Force Systems Command general said. 'The meeting's over, so what did you wish to ask?'

'I have to report to Wilson, sir, about your recommendations regarding the Condon Report.'

'Christ, I wish we could get ahead of that bastard and blow him away,' the representative of the Air Defence Command said vehemently.

'We might eventually get to do that, sir, but I'm afraid it's still a long way away.'

'Unfortunately, yes.'

'And what are your recommendations, sir?'

'We've chosen to ignore the widespread criticism of the Condon Report and instead implement its recommendations.'

'I welcome that decision, sir. I'm sure Wilson will be pleased. But I have to warn you that those recommendations have already been widely viewed as notorious – an Air Force snow job – so we have to be careful how we handle it.'

'The Report was widely viewed thus by the civilian UFO groups and UFOlogists, who hardly concern us here.'

'The Condon Report was also widely attacked by the press.'

'The press is filled with communists, Fuller, so we don't need to heed them. Frankly, we're more concerned with not offending Wilson than we are with inviting squeals of rage from reds under the beds.'

'What about Blue Book?'

'Project Blue Book has been officially closed down at this meeting. Project Blue Book is dead and gone.'

'I have to say, sir,' said the representative of the Office of Scientific Research, 'that I strongly disagree with closing Project Blue Book completely. I agree that interest in UFOlogy must be dampened, but Blue Book now has historical roots and should be preserved in some form, no matter how modest, to give the illusion that we did, at least originally, sincerely believe in it.'

'I agree,' Fuller said, 'and even presented the notion to Wilson; but he said all roots, even historical ones, die quickly and crumble to dust when torn out of the ground – so he insisted that we kill Project Blue Book entirely.'

'Do we have to do *everything* that bastard says?' asked one representative from the Office of Information.

'For the time being, yes,' Fuller said. 'I should remind you that Wilson has kept his promise by ensuring the US is in the lead in the space race and that an American, Neil Armstrong, will certainly be walking on the Moon this coming July – the first man in history to do so.'

'I second that,' said the gold-braided representative of the Office of Aerospace Research. 'Even though we pay dearly, we *have* been given some extraordinary aid from Wilson, so we must keep him happy until we're perfectly sure we can move against him.'

'Exactly,' Fuller said. 'Now may I suggest that the Blue Book records be made as inaccessible as possible to make life difficult for future researchers. Any suggestions?'

'I recommend Maxwell AFB in Montgomery, Alabama,' said the representative of the Office of Information. 'It's not a place too many people want to visit unless they really have to. Also, those southern officers are notoriously prickly to deal with and even hardened researchers give up more often than not when trying to get something out of them.'

'That's fine by me,' Fuller said. 'Anything else to pass on to Wilson?'

'No,' the chorus came back from that cloud of cigar smoke.

'Fine,' Fuller said. 'Thank you one and all.'

Leaving the meeting, he drove to a dark field in a pastoral, empty area of Virginia and sat patiently in his car until a flying saucer, vastly more advanced than the Canadian-US saucers he was protecting, landed in the field right beside him. It came down silently, with no lights flashing, and was only revealed by the moonlight shining off its silvery dome. When the front ramp fell down, the light beaming out was extremely pale and would have shown little to the cars passing by on the distant road.

Wilson emerged from that light, followed by the usual hideous, frightening cyborgs. Wilson, his blue eyes still intensely bright in the moonlight, wore his usual faint smile of disdain when he walked up to Fuller.

His greeting was: 'So what did they say?'

Fuller told him what had taken place at the meeting in Air Force Headquarters. Wilson was pleased, but wanted to know what President Nixon thought about the UFO situation in general and him in particular.

'Nixon's the supreme pragmatist,' Fuller said, 'and accepts the status quo. He doesn't like it, but he accepts the necessity of dealing with you. No need for anxieties there.'

'There's no-one more pragmatic than I,' Wilson replied, 'and I *never* suffer anxieties.'

Ignoring the remark, Fuller removed a piece of notepaper from his billfold, checked the details written on it, then put the paper back in his billfold and put the billfold away.

'I thought I should tell you,' he said to Wilson, 'that Tony Scaduto, that UFO researcher I mentioned before – works for NICAP, but also does a lot on the side for Dr Epstein's APII – recently chartered a private aircraft piloted by flight-trainer Hank Lomax. Accompanied by that former ATIC officer and present APII investigator, Dwight Randall, he flew over a US-Canadian flying saucer plant in British Columbia. There, after clearly viewing the saucers resting outside the hangars – that advanced one hundred and twenty-five-footer recently delivered by you – the airplane was pursued and harassed until it left the area.'

'Did they take photos?'

'We assume so, but a laser-beam weapon and force field would have put paid to his film.'

'Very good.'

'Do you think we should do something about him?' Fuller asked.

'Just scare him for now,' Wilson replied. 'I don't wish to be involved. But if your fright tactics don't make him shut his mouth, let me know and I'll deal with him as I've dealt with that increasingly irksome troublemaker, Dr James E. McDonald.'

'McDonald's still around,' Fuller replied.

'It's an illusion,' Wilson said.

Instead of explaining what he meant by that ambiguous remark, he changed the subject by pointing out that since American astronauts had recently orbited the moon in the

Apollo 8 spacecraft and would, indeed, soon be actually taking their first steps on it, he wanted no reports to filter through regarding the debris of his own previous landings there. He insisted, furthermore, that the UFO reports being submitted with increasing frequency by astronauts were to be treated as the sightings of previously unseen natural cosmic phenomena.

When Fuller agreed, Wilson returned to his flying saucer and left the otherwise cynical CIA agent to stare in wonder at its magical ascent until it was lost in the stars.

Time moved on, Fuller realised.

Chapter Forty-Six

A shocked Randall felt that he was reliving his life. Back in 1952, with his late friend Bob Jackson, he had passed a newspaper stand in Washington National Airport Terminal Building and seen from the headlines that UFOs had invaded the capital and felt outraged that he had not been informed. Now, his old friend long gone, he saw from the headlines dated December 17, 1969, in the very same airport, that the Secretary of the Air Force, Robert G. Seamans, Jr., had just officially announced the termination of Project Blue Book and the Air Force's twenty-two-year study of unidentified flying objects.

With his shock turning into disbelief, anger and despair, Dwight caught a cab and continued on his journey to what could be a crucial meeting with Tony Scaduto. He was dropped off outside a nondescript bar in M Street, not far from where Bob Jackson had died of a 'heart attack' which Dwight then, and now, believed had been murder.

The flamboyant Scaduto was like a different man: dressed like a Haight-Ashbury hippie, smoking a joint of marijuana, drinking too much, listening to a jukebox playing Zager and Evans, Blood, Sweat and Tears, The Rolling Stones, and Jethro Tull while psychedelic lights flashed on and off the walls. He was also practically gibbering with fear.

'I tell you, man, wow, right,' he said, inhaling, exhaling, glancing left and right, avoiding Dwight's gaze and doing everything to avoid the issue of UFOs or the termination of Project Blue Book. 'What a year, right? I mean, I really dig it that a US astronaut's become the first motherfucker to land on the Moon and that just last month two more astronauts did the same. Superheroes, those guys.'

'There are no superheroes,' Dwight replied, already beginning to despair of this conversation.

'Yeah, well, right,' Scaduto continued rambling while sucking on Mary Jane, putting his head back, closing his eyes, then exhaling slowly. 'Yeah, but we really beat those goddamned Russkies in the end. That's one hell of a thing, right?'

'Right,' Dwight said. 'I really wanted to talk about the termination of Project Blue Book.'

'Yeah? Well, you know, I really don't know anything about that, man. I mean, what the fuck, they've been trying to kill it off for years and it was practically dead on its feet long before it was terminated. Not much lost anymore, right?'

'Who do you think was behind it? Jack Fuller's gang?'

'Yeah, probably, but who knows? I mean, I don't wanna know anymore. And neither do you, man. You shouldn't ask questions about things like that. Things like that can be messy.'

'I haven't heard from you in a long time, Tony. You don't reply to my letters anymore. Have you given up your UFO investigations?'

'Yeah, right, I gave it up.'

'Why's that?'

'I just got fed up with it, is all. I mean, I just got the urge to do other things,' Scaduto raised his fat joint in the air, waved it, then giggled. 'Yeah, man, other things.'

'You didn't just get interested in other things, Tony. You got scared.'

'Bullshit!'

'You're scared right this second.'

'Just stoned, man. Bit sweaty. Fucking hot in here. And those lights man, they make your heart race. It's the new generation.'

'You're a bit old for it, Tony.'

'I'm okay. I still pull the chicks.'

'The use of the word "chicks" already dates you.'

'Okay, man, just lay off.'

Flickering constantly, rapidly in the gloom, like the lights seen on many UFOs, the psychedelic lights in this crowded bar were creating bizarre patterns on the walls and on the bodies, faces and limbs of the young people packed tightly together, most wearing hippy clothes – baubles, bangles and beads – and talking in a haze of marijuana smoke. In that disorientating combination of kaleidoscopic lights and the smoke from the pot, Scaduto looked gaunt and haunted.

Determined to get to the bottom of the dramatic change in his old friend, Dwight ploughed ahead. 'So why are you frightened? Did they get to you, Tony?'

Scaduto sighed. 'Okay, man, I confess. I recently received a visit from three bastards in black suits. They claimed to be CIA agents, scared the hell out of me, and demanded that I drop my UFO investigations and forget what I saw over British Columbia. They said that if I ever flew over British Columbia again I wouldn't come back. They also quoted the name of our pilot, Hank Lomax, and told me to give you their regards.'

Dwight was shocked almost rigid. Sitting up straight in his chair behind the small, round table, he found himself squinting automatically into the flashing strobe lights, trying to see if he was being observed. Realising that he had become paranoid again on the instant, he then understood, also, just why Scaduto was behaving in this manner. Yes, Scaduto was helplessly frightened – just like himself.

Oh, God, he thought. *Not again*.

Trying to get a grip on himself, he said: 'For both flights – the one from Dayton to Calgary and the one in Lomax's plane – I was listed under another name. How the hell could they have known I was present?'

Scaduto threw his hands up in the air, pleading innocence. 'I swear to God, man, I didn't tell them. If they'd asked, I think I would have, 'cause I was so damned scared, you know? But they didn't ask. They just told me they knew Lomax was the pilot and then said – kinda grinning maliciously – to give my regards to you. So they know you were there.'

'Jesus Christ, *how*?'

'I think it was the beam of light. You remember? That pyramid of light that beamed down from the saucer to cut our aircraft's engines then somehow keep us up there in the air, still moving forward. That light scorched and destroyed the film in my camera, thus destroying our evidence for the existence of the man-made saucers. I think it also somehow photographed us – or at least sent up an image of us to them. They identified us from that.'

'Oh, my God,' Dwight said, briefly covering his face with his hands and now feeling as frightened as Scaduto looked. 'What have I done?' He uncovered his face and stared straight at Scaduto who, in the distorting, kaleidoscopic strobe lights, looked oddly inhuman. 'What about Beth?'

Scaduto leaned across the table, waving his thick joint between the fingers of one hand and grabbing Dwight by the lapels of his jacket to shake some sense into him. 'Fuck flying saucers,' he said to Dwight. 'I just want to stay alive. And so should you, man. For your own sake. For Beth's. This is the last time we meet, Dwight. Good luck. Adios.'

He released the lapels of the jacket and gave Dwight a gentle shove. Dwight pushed his chair back and stood up to hurry out of the bar. Once outside, on the pavement, in the early afternoon's wintry light, he caught a taxi straight back to the airport. There, instead of catching his return flight to Dayton, Ohio, he caught the next plane to Phoenix, Arizona. He had a window seat and during the lengthy flight he couldn't take his eyes off the sky. He kept imagining he was seeing flying saucers moving eerily through the clouds, but nothing materialised.

Arriving in Phoenix late that evening, Dwight hired a car

and drove to a residential area near the University of Arizona, where he booked into a small hotel for the night. He did not sleep well. Rushing back in upon him, as if stirred up by his talk with the equally frightened Tony Scaduto, were all the old dreams of flying saucers and mysterious men in black. Mixed in with such dreams were dreadful visions of Beth surrounded by other creatures, some human, others alien, bathed in a radiant white light and being probed in her most private places with what looked like surgical instruments. He thought he could hear Beth screaming. In fact, it was himself. He awakened more than once in that endless, sweaty night to find himself screaming.

At ten the following morning, after a breakfast of black coffee (since he could not stomach even the idea of food) and after making a quick call to check that Beth was okay, he drove to the University of Phoenix and was escorted to his pre-arranged meeting with Dr James E. McDonald.

Over the past few years McDonald, who was strongly pro-UFO and anti-CIA, had become a troublesome thorn in the side of the latter, as well as the Air Force. This had led him into doing freelance work for APII and it was through this work that Dwight had gotten to know him and respect him. Though very much the scientist, living in a cloistered world, McDonald had taken the bit in his teeth and gone out to fight all those in the CIA and Air Force who were trying to stifle information about UFOs or intimidate or harass witnesses. He had done so with tremendous energy and a surprising eye for publicity, thus placing APII more vividly on the map, even while making himself a leading target for those he was exposing. Dwight had to admire that.

Now, however, entering McDonald's office, Dwight was shocked to find that McDonald has changed almost as much as Scaduto. A kind-faced, academic man with short-cropped hair and spectacles, he had recently lost a lot of weight and looked like someone in a state of permanent exhaustion. Behind the spectacles, his eyes seemed slightly glazed and distracted, possibly even fearful.

After welcoming Dwight into his office as warmly as possible given his condition, McDonald confessed that he no longer wished to discuss UFOs and had almost refused Dwight the interview.

'So why did you change your mind and let me come?' Dwight asked, when he was seated in the chair in front of McDonald's desk.

McDonald shrugged and smiled with what seemed like an air of sadness. 'I guess in deference to all we shared in the past,' he said. 'By which I mean our work for APII.'

'You were doing so well,' Dwight told him, 'then you suddenly stopped. Why was that, James?'

McDonald stared steadily at him for a moment, then shrugged again, this time forlornly. 'No reason, Dwight.'

'You look terrible,' Dwight said. 'You look sleepless. What happened, James?'

McDonald was silent for what seemed like an eternity, his gaze focused on the ceiling, then he sighed with what could only be deemed despair and lowered his gaze to look at Dwight – not directly at him, but as near to that as he could manage in his state of dreadful distraction.

'All right,' he said. 'In deference to our friendship, I'll tell you this once, off the record, on the condition that you never visit me again.'

'Never?'

'Never.'

Though immeasurably shocked, thinking of Scaduto's dismissal yesterday morning, Dwight nodded: 'Yes.'

There was another lengthy silence from McDonald, as if he was struggling to find the courage to speak, but eventually, after another mournful sigh, he said: 'About the middle of March last year – I can't recall the exact date – feeling restless, I went for a night drive into the desert just outside of town, which is something I've done all my life. This time, however, I blacked out. I awakened fifty miles from where I last remembered driving . . . and my car was pointing back in the direction of home.'

'Just like Beth,' Dwight said.

'Exactly.' McDonald clasped his hands together, placed them on his desk and studied them distractedly for some time, before eventually continuing: 'From that day on, I've been suffering from dreadful headaches and the conviction that I'm being observed in some inexplicable manner. This conviction is so strong that often I think I'm going mad. It's given me a lot of sleepless nights – in fact, I'm now almost permanently exhausted – and naturally this, apart from its effect on myself and my family, hasn't helped when it comes to dealing with what's presently going down.'

'What's that?' Dwight asked.

When McDonald next sighed, Dwight realised that it wasn't actually sighing; it was the gasping for breath that denotes the repression of panic. McDonald spoke very softly, in short bursts, catching his breath in between.

'As you know,' he said, 'since the implementation of the Condon Report recommendations . . . notably the closing of Project Blue Book and all other . . . UFO investigations . . . the UFO controversy has practically become a . . . a . . . forgotten issue in the press.'

'Yes, I know.'

'Behind the scenes, however,' McDonald continued, gradually regaining control of his panicky breathing, 'the ridicule attached to the study of UFOs has actually . . . increased. For that reason, as I was still insisting that UFOs were physical, metallic objects and their origins possibly known to the Air Force, I was . . . ridiculed relentlessly at committee hearings and in the institute as . . .' He shook his head in unutterable despair and humiliation. 'As a man who believes in little green men and other science fiction or comic-book inventions. Now most of my serious work is being ignored and my career is in jeopardy.'

He glanced down at his desk again, studying his hands, then managed to redirect his troubled gaze to Dwight.

'If what happened to me in that desert is the same as

what happened to Beth, then God knows what they did to me when they got me. I feel I'm being controlled. Not just watched – but manipulated. And now, like Beth, I'm haunted by dreams of UFOs and men in black – of being inside a UFO, surrounded, blacking out. And because of that I'm now exhausted from lack of sleep, my career's crumbling, and my marriage is rapidly breaking down. I'm in trouble in more ways than one, Dwight, and that's why this is finished . . . So I've told you. Now don't ever return. I'm sorry Dwight. Goodbye . . . and good luck.'

Feeling as if he was going mad, Dwight stood up, shook McDonald's hand, then left the building. After driving too quickly, dangerously, to the airport, he commenced the first leg of his journey back to Dayton, Ohio.

As with the flight in, he asked for a window seat and spent the whole of both flights staring through the window at the clouds below. He kept thinking there were objects moving down there, but again nothing materialized.

Feeling ever more fearful, Dwight picked up his car where he had left it in the airport in Dayton and headed for home as quickly as possible, growing ever more fearful for Beth's welfare.

It was already dark when he left the airport and once away from the ugly clutter of the industrial belt, with its gas stations, warehouses, and factories for the production of refrigerators, air-conditioning equipment, cash registers, machine tools and, especially, aircraft instruments, the land became emptier, mostly agricultural land, pretty in the daytime, but flat and featureless in the darkness, though the sky contained a large moon and a spectacular display of stars. There were very few clouds – just some candy-floss wisps here and there – but enough to cast shifting shadows on the broad, moonlit fields.

Dwight drove pretty fast, too frightened for Beth to be careful, trying to distract himself with the feeling of power, of magical omnipotence, that came with being isolated from the world while moving through it at great speed. He normally loved the land at night, the play of shadow and light, but tonight, given the couple of days he'd just had, he felt threatened by it.

Then he started feeling odd – no longer alone . . . aware of some unseen presence.

'What the hell . . .?'

He spoke aloud to break the silence, suddenly frightened of being alone out here, then he automatically glanced at his rear-view mirror.

He saw only dark clouds crossing the stars and reaching out to gently stroke the moon.

Nothing else . . . just the darkness . . . the stars seeming to move away . . . the sky unfolding radiantly in his wake as the car barrelled forward. Nothing else in the mirror . . .

Yet his heart started racing.

He glanced left and right, convinced that something was out there. Seeing nothing, he glanced up, where there was nothing unusual, so once more he concentrated on the road straight ahead, uncomfortably aware that he had started sweating.

'Damn it, Dwight!' he whispered to himself. 'It's just your overwrought imagination – that's a dangerous thing.'

Talking to himself . . . Speaking aloud to calm his nerves . . . There was nothing out there but moonlit darkness, starlit sky, shifting shadows . . .

No, something *was* out there . . . What was *that*? Something moving . . . A flashing light . . . Growing bigger. Approaching . . .

Yes, damn it, *approaching*!

He saw the light, then it was gone, though it hadn't flashed on and off. It had flown from east to west at tremendous speed, then maybe shot upwards – so fast it just disappeared.

Where was it now?

Dwight felt his skin crawling with a dreadful, clammy fear. He was aware of something out there. He couldn't see it, but he could *feel* it, and his hands became slippery on the steering-wheel as his heart raced in panic.

'Imagination!' he whispered again, trying vainly to convince himself that this was the truth . . . Then, as his helpless fear deepened, something flashed in his eyes.

He almost swerved off the road, but blinked and straightened out. He squinted into the darkness, trying to see between the headlights. Seeing nothing, he looked to the side.

A pool of light was brightening on the road beside the car, keeping abreast of the car, speeding along and growing brighter and wider until it covered the whole road.

Dwight glanced up and was blinded by dazzling light . . . then he lost control of the car.

'Damn!' he exclaimed, his voice reverberating in his head as he fought with the wheel and the car swerved off the road, out of the light beaming down, then back onto the road and into the light again. 'Jesus Christ! What the . . .?'

The light disappeared abruptly. The car barrelled into the darkness. Its headlights had gone out and Dwight frantically worked the switch – and then a bass humming sound, an infrasound, almost *physical*, filled the car and tightened around his head as the engine cut out.

Dwight slammed on the brakes. He went into a skid, managed to straighten out, and was slowing down when something passed above, shot into the darkness ahead, then became an enormous, burning globe that froze right in front of him.

The car came to a halt. It just rolled to a stop. Dwight sat there, hardly believing what he was seeing, but too stunned to move.

He was looking at an enormous, slightly glowing flying saucer that was hovering in mid-air along the road, almost as wide as the highway. It had a silvery, metallic appearance, no surface protuberances, and possessed a perfectly seamless surface beneath that eerie white glowing.

Dwight sat in the car, too stunned to move, mesmerized

as the flying-saucer sank lower and settled onto the ground. It didn't appear to have any legs – it just settled down on its base. No, not quite on the ground: a few inches above it; hovering just above the ground. Then the base humming sound increased, tightening around Dwight's head, and he saw a large panel opening up in the sloping surface of the saucer, emitting a brilliant light, then falling forward to form a ramp that led down to the ground.

Three figures walked down the ramp, the smaller two moving awkwardly, to spread out across the road and walk towards the car.

Dwight was terrified. The middle figure was a tall, slim human being dressed all in black, but the other two, one on each side of him, were creatures little more than four feet tall, wearing silvery-grey coveralls, but with studded helmets on their heads, lower faces made of moulded metal and devoid of noses or lips, and hands that looked from Dwight's view point like vicious steel claws.

They looked just like creatures from another world.

As they deliberately advanced upon Dwight, spreading out as they came closer, emerging from silhouette, he wanted to get out of the car and flee, but he felt paralysed.

Then the infrasound faded away and the tightness left his head. Immediately, he reached for the ignition key and turned it, but he heard only a dead click. Jerking his hand away, thinking it had been scorched, he tried to still his racing heart as he waited for the two alien creatures and the man in the middle to reach the car.

One of the alien creatures stopped right in front of the car, the other went to the far side, and the tall, silvery-haired man dressed all in black walked around to stop by Dwight's door.

When he bent down to look through the window, Dwight wanted to scream.

'Roll the window down, Dwight.'

The man's voice was like a whisper. It was also oddly flat. It was the voice of a man with no feelings, but a lot of authority. Dwight did as he was told. He didn't seem to have a choice. That voice, though quiet and unemotional, would brook no disobedience. Dwight rolled the window down, his hand shaking, then he stared at the man.

He had silvery-grey hair, unnaturally smooth white skin, curiously immobile, handsome features and icy blue eyes.

'You're Dwight Randall,' he said.

'That's right,' Dwight replied.

'You were with Project Blue Book at ATIC, then worked for APII.'

'That's right, as well,' Dwight said.

The man smiled without warmth. 'You also flew over a construction plant in British Columbia and saw some of our saucers.'

'Yes,' Dwight confessed.

'You will stop this, Dwight. From this moment on. You've already done considerable damage to your wife and could do a lot more. As for your friends, Tony Scaduto and the meddlesome Dr James E. McDonald, you've seen the state they're in – and let me assure you that they're going to get much worse. Is that what you want for yourself, Dwight?'

'No.'

'For your wife?'

'No.'

'Your daughter?'

'Please, no!'

'Well, if you don't want that to happen to your wife and daughter, not to mention yourself, you must stop your involvement with UFOs and never return to it. Do you understand?'

'Yes.'

'Good. However, just as a precaution, Dwight, to ensure that you keep your promise, I'm going to give you a final warning. Not right now. Not this year. Maybe not next. It will happen when we feel you've had enough time to consider all this and have to make a decision about whether or not to stay silent about us. This warning will help you make the right decision should you be feeling less fearful.'

'What kind of warning?' Dwight asked.

The man offered his chilling smile. 'Wait for word about your friend Dr James E. McDonald. When it comes, you will know. That will be your final warning. The next in line will be you and your family should you ever again displease us. Do you understand?'

'Yes.'

'Then return to your home, Dwight, and look after your family. Goodnight, Dwight. Goodbye.'

Dwight felt that he was dreaming. In his dream the fear returned. He kept thinking of Beth and Nichola, of that warning, and he knew he would stop here.

'Goodnight,' he replied.

The tall, silvery-haired man with the oddly immobile features managed a chilling smile and a nod before walking away with his two hideous cyborgs, back to the enormous flying saucer. He and the two cyborgs walked up the ramp and disappeared back into the saucer's brilliantly lit hold while Dwight sat on in the car, still unable to move. The saucer's ramp lifted up and folded back until it again became part of the seamless body, cutting off the light and leaving the immense saucer to reflect the moonlight from its curved metallic surface. Then Dwight heard the bass humming sound, almost *felt* it, an infrasound again – and as his head started tightening and his skin became numb, the flying saucer started glowing, its silvery body brightening magically, until it became encased in a cocoon of pulsating white light and lifted off the ground.

Dwight heard the noise, *felt* it, was surrounded by it and became part of it, as the saucer ascended slowly, gracefully – yes, even majestically. Then it suddenly shot upwards, about one hundred feet up, but stopped again, as if by pure magic, to hover high above and to the side, where he could just about see it.

The infrasound cut out abruptly, allowing Dwight to move again, though he didn't dare get out of the car. The saucer looked small up there, about the size of a dime, and it seemed to be spinning on its vertical axis and filling the sky with light. Then it shot up even higher, shrinking rapidly, but still shining, until eventually it merged with the stars and suddenly winked out.

Dwight saw the moon and stars, the vast web of the cosmos. They made him think of the beauty and terror of life – and of those he most loved and were most threatened: Beth, Nichola and Nichola's baby son, still only eight months old.

Determined to protect them, he turned the ignition key, found that it worked perfectly, and drove home as quickly as possible, obsessed with the notion that his family might have been visited by the man who had just left and, even worse, might be in that saucer this very moment.

He was therefore overwhelmed with relief and love when he found that Beth, though telling him that she had been visited by men in black and haunted by a UFO that circled over the house the previous evening, was unharmed, as were Nichola, her husband and the eight-month-old baby, named after Bob Jackson.

Nevertheless, when he took her in his arms to kiss her, he knew that both of them were still in danger and would probably remain so for the rest of their days. Though he suspected that he could never hide from that nameless man for long, he was determined to try.

'We're selling up and going to Oregon,' he told Beth, 'where you've always wanted to live. It's time we moved on.'

'I understand,' Beth responded. 'It's all ended, hasn't it?'

'Yes,' Dwight said. 'It's ended.'

His kiss told her the rest of it: that love, which could not protect a single soul in the world, could at least heal old wounds and soothe fear. It was a kiss of renewal.

Chapter Forty-Seven

Eighteen months later, in June 1971, Dwight had settled comfortably into his new life with Beth, Nichola, her husband Larry and baby Bob in a rambling old farmhouse in Vida, Oregon. Out of deference to Nichola's fears for her own child, as well as for Dwight and Beth, Larry had generously agreed to give up his job as a civilian engineer with Wright-Patterson AFB in Dayton, Ohio, and move with them in relative anonymity to Oregon, where he settled for a job as a maintenance engineer with a local private airline that combined commercial flights to local towns with crop-dusting. Dwight, on the other hand, was happy to get a job as a truck driver, delivering farm produce to the shops of the various small towns in the area. Nichola looked after baby Bob and Beth looked after Nichola and the baby, as well as tending the house. All in all, it was a quiet pleasant life in pastoral, postcard countryside dominated by the spectacular Cascades where, as Dwight often recalled, some of the earliest and most famous flying saucer sightings had been made.

Dwight knew in his heart of hearts that if that nameless silvery-haired man or any of his equally mysterious friends wanted to find him, they would doubtless be able to do so – and, indeed, probably knew where he was right now. Nevertheless, the move to Oregon had not only been made to satisfy one of Beth's oldest dreams – she had always wanted to live in Oregon – but to let 'them' out there know that Dwight had moved away from all his old friends and associates and was now living in relative obscurity.

In other words, he was telling them that he had well and truly retired from the UFO business.

As if being thanked for keeping his word, Dwight was pleased to note that Beth's nightmares and physical 'hauntings' had disappeared within days of leaving Dayton and had not returned in the eighteen months they had been in Oregon. As for himself, since leaving Dayton he had not seen or heard anything of a disturbing nature, and he was grateful for that.

During that eighteen months few days went by when Dwight did not think of his many years in search of UFOs, but he certainly harboured no regrets. Gradually, however, as the more frightening recollections began to dim in his memory – or, at least, to seem less frightening than they had been at the time – he began wondering more and more about finding a way of imparting all he had learned about the man-made UFOs to those who could use the information best, notably Dr Frederick Epstein and Robert Stanford of APII in Washington DC.

No sooner had he started doing so than he was reminded of that nameless, silvery-haired man's threat to send him a warning through Dr James E. McDonald.

He started thinking of that warning about a week before the warning actually came. Wondering why, suddenly, he could not get Dr James E. McDonald out of his head, he spent a troubled week, then decided to take a day off and go fishing in the local lake. Arising just after dawn, he drove into Vida, picked up the local newspaper, then drove out to the lake. Still sitting in his car, he poured a cup of hot coffee from his thermos flask, then settled back at the steering wheel to read the newspaper.

Instantly shocked, he sat forward again, resting the newspaper on the steering wheel to prevent it from shaking.

The first page contained an article stating that two days ago Dr James E. McDonald, B.A. in Chemistry, M.S. in Meteorology, Ph.D. in Physics, Professor of the

Department of Meteorology and Senior Physicist at the Institute of Atmospheric Physics of the University of Arizona, after suffering from depression and a broken marriage, had committed suicide by driving out into the desert in the middle of the night and shooting himself in the head with a pistol.

Shocked, Dwight let the paper slide off the steering wheel, onto his feet, as he stared out over the lake, at the Cascades soaring beyond it, thinking about what he had been told.

Dwight was instantly convinced that McDonald, though he may indeed have shot himself, had not committed suicide – he had merely pulled the trigger. Though the evidence would never come in, he sat there in his car, looking at the distant Cascades where the whole UFO flap had first begun, and tried imagining the most likely scenario, given what McDonald had told him.

Dwight's hypothesis, based on his own knowledge of UFO abductions, Beth's personal experience, and McDonald's confession to him, was as follows . . .

Already in a bad way after a combination of overt Air Force and CIA harassment and inexplicable set-backs in his formerly illustrious career, now suffering additionally from severe depression and a broken marriage, McDonald awakens in his bed in the middle of the night, dresses in his normal clothing, including suit, shirt and tie, and goes down to his kitchen for a hot drink.

Sipping his coffee, he remembers the visit he had from the impassioned Dwight Randall who, like him, had gradually become obsessed with UFOs.

McDonald then broods on how a relentless barrage of private and public ridicule is being used against him to discredit his professional credibility.

Of all the ridicule he has suffered, nothing had been worse than when the House Committee on Appropriations had called him to testify about the supersonic transport

(SST) plane and how its use would affect the atmosphere.

McDonald had discovered (correctly) that the SST would reduce the protective layer of ozone in the atmosphere and that this could cause an additional 10,000 cases of skin cancer each year in the United States, as well as having other dramatic effects on animals, crops and the weather.

However, during his testimony he was constantly ridiculed as a believer in flying saucers and 'little men flying around the sky' and treated generally as someone deranged.

Sitting at his kitchen table in the middle of the night, brooding about this, as well as the loss of his wife and career, McDonald takes a pistol out of a drawer under the table and thoughtfully studies it.

As he does so, an almost palpable bass humming noise, an infrasound, fills the room and an eerie, pulsating light pours in through the window. McDonald clutches his head and groans until the light and sound fade away.

He then looks up with tears in his eyes and walks out of the house, still carrying the pistol.

He gets into his car and drives into the desert beyond Phoenix, Arizona, taking the same route he had taken a few years ago when he had first blacked out during a night drive.

He parks in the middle of the desert and stares up at the vast, star-filled sky.

When he does so, an enormous UFO in a pulsating aura that changes repeatedly from green to silver descends until it is hovering directly above him, blotting out the glorious sky and revealing only a pitch-black base that appears to have no depth.

As McDonald stares up at the terrible beauty of that sight, he has fragmented memories of being picked up by the same craft when last he parked here and of being deposited back on Earth much later, his head as tight as a drum.

Eventually, as the infrasound increases, deafening him

and also making his head tighten as if about to explode, McDonald obeys an inner voice – the one voice he cannot resist – and helplessly raises the pistol to his head and presses the trigger.

His last memory – if such it can be called – is of an exploding galaxy.

He falls forward and dies.

Dr James E. McDonald was now only an illusion of the mind: a warning to Dwight that he should not change *his* mind, nor forget the terrors of the past and attempt to pass on his secrets to Dr Epstein, Robert Stanford or anyone else.

Thus, when Dwight, still sitting in his car, managed to regain control of himself and shake off his shock, he tugged the newspaper off his boots, clambered out of the vehicle, threw the newspaper into a rubbish bin and walked down to the river. There, he climbed carefully into his boat, rowed out to the centre of the lake, unreeled his line and sat down to fish, surrounded by the dark, mysterious water and the soaring peaks of the Cascades. Thoroughly distracted, he let the boat drift where it would as he gazed at the sky above the distant, soaring mountains.

He had the feeling that the flying saucers were still somewhere out there, gliding eerily through the clouds, keeping him under surveillance . . . and he knew that this feeling would haunt him for the rest of his days.

He sat there all day drifting aimlessly in the canoe, until the stars came out . . . and even then he did not move.

He could not feel safe even out here.

It was best to be silent.